FORGOTTEN REALMS

SHADOWBRED

THE TWILIGHT WAR · BOOK I

PAUL S. KEMP

The Twlight War, Book I

SHADOWBRED

©2006 Wizards of the Coast, Inc.

Cover art by Raymond Swanland
Map by Todd Gamble
First Printing: November 2006
Library of Congress Catalog Card Number: 2005935524

9 8 7 6 5 4 3 2 1

ISBN-10: 0-7869-4077-8
ISBN-13: 978-0-7869-4077-6
620-95616740-001-EN

U.S., CANADA,
ASIA, PACIFIC, & LATIN AMERICA
Wizards of the Coast, Inc.
P.O. Box 707
Renton, WA 98057-0707
+1-800-324-6496

EUROPEAN HEADQUARTERS
Hasbro UK Ltd
Caswell Way
Newport, Gwent NP9 0YH
GREAT BRITAIN
Save this address for your records.

Visit our web site at www.wizards.com

For Jen, Riordan, and Roarke, my loves.

Thanks to Phil Athans and Bob Salvatore,
my friends.

Hey now,
all you sinners,
put your lights on.

PROLOGUE

23 Eleint, the Year of Lightning Storms (1374 DR)

Aril could not contain a smile. Five good skipping rocks filled his pocket and a pouch of squirming bole slugs hung at his belt. And there was no better bait for catching greengills than bole slugs, especially fat bole slugs like the ones he'd just caught.

When the sun rose, he and Mother would take the path to Still Lake. Aril would skip some rocks, and they would catch a few fish, always a welcome addition to the supper table. It would be the best Nameday ever. Aril only wished Mother would have let Nem come along, too.

Mother walked beside him, slowly, to accommodate Aril's awkward gait. As always, her right arm hovered near his back.

"I won't fall, Mother," he said. She was always afraid he would stumble or fall, but he never did. He was awkward on his clubfoot, but not clumsy.

"Of course not, sweetdew."

Her arm dropped for three strides before drifting back to its usual position.

A yawn snuck up on Aril. He had not been awake so long after moonrise in a long while.

"Sleepy?" Mother asked him.

Aril *was* sleepy, but did not want to say so to Mother. He did not want her to think him a wee.

"No, Mother," he fibbed, and turned his head as another yawn tried to betray him.

"Well, you should tell your yawns that, then, or they'll soon have your mouth filled with mosquitoes. And I know how much you like that."

Aril winced, in part because Mother had caught him in the fib, and in part out of disgust. He knew exactly what a mouthful of insects tasted like. Once, on a dare from Nem, he had run through a cloud of gnats with his mouth open. He'd spent a good long time gagging and spitting out gnat fragments. Nem had nearly split his sides laughing. Thinking back on it caused Aril to giggle. Mother smiled, too. Then a thought occurred to him.

"Hey! How did you know about that?"

She looked down at him and winked. "Mothers know everything, Aril. How do you think I knew where to look for bole slugs in the middle of the night?"

Aril frowned, his mind racing. She could not know *everything*, could she? What if she knew about Matron Olem's pie? Or that time he and Nem had hidden in the peddler's wagon and ridden halfway to Ashford?

He decided he should tell her the truth from then on, to be safe.

"Maybe I am a little sleepy," he acknowledged. "But only a little."

Mother smiled and tousled his hair. "There's a good boy. Maybe you can sleep late tomorrow, before we go to the lake."

"Do you mean it, Mother?"

The next day was the last of the tenday, and even though it was a day of rest in the village, Mother never let Aril sleep late. Usually, she took him to hear Hearthmistress Millam give a sermon about Yondalla. And the hearthmistress said the same thing every time: the harvest would be better next year, the drought and wild weather could not last, the dragons had all gone back to sleep. Millam's voice always made Aril drowsy.

"It's your Nameday," Mother said. "So if you like, you can sleep in."

He knew what she wanted him to say, so he said it, though without much enthusiasm. "No, Mother. We should go to temple and hear the hearthmistress. We can go to the lake after that."

Mother smiled and took his hand in hers. He did not resist. He still liked holding Mother's hand when they walked. If his friends had seen it, they would have laughed and called him a wee. But his friends were not around. It was just him, Mother, the Old Wood, and the night.

A full Selûne floated in the sky, but her light fought its way through the forest canopy with difficulty. Aril was not usually afraid of the dark, but night in the tangled Old Wood was a little scary. He knew it was safe, though. Halflings had been hunting game and chopping timber in the Old Wood for generations.

"Look, Mother!"

He grabbed her cloak and pointed up through an opening in the trees. A shooting star chased a glowing path across the sky. He watched it until it faded to a pale scar, then vanished.

"Did you see it?"

"I saw it, Aril," Mother said, and she offered a brief prayer to Yondalla.

Aril remembered the previous autumn, the night that a whole rain of flaming stars had streaked from the dark sky. He'd heard from a peddler that the falling fire had destroyed villages and burned down forests and caused destructive waves and made the drought, but he doubted it. They had been too beautiful. He wished with all his heart that he could find a piece of one of those falling stars—he imagined they were probably orange, or maybe red—and carry it around in his pocket with his skipping stones. But none of them had struck near his home. If one had, he and Nem could have found it and taken it out to look at it anytime they wanted. That would have been wonderful. And Jase would have been so jealous.

Thinking of his friends, Aril decided to ask Mother just one more time if Nem could accompany them to the lake on the morrow. He held his tongue for a time, thinking to wait for just the right moment.

They picked their way through the trees and brush in silence. Quiet shrouded the wood. Even the insects were sleeping. Aril could hear himself breathing. He and his mother moved lightly through the undergrowth—quiet and light was the halfling way, his mother always said. Aril could have sneaked up and touched the three brown hares he saw nibbling on foliage near the base of a pine. He was hardly quick or graceful on his clubfoot, but he was quiet.

Fighting another yawn, he suddenly longed for his bed. He asked, "How much farther to the village, Mother?"

"Not far, Aril. The edge of the forest is just ahead."

Aril was glad of it. He decided the time was right to ask about Nem. He clasped his mother's hand a bit more tightly and adopted his wee voice, the one that usually got him what he wanted.

"Mother?"

She looked down at him.

"May Nem—"

A sound from ahead of them rushed through the trees and bit off the rest of his words. As one, he and his mother crouched in the undergrowth and froze. Aril was glad they had relied on only the moon for light.

"What was that?" Aril whispered.

It sounded like a growl, but unlike any growl Aril had heard before. His heart beat fast. He reached into his pocket and clutched a skipping stone in his fist. Mother's grip on his hand tightened and she shushed him.

The sound had come from the forest's edge, from the direction of the village.

Mother stared into the trees, her head cocked, worry lines creasing her forehead. She caught Aril looking at her and forced an insincere smile.

Aril opened his mouth to speak but she shook her head and put a finger to her lips for silence. That made him more nervous, but he held his tongue and nodded.

They stood as still as the shrubs. Time passed slowly, but when the sound did not repeat, Mother's grip on his hand loosened. She visibly relaxed. Aril took a sweaty hand from his skipping rock and let out a breath.

He pulled Mother down by her cloak to his level, leaned in close, and whispered, "What made that sound, Mother?"

He imagined in his mind a passing bear, or maybe a wolf. Two months earlier a bear had killed Matron Ysele and her dog. Aril had not seen her body but he had heard enough from Nem that for a tenday he'd had to sleep in Mother's bed with his feet touching hers. Sheriff Bol had said the bear was just hungry, the same as the villagers, and that he would not return.

"I don't know, sweetdew," Mother answered. "Let's be still for a bit longer. To be sure it's gone."

Aril nodded.

An autumn wind rustled through the trees. Limbs rattled. Aril wished for the thousandth time that his father was still alive, that the red pox had never come to the village. Father would have come with them into the Old Wood. Father would have protected them from any old bear.

He leaned against Mother. Her warmth and smell—like fresh bread—comforted him. She crouched and put her arms around him.

A limb cracked sharply somewhere in the woods behind them. Both gave a start and looked about. Aril's heart raced anew. He saw nothing through the filtered moonlight but trees and undergrowth. Aril had heard that dwarves could see in the dark. He wished with all his might that halflings could.

Mother was breathing fast and Aril did not like it. He tried to swallow but his mouth was dry; he clutched a handful of Mother's cloak and bit his lower lip.

Another limb cracked behind them, in the dark.

Mother put her mouth to Aril's ear. "Quiet. We must hide."

He nodded.

He still saw nothing, but he knew something was out there. Mother was afraid—he could feel it. He started to shake and Mother hugged him tighter. He was breathing as fast as she.

"It will be all right," Mother whispered to him, but he was not sure if she was really talking to him. She half-stood out of the undergrowth and looked around the forest for a better hiding place.

Aril wondered if maybe they should dash for the village. Or shout for help? Surely someone would hear them. Maybe even Sheriff Bol. "Momma . . ."

He had not called her Momma since he was a wee, since Father had died.

"Momma, shouldn't we—"

One of the village's dogs barked. Another joined it. Soon it sounded as if every dog in the village was barking.

Aril looked to his mother for reassurance but she was not looking at him. She was looking through the trees, toward the village.

A shout of alarm sounded—a man's voice—then another, and another. Before Aril could ask any questions, a woman's scream tore through the night. Aril did not recognize any of the voices, but he knew they were his neighbors, his friends.

Growls answered the shouts—lots of growls. Worse than before. They sounded like Aril's stomach after he ate too much rhubarb pie, only worse. A man's voice shouted for arms and Aril thought it might have been Farmer Tyll. There was fear in his voice, and the sound made Aril's skin turn gooseflesh.

Mother squeezed him so hard that he could hardly breathe. Aril's heart beat so fast it hurt his chest. His stomach fluttered.

"What's happening, Momma?"

"We stay right here, Aril," she whispered. "No matter what."

The growls turned to roars and Mother paled. More shouts answered. The dogs barked themselves into a frenzy, doors slammed, wood cracked. Aril could not see it but he knew the village was in tumult.

"What is it, Momma? What is it?"

"I do not know, Aril. Cover your ears. Don't listen."

But Aril could not help but listen as the shouts turned more and more to screams. He heard a dog yelp in pain and go silent. A second dog did the same. A man screamed, then a woman. He thought he heard Sheriff Bol barking commands. And throughout all of it came the roars, the terrible roars.

He buried his face in Mother's cloak.

Mother picked him up, stood, and started back into the woods.

Fear seized Aril. He did not want to go back into the woods.

"Where are we going?!" he said, too loud.

From the trees behind them came another growl, almost thoughtful. Saplings snapped, and the sounds came closer.

Mother froze in her steps. Aril felt a tremor run through her body.

Something was moving through the brush toward them—something big, snapping trees.

"No," she said, so low that she probably had not thought Aril would hear. "Please, Yondalla, not my boy, not my son."

Terror rooted in Aril's chest. Whatever monsters were in the village, more of them were in the woods. He wrapped his legs around his mother's waist and buried his face in her neck. Tears filled his eyes.

"What do we do, Momma?" he whispered through his tears. "I want Papa. Where's Papa?"

The words made no sense but they poured out anyway.

"We must hide," she said again, her voice a hiss. "Yes, we will hide."

She whirled a circle and fixed her eyes on a stand of pines near the edge of the forest, off to the side of the village. A dead log lay near it—a good hiding place for them.

Mother balanced his weight in her arms and ran. She sometimes struggled to carry him lately, but at that moment she bore him as easily as a babe.

The creature behind them in the woods growled. Mother stumbled and Aril squealed in terror, but her grip on him never faltered. She kept her feet, crashed through low-hanging tree limbs and undergrowth, and fell to her knees under the pines, near the log.

They both turned to look behind them, breathing heavily. Aril saw nothing but trees and darkness. Perhaps the creature had not seen them?

Another crash sounded from the trees, so loud that Aril thought the creature must be not more than a stone's throw away. More roars from the village. Aril covered his ears and squealed.

Mother pried his hands away and put her mouth to his ear. She spoke in a whisper.

"I don't think it has seen us, Aril. Squeeze under the log and do not move. Like when you play hide and find with Nem."

Her voice calmed him and he nodded, though the screams from the village made him think of his friends. He was worried for Nem.

With Mother's help, he hurriedly squirmed under the log. It was a tight fit, but the hills and hollows of the ground gave him space. The earth filled his nostrils with their loamy scent. Dry pine needles poked his flesh and made him itchy. Mother laid herself behind him, like a pair of wooden spoons, sheltering him. She pulled armfuls of leaves and branches over them both. He could feel her breathing in his ear, feel her body trembling. He worried that she was not well hidden.

"Do not move, sweetdew," she whispered. "No matter what happens. No matter what. Nod if you understand."

He nodded and got a face full of pokey pine needles for his trouble.

"Momma loves you, Aril. More than anything. Papa did, too."

Aril tilted his head to get a needle out of his ear and saw that a thin gap between the log and the ground offered a window through which he could see part of the village commons. He pressed his cheek into the ground so he could see better . . .

. . . and wished immediately that he had not.

His view was limited but he caught a glimpse of long-limbed, lumbering creatures loping across the green, tearing at any halflings within reach. In the village torchlight, he saw flashes of claws, huge mouths full of teeth. He knew what they were, and the knowledge made him sick to his stomach.

Trolls. There were trolls in the village. And there were more trolls behind them in the woods, hunting him and Momma.

He knew what trolls did. He'd heard the stories. He knew they could smell as well as Farmer Tyll's hounds. He and Momma would be caught. He knew they would be caught.

And they would be eaten alive.

Tears flowed anew but Aril bore them in silence. He clenched his eyes shut and wished the horrible images away but the sounds coming from the village, the screams, the roars, preyed on his imagination. He saw with his mind what he no longer saw with his eyes: trolls killing and eating, claws and fangs dripping with the blood of friends and neighbors. He imagined Momma screaming. . . .

He heard a rush of motion behind them, the slow footfalls of something large prowling the undergrowth nearby. He heard heavy respiration. It was sniffing for them; a troll was sniffing for them.

He felt Mother tense.

Aril felt dizzy. His heart beat so hard and fast he thought it might jump out of his chest. His breath left him. He could not breathe. He could not breathe! Panicked, he squirmed and his body pressed against one of the branches Mother had used to cover him.

It cracked.

The troll near them went still.

Momma's hand squeezed him. Both of them held their breath.

More screams from the village, and a long, high-pitched wail of pain.

Aril pressed his face into the dirt to muffle any more sounds but that only made it harder to breathe. He wished so hard for his Papa. He wished that he was one of the bole slugs so he could burrow into the ground under a tree where no troll could ever find him. He wished he could hide in the earth and never come out again. He promised Yondalla that if she made him and Momma into worms he would live in the ground and never bother anyone ever again.

His mother gave him another squeeze. He felt her tears warming his ear. A limb broke right behind them. He heard sniffing, then a rumbling, curious grunt.

The troll started tearing through the debris under the pines and he knew, with perfect clarity, that he would die.

"Stay here," Mother whispered, and jumped to her feet.

The troll roared.

Aril immediately ignored her words and squirmed out from under the log. He stood, raining dirt and leaves and twigs. He was already on his feet before he thought about what he had done.

"Aril, no!" Mother said, and he heard despair in her voice.

A troll stood five paces from them. Though hunchbacked, it still looked as tall as a tree. Warty green skin with patches of coarse black hair wrapped a frame that looked to Aril to be composed solely of muscle, claws, and teeth. It looked at them and inhaled deeply, as if testing the air for their scent. It smiled a mouthful of fangs, and a low rumble emerged from somewhere deep in its throat. Moonlight gleamed on the drool dripping from its lips.

Aril wanted to scream, but no sound would come from his mouth. It just hung open, waiting to be filled by mosquitoes. He was frozen.

The troll stared right at them. Its eyes were as black as the night.

Mother held out her arms to shield Aril. "Into the woods, Aril! Run! Run now!"

But Aril could not run. He could not move.

The troll cocked its head at Mother's audacity. It flexed its claws and took a step toward them.

"Now, Aril!" Mother ordered. She picked up a stick and brandished it at the troll. "Here, creature!"

Aril was tempted to run, but only for a moment. He would not leave his Momma. Papa would not leave her, and he was Papa's son. He grabbed a skipping stone from his pocket.

The troll growled and took another step toward Mother.

Aril hurled the stone and hit the troll squarely in the chest. It sounded like it had hit a log, and the huge creature barely flinched. Its eyes fixed on Aril, and it said something in a foul language and licked its lips.

Mother exclaimed, "No! Here, beast!" She waved her makeshift club and tried to charge, but slipped and fell on her stomach.

Aril did not think. He did what Papa would have done. He jumped in front of his prone mother, planted his clubfoot in the earth, and prepared to stand his ground. He took another stone from his pocket and prepared to throw.

"Leave us alone or I'll hit you again!" he shouted.

The troll bounded forward with terrifying speed and Aril knew he had made a mistake. His arm went limp. His legs weakened and the stone fell from his fist. He screamed in terror.

Mother pulled him to the ground and threw herself over him.

"I love you, Aril!"

Aril hit the ground on his back and could not help but stare, eyes agog, as the troll loomed over them. Claws, teeth, and a wall of green flesh filled his vision. The night grew darker. The troll stank like rancid meat. Sounds faded. Aril's vision blurred and the darkness swirled. He was spinning, spinning.

The troll opened its mouth.

The night clotted into a blackness deeper than pine pitch.

The troll reached down for them, its claws as long as Aril's fingers.

Shadows haloed the troll like black fire.

The troll's mouth was so wide Aril thought it would swallow him whole. He saw its black tongue, its sharp teeth. He could not close his eyes. He wanted to, but he could not.

A man appeared beside the troll, a dark man with a dark sword.

Aril knew the man had come to carry him away to death. He realized that all of the Hearthmistress's sermons had been a lie. Yondalla had not come for him. There were no Green Fields. There was just a dark man with a dark sword.

The troll took hold of Mother's arm and she screamed. The sword flashed and the troll lurched and released Mother. Aril screamed as the massive body of the creature fell to the ground.

Fell to the ground.

Fell to the ground.

Aril blinked, confused. He stared wide-eyed at the body of the troll. This did not make sense. Wasn't he dead?

Still lying atop him, Mother was crying wracking sobs that shook her whole body.

Black blood pumped from the stump of the troll's neck. Aril watched it soak the forest floor. The headless body still scrabbled at the ground near them, as though trying to reach them—or dig its own grave.

Next to the body, the dark sword pierced the troll's severed head, pinning it to the forest floor. Pennons of shadow twirled around the blade. The troll's jaws gnashed futilely in an effort to reach the steel.

Aril still did not understand. He blinked rapidly, unconvinced that he was seeing something real. He closed his eyes, held them shut, opened them.

Everything remained as it was. Mother continued to cry. The troll continued to bleed.

Aril forced his stare away from the troll's head. His gaze wandered up the blade of the sword to its hilt, then to the dusky, shadow-enshrouded hand that held it, and finally rested on the face of a tall, dark-haired human man. Aril met his eyes and they flared yellow.

Aril realized what had happened.

The shadowman had saved them.

"Back away," the shadowman said in the halfling tongue, and he nodded at the twitching body of the troll. His voice was deep, and it scared Aril.

Aril had never before met any big folk who spoke the language of halflings. But the shadowman did.

Mother, still shaking and crying, was beginning to bleed from where the troll had grabbed her arm. She scooted backward and pulled Aril with her, away from the body of the troll.

Blood soaked Aril's trousers, but it was the troll's blood. Or maybe Momma's. It was warm and sticky. He had not noticed it at first.

"Thank Yondalla," Mother said through her tears, the words barely recognizable. "Whoever you are, thank you. Thank you."

"He's the shadowman," Aril tried to say, but the words did not come out.

The shadowman did not answer Mother, did not even look at

her. He removed a small flask from his cloak and soaked the troll's body with the contents.

Lamp oil. Aril knew the smell.

The shadowman took a tindertwig—like the ones peddlers sold in the village—from a belt pouch, ignited it on one of his boots, and tossed it on the troll. As flames engulfed the body, it thrashed in agony. The skewered head twitched and gnashed frenetically as the body burned. The shadowman held an open palm over the blaze. Darkness shrouded the fire and masked its light. At first Aril did not understand why he did it. Then he remembered the other trolls. The shadowman did not want them to see the flames.

The shadowman pulled his sword free to toss the troll's head into the fire. It gnashed as it burned. Then its eyes popped.

The man—he was so tall!—looked at Aril and Mother. Shadows wrapped him. Aril could not quite tell where the man ended and the night began.

"You are safe for now. I will do what I can for the village."

He looked past them to Oakthorne, where screams, roars, and shouts of combat and slaughter continued. The shadows around his body alternately coiled and flared.

"You are the shadowman," Aril said, finally croaking the words out.

The man regarded Aril with narrow eyes. The wind stirred his long hair.

Mother drew Aril close. "Thank you for saving us, goodsir. Please, help our folk."

The shadowman ignored her. He had eyes only for Aril.

"What did you call me?"

His sword was as long as Aril was tall. Darkness poured from it like steam off the lake on winter mornings.

"He meant no offense," Mother said.

Aril said, "The shadowman. You don't like that name? That's what Nem said the peddler called you. Hunters have seen you, too. In the forest. Some said they spoke to you but I thought it was all a tale. Nem said he heard you rode here on a shooting star. He said you came here to protect us because . . ."

Aril trailed off, suddenly nervous about continuing. He did not like the frown on the shadowman's face. The dark eyes—they weren't yellow anymore—bored into him.

"Because?" the shadowman prompted.

"He meant no offense, goodsir," Mother said, her voice quavering. "Please . . . leave us alone, now."

Aril summoned his courage and said, "Nem said he heard you protect us because you had a friend who was a halfling and you . . . could not protect him."

The shadowman's face was frozen. Aril could not tell if he was angry or sad.

The shadowman appeared next to him—had he moved?—reaching to touch Aril's head, maybe to tousle his hair, but he stopped short. He studied Aril's face and said, "Your friend has the right of it. My name is Erevis. Erevis Cale." He paused then said, "But I like 'shadowman,' too."

Mother audibly exhaled.

The roars and shouts from the village drew the man's attention back to the slaughter. Without another word he was gone.

Aril twisted in his mother's grasp and looked about. He did not want to be left alone in the forest.

He spotted the shadowman not far from them, crouching in the undergrowth, looking toward the village, and said the first thing that came to his mind.

"Tomorrow is my Nameday."

"Let the man go," Mother said to Aril, in the tone she usually reserved for telling him to do chores. "He's going to help the others."

The shadowman turned so that Aril saw his face in profile. Darkness gathered around him.

"I do not want him to go," Aril blurted. "I'm afraid."

Aril did not see the shadowman move. The man looked back on Aril, the darkness blurred, and he was suddenly kneeling at Aril's side. Mother and Aril gasped.

"Everyone is afraid," the shadowman said, his tone soft. Ribbons of shadow leaped from his flesh and touched Aril with cold fingers. "Even me. There's no shame in it. Do you really want me to stay here while the trolls attack your village?"

Aril understood the question. It was the same as when Mother had offered to let him sleep in the next day. He was supposed to say no. He struggled to find words.

"I was just . . . I was praying for Papa to come, and you came. I thought . . ." He trailed off. He did not know what he had thought.

The shadowman stared at him for a moment. Finally, he asked, "What number Nameday is it? Eighth?"

Aril felt indignant that the shadowman had taken him for a wee. "My tenth," he corrected, and his tone made the shadowman smile.

"You are small for your age," the shadowman said. "But only in your body, not in your heart. What is your name?"

"His name is Aril," Mother answered. Aril frowned that she had stepped on his answer.

The shadowman nodded. "Aril is a good name. My friend's name was Jak. And he was a halfling like you. Not from this village, but from another like it."

The screams from the village continued.

"Can you count, Aril?" the shadowman asked.

Aril nodded.

"To one hundred?"

Aril nodded again.

The shadowman stood and looked down on them. "When you reach one hundred, this will all be over. Those trolls will never bother you or your village again."

Aril nodded, wide-eyed.

The shadowman looked at Mother. "This is nothing you'll want to see. Same for the boy. Trust me, and stay where you are. I'll save who I can."

Mother just stared.

The darkness around them began to deepen. Before it was too dark to see, Aril took a skipping stone from his pocket and tossed it to the shadowman.

"You might need it," he said.

The shadowman caught it, smiled, and slipped it in a pocket.

"I might at that. Your papa would be proud of you, Aril."

The shadowman vanished as the darkness grew impenetrable. Aril held his hand before his face and saw nothing. His mother's arms were around him though, so he felt safe enough.

The shadowman's voice cut through the darkness. "Start counting, Aril. Aloud."

Aril did. "One, two, three, four . . ."

By ten, he heard roars of surprise from the trolls. By fifteen, he heard the first of them die. Others followed quickly—at twenty, twenty-three, thirty-one. Roars of pain came one moment from Aril's left, then from his right, one moment nearby, the next farther away. He imagined the shadowman stepping out of the shadows, killing, and disappearing, only to materialize across the village and slay again. By sixty, Aril stopped counting. The surviving trolls were trying to flee. He could tell by the way their terror-filled shrieks grew more and more distant.

Mother held him throughout, rocking him, humming a lullaby. He thought perhaps she was more frightened than he was.

"It's all right, Mother," he said, and patted her hand. "He is here to save us."

He felt his mother shake her head. "No, sweetdew. Not us. He's here to save himself."

After a time, quiet settled over the woods. Then Aril heard a *whooshing* sound. The smell of smoke and burning flesh grew powerful.

He and Mother remained still, as the shadowman had told them. He heard no trolls, no combat, merely the moans of wounded villagers, the soft crying of mourners, the barking of a few dogs.

"Shadowman?" Aril called.

The darkness lifted. He blinked in the flickering orange light of a great bonfire that burned in the communal fire pit between the forest's edge and the village. Aril and his moher walked cautiously to the forest's edge. A pile of a dozen or more troll bodies, all of them dismembered and squirming, lay within the flames. Thick, stinking black smoke spiraled up from the corpses. The smell was foul and sickening.

The shadowman was gone.

The survivors from the village wandered slowly, dazed, confused. A few tended the wounded or knelt over fallen friends. Aril avoided looking too long at the dead. He would have cried but he felt too numb to do anything more than stare.

Some of the survivors walked cautiously toward the fire. Many held weapons—mostly pitchforks—but a few carried swords. Others leaned on their fellows, whether from wounds or fatigue Aril could not tell. They murmured amongst themselves as they neared the pyre. Aril could see them pointing, explaining, trying to make sense of what had happened. Some prodded the burning troll corpses with their weapons. Sparks mushroomed into the air.

Thunder rumbled in the distance. A storm was threatening. Aril doubted it would rain, though. It rarely did.

"None escaped," Aril heard someone say.

"Did you see him?" said another. "Who was it? *What* was it?"

Aril and his mother limped out of the woods toward the fire. Mother took Aril's hand firmly in her grasp.

"It was the shadowman," Aril called, and all eyes turned to him. "The shadowman saved us, all of us. His name is Erevis Cale. We saw him. He talked to me."

Aril spotted Nem in the village beyond, standing near his father, who held a woodsman's axe resting on one shoulder. Aril waved, relieved to see his friend. Nem returned the gesture and both forced smiles. The numbness left Aril abruptly and he began to cry. So did Nem.

"The shadowman is a hero," said another, and everyone nodded.

"Where did he go, Aril?" asked Matron Steet.

Aril glanced around through his tears and could only shrug.

"Back into the shadows," Mother said.

Aril gazed into the woods, into the dark.

"Come into the light," he whispered to Erevis Cale.

CHAPTER ONE

25 Eleint, the Year of Lightning Storms

Black clouds roiled in the night sky. Lightning flashed, splitting the dark. Thunder rolled and boomed. Swells like mountains rose and fell on the sea. Rain fell in torrents. The mizzenmast of *Night's Secret* bent in the wind. The whole of the caravel creaked from the battering of the storm. Loose rigging and shredded sails snapped like whips in the gusts, but the dark pennon bearing the symbol of Shar and flying from high atop the mainmast held its ground against the storm. Rivalen smiled at that. The black circle bordered in violet looked like an eye, Shar's eye, guiding them to their goal.

Rivalen stood on the lurching deck of *Night's Secret* and tried to keep his footing as the bow again rose skyward, crested a swell, and skidded down a mountain of water. The crew, experienced hands all, gripped lifelines nervously as they lurched across the slippery deck to obey Captain Perin's shouted commands.

Rivalen knew they were close to Sakkors. The augury he had cast whispered as much in his ear. The first part of his quest would soon reach its end.

More than a year earlier, a cry had sounded across the Weave and the Shadow Weave, the warp and weft of magic, and resounded across Faerûn. Every spellcaster of power had heard it, though probably only a handful had understood the language, that of ancient Netheril.

I am here, proclaimed a voice in Loross. *Help me.*

Rivalen's father, the Most High Telemont Tanthul, had immediately deduced the origin of the plea, as had Rivalen himself. Its only possible origin was the mythallar of Sakkors, a sentient artifact created thousands of years earlier by one of Netheril's High Arcanists, Xolund the Maker. The revelation that a second mythallar had survived Netheril's fall had sent a ripple of excitement through the rulers of Shade Enclave. Divinations had been cast, auguries consulted. Eventually, Rivalen's brother, Brennus, a prodigy in the use of divinations, had located the site of the mythallar. Rivalen and Brennus had been dispatched to find it.

And they were nearly upon it.

Rivalen reached into the pocket of his rain-soaked cloak and removed a worn platinum coin. The octagonal currency had been known in ancient Netheril as a *thurhn*. Time had rounded its corners and worn the stampings—twin lightning bolts crossed over a mountain on the obverse, a date on the reverse—almost into illegibility. The coin had been minted in Sakkors long ago, when the city had flown in the sky on an inverted mountaintop. Like all the other floating cities of Netheril, save Shade Enclave, Sakkors had plummeted to earth when Karsus the Mad had attempted to achieve godhood. His meddlings temporarily unraveled the Weave, and the Empire of Netheril had died in a rain of falling metropolises.

Shade Enclave had survived only because the dark goddess Shar had helped Rivalen's father shunt the city into the Plane of Shadow. Shade Enclave had abided there for centuries, had absorbed the darkness of the plain, and had only recently returned to Faerûn.

Rivalen squinted against the rain and watched the coin, waiting. He nodded with satisfaction when his eyes, attuned to see dweomers by merely looking for them, saw a soft red glow emanate from the center of the platinum piece. The spell on the *thurhn* was of negligible power, little more than a magical mintmark designed to prevent counterfeiting, but its appearance indicated that they were nearing Sakkor's mythallar.

The quasi-magic in the coin had been common in ancient Netheril, but was nearly unknown in Faerûn's present era. The coin derived its power from a mythallar, and the mythallars of the empire had done far more than fly cities through the sky. They allowed spellcasters to create magical items in the mythallar's presence without physically or psychically taxing the caster. The physical and mental drains of spellcasting, ordinarily natural boundaries that limited a spellcaster's ability to forge magical items, were thus overcome by the presence of a mythallar.

The quasi-magic went quiescent if items were taken out of proximity of the mythallar, but that had not stopped a profusion of quasi-magical items from rapidly transforming society in the empire. Rivalen remembered those days well—magic had permeated almost every facet of society and culture. The ancient Netherese had used magic and magical items for even the most mundane tasks, from street cleaning and waste disposal to flavoring food or carving a joint of beef.

The presence of such vast quantities of magic had served only to make the empire's fall all the more spectacular when the Weave unraveled and magic failed.

But before the Fall Xolund of Sakkors had improved on the mythallar's design. He had infused his enclave's mythallar with a rudimentary sentience. The self-aware artifact called itself the Source, and unlike all other mythallars, its sentience allowed it to direct or withhold its magical power as instructed. Instead of powering all items in its proximity, it could focus all its power on a single item, on none, or on many.

The development of a sentient mythallar had caused a stir among the arcanists of the empire, but the Fall had ended any attempts to duplicate Xolund's feat. Sakkors's mythallar was unique. And Rivalen wanted it.

He peered through the storm and across the churning sea for *Secret*'s twin, *New Moon*. The darkness did not hamper his vision—Rivalen was a creature of darkness, bonded to it, and saw through it as if it were day—but the rain obscured his surroundings. He spotted the caravel two long bowshots to starboard, bobbing on the swells like a toy. Both *Moon* and *Secret* would have been lost to the storm but for the water elementals Rivalen had bound to his service. The living waves surged through the turbulent ocean alongside both ships, righting them when they listed, shielding them from swells that would have swamped them.

Rivalen's younger brother, Brennus, stood beside him, clutching one of the many hemp lifelines that webbed the deck. Shadows crawled over Brennus's exposed skin, betraying his nervousness. Like Rivalen, like all the Twelve Princes of Shade Enclave, Brennus was a shade. He usually traveled in the company of two homunculi, but the storm terrified the little constructs. They cowered belowdecks.

"The storm is sent by the kraken," Brennus said, and he lurched as the ship slid down another swell. His shining eyes, the color of polished steel, glittered in the darkness. "It's not natural. We must be close."

Rivalen held up the Sakkoran coin for Brennus to see. "Not close. We're here."

Abruptly, the storm abated. The rain, thunder, and lightning ceased. *Secret* and *Moon* floated on a quietly rolling sea. The clouds parted to reveal a starry night sky.

The soaked crew of *Secret* was too exhausted to do much more than give a hoarse cheer. Captain Perin issued orders to assess the damage to the masts, sails, and rigging, and to get a headcount. The men snapped to.

Rivalen and Brennus used minor magics to dry their clothing and gear.

"How fare you?" a sailor on *Secret* shouted across the water to *New Moon*. His voice carried easily over the calming sea.

"Wet but no worse!" came the shouted answer. "All hands accounted for."

Rivalen's augury was nearly at its end, but before expiring, it revealed to him an approaching danger. He secured the *thurhn* in his pocket.

"It's coming," he said to Brennus.

"Now?"

Rivalen nodded.

"Ready yourself and the crew, Captain Perin!" Rivalen shouted to the captain. "Something comes."

The brothers shadowstepped from mid deck to the rail, covering the distance in a single stride. There, they scanned the sea while the crew heeded Rivalen's warning and took up crossbows and belaying pins.

"My princes?" the captain called from the sterncastle.

Rivalen did not reply, but gripped the medallion of Shar he wore on a chain around his throat and stared at the water. Brennus held a duskwood wand in his hand. Shadows leaked from their flesh and cloaked them both.

"I see nothing," Brennus said.

"Wait," Rivalen cautioned.

They waited, waited . . . then saw it.

About midway between the two caravels, a soft red glow rose up from the depths and stained the sea crimson. It grew brighter like a rising sun, spreading through the water like pooling blood.

The crew saw it, too. They shouted, pointed, rushed to the rail, not knowing what they would soon see. Rivalen had said nothing about the creature, fearing he would not have been able to secure a crew.

"The glow . . ." Brennus said.

"Must be from the mythallar," Rivalen finished.

Brennus nodded. "It bears the mythallar with it?"

Rivalen nodded and frowned. Caution would be necessary in defeating the kraken. They could not risk damaging the mythallar with poorly chosen spells.

Brennus turned to Rivalen, a question in his eyes. "Strange that the Source has not contacted us, is it not? We know it to be sentient. We are close enough. It should have contacted us. It called to us before."

Rivalen nodded and said nothing. He'd had the same thought but did not want to give his concerns a voice. Brennus tapped his wand on the rail, demonstrating enough anxiety for both of them.

"Perhaps an attack has weakened it, or destroyed its mind? Perhaps it is now too weak to suit our purposes? Perhaps . . ."

Rivalen pointed a finger at his brother. Shadows poured from his flesh, betraying his agitation. "Enough, brother. We will know soon. Speculation is pointless."

Brennus looked chastened. "Of course."

The red glow grew brighter.

"What is it, my princes?" the captain asked. "What comes?"

The crew's curiosity was giving way to alarm. They eyed the brothers and the sea nervously. All were Sharrans, and all would die for Rivalen, but that did nothing to quell their fear. They would have been more frightened had they known the truth.

"We capture it, if possible," Rivalen said.

Brennus looked at him sidelong. "That will be quite a capture, brother."

Rivalen allowed himself a tight smile before he drew on the Shadow Weave and incanted a series of arcane stanzas. Brennus watched for a moment, noting the spell Rivalen was casting, then put aside his wand and mirrored Rivalen's efforts. Their voices merged, arcane power gathered, and both moved their hands through an intricate set of gestures.

The magic of their spell gave substance to the darkness and a net of shadows formed on the surface of the water, backlit by the red glow of the mythallar. The lines of the net's mesh were as thick as a man's arm. The brothers poured power into the spell until the net of shadows reached across the water, nearly touching both *Night's Secret* and *New Moon*. The water between the ships looked not unlike an enormous chessboard.

"That must be quite a fish," one of the crewman jested. No one laughed.

Rivalen and Brennus held the magic of the shadow net taut, waiting.

The glow grew brighter.

"Now!" Rivalen said.

He and Brennus released the pent-up magic of the spell and the giant net shot downward at the kraken, closing as it went. The net was powerful enough to scoop up everything in the sea between the ships to a depth of a hundred fathoms, killing most everything it touched, and trapping and weakening the kraken.

A rush of bubbles rose to the surface as if the sea were boiling. Hundreds of dead fish bobbed upward, their lives extinguished by the enervating touch of the net. A shriek, like nothing Rivalen had ever heard, carried up from the depths and out of the sea.

As one, the crew of *Night's Secret* backed away from the rail. Sailors exchanged alarmed glances.

"Steady, seajacks," shouted the captain. "We've a sound ship under our feet and two princes of Shade aboard. Steady."

"We have him," Brennus said, and leaned over the railing.

Rivalen was uncertain.

The red glow flared as the kraken broke free of the net, shot upward, and breached the sea. A glistening, dun-colored mountain of flesh exploded out of the water. Spray flew as high as a bowshot into the sky. Tentacles as tall as towers squirmed into the air and blotted out the stars. The tatters of the net of shadows clung to the massive limbs and dissipated into nothingness.

The crew of *Night's Secret* shouted in terror. Crossbows twanged but the bolts were too small to affect the kraken. The roiling sea set the ship to rocking, nearly tossing Brennus overboard. Rivalen grabbed his cloak and jerked him backward. Brennus steadied himself on the gunnel and cursed.

"At your stations, seajacks!" Captain Perin shouted. "At your stations! Harpooners to starboard!"

The tentacles retreated under the sea and the head of the kraken—sleek despite its enormousness—broke the surface. Rivalen saw what he had never expected to see outside of Shade Enclave: a Netherese mythallar.

Another shriek from the kraken split the night.

The glowing, crystalline shard of the mythallar, as big as a mature oak, stuck out of the kraken's head like an enormous unicorn's horn. The creature's flesh had grown over to enclose the huge crystal.

One of the kraken's huge eyes—partially visible above the waterline—fixed on *New Moon*, and the great creature dived under the surface. The mythallar's glow highlighted the kraken's form in silhouette. Its massive size surprised even Rivalen.

With a single undulation of its body, the kraken darted like an arrowshot toward *New Moon*. The panicked shouts of the crew carried over the water.

Brennus began a series of complex gestures and incanted the words to a spell to blast the kraken with dark energy. Rivalen took hold of his brother's hands and interrupted the spell.

"No. You could damage the mythallar."

Brennus's eyes flared. "Those are worshipers of Shar, brother. Men serving us."

"I know." But Rivalen also knew that he could not risk the mythallar. He needed it; Shar needed it.

The kraken plowed into *New Moon* without slowing. The ship, a three-masted caravel from the Pirate Isles, disintegrated in a cacophony of cracking wood, roiling water, screaming men, and the shriek of the kraken. The creature dived under again, circling below the floating debris.

Flailing men and hunks of broken ship dotted the sea's surface, lit from below by the light of the mythallar. The kraken's silhouette glided under the men. They screamed in terror.

The crew of *Night's Secret* watched it all in fearful, silent awe.

"My princes," shouted Captain Piren, the fear evident in his tone. "No ship on the sea can outrun that beast."

"We are not running, Captain," answered Rivalen over his shoulder.

Two harpooners hurried to the rail. Rivalen eyed the powerfully built men bearing iron pikes tipped with sharpened hooks. Rivalen waved them back. Harpoons would not harm the kraken. Nor would most of his spells, at least not before the creature could destroy the ship. He would have to try something else.

The kraken swam under *New Moon*'s surviving crew and jerked several of the men under the waves. They left behind only ripples; they did not even have time to scream. The kraken abandoned its sport with *New Moon*'s survivors and turned toward *Night's Secret*.

The wide eyes of *Night's Secret*'s crew darted back and forth between the onrushing kraken and the two princes of Shade. Rivalen felt Brennus's gaze on him, too.

"See to the rescue of *Moon*'s survivors," Rivalen said. "At least a dozen men are still in the water. Use the elementals."

Brennus cocked his head in puzzlement. "What do you intend?"

"To end this," Rivalen answered, taking his holy symbol in hand.

Brennus grabbed him by the wrist. Shadows coiled around them both.

"This is not a time to test your faith, Rivalen. A stronger shadow net might hold it still."

Rivalen removed his brother's hand from his arm. He had made a lifelong habit of testing of his faith, and Shar had rewarded him for it. He saw no reason to change his practice.

"No net will stop it, Brennus. But faith will. Watch."

With that, Rivalen spoke an arcane word and empowered himself to fly. He stepped off the deck and streaked toward the kraken. The dorsal hump of the creature's body rose above the surface, so large it could have been an island. The glowing mythallar spike rose from the sea like a standard and led its charge.

Rivalen felt the weight of the enormous creature's gaze, but answered with his own. The kraken's body pulsed, churning the sea behind it, and accelerated toward him. It shrieked from an unseen beak.

Rivalen pulled up, hovering just above the surface of the sea. He recited a prayer to the Lady of Loss and felt her presence near him, frigid and calm. He took comfort. He was her instrument and would not fail.

Drawing on the Shadow Weave—Shar's Shadow Weave—he

spoke the arcane stanza for one of his most powerful charms. He completed the spell as water and tentacles exploded out of the sea and reached for him.

Rivalen's magic reached into the mind of the kraken, established a link between man and beast. The spell pitted Rivalen's will against that of the kraken.

"Stop," Rivalen said, and the spell sent his voice careening through the corridors of the kraken's brain.

The creature's mind and comprehension were as immense as its body. The kraken had lived centuries, spent decades in contact with the sentient mythallar, learning, growing, knowing. Its mind was keen, incredibly powerful.

But it was no match for Rivalen Tanthul.

Rivalen had lived for millennia, had learned spellcraft at the sides of the most powerful arcanists Toril had ever known, had survived the horrors of the Plane of Shadow for centuries, had battled the primordial malaugrym on their home plane, had melded his physical body with the stuff of shadow, had served and continued to serve as high priest to one of the most powerful goddesses in the multiverse.

The kraken's mind quailed before Rivalen. The huge creature submitted and stopped.

Rivalen hung in the air, surrounded on all sides by tentacles as thick as wine vats. He could have reached out and touched them. They smelled of fish and the sea. Suckers dotted the limbs, each of them as large as a war shield.

"Lower your limbs and be still," Rivalen ordered.

The tentacles sank into the sea and the kraken held its position below him. Rivalen reached into the kraken's mind and learned its name: Ssessimyth.

Behind him, the crew of *Night's Secret* cheered and praised Shar. A cloud passed before Selûne, obscuring its light. Rivalen knew it to be a sign of his goddess's approval.

He looked over the sea to the survivors of *New Moon* and saw the water elementals scooping them up in turn, bearing them toward *Night's Secret*. More than half the crew of *New Moon* had been lost to the kraken. Rivalen felt pangs of regret. They had been loyal servants.

He flew along the kraken's body until he reached its head. There, he studied the mythallar. The flesh of the kraken's head grew along much of its length, and the open wound and folds of rubbery skin out of which the crystal protruded looked swollen and inflamed. Removing it from the creature would be difficult and painful for the kraken, but probably not fatal. That was well. Rivalen was certain he could find a use for the enspelled creature.

Rivalen found the swirling whorls of color within the artifact's crystalline depths seductive, hypnotic. He lowered himself and placed a hand on it. The shadows around his body swirled about him defensively. The kraken spasmed as though startled.

"Be still," Rivalen commanded the creature, and it was.

You are the Source, he projected to the mythallar. *Do you understand me?*

No response.

He frowned. He had neither the time nor the resources to spend repairing another mythallar. The arcanists of Shade Enclave had only recently repaired the damage Mystra's Chosen had done to his own city's mythallar.

Brennus, powered by his own spell of flying, flew out to him. The two brothers hung in the night air over the subdued kraken, in the light of the mythallar, while the crew of *Night's Secret* took aboard *New Moon*'s survivors. Brennus eyed the kraken and shook his head.

"Shar favors you indeed, brother. Forgive me for doubting."

Rivalen waved away the apology and ran his fingertips over the mythallar. His touch left fading streaks of shadow on the glowing crystal.

"I tried to contact it and received no response. It does not appear damaged. What can you see?"

Brennus cast a series of divinations. With each spell, his expression showed increasing puzzlement.

Rivalen knew his brother could study a subject for tendays at a time. "Speak, Brennus. What is it?"

Brennus shook his head. "I am not certain. The mythallar is weakened, though it appears to hold enough power for our purposes. But . . ."

"But?"

"But I cannot elicit even a superficial response from the sentience. For the moment, it's as inert as any other mythallar."

Rivalen frowned. "Has its mind been destroyed?"

Brennus shook his head.

"No. The intelligence still exists. My spells detect the mind. But it is . . . torpid." He looked down on the mythallar in puzzlement. "As if hibernating." He looked at Rivalen. "To heal, perhaps?"

"Can we awaken it?"

Brennus shrugged.

Rivalen offered his disappointment to the Lady of Loss as sacrifice. Even if the mythallar's sentience was forever lost, the crystal might still be used.

"It can serve our purpose, asleep or awake."

Brennus nodded absently, still puzzling over the mythallar.

"I am going below," Rivalen said.

Brennus cocked an eyebrow and looked at his brother in astonishment. "Below? Now?"

Rivalen nodded and removed the ancient Sakkoran coin from his pocket. Thousands more were probably scattered on the sea floor. If he found a quality specimen, perhaps he would add it to his collection.

Seeing the coin, Brennus jested, "I do not think the kraken will charge you a fee for transport."

Rivalen smiled and said, "I want to see the ruins."

Brennus grew solemn, nodded.

Rivalen lowered himself onto the kraken's head. Ssessimyth's flesh was rubbery, cold, and slick, but Rivalen sat on his knees and kept his balance. He took his holy symbol in hand and offered an imprecation to Shar. Magic coursed through him and the tingle in his chest told him the spell had taken effect—he could breathe water.

He followed with the arcane words to another spell and when he felt the magic charge his hands, he spun shadows from the air and shaped them with his fingers into a short rope and a barbed piton as long as his forearm. By the time he was done, both were as solid as if they were real.

"What are you doing?" Brennus asked, but he must have guessed, for he floated backward a few paces.

"Remain still," Rivalen ordered Ssessimyth, and he drove the shadow spike deep into the kraken's flesh. The gargantuan creature seemed not to notice. Rivalen looped the rope of shadows through the piton's eye and held both ends in his hands.

Brennus shook his head and smiled. His fangs—a royal affectation—glinted in the starlight.

"Descend to the ruins," Rivalen said to Ssessimyth.

The kraken immediately dived under the surface and shot downward like a bolt from a crossbow. The terrific speed almost stripped Rivalen from his perch, but his great strength, enhanced by the darkness, allowed him to keep his hold on the shadow rope. He expelled the air from his lungs and inhaled to fill them with water. The ever-present shadows around him held the cold and pressure of the depths at bay.

Led downward by the soft red glow of the mythallar, the kraken dived for the bottom of the Inner Sea toward a city that had last been in the light of the sun over two thousand years earlier.

The silence and isolation underwater surprised Rivalen. Sediment clouded the sea, probably churned when the kraken had left the bottom. It was like moving through mist. Rivalen could see only a short distance in front of him despite the light of the mythallar.

After a time, the kraken leveled off, partly rolled its body, and began to wheel a slow circle. Rivalen clutched the rope, leaned over, and looked down.

The ruins of Sakkors materialized out of the misty murk like a specter. The destruction shocked Rivalen. The inverted mountaintop upon which the flying city had stood had come to rest on its side. The position made the once-horizontal plateau into a vertical cliff. Caves in the cliff suggested the activity of creatures, but Rivalen saw no life. Perhaps whatever creatures had lived there had moved on or died.

The sideways landing had dumped the city off the plateau. Thousands of buildings lay in a heap on the sea floor at the base of the artificial cliff. Rivalen recognized the outlines of some of the structures—the shattered dome of the temple of Kozah, the once-tall spire of Xolund's tower. Rivalen wondered what Xolund's final thoughts might have been as his city fell into the sea. He wondered what the Source's thoughts must have been. He shook his head and remembered a day, thousands of years earlier, when he had walked the streets of Sakkors, when he had taken counsel with Xolund himself. Sakkors had not been as grand as Shade Enclave, but it had been a beautiful city nevertheless.

And it would be again.

Rivalen thanked Shar for sparing Shade Enclave the fate of Sakkors. He promised her that he would resurrect the sunken city. He would bring it up from the bottom and back into the air, just as Shade Enclave had emerged from the shadows to fly again in Faerûn's sky.

Through the mental connection of his spell, Rivalen willed the kraken to move closer. He longed to examine the mountaintop in more detail.

The powerful magic that had first severed the top of the mountain from its root appeared also to have preserved it nearly intact, despite the impact and the passing of years. This bade well. The Shadovar of Shade Enclave could repair a damaged mythallar, could use magic to rebuild a city in a month, but Mystra's Denial—an edict issued by the goddess of magic in response to Karsus's Folly, an edict that prohibited the casting of certain powerful spells once common in ancient Netheril—made it difficult and costly for even the most high to cast the spell necessary to remove the top of a mountain and use it as a base for a floating city. Mystra's Denial meant that the empire could never be fully replicated.

But a new Netheril could rise. The raising of Sakkors would be its harbinger.

Rivalen decided that he had seen enough. He took the *thurhn* from his pocket and dropped it into the depths. It reflected the red light of the mythallar as it sank, tumbling, to the ruins. He would recover his coin when he recovered the city.

He took one last look behind him, committed the ruins to memory, and commanded the kraken to surface.

He found Brennus waiting for him, still hovering over the sea. Rivalen was still able to use his spell to fly, so he leaped off the kraken's back and recited a minor magic that dried his clothing and gear.

"What did you see?" Brennus asked.

"The destruction of the city is complete," Rivalen answered. "But the mountaintop is intact. You should see it, Brennus. The spire of Xolund's tower is discernible, as is the temple of Kozah."

"Kozah. That is a name I have not heard in a long time." Brennus smiled slightly. "But, no. I do not want to see it until it joins Shade Enclave in Faerûn's sky."

Rivalen nodded and smiled, feeling satisfied. The first task set to him by Shar and his father was almost complete.

"We should inform the most high that we have been successful," Brennus said.

"Agreed."

Brennus put a hand on Rivalen's shoulder. "And I have some thoughts about how to awaken the mythallar's sentience."

Days later, far removed from Sakkors and the Inner Sea, Rivalen sought his father, the Most High Telamont Tanthul. Striding into his father's parlor, pennons of shadow formed spontaneously in the caliginous air and clung to his high collared silk shirt and linen breeches. Rivalen had become so accustomed to the touch of the shadows over the centuries that he scarcely noticed them anymore. Shadows saturated Shade Enclave just as the Inner Sea saturated Sakkors.

Dim lights provided the only illumination in the rich, duskwood-paneled chamber. A thick gray rug decorated with an azure spiral motif covered the floor. Plush chairs and two claw-foot divans provided seating. Books and scrolls covered most of the walls in the circular chamber. The Most High's mammoth darkwood desk sat centermost, itself covered in scrolls and tomes. Rivalen's father read voraciously everything he could find. Rivalen knew that the Most High had made a secret arrangement with the keeper of tomes, the master of Faerûn's greatest library, Candlekeep. The most high had provided the keeper with some rare tomes from ancient Netheril, written in the original Loross. In return, the keeper allowed the most high—through his agents, of course, or in disguise—full access to Candlekeep's collection.

Rivalen spotted his father on the far side of the parlor, standing before a magical wall map of Faerûn. Rivalen saw no sign of Hadrhune, his father's counselor and Rivalen's chief rival for his father's ear.

"Central Faerûn," said the most high, and the magical map changed perspective, expanding to show the details of the heartlands of Faerûn—Cormyr, Sembia, and the Dalelands.

Rivalen prepared to announce himself but the most high said, "You and Brennus have found Sakkors. Its mythallar is ours."

Rivalen no longer bothered to ask how his father knew what he knew.

"Yes, Most High."

The most high turned to face him. His knowing, platinum-colored eyes stared out of a narrow, expressionless face. Rivalen had inherited his father's sharp nose and imperial bearing. His father's royal cloak, originally violet, was so dark as to be almost black. As much shadowstuff as flesh, Telamont seemed to float rather than stand. The outline of his body blurred with the darkness in the room. Shadows swirled constantly around him, longer and thicker than those that circled Rivalen. The shadowstuff had not yet so consumed Rivalen. But it would.

"Well done, Rivalen."

The most high's praise was hard won. Rivalen enjoyed the moment.

Telamont moved past Rivalen to the darkwood desk and removed the crystal stopper from a bottle of nightwine. He poured two glasses and gave one to Rivalen. Rivalen held it but did not drink; he never did.

"The mythallar is undamaged?" his father asked.

Rivalen swirled the nightwine, inhaled its piquant aroma. "Structurally it is undamaged. And its magic appears intact, if somewhat weakened. But the sentience within is . . . unconscious. At this point, it is nothing more than a slightly weakened, ordinary mythallar."

The most high sipped his drink and frowned. "The sentience in the mythallar would be a formidable weapon to add to our arsenal. Awaken it, Rivalen."

"Easier spoken than accomplished, Father. Brennus has learned the name of someone we believe may be able to awaken it. I wanted only your permission to proceed."

"Who is this person you seek?"

"A mind mage who travels the Dragon Coast. He is of no political consequence and will be missed by no one."

"A mind mage? Unusual in this age. This will not distract you from other matters?"

"What other matters?" Rivalen asked.

Telamont smiled enigmatically. "You have my permission, Rivalen." He clasped his hands behind his back and floated back to the wall map.

Rivalen followed, thoughtful.

"We should proceed with the raising and reconstruction of Sakkors," the most high said. "Your brothers Yder and Clariburnus should lead the effort while you and Brennus pursue this mind mage."

"As you wish, Most High."

"Yder and Clariburnus are to use all resources at our disposal. I want the city rebuilt within the month."

"Yes, Most High."

A month would be an ambitious timeline, but with magic and slave labor—especially that of the krinth, a strong but dull race born of slaves and shadow demons—it could be done.

Rivalen stood at his father's shoulder and studied the map. It showed Sembia centermost: roads, cities, towns, temples, all clearly marked. Rivalen had long advocated moving against Sembia, a rich realm with fertile upcountry farmland and several southern ports.

Rivalen had discussed the plan with his father at length, had planted the roots of Sembia's overthrow long ago, even before Shade Enclave had returned from the Plane of Shadow. Rivalen controlled cells of Sharrans in almost all of Sembia's major cities.

The most high said, "The Heartlands are ripe, Rivalen. The Rage of Dragons has weakened them. Drought has weakened them. The Rain of Fire has weakened them. Their internal political squabbles and this elven Return have weakened them. We must not let them rot on the vine."

"Most High?" Rivalen asked, not daring to hope.

Telamont continued, "We have spent over a year scrabbling in the dirt, looking for trinkets from the empire while we sought alliances with the child kings who now rule Faerûn. Wasted efforts, I think. Do you agree?"

Rivalen licked his lips and carefully worded his reply. "We have recovered what magic there is to recover from the ruins of the empire, Father. That time is past. And our attempts at diplomacy have been met with scorn and mistrust. Cormyr and Evereska still blame us for the depredations of the phaerimm. The elves that have Returned to Cormanthor gather strength while we speak. The time for diplomacy, too, seems past."

The most high gestured at the map, indicating all of Faerûn with a wave of his arm. "Faerûn is covered by petty realms ruled by petty kings, little better than the Rengarth tribesmen who once peopled the lands under the flying cities of the empire. Even the elves have degenerated into barbarism. What have any of them accomplished since the Fall? The Empire of Netheril gave them the pinnacle of magic, arts, and science, and they preserved none of it." His father faced him, his platinum eyes aglow. His voice softened. "What is now Sembia once was called Arnothoi by the elves. Did you know that, Rivalen? It was all rolling forest and grassy meadows."

"I did, Most High." Rivalen's collection included a coin of magically preserved, polished wood from Arnothoi. He knew the elven realm's history.

The most high pointed to upcountry Sembia, not far from Daerlun. A wisp of shadow spiraled from his fingertip and kissed the map. "I walked a meadow there with Alashar, long ago. A stream divided it in two. Goldslips covered the banks. Your mother loved how the flowers looked in the sun."

Uncomfortable, Rivalen said nothing. His father seldom waxed sentimental, and the subject of Rivalen's mother, Alashar, always made him squirm. Rivalen had murdered her, after all.

Telamont exhaled a cloud of darkness. "Let the Sakkoran mythallar be the last artifact of old Netheril that we seek. Trying to resurrect the old empire is a fool's task. Instead, we will build a new one. Do you agree?"

"You know my thoughts on this, Most High."

"You have prepared the way in Sembia, yes?"

"All is ready, Most High. "

"Proceed, then."

A thrill went through Rivalen and he saw Shar's will made manifest in the news. "Shar favors your course, Father."

The most high's eyes narrowed. "She has given you signs?"

Rivalen's hand went to the holy symbol around his neck. "Yes. Ever since Variance recovered *The Leaves of One Night,* the Lady has been generous with her favor."

Variance Amatick was Rivalen's underpriestess and archivist, second only to Rivalen in Shar's hierarchy in Shade Enclave. Over a year and a half earlier, she had recovered a lost book long sought by Shar's faithful—*The Leaves of One Night.* Rivalen purported to have locked it away in the temple's vault. In truth, he bore it with him always. The book revealed Shar's one moment of weakness. Most of the faithful believed that the moment had passed long ago; Rivalen knew that it had not yet occurred. But that was a secret he kept to himself.

Telamont said, "If Shar has spoken to you clearly, Rivalen, inform me of her words."

"You know I should not," Rivalen answered. "The Lady's secrets are for the ears of her high priest. Forgive me, but that is the way of her faith, Father. Of your faith."

The most high's eyes flared.

"I am the Most High, Rivalen. And your father."

Rivalen did not quail. "I am her high priest and servant."

"You are also a servant of the most high," said a voice from behind them—Hadrhune's sibilant, reptilian voice. Rivalen turned to see Telamont's chief counselor rise from one of the parlor's chairs, dripping shadows. He clutched his ever-present darkstaff in his hand.

Rivalen had not noticed him upon entering. He wondered if Hadrhune had been in the room the entire time.

Hadrhune continued. "Your loyalty is to the most high first, Rivalen Tanthul. To Shade Enclave second, and to your goddess only third. Or so it should be."

Rivalen glared. "A false choice, Hadrhune. The interests of all three are aligned."

Hadrhune smiled. "I wonder what would happen should they become misaligned? What would you do, Prince?"

Rivalen held Hadrhune's gaze. "I would never allow them to become misaligned."

"So you say," Hadrhune said, and waved a hand dismissively.

"Enough, Hadrhune," Telamont commanded. "Rivalen, enough."

Both men stared at one another but bowed before the most high's anger. Rivalen's father went on. "We must respect my son's religious zeal. He answers to what he believes to be a higher calling. Isn't that so, Rivalen? Shar has called you to a greater purpose, has she not?"

Rivalen stared at Hadrhune and nodded.

"And Hadrhune seeks only to serve me and this city."

"As do I," Rivalen said tightly.

Telamont nodded and shadows flowed from him. "The time has come to build a new Empire of Netheril. See it done, Rivalen. Find this mind mage first, if you must. But see it done."

"As you wish, Most High."

Rivalen gave Hadrhune a final look and turned to leave. As he walked from the parlor, he realized that he had been standing in the room at the very moment when a new Netherese Empire had been conceived. He gave Shar praise and thanks.

Now he had one man to kill and another to capture.

CHAPTER TWO

29 Eleint, the Year of Lightning Storms

Rivalen and Brennus stood in the doorway of a scrying chamber in Brennus's mansion. Shadows cloaked the room, cloaked the brothers. Rivalen had decided to do the killing before the capturing.

A domed ceiling of dusky quartz capped the scrying chamber, and the starlight that crept timidly through did little to dispel the murk. No moonlight marred the darkness. Selûne was new, in hiding, as if she knew what was to come.

Rivalen brushed his fingers over the enameled black disc that served as his holy symbol. He wished the Lady's eyes to be upon him, so he pronounced a bit of her liturgy into the room.

"In the darkness of night, we hear the whisper of the void."

"Heed its words," answered Brennus.

Rivalen heard only partial sincerity in his brother's rote response but did not let it bother him. While the most high and all of the princes of Shade worshiped Shar, only Rivalen *served* the Lady of Loss. His father and his brothers craved worldly gain, for themselves and for their city. For them, Shar's worship was a means to that end. Rivalen, on the other hand, craved gain for the world—by returning it to the peace of Shar's nothingness. For him, Shar's worship *was* the end.

None of them fully understood that. But none of them needed to.

Few men were called to true faith. Rivalen's father and most of his brothers were powerful wizards—several were even more powerful than Rivalen, but they were only wizards. Their understanding was therefore limited. Rivalen was more—he was both archwizard and priest, a theurge. Among the Twelve Princes of Shade Enclave, he was unique. Among all men, he was unique.

Rivalen had received Shar's calling as a young man, when Netheril still had ruled much of Faerûn. To prove his faith, Shar had required him to arrange the murder of his own mother, Alashar, and Rivalen had done it. The death of Alashar had sunk the most high into despair and that, in turn, had led him to Shar, the Lady of Loss.

Through the ensuing years, Telamont had turned all of Shade Enclave to the worship of Shar. Rivalen had taken the dark rites and become first her priest, then her high priest. As a reward for their service, Shar had gifted the Tanthuls with special knowledge—how to bind their essence with shadowstuff. She had taught them of the secret weft of magic, the Shadow Weave, and had helped Shade Enclave avoid the otherwise complete destruction wrought on Netheril by Karsus's Folly.

She had given Rivalen still more. She had whispered to him his Own Secret: Rivalen would bring about the destruction of the world. She had birthed a plan then that would only see fruition two thousand years later.

Rivalen still marveled at the depth of Shar's planning, at her patience. He did not regard the murder of his mother as a betrayal of his father. Alashar's death had served a more important purpose than her life. All was according to Shar's plans.

"Come," Brennus said, and gestured him from the doorway into the chamber.

The brothers crossed the smooth floor of the scrying room. The shadows gave way before them to reveal a massive cube of tarnished silver, half again as tall as Rivalen—Brennus's scrying cube. Dim images played across one of the four vertical faces.

Brennus's two homunculi sat cross-legged on the floor, their backs to the brothers, watching the images displayed on the cube. The tiny humanoid creatures, each constructed by Brennus, absently fiddled with their toes while they watched intently. When they noticed Brennus, one nudged the other and both jumped nimbly to their feet. Toothless smiles opened under flat noses. Both had droopy eyes the same steely color as Brennus's. Their gray skin creased like old leather as they bowed. To Rivalen, they looked like unfinished clay sculptures.

One of the homunculi croaked, "The master arrives. We have observed the images as you commanded. There is nothing of interest to report."

"Well done," Brennus said.

The homunculi preened at his praise. They asked, "Up? Up?"

Brennus smiled and extended an arm downward. The homunculi grinned and gripped his shirt sleeve to clamber up his arm, then took station on either shoulder. From there, they eyed Rivalen through narrowed eyes.

"I do not understand your fascination with constructs," Rivalen said, studying the creatures. His brother was also adept at crafting golems.

The homunculi stuck their tongues out at him.

"No more than I understand your fascination with numismatics," Brennus answered.

"Coins are bits of history, Brennus. Countless realms rose and fell during our two-thousand-year absence from Faerûn. Collecting the coins of those failed kingdoms reminds me of the fragility of empire. A useful lesson, as we craft another."

"Crafting constructs reminds me of the fragility and delicateness of life," Brennus retorted. "A useful lesson, as we take those of others." He grinned and his fangs gleamed. "You see? We are similarly motivated, Rivalen."

The homunculi giggled.

Rivalen smiled and tilted his head to concede the point. He studied the images that the homunculi had been watching. Brennus waved his hand before the device and the images cleared and brightened. The homunculi clapped.

In one of the images, two women sat in solemn counsel across an ornate wooden table. A blue tapestry featuring a purple dragon hung on the wall behind them. The younger of the two, an attractive woman with blond hair, gestured intensely as she spoke. The other, a dark-haired, dark-eyed woman with a serious countenance, remained still and listened, sometimes offering an observation.

"The Regent of Cormyr and Lady Caladnei," one of the homunculi observed.

Rivalen nodded and turned to the other image. A man with long gray hair and a thick beard sat in a padded chair, studying a thick tome in an expansive library. Smoke spiraled toward the ceiling from an ornate, dragon-headed pipe set on the desk before him.

"Elminster of Shadowdale," the other homunculus said.

Rivalen recognized Mystra's Chosen. He faced his brother. "Impressive. No doubt the most high is pleased."

Brennus smiled distantly. "Perhaps not as much as you think. The Steel Regent and Caladnei incessantly discuss and debate the plots and counterplots of her nobility. They are convinced, correctly, that some of the rebellious nobles are allied with us. But they do not know which. Other than that, we have learned little of value. As for Elminster, the image is fake. He thinks to deceive us by feeding us an illusory image."

"A fake, a fake, a fake," one of the homunculi chanted.

Rivalen raised his eyebrows and more closely examined the image of Elminster.

"Are you certain? The detail is extraordinary."

Even as he watched, the false Elminster leaned back in his chair, took up his pipe, and studied the ceiling, as if pondering a point he had read in the tome before him. Care lines creased his face, though his eyes looked as young as a man in his prime.

"I am certain," Brennus answered. "The illusion is a spell tag. It is designed to attract divinations, twist the magic, and turn them back on the caster, allowing Elminster to scry those who would scry him. I prevented that, of course." Brennus eyed the image with open admiration. "Still, it is extraordinary work. He is clever, and his spellcraft formidable. I have been unable to pierce his defensive wards."

"Yet you continue to scry the illusion? Why?" Rivalen asked.

"It amuses me to do so. And I hope to turn his own spell against him. It must reach back to the real man somehow. I simply have not figured out the method. But I will."

Rivalen had no doubt. Few could match Brennus's skill with divinations.

Brennus gestured at the cube and the images of Elminster and Alusair went dim.

"Bye-bye," said one of the homunculi.

"Shall we proceed?" Brennus asked.

Rivalen nodded.

Brennus asked, "The most high is aware of your plan?"

"Only you and our father are aware of my plan," Rivalen answered, deliberately leaving out any mention of Hadrhune. "And the most high wishes it to remain just so until events progress further."

The two took positions before one of the blank faces of the scrying cube. Speckles of black tarnish marred the silver face.

Brennus held up his hand and the homunculi mimicked his gesture. Streams of shadow leaked from his flesh. He spoke an arcane word and the tarnish on the cube face began to swirl and eddy.

"What do you hope to see?" Brennus asked, as the magic intensified.

"Shar teaches that hope is an indulgence for the weak," Rivalen answered.

"Of course," Brennus answered with a half-smile.

Rivalen said, "Therefore, let us not hope. Instead, let us *expect*. And what I expect to see is opportunity. Consider it yet another test of faith."

Brennus smiled at that.

The swirling cube face took on depth, dimension. Rivalen felt as though he were looking into a hole that never ended. He felt nauseated, as he always did when scrying, and had to look away for a moment.

Brennus extended both arms and pronounced the name of the Overmaster of Sembia: "Kendrick Selkirk."

Rivalen looked back to see colors spinning on the cube face as the magic of the device sought its target, found him, and wormed its way through a number of wards against observation. The colors slowed, expanded, and an image began to take shape.

The homunculi clapped with glee.

Rivalen put a hand to his holy symbol as the image cleared. With his other hand, he took from his pocket one of the coins from his collection that he had pocketed for the occasion: a five-pointed Sembian fivestar, stamped in 1371 Dalereckoning to commemorate Overmaster Selkirk's ascendance to power. He flipped it over his knuckles, a nervous habit, and waited.

The face of the scrying cube showed a balding, bearded man asleep in an ornate bed. Dyed silk sheets covered his tall frame. The soft glow of embers provided the only light.

He was alone.

Rivalen smiled and ran his tongue over his left fang. Another test—passed. He slipped the fivestar back in his pocket. Sembia would need another fivestar designed and stamped for 1374, to commemorate the beginning of a new overmaster's reign.

"Opportunity, indeed," Brennus said. "He is alone."

Rivalen concentrated to engage the magic-finding in his eyes, then examined the overmaster through the viewing cube. His enhanced perception showed him magical auras as fields of glowing color.

Two protective dweomers warded the overmaster, probably emanating from the two magical rings he wore. But neither would protect him against what Rivalen planned to do. Rivalen also saw the glowing lines of a spell of alarm that warded the overmaster's chambers. He frowned, even though he had expected a magical alarm. It could be defeated by dispelling it, which Rivalen did not wish to do, or by speaking the password, which Rivalen did not know.

"The wards are easily dispelled," said Brennus, who had his own ability to see magic.

"Dispelling them will not serve my purpose," Rivalen answered, but he had another idea. "Maintain the image."

Brennus did as Rivalen bade him, asking no further questions.

Rivalen lowered himself to a sitting position on the floor, drew on Shar's Shadow Weave, and spoke a series of arcane words. As he cast, he stared at the sleeping overmaster, let the image sink into his brain, and completed the spell by speaking aloud Kendrick Selkirk's name.

Instantly his consciousness separated from his body and streaked through the scrying cube at dizzying speed until it reached the overmaster's chambers. There, it oozed into the overmaster's mind and infected his dreams. The phantasm allowed Rivalen to adopt a guise pleasing to the overmaster in his dream, to use that guise to cause the overmaster to do what Rivalen requested upon waking.

Rivalen did not see Selkirk's dreams, nor did he know what guise the spell adopted for him. Instead, his mind hovered around the edges of the dreams until the spell captured the overmaster's attention. Rivalen felt the connection open.

He projected a compulsion through the spell and into Selkirk's dream: *Upon waking, speak aloud the password of the alarm spell that wards your chambers. Otherwise, all will be lost.*

The spell allowed no more, so Rivalen pulled himself out of the overmaster's sleep. In a fraction of a breath, his mind returned to his body. He opened his eyes to find himself once more in the scrying chamber.

"And now?" Brennus asked.

"And now we wait until he awakens and speaks the password. Then I will kill him."

Brennus nodded. "Do you wish me to accompany you?"

Rivalen shook his head. He was Shar's servant. He would do her will and he would do it alone.

"This is a task set by Shar for me alone," he answered.

Brennus accepted his statement with a nod. None of the other Twelve Princes disputed Rivalen on matters of religion. Even the most high accorded great respect to Rivalen's views when it came to Shar's faith.

"My gratitude, however, for the offer," Rivalen added.

The homunculi grinned, as did Brennus.

They spent the next few hours watching the scrying cube, waiting. Rivalen used the time to pray, to rehearse his plan, to toy with the Sembian coin. He had already committed to memory the many spells he would need, including several that he had memorized so they could be cast with only a thought.

"He stirs," Brennus announced.

Rivalen tensed, placed the coin back into his pocket.

The overmaster rolled over in his bed. His eyes opened, he blinked, and he sat up, a glazed look on his face.

"Machinations," he announced.

Rivalen knew that the puzzled frown on Selkirk's face would soon change to worried alarm, so he wasted no time. He spoke aloud the single arcane word that would transport him bodily across Faerûn. The magic whisked him into the bedchamber of the Overmaster of Sembia.

"Machinations," he said as he appeared, preventing the magical alarm from functioning. He followed this immediately with one of the spells triggered only by his thoughts.

The magic took effect and silence cloaked the room. No sound could be made or heard within the chamber.

Selkirk saw him and recoiled. His mouth opened but his shout made no sound. His eyes went wide and he lunged for an exquisitely carved night table beside his bed.

Rivalen triggered a second spell and a swirl of magical shadows went forth from his outstretched hand. The dark tangle struck the overmaster, expanded, and wrapped his arms, torso, and legs in chains of shadow.

Selkirk struggled futilely against the bindings but managed only to fall off the bed to the floor. The Sembian's labored breathing, though silent, was visible even through the shadowy chains.

Rivalen stepped through shadowspace, covering the length of the chamber in a single stride, and knelt at the overmaster's side. The acrid smell of fear rose from the Sembian's body. Words spilled out of his mouth—desperate words, to judge from his expression. Probably he was offering Rivalen wealth, station, trying to make a bargain. Rivalen had come to expect as much from Sembians. But even if Rivalen could have heard the words, he would not have cared what the overmaster had to say. Rivalen had not come to bargain; he had come to kill.

He put his hand gently on Selkirk's brow. The man's body went rigid and he shook his head over and over again. Rivalen would have respected him more had he shown defiance.

With a thought, Rivalen tapped the Shadow Weave and triggered a powerful necromancy spell. The overmaster might have been powerful enough to resist the spell, so Rivalen poured his power into the casting to make his fate certain and quick. The shade had no desire to prolong the Sembian's suffering.

Energy flowed out of Rivalen's hand and into the overmaster's body. It drove an arcane spike into the Sembian's heart. Selkirk arched his back, grimaced in pain, convulsed for a few moments, and died. His eyes stared upward; foamy spittle glistened in his beard.

Rivalen dispelled the bindings on the overmaster's corpse and they vanished. Using the strength granted him by the darkness, he lifted the body into bed and covered it neatly with the sheet. Wondering what Selkirk had been lunging for, Rivalen examined the night table. A glass vial stood near an oil lamp and a small pile of coins. The vial's contents glowed with a faint magical aura. Within it was a clear liquid. Rivalen tilted the bottle and the liquid grew cloudy. He smiled.

The potion would have turned the overmaster into mist, allowing him to escape the room, probably through a tiny bolt hole. It was a simple but prudent bedside elixir for a head of state. Rivalen placed the vial where he had found it and eyed the coins, tempted. One of the fivestars was dated 1374 Dalereckoning, the year Overmaster Selkirk had died. The overmaster's profile was featured on the obverse.

Rivalen could not resist. He pocketed the coin. In his pocket, he had a fivestar minted in the year of Overmaster Selkirk's ascendance and a fivestar minted in the year of his death.

Coins are history, he thought.

He waved his hand to dispel the magical silence. Placing his hands over the overmaster's nose and mouth, he softly uttered the words to a powerful spell that severed the metaphysical tie between the Sembian's body and his soul. There would be no resurrection for Kendrick Selkirk.

He evaluated the room to ensure that nothing betrayed his presence, then took some time to cast several masking spells that would make his presence undetectable. Under the best of circumstances, Weave users had difficulty detecting spells cast through the Shadow Weave. Riven's masking spells made it nigh impossible.

His plan was almost complete. He had but one final spell to cast.

He stepped before the limestone hearth that filled nearly half of one wall of the chamber. The night embers glowed red. Crossed sabers and a shield featuring a coat of arms, a silver raven on a blue field, hung over the mantle.

Rivalen turned his back to the fire and the light from the embers stretched his shadow out before him on the carpeted floor. He held his holy symbol in his hand and intoned a prayer to Shar. As the spell progressed, it drew off some of his essence—he gasped as part of him drained away—and funneled it into his shadow, giving it rudimentary life.

The moment the shadow animated, it began to squirm free of the floor. Rivalen took it by the armpits—it felt slippery in his grasp, as if coated in oil—and helped draw it forth. He turned it and held it before him like a cloak—it had no weight—and looked into its face. A duller version of his own golden eyes looked back at him. He smiled. His shadow self was as much a construct as his brother's homunculi.

"You know what you are to do?" Rivalen whispered.

"I am you," the shadow self hissed.

"Then do it."

Rivalen released the shadow and it floated to the overmaster. It hovered over the bed for a moment, leering, then stretched itself into little more than a ribbon and wormed its way into the Sembian's body through one of the nostrils.

When it was gone, Rivalen cast another concealment spell on the body and surveyed the chamber one final time. The chamberlain would find the overmaster dead in his bed of a failed heart, his personal wards and the alarm spell still intact. Perfunctory divinations would be cast but would reveal nothing. Resurrection would fail, if tried, and the customary attempts to speak with the dead would reveal only what Rivalen wished.

Satisfied, he thanked Shar, drew the shadows about him, and rode them in an instant back to Brennus's scrying room. The homunculi greeted his return with applause.

"Well done," Brennus said.

Rivalen did not acknowledge the praise. Events would move quickly. He needed to contact Elyril.

The Lord Sciagraph entered her dream, dwarfed her consciousness. The proximity of the Divine One hollowed out Elyril, reduced her to an empty rind of flesh. Her dream-self trembled with awed anticipation. It had been two decades since she had last felt the oblivion of the Lord Sciagraph's presence.

Then, she had been a mere adolescent, the daughter of a Sembian noble family. The Lord Sciagraph had entered her dreams for the seven consecutive nights of the new moon and ordered her on the last night to do Shar's will by murdering her parents and older brother in their sleep.

Awed by the magisterial void of Volumvax, the Divine One, the Lord Sciagraph, the Voice and Shadow of Shar, Elyril had obeyed. Her parents had been planning to murder her anyway. She knew that for certain.

The memory of that blood-spattered winter night in Uktar still pleased her. The murders became her Own Secret, an event known only to Elyril, Volumvax, and Shar, and as reward for the deed Shar had granted her a secret name: Nightbringer.

The murder had resulted in Elyril being fostered in the house of her aunt, the Countess Mirabeta Selkirk. Elyril assumed her fostering to be Shar's plan all along, so she wasted no time worming her way into the confidence of her aunt, a dark-hearted, petty woman whose only virtue was unbridled ambition. Over the years, Elyril became the daughter Mirabeta wished she'd had, so much so that the countess sent her own sons away from the capital and paid for Elyril's tutors. By the time Elyril reached womanhood, she had become the countess's chief advisor and confidante. Elyril made it a point to dismiss all suitors, which only pleased her aunt further.

"I serve only the Countess Mirabeta," Elyril always told them.

So positioned, Elyril had bided her time and waited for word from the Lord Sciagraph to learn what Shar wanted next. The wait had been long, but it appeared to be over.

Elyril let her dream-mind careen into the cold, empty abyss of Volumvax's manifesting eminence. She tumbled downward toward infinity, and the metaphorical fall went on for a time that felt like years. Her body smashed flat as her fall was arrested on a bleak gray dreamscape, as level and featureless as a board of slate. The abrupt stop elicited a gasp but otherwise left her unharmed. Naked, small, and merely human, she rose to her knees and waited for her lord and intercessor to reveal himself fully.

Within moments a heaviness suffused the air, its presence more tactile than visible. An oiliness formed on Elyril's skin, black, thick, and viscous. From her earlier experience, she knew it to be the precursor to the manifestation of Volumvax. She waited, eager, awed, shaking with anticipation.

Slowly, like sweat squeezed from pores, darkness oozed from the slate of the dreamscape. She kept still as it formed an expanding pool at her feet. The touch of the shadowstuff elicited shivers. She sensed her physical body, still asleep in her bedchamber, trembling with the ecstasy and exquisite terror that accompanied contact with the divine.

Her heart thumped like a war drum, her flesh tingled, and blood pulsed in her pelvis. She knew that she would awaken with the flushed skin and weak legs that always afflicted her after sexual release, but she did not care. She was in the presence of Volumvax, the highest servant of her goddess, himself a demigod, and she trembled.

The shadowstuff rose up and began to take shape before her, solidifying, twisting itself into a form that Elyril's mind could not fully comprehend, whose dark borders reached into the secret corners of the world, whose presence murdered light.

Elyril averted her gaze and abased herself before her manifesting lord, pressing her forehead into the slate of the dreamscape. She knew that she was unworthy to look upon Volumvax, even in a dream. The Divine One was too beautiful in his darkness for a human to see unveiled.

A palpable wave of bitterness went forth from the forming demigod and washed over Elyril. Primal emotion pressed against her mind until she screamed. The sound died the moment the scream left her lips, absorbed by the nothingness around her. Terror and excitement drew her breath forth in gasps.

After a timeless moment, she felt a presence before her, so heavy, so substantial that it surely must shroud the world.

Elyril knew when Volumvax's gaze fell upon her trembling form. She felt his eyes on her back like the stabs of twin spears. The weight drove her chest flat against the floor and she lay there, pinioned by his might, impaled by his eyes.

Drool dripped stupidly and unheeded from her lips as she mouthed the words to the Supplication: "I kneel before Shar's Shadow, who shrouds the world in night. I kneel before Shar's Shadow . . ."

Elyril knew that the Lord Sciagraph would not speak in her dream. He never did. But she heard him nevertheless; she *knew* him nevertheless. She waited, her breath like a bellows. As one moment stretched into another, she tried to brace herself. Her fingers gouged grooves into the dreamscape. Her heart bounced in her chest. Her lungs rose and fell, rose and fell.

"I kneel before Shar's Shadow, who shrouds the world in night. I kneel before Shar's Shadow . . ."

Volumvax touched her, the gentle caress of the demigod who would rule the world in Shar's name.

An instant of excruciating pain wracked her body. She convulsed, and swallowed her scream only by biting down hard on her tongue and pressing her forehead into the ground. Back in her bed, blood from her mouth joined the drool that already dampened her pillow.

The pain passed quickly, replaced by indescribable pleasure. The touch of divine fingers excited such arousal in her already sensitized body that she experienced wave after wave of sexual release, one rapid, agonizing, ecstatic pulse after another. The wail elicited by that ecstasy was uncontainable, even in the dream. She arched her back and groaned her pleasure into the nothingness.

Volumvax's fingers lingered on her flesh as he communicated his intent. His eyes burrowed through her back and into her soul to impress upon her his will, Shar's will: *So says Shar, the Lady of Loss, through her instrument and Shadow, the Lord Sciagraph. Follow the Nightseer until the sign is given and the Book is made whole. Then, summon the Storm to free the Divine One. This to be a secret known only to we three.*

Elyril sagged, began to weep. She had waited for so long to be Shar's instrument. The time, at last, was at hand.

Now see the Lady's vision for you, secret even from me.

The Lord Sciagraph removed his hand from Elyril, leaving her bereft, and the gray plain instantly fell away. She found herself alone, suspended within the nothingness. Elyril's stomach rushed into her throat. Vertigo made her dizzy. Back in her bedchamber, she felt her body vomit its evening repast.

Mountains, seas, rivers, and plains took shape far below her. Her nausea passed and she recognized the landscape. She was floating as high as the clouds above an image of Faerûn's heartland. She could see for leagues in all directions. The landscape stretched from the sandy wastes of Anauroch and the Dalelands in the north to the Dragon Coast in the south, from the jagged Stormpeaks that bordered Cormyr on the west, to Sembia and Ravens Bluff in the east. She recognized the dark lesions on the land as cities:

Arabel, Selgaunt, Urmlaspyr, her own home of Ordulin.

She waited.

After a moment a thin, purple-veined tendril of shadow formed in Anauroch, within Shade Enclave, home of the Shar-worshiping Shadovar and their high priest, the Nightseer, Rivalen Tanthul. The tendril expanded southward and east, toward Sembia. At the same time, a second shadowy tendril, thick and blunt but also lined with veins of purple, burst out of Ordulin and made its way west across Sembia.

Elyril smiled to see Sembia caught in the vise of her goddess's will. She smiled even more to see one side of that vise originate in Ordulin, presumably with her.

Summon the storm, the Lord Sciagraph had commanded.

The two fronts moved inexorably toward one another, swallowing the light, shrouding the land. Darkness devoured Sembia, and all of Faerûn cowered. Elyril watched it all, satisfied that she would live to see Shar's final victory in Faerûn, until . . .

A third tendril of darkness, narrower but deeper than the other two, arose in central Sembia and expanded rapidly outward in both directions to meet the onrushing shadows of Shar. This tendril bore no trace of Shar's holy purple.

The competing fronts of shadow met and did battle. Elyril shouted in rage as darkness warred against darkness. Who would dare stand in the path of the Shadowstorm? How would—

Without warning, the vision ceased and Elyril was alone in the nether. She screamed her frustration into the void.

Some time later she awakened in her bed, sweat-soaked, exhausted, and staring up at the beamed ceiling of her bedchamber in her aunt's mansion east of Ordulin.

"No!" she said, and sat up, disturbing the vomit, blood, and drool that stained her silk sheets and pillow. Her tongue ached from where she had bitten it in her dream. She ignored the pain and the sloppy mess on the bed.

Volumvax's will throbbed at the forefront of her consciousness and she whispered it aloud: "Summon the storm to free the Divine One."

She wanted to know more, needed to know more, but she knew she would learn nothing else. The Lord Sciagraph and the Lady of Loss kept their secrets. Such was the nature of the faith. As a priestess of Shar, Elyril often had to act while ignorant of Shar's plans.

Near the foot of her bed, she heard Kefil stir. The black mastiff climbed to his feet, stretched, and uttered a contented rumble from deep in his huge chest. The dog's shoulder stood even with the top Elyril's bed and his bloodshot brown eyes fixed on her.

You thrashed about in your sleep, Kefil projected. Gray hairs dotted his massive jaws, and his bleary eyes showed their age.

Elyril smiled in spite of her concerns. The dog spoke to no one but Elyril—it was their secret. Kefil had first spoken to her the night after she had murdered her parents. He had been a pup then, and his name had been Mors. Elyril had renamed him after her dead brother. She assumed his intelligence to be a gift granted by Shar. Over the intervening years, he had become a trusted confidante. Her aunt hated the dog, but allowed Elyril to keep him in her room anyway.

Kefil whirled around to nibble at an itch in his hindquarters.

"The Lord Sciagraph spoke to me," she said to him, and offered no further explanation. She would not share even with Kefil the intimacies of her relationship with Volumvax.

Kefil continued biting his itch, and respectfully asked no further questions.

Mindful of her soiled sheets, Elyril carefully pushed the silk from her legs and swung them off the huge bed. Her head felt as if it were stuffed with rags; her temples pounded. She cradled her brow in her hands.

"Thank you, my lord," she said to Volumvax, wincing at the pain in her tongue and head. "It is my humble pleasure to serve."

Kefil abandoned his itch and devoured some of the darkness in the room.

Elyril smiled. Kefil always hungered for shadows. The mastiff sank back to the floor with a grunt.

A tingle under her scalp told her that the Nightseer was trying to contact her through the magical silver and amethyst ring she wore. She looked down, saw the amethyst set into her ring sparkle as its magic linked into the Shadow Weave. The connection opened.

You have received a sign, dark sister, Rivalen said, and it was not a question.

Elyril's breath caught. Volumvax had commanded her to keep the sign a secret. How could Rivalen have known? He could not know of Elyril's relationship with Volumvax, could he?

Elyril could not answer the Nightseer for a moment. Finally, she responded. *Yes, Prince Rivalen. I have received a sign. I believe the Cycle of Shadows is beginning.*

A long pause passed before Rivalen answered. *No, dark sister. The Cycle was begun long ago, thousands of years before your birth. Know that the Overmaster is dead.*

Elyril gave a start. *Dead? When?*

This night. He appears to have died in his sleep.

Elyril giggled. She had never fancied her aunt's cousin.

All will suspect murder, she projected. And most would suspect her aunt.

And they will have their murderer, Rivalen answered. *Resurrections will fail and none but a user of the Shadow Weave will be able to learn the true cause of death. Speaking with the spirit of the dead will reveal a name—the name of he who we wish known as the killer. Be certain that it occurs in public, before the High Council if possible. Prepare your aunt to take power. Prepare yourself to steer her as I and the Lady direct.*

Elyril's aunt had been positioning herself for over a decade to challenge Kendrick for power. With Elyril's aid, Mirabeta had bribed or extorted alliances from fully half of Sembia's High Council. She would be among the leading candidates to replace the dead overmaster.

That should not be difficult to arrange.

That is what I expected, Rivalen said, and Elyril thought she heard a smile in the tone.

Night shroud you, Nightseer.

And you, dark sister.

A gentle hum in Elyril's ear indicated that the magic of the sending ring had gone quiescent. Rivalen was gone.

Elyril sat on the edge of her bed for a moment, letting the import of the night's events settle on her. She had been directly contacted by the two most powerful servants of her goddess. She must indeed be Shar's instrument. Now she needed only to await the sign, and for the book to be made whole.

But what book?

She did not know. For the moment, it was Shar's secret.

She touched the disc she wore on a chain around her neck. Years earlier she had paid a wizard to make the black and purple disc permanently invisible, then used it in a ceremony sacrificing him to Shar. No one but Elyril, Volumvax, and Shar knew of the symbol. Its existence was their secret. So, too, was the fact that the holy symbol stored the souls of those Elyril had killed, including her parents.

Elyril's headache reminded her that divine visions did not come without a physical price. She stood, and her legs, weakened from sexual release and the exhaustion that accompanied contact with the Lord Sciagraph, wobbled under her. She touched a fingertip to her tongue, looked at the blood, clasped the invisible holy symbol that hung from her neck, and whispered a healing prayer to Shar. The wound in her tongue closed; the pain in her head subsided.

She noticed a chill in the room. Embers glowed in the huge stone hearth that dominated her bedchamber, but they offered scant warmth to her body, covered as it was only in a thin nightshift. She crossed the chamber, stirred the embers with a poker, and added a log. She caught Kefil leering at her out of the corner of her eye. She knew her lithe body pleased the dog.

Flames rose from the stirred embers and caught quickly, sending flickers across the room. The wood crackled.

She walked to the night table and rang a small, magical brass bell. Her personal servants, all magically attuned to the bell and others like it, heard its ring no matter where they were or what they were doing.

After ringing, she began a mental count. She had adopted her aunt's rule that servants had a twenty count to attend her after the ring, no longer, or they would be flogged. Before she reached ten, she heard the sound of feet rushing down the hall, the tinkling of bells, and a hesitant knock on her door.

"Enter," she commanded.

The door opened. Daylight from the hall outside cascaded into the room. She blinked in it. She had not realized that the sun was well into its daily course.

"Close that door," she snapped.

Kefil growled at the sudden light.

A skinny adolescent boy hurried in, eyes on the floor, and closed the door behind him. The room returned to darkness. The youth wore the black tunic, belled head wrap, and calf-length trousers that Mirabeta required of all the servants. Bony legs and arms jutted from the clothes, the limbs like those of a scarecrow. Elyril did not know his name and did not care. Probably the boy was the result of one of the sexual unions that Mirabeta had arranged between her servants. Her aunt enjoyed breeding the staff, selling some to slavers, some to fighting rings, some to brothels, and keeping those who pleased her. She had done so for decades.

"Mistress," the boy mumbled. "You summoned me?"

The boy's eyes never left her bare feet.

Kefil stood up and the boy gulped. The mastiff cocked his head and eyed the boy as he might a piece of meat.

"My sheets and bed pillow require laundering," Elyril said. She reached for the tiny iron snuffbox she kept in the drawer of her night table.

"Yes, Mistress," replied the boy. He stepped to the bed, keeping as much of it between him and Kefil as possible, and began to gather the sheets.

Elyril popped the snuffbox with her thumb. The piquant, bitter aroma of dried and powdered minddust filled her nostrils. The drug was a poor substitute for Volumvax's touch, but she found it pleasing nevertheless. She'd once heard from an apothecary that prolonged minddust use drove its users mad. Elyril found the notion absurd.

She'd been using the powdered leaf for nearly a decade and showed no ill effects.

She took a pinch between her fingers, brought it to her nose, and inhaled sharply. The drug danced over the back of her throat, tickled her senses. She felt the effects almost instantaneously. Her head went light, she heard a melody in the crackling of the fire, and the hairs on her arms stood on end, tingled in the air.

She caught the servant-boy watching her from the corner of his eye as he leaned over her bed and pulled in the sheets and pillow. He bunched the bedding into a ball, bowed—Elyril heard a poem in the tinkling of the head wrap's bells—and prepared to leave.

Elyril held out the snuff box and purred, "Do you wish to try some?"

He froze for a moment, shook his head, and refused to look at her.

"I wish you to try some," she said. "Come here."

He lifted his eyes to hers for only a moment before restoring his gaze to her feet. She could smell the fear in his sweat and it intoxicated her nearly as much as the minddust. She took another pinch from the box, inhaled it, and laughed aloud.

"Come," she ordered. "This instant."

He took a slow step toward her, another, and she glided the rest of the distance to him. Her shift clung to her as she moved and showed her body to best effect.

The boy trembled, uncertainty and fear writ clear on his troubled brow.

"You are a pretty boy," she said.

Still looking at the floor, the boy said, "The mistress is gracious, but I should see to these sheets immediately, lest the stain become difficult to remove."

Elyril smiled and clapped her hands. The boy was clever, moreso than most. Mirabeta's breeding program had resulted in a fine specimen.

"You are articulate," she said, and leaned in close to let her breath warm his cheek. Before he could frame an answer, she lightly ran a fingertip over his arm.

Startled by her touch, the boy stumbled backward a step and nearly fell down. The bells on his wrap tinkled loudly. Their melody told her to kill the boy.

The youth scrambled to his feet, holding the bedding defensively between himself and Elyril. Vomit from the sheets smeared his clothing. "Mistress, I—"

Kefil padded around the bed and the boy froze. Kefil sniffed around his legs.

May I maul him? Kefil projected.

Elyril considered it but decided that she did not want blood in her chamber. She could chop him up and feed him to the dogs later.

Devour his shadow, she answered.

The mastiff seized the boy's shadow from the floor, shook it, and devoured it as it screamed. The boy never made a sound, never moved. Kefil finished his repast and let out a satisfied grunt. He sank to the floor beside the boy.

"What is your name?" Elyril asked the slave at last, keeping her voice level. She liked to know the names of those she would sacrifice to Shar.

"Mard, Mistress," the boy said, and she could hear the beginnings of tears in his voice.

"Mard," she said. She let the word hang between them for a long, delicious moment before deciding to end the game. "Mard, do not get your tears on my sheets. Begone from me. Alert one of the kennel boys that Kefil requires a walk."

Mard stared at her for a moment, as if unsure what she had said.

"This instant," she ordered.

"Thank you, Mistress," he said, and fled the room.

She watched him go, thinking how pleasant it would be to hear him scream as he died.

Kefil belched, sated on shadows.

In the darkened chambers of his mansion in Shade Enclave, Rivalen stared at his coin collection and let the ache in his temples subside. He always found mental contact with Elyril uncomfortable. Her minddust madness polluted the connection and made his head throb, and it had grown worse over the years. Still, she was a useful tool to him as he prepared to bring his plan to fruition. The most high wanted a new Netherese empire. His goddess wanted the Shadowstorm. Rivalen knew that the two goals were compatible. He would use the one to bring about the other. And a Sembian civil war would be the means.

Over the centuries, Rivalen had spent much intellectual energy finding ways to make the requirements of his faith compatible with his duty to his city, his people, and his father. So far, he had been successful, but Hadrhune's words made him worry that the day would arrive when he would not.

Rivalen did not know the entirety of the Lady's plan—such was the nature of Shar's faith. Through the years, Shar had revealed to Rivalen only bits at a time. But Rivalen had faith that she would reveal to him what he needed to know when he needed to know it, and that she would reward his successes. While he dared not hope to be Shar's Chosen, after experiencing firsthand the power of Mystra's Chosen, he had allowed himself to . . . consider the possibility.

He dismissed such thoughts as unproductive and continued with his sendings. He activated the magic of his sending ring and thought of another of his Sembian agents, the Sharran dark brother in Selgaunt. The familiar tingle of the magic tickled his scalp. He sensed the channel opening.

Prince Rivalen, answered the dark brother, an heir to a wealthy Sembian family.

Rivalen knew him to be an effective servant of the Lady, posing as a rich dilettante.

Is all prepared? Rivalen asked.

As well as it can be. Construction proceeds apace. None suspect the truth.

See that it is complete within the next three months, Rivalen said. *There will be still more for you to do afterward.*

The night shroud you, Nightseer.

And you, Rivalen answered, and terminated the magical connection.

Rivalen went on to contact the leaders of each Sharran cell in Sembia, over two dozen of them. Each wore a sending ring paired to his master ring, though none knew the other powers of the rings. To each, he gave a variation of the same message: *Be prepared. The Shadowstorm is brewing.*

None asked him questions, for they all knew they would receive no answers.

Prior to Rivalen's involvement, the Sharran cells in the heartlands had operated independently, mostly ignorant of each other. But after Variance, at Rivalen's command, had recovered *The Leaves of One Night,* Shar had revealed to him the identities of the leaders of the cells. One by one, he and Variance had contacted the cells and brought them all under his leadership, until finally Rivalen commanded the grandest conspiracy in Faerûn. A small army of Sharrans lurked beneath the veneer of Sembian society, eating away at the core.

His sendings complete, Rivalen relaxed by sipping tea and examining his coin collection. He stored his coins in a large case of magically hardened glass, each piece placed in a black velvet setting. He had an electrum falcon from the year of Cormyr's founding, one-hundred-year-old gold belbolts from Chessenta, a cursed copper fandar from Amn that caused the bearer's business decisions to go poorly, a magical platinum Calishite kilarch that returned to its spender thrice, and a host of other coins, both magical and mundane, from all across Faerûn, from almost all eras of its history. He looked to the empty place in his collection where he had kept his Sakkoran *thurhn.* The hole in his collection reminded him of the magnitude of his tasks. He had many holes to fill in the coming years.

He finished his tea and turned his mind to the first of his holes— the problem of awakening the sentience in Sakkor's mythallar. He would need Brennus's divinations to find the mind mage.

CHAPTER THREE

30 Eleint, the Year of Lightning Storms

The sight of the oak brought a smile to Magadon's face. He had passed the soaring old tree many times in his journeys to and from Starmantle, though it had been almost a year since he had seen it last. It looked almost exactly as he remembered it—a lone soldier standing sentry over an expanse of knee-high whip grass. Other trees dotted the plain here and there, but none were as large as the oak. He was their general.

Magadon ignored the chatter from the camp behind him and ran his fingertips over the tree's bole. The deep ridges of the bark and the size of the bole put the tree's age somewhere between seventy and eighty winters—a grand old man. A few tumors bulged here and there from the trunk, and the crotch showed a ragged scar from a recent lightning strike, but Magadon thought the tree hale. The world had thrown another year at it, and there it stood.

Magadon figured there was a lesson in that. Too bad he had not learned it sooner. Magadon had not had the oak's strength. The last year had broken him.

"Or bent me, at least," he murmured.

The oak's leaves were changing from green to autumn red. They looked beautiful even at night, especially at night, framed against the starry sky and glinting in the silver moonlight of the newly risen crescent of Selûne and her Tears.

Magadon flattened his palm against the oak. He had missed the tree, or he had missed . . . the part of his life it represented.

But he was reclaiming that part of his life, reclaiming himself.

Droppings at the base of the tree caught his eye. He knelt to examine them, and recognized raccoon pellets. He stood, smiling. Things were coming back to him. He had not forgotten his woodlore.

A soft skitter sounded up in the tree. Magadon looked up and found two pairs of masked eyes peeking down at him—a mother raccoon and one of her young. He would not have seen the creatures but for the nightvision granted him by his fiendish blood.

"You've picked a good home, mother," he said to the larger raccoon.

Mother and baby cocked their heads to the side, chittered, and ducked back into their hidden den.

Magadon patted the tree's trunk.

"Can you bear some more company, old man? I promise you will find me an easy guest."

The oak kept its own counsel, so Magadon unslung his pack—stuffed full with gear, as always—and sat with his back against the trunk, facing the camp. The campfire was going strong, and merchants and men-at-arms sat around it on barrels, crates, and logs, talking, drinking, laughing.

Magadon stretched out his legs, interlaced his fingers behind his neck, and blew out a sigh. The oak felt good at his back. His friend Nestor had once said, "There's naught steadier than an old oak." Magadon knew it to be true. And he knew there was much to be said for steadiness.

He hoisted his waterskin in remembrance of Nestor and took a long drink. Thinking of Nestor and his death brought back a wash of memories, some good—of Erevis, Riven, and Jak—and some bad—of the Sojourner, the slaads, the Weave Tap, and . . . the Source.

Recalling the Source made him squirm. He cleared his throat and tried to forget what it had shown him, what he had known, what he had been, for those few moments of contact. But memories were stubborn things.

He unclenched his hands from behind his neck and held them before his face. A tremor shook them, softly at first, but growing stronger. He knew what was coming. He stuffed his hands in his pockets and waited. He had seen the same shaking in minddust addicts who had gone too long without their snuff.

The need came on him, the hunger. A tic caused his right eye to twitch.

The Source had given him so much knowledge, so much *power*. He could have done such good with it. . . .

He should find it, go to it, and bond with it once more.

"No," he said, and shook his head. Even if he had surrendered to his need, he could not have gone to it. The Source lay at the bottom of the Inner Sea, sticking out of the head of a creature as large as a city.

Magadon recognized what was happening and fought, as he did every day, to keep hold of himself. His mental addiction to the Source had caused him to lose himself once. An entire year of his life had vanished into a haze. He would not allow it to happen again.

He took a deep, shaky breath, felt the oak at his back, the breeze on his face, and the clean air in his lungs, and heard the laughter of the caravaneers, and rode out the pull.

After a time, it passed, more quickly than the day before. He was beating it. The realization strengthened him further.

Another chitter came from above. He looked up to find not two, but a row of six raccoon faces staring down at him, presumably the mother and all of her young. He could not help but smile at their wide-eyed, curious expressions. One of the young climbed over another and the mother chittered at them.

"Very well," he said. "I will be on my way, but only after I eat."

The raccoons continued to stare at him with bright eyes through their masks.

Magadon pulled a half-wheel of cheese and two mostly-brown apples from a leather bag in his backpack. He habitually ate alone, separating himself from the caravaneers. He did not quite feel up to companionship. He thought the men of the caravan decent fellows, but he needed meditation more than company. Or so he told himself.

The raccoons chittered at him in irritation.

He took another bite of apple. "You don't frighten me," he said to them with a smile. "I have seen angry eyes behind a mask before."

He took another bite of apple and noticed the black, clawed nails that had once been his normal fingernails. He sank them into the apple to hide them.

Inexplicably, his contact with the Source had changed not only his mind but also his body, somehow stirring the blood of the archdevil father that polluted his veins. As his mental powers had expanded, his body had come to more closely resemble that of his diabolical sire. As had his proclivities.

Soon after his separation from the Source, the nightmares had begun. The Nine Hells haunted his dreams. When he slept, he saw souls burning, writhing, screaming in pits of fire while leering devils looked on. The visions had grown worse over time. He felt as if they were moving toward some climax that would drive him mad. For months, he had feared sleep.

He had grown desperate, had sublimated his desire for the Source and his need to escape the dreams by turning first to drink, and when that did not stupefy him adequately, to drugs. He had lost himself for months. The dreams had not stopped, his need for the Source had not stopped, but he had been so dulled that they had bothered him less.

He scarcely remembered those days. He did remember that during the all-too-rare moments of clear-headedness, he had considered reaching out with his mind to Erevis or Riven, his friends, but had lacked the courage. His stupor had not dulled his shame over what he had become. He had not wanted his friends to know of it.

Besides, each of them had their own burdens to carry.

The visions of the Hells had eventually left his dreams and invaded his waking hours. He'd hallucinated immolations on the city streets at midday, heard his father's voice in the call of street vendors, seen devils in the darkness of every alley. He was falling into madness, but could not stop the descent.

Blood of my blood, his father assured him in a voice smoother than Calishite velvet. *I can end all this and give you what you want, what you need.*

Magadon had never been sure if the voice had been real or imagined, but he had been tempted. He awoke one night in a dust den, his shirt stained with blood—someone else's. He'd known then that he had to do something to save himself or he would die, in spirit if not in body.

Ironically, the Source, by expanding his mental powers, had given him the tool he needed. He used it, performing a kind of psychic chirurgery on his own mind, walling off most of the dark, addicted portions of his consciousness from the rest. He likened it to cutting off a gangrenous limb, but this was more like splintering himself. He'd had to divide himself to save the whole. He could not cut off all of the addiction or all of the dark impulses, but he had severed most of them from his core.

And it worked. Mostly.

He still dreamed of the Hells. His body told him that he had not slept well in months, but his conscious mind did not remember. That was the important thing. He worried what kind of rot was occurring within him, unnoticed behind the mental wall, but he figured a man half-saved was better than a man wholly-damned.

A loud round of laughter from the merchants shook Magadon from his ponderings. One of the merchants, a brown-haired man with a pot belly and receding hairline, stood up and called over to him. Magadon thought he remembered his name was Grathan.

"Woodsman! We've a wager here. We all know that you never doff that hat."

"Even when you sleep," one of the men-at-arms shouted.

Grathan nodded. "Even when you sleep. I say you've something even more peculiar than your eyes under it."

Magadon's eyes—colorless but for the pupils—often drew comment. He had explained them to the merchants as a defect of birth, and he supposed it was, coming as it did from his fiendish blood. Most called them "asp eyes" because they looked like single pips on the dice: an unlucky roll.

"A scar or somesuch, perhaps," Grathan said.

"Or maybe a balder head than Grathan's," shouted another of the merchants, bringing the rest to hoarse laughter.

"That'd be bald, indeed! A scar'd be better."

Grathan waited for the laughter to die down, then gestured at a young merchant who sat near him. "Tark here says you wear it out of superstition, for luck or somesuch. Which is it? There are twenty silver falcons to the man with the right of it."

Magadon pushed his floppy, wide-brimmed hat back on his head, though he took care to keep it over his horns.

"This hat?"

"None other," said the merchant.

Magadon decided to amuse himself by telling them the truth. "I wear it to hide the devil horns sticking from my brow. Or somesuch. And that makes you both as wrong as an orc in a dwarfhold, so you can add the twenty falcons to my fee."

The merchants and men-at-arms loosed raucous guffaws.

"Has you by the danglies there, Grathan!"

Grathan laughed along with the rest, even toasted Magadon with his tankard. When the group quieted, he said, "Done, sir. Such sum to you . . . or somesuch."

Magadon appreciated the turn of phrase. He tipped his hat in a salute.

"But the added fee only if you share a drink with us," called Tark, who had a much more commanding voice than his willowy frame suggested. "You abstain with such fortitude that Noss here," he jerked a thumb at a burly man-at-arms near him, "claims you're an ascetic Ilmaterite monk in disguise."

Noss's face wrinkled with puzzlement and he slurred through his beard. "Huh? Ascetic? What is that, a drunkard?"

More laughter.

"A drink, sir," seconded Grathan, and the others around the fire nodded and murmured agreement. "Come, join us. Our journey is almost done and custom demands we share a drink with our guide while still on the road."

Noss filled a tankard with ale and held it up for Magadon.

Magadon rehearsed an excuse in his head, prepared to offer it, but surprised himself by changing his mind. It *was* custom around the southern shores of the Inner Sea to drink with a guide while on the road; and more than that, he suddenly wanted company more than privacy.

He adjusted his hat, collected his bow and pack, and rose to his feet.

To the raccoons, he said, "I'm away, Mother." To the merchants, he said, "I can put your minds at ease that I am no ascetic, goodsirs, not by a wide margin. I've had everything from homebrewed swill in Starmantle to firewine in Westgate. But these days, I have sworn off spirits."

The merchants booed and hissed, but all held their smiles.

"You still must shed the hat," someone called.

"Yes! The hat!"

"Yes!"

Magadon realized that his hat had become the focus of too much attention, albeit intended as jest. He had to do something to diffuse the matter or one of the men would grab it off his head as a fireside prank. And if the caravaneers learned that he was fiendspawn, the smiles and camaraderie would vanish as quickly as they had appeared. He had seen it happen before when someone discovered his horns, or the birthmark that marred his bicep.

As he approached the fire, he summoned some of his mental energy, used it to extend his consciousness, and lightly reached into the minds of the dozen caravaneers around the fire. None showed any sign of noticing.

He took a subtle hold of their visual perception, pulled off his hat, and modified what they all witnessed. Instead of horns, he caused each of them to see only a smooth brow and his long dark hair.

"Not even bald!" one of them shouted.

"You see?" he said, and fixed the hat back on his head. He released his hold on the caravaneers' senses and offered a lie. "Neither scar nor bald head. I wear the hat because it belonged to a close comrade who fell to gnolls while we were on the road together. So when I am on the road, I rarely take it off. Well enough?"

The men understood that. "Well enough," most said in more subdued tones, and all nodded. Two even raised a drink in a salute. Others cursed the gnolls.

Magadon drew tight the drawstring on the hat and took a seat by the fire. As the jests, tales, and insults flew, he held his conversational ground as well as any. For the first time in almost a year, he truly felt like his old self. He was pleased to see that his hands remained steady throughout the evening, even when his thoughts returned to the Source, as they continually did. The pull was weakening, albeit slowly.

As Grathan and another merchant debated the intricacies of Sembian contract law, Magadon's mind drifted back to a night long ago, on the Plane of Shadows, when he and Erevis had shared a conversation across a campfire. Not banter or debate, but honest words between men. Magadon had admitted his lineage to Erevis and Erevis had admitted his fears to Magadon. Neither had judged the other. They'd become friends that night. Later events had only strengthened the bond.

Magadon missed Erevis and Riven, missed them both more than he missed the Source, more than he had missed the oak.

He realized all of a sudden that he had been foolish to isolate himself. His friends had not judged him for being born of a devil and they would not have judged him for his addiction to the Source. He had lost himself all the more easily for not having his friends around him. He resolved to find them as soon as the caravan reached Starmantle.

His mind made up, he allowed himself to enjoy the camaraderie around the campfire. After a few hours, the drink took its toll on the caravaneers. By the time Selûne passed her zenith, the merchants and men-at-arms had begun to wander to their wagons for sleep. A few, including Tark, nodded off where they sat.

Grathan stood. "I'm off to sleep."

"Goodeve to you," Magadon said. "We'll reach Starmantle in a few days."

Grathan nodded and started off, but turned back to Magadon. He came close and said in a low tone, "Woodsman . . . I've seen worse than your horns."

Magadon was too shocked even to stammer a denial. He felt himself flush. His mind raced. Before he could frame a reply, Grathan went on, "If a man keeps his word and cares for his own, I don't care what his appearance may be, or his bloodline. There are some here you could have trusted. And we could have managed the rest."

Magadon looked quickly around to see if any of the few remaining caravaneers were watching or listening. All were sleeping, or nearly so. Magadon looked up at Grathan.

"I hear your words," he said softly, studying the merchant's jowly face, "and appreciate them. But how . . . ?"

The merchant smiled and touched his silver cloak clasp. "This shields me from whatever trick you used on the rest. A valuable gewgaw for a merchant, no? I picked it up from a Red Wizard in Daerlun." Grathan sat down beside him.

Magadon stared at him and asked, "What now?"

"Now, nothing. You've naught to fear from me. If you wish the horns and whatever else a secret, a secret it shall remain. And I'll ask no more questions. I meet all sorts in my travels and here's what I know: All men keep a coffer full of secrets in their souls. It's what makes us men. You are no exception to that. But I will tell you this. You must open up that coffer and show the contents to another sometimes, or it rots in you."

Magadon heard wisdom in his words. He extended his hand and said, "You have my gratitude, Grathan."

"And you have my respect," the merchant answered, clasping Magadon's hand. "That cannot be an easy load to cart."

"Easier some times than others."

"Or somesuch?" Grathan said with a grin.

"Or somesuch," Magadon answered with a nod and smile.

"Goodeve to you, woodsman," Grathan said, and patted Magadon's shoulder. "Remember to take off your hat sometimes."

He rose and walked toward the wagons.

Magadon stared into the dying fire, thoughtful, playing with the drawstring of his hat. He reminded himself that he should not always assume the worst of men. He had grown so accustomed to thinking so little of himself that he automatically thought little of others.

The realization lightened his mood. He resolved again to contact Erevis and Riven—

Sudden motion near the oak drew his eye. The mother raccoon and her young scrambled up the tree. The young climbed awkwardly but fear lent them speed.

Frowning, Magadon scanned the area near the tree for a predator, but saw nothing unusual out to the limits of his nightvision.

A cloud bank swallowed the crescent of Selûne and the drone of insects immediately went quiet. The horses and train mules, tied to the wagons, snorted and pawed at the ground. The temperature dropped noticeably. A tingle tickled Magadon's exposed flesh. He felt magic in the air. The few snoring men around the fire stirred restlessly and waved a hand in the air, as if fending off nightmares.

Magadon's heart began to thump. For a moment, he feared that he had fallen asleep, that Grathan's words had been a dream, that the walls he had built in his mind had crumbled and that he would soon hear his father, see the men around the fire burst into flame. His hands started to tremble but he steeled himself, told himself that it was no dream.

He took up his bow, rose to his feet, and with difficulty, nocked an arrow. The familiar movement steadied him. He turned in a circle and looked out on the plain but saw nothing to alarm him—just rolling grass, the old oak, and few other scattered trees. He stepped around the fire and nudged Tark, who was sleeping.

"Up," he ordered. "And the rest. Be quick and quiet. Something comes."

Tark did not move. Neither did anyone else.

"Up!" Magadon said, and kneed him hard.

Tark fell off his barrel, but neither he nor any of the other caravaneers around the fire stirred.

Magadon cursed. Tark and the other men had been enspelled. He weighed whether to raise the alarm and tip off the attackers that he knew of their presence. He decided there was no other way.

"Is anyone awake?" he shouted at the wagons. "Grathan!"

His shouts agitated the pack animals further, but no one in the caravan answered his call.

He was alone. Perhaps his mental abilities had spared him the effect of whatever spell had rendered the rest of the men unconscious. He licked his lips, swallowed, and focused his mind on his arrow tip, charging it with mental energy. Power filled it and it shone red. It would pierce plate armor.

Magadon scoured the terrain with his eyes. He controlled his breathing, steadied his hands, and held his calm. He drew on his mental power, transformed energy into a physical force, and surrounded himself in a translucent barrier that would deflect incoming projectiles. Wrapped in the power of his own mind, he turned a slow circle and sought a target.

"Father?" he shouted, nervous as the word left his mouth. "Show yourself!"

A sound like rushing wind filled his ears, though there was no wind. He scanned the night for the source but saw nothing. The sound grew, louder, louder, until—

At the limits of his darkvision, a mass of squirming tendrils seeped into view. As thick around as the oak, as black as ink, they wormed sickeningly over the terrain. Their motion reminded him of the kraken's tentacles, of the grotesque limbs of the darkweaver that he had faced on the Plane of Shadows.

The tentacles brought a fog of darkness in their wake.

Two pinpoint pairs of light formed in the darkness above the tentacles, one pair the cold gray of old iron, the other pair a dull gold.

Eyes.

The rushing sound grew still louder, as loud as a cyclone. Magadon thought his eardrums would burst. The horses and mules panicked. Two snapped their lines and sped off into the night.

"Who are you?" Magadon shouted, his voice barely audible over the roar.

The tendrils drew closer; so did the eyes.

"Show yourselves!"

No response, so Magadon loosed an arrow at one pair of eyes. The missile streaked from his bow, leaving a red trail of energy in its wake. When it hit the darkness, it vanished with no visible effect.

Screaming, Magadon fired another arrow, another. The rushing sound ate his battle cries; the darkness ate his arrows.

The rush reached a crescendo, so loud Magadon felt his head would explode. How could the caravaneers sleep through it? It was like a pair of knives driven into his eardrums. He dropped his bow and clamped his hands over his ears. He screamed in pain but the roar swallowed the sound.

Without warning, the roar ceased.

But for his gasps, silence ruled the night.

Magadon's ears rang; his temples throbbed. He looked up and saw that the tendrils were gone, the eyes were gone. He was alone. He looked at his palms to see if there was any blood, saw none.

He almost collapsed with relief.

"Tark," he nudged the young merchant. "Tark!"

Still no response.

A rustle from above drew his gaze. He looked up and what he saw stole both strength and breath. His hands fell to his sides.

"Gods," he mouthed.

The night took him.

Elyril wore a false face—that of a solicitous young niece and trusted political advisor to Lady Mirabeta Selkirk—and stood beside her aunt next to the bed of the dead overmaster. They had traveled by common coach rather than carriage across the streets of Ordulin, and both wore heavy, plain, hooded cloaks. After hearing what the messenger had to say, they had not wanted their passage noted. The city was in enough turmoil. All of Sembia was in turmoil.

Kendrick Selkirk the Tall lay cold, pale, and very dead between his sheets. The overmaster's balding, gray-haired chamberlain, Minnen, stood in the doorway behind Elyril and her aunt, wringing his age-spotted hands. Beside him stood the bearded house mage, Saken, arms crossed over his ample belly, chapped lips pressed hard together. The circles under his eyes looked as if they had been drawn with charcoal.

Seeing the dead overmaster for herself, Elyril felt an uncontrollable urge to smile. She masked her mirth with a hand before her mouth and a feigned cough.

"I have sent for priests of Tyr, Countess," Minnen said to Mirabeta. "To certify the death and prepare the body."

Mirabeta nodded. "Well done, Minnen. You have sent word to Selkirk's family?"

Kendrick Selkirk's immediate family consisted of only his two sons, Miklos and Kavil. His wife had been dead almost a year.

Minnen fiddled with the flare at the end of his shirt sleeve. "I have dispatched messengers, but contacting Miklos or Kavil is always difficult. As is their wont, they are away from Ordulin. No one seems to know their current location. That is why I hurried a messenger to your estate, Countess. You are the overmaster's cousin, his only family in Ordulin. Despite your . . ." he cleared his throat and looked embarrassed, " . . . political differences, you must speak for the overmaster's needs until his sons arrive."

Mirabeta and Elyril shared a glance and Elyril could read her aunt's mind: *If* the overmaster's sons arrive.

No doubt it amused Mirabeta that Kendrick Selkirk's body and estate were in her charge, if only temporarily. Most of Ordulin saw Mirabeta as a respectful rival of Kendrick. Elyril knew better. Mirabeta had thought her cousin little more than a weakling and dolt whose incompetence had led Sembia in the direction of disaster. Probably Mirabeta would have had him killed herself if she had thought she could have avoided suspicion.

The countess ambled around the chamber, eyeing the rugs, the sideboard, the swords and shield over the large fireplace. "That was well conceived, Minnen. Kendrick and I disagreed on political matters, but he was ever my beloved cousin."

Minnen wisely held his tongue.

"Should we examine the body, aunt?" Elyril suggested, an idea born of a desire to provide political cover for her aunt, and a desire to touch something dead.

The old chamberlain looked appalled. "Why, Mistress?"

Before Elyril could answer, Saken unfolded his arms and said to Mirabeta, "There is no sign of violence, Countess. The wards on the room were intact and my preliminary divinations have detected nothing untoward." The mage looked pointedly at Elyril. "There is no reason to examine the overmaster's body."

"A skilled assassin would leave no sign," Elyril said to the room.

Minnen frowned. "The mistress seems to know much of the quiet arts."

Elyril smiled politely to hide her hatred.

Minnen looked to Mirabeta. "None passed his door last night, Countess. Of that I am certain."

Mirabeta looked from Elyril to Minnen. "And I am certain of no such thing. As my niece observed, a skilled assassin would leave no sign, magical or otherwise."

Elyril was pleased. Mirabeta's political instincts, honed through years of maneuvering in Sembia's capital, were as sharp as ever. The countess did not know that Selkirk had been murdered. But she did know that *she* had not been involved in the murder, if murder it was. She therefore realized that she would be best served politically by insisting on a zealous and thorough investigation. She could only gain from it, whether she found a murderer or determined that Overmaster Selkirk had died of natural causes.

Elyril knew the truth, of course, and the secret she held made her smile.

"My cousin was as healthy as a cart ox," Mirabeta said. "I saw him just two days ago. He showed no signs of illness, yet we are to believe that he just died in his sleep?"

"Men die," said Saken with shrug.

"And men are murdered," Mirabeta said with a dismissive wave of her hand. "I will determine which occurred here."

Without waiting for permission, Elyril bent over the overmaster's corpse, pried open his mouth, and examined his gums. Finding nothing—as she knew she would not, for the Nightseer would not use poison—she peeled back his eyelids and studied the eyes. Then she lifted his arms and looked in his armpits.

"Mistress!" the chamberlain said, appalled.

Elyril let the overmaster's arms drop to the bed and spoke a lie. "I have heard of poisons that discolor the skin for only a short time before all signs vanish. I do not want evidence to go unnoticed."

"Poison!" Minnen exclaimed.

Saken nodded thoughtfully. "I, too, have heard of such poisons."

"As have I," Mirabeta said.

Overruled, the chamberlain quieted.

Elyril went through the motions of thoroughly examining the body. Touching the cold, dry flesh of the corpse aroused her, but she kept her face expressionless. Attuned as she was to the Shadow Weave and Shar, she felt the squirming, dark thing hidden within the corpse.

"I can find nothing," she said to her aunt. "But that means nothing."

"Who else knows of this, Minnen?" Mirabeta asked.

Minnen answered. "The messengers I dispatched, but they are all trusted men. The priests of Tyr, by now. No others."

"Keep it so for now," Mirabeta ordered. "Do not let the household staff leave the grounds. All are to be questioned under spell by the priests. Including both of you."

Both reddened, but both nodded.

"Perhaps he did die in his sleep," Mirabeta said, and Elyril could see in her aunt's expression that she hoped it was otherwise. "We will know soon enough. A resurrection should be attempted. I will pay for it, of course."

Elyril could tell from the marked lack of enthusiasm in her aunt's tone that she begrudged the idea; she made it only to maintain appearances. No doubt she hoped the resurrection would fail, as they sometimes did. Elyril, of course, *knew* a resurrection would fail. Rivalen had assured her of as much.

Minnen said, "That is most gracious, Countess. But . . ."

"Speak, Minnen," Mirabeta ordered.

Minnen nodded. "I am aware of the contents of Lord Selkirk's testament, Countess. He specifically forbids any attempt to resurrect him after his death. As you know, he was a faithful follower of Tyr. He regarded his end as his end."

For a moment, Mirabeta said nothing. She looked at Elyril and Elyril felt certain that her aunt would not be able to contain a smile. But she did, somehow, and returned her gaze to Minnen.

"I understand, Minnen. Thank you. Then I shall pay all costs of the investigation into his death. That is the least I can do for my cousin."

"Countess, I am certain the High Council would appropriate—"

"He was my cousin and I will pay," Mirabeta said, cutting off discussion.

More positioning, Elyril knew.

"Of course, Countess," Minnen said.

Mirabeta turned to Elyril and Elyril saw the pleasure in her aunt's expression. The wrinkles around the countess's eyes looked less pronounced than usual.

"I will await the arrival of the priests with Minnen and Saken," Mirabeta said to Elyril. "Return to our estate. Send out messengers under seal. The High Council is to meet in emergency session as soon as possible. A successor must be chosen."

Elyril started to go, but turned and said, "May I offer a suggestion, Aunt?"

Mirabeta nodded and Elyril spoke the Nightseer's wishes. "A ruler is dead. The stability of the state during the transition is paramount. All suspicions must be laid to rest. My cousin cannot be resurrected, true, but would it not be prudent to put questions to his body about the circumstances surrounding his death, and to do so before the High Council?"

"Necromancy," Minnen murmured.

Saken raised his eyebrows thoughtfully and nodded. "There is precedent. Four hundred years ago, Overmaster Gelarbis was murdered by a mob. The questioning of his body by priests, in the presence of the members of the High Council, helped locate the murderer."

Elyril could have hugged the fat house mage, though his words were probably unnecessary. Mirabeta would have seen the political benefit of a magical inquiry before the council. It would publicly exonerate her of any involvement and solidify her guise as a concerned cousin. Her aunt wore false faces almost as well as a Sharran.

"Your idea has merit," Mirabeta said. "I will think about this. My cousin's wishes must be considered. Does his testament speak of such matters, Minnen?"

Minnen did not look her in the eye. "It does not, Countess."

Again, Mirabeta managed not to smile. "Off now, Elyril," she said.

As she walked to the door, Elyril noticed Saken's ragged shadow on the floor. She could tell from looking at it that the mage would be dead within a year.

"I have a secret," she whispered to him, grinning, and exited the chamber.

Sometime later—perhaps days, Magadon could not tell—he opened his eyes to darkness. He did not feel a blindfold against his face. Ordinarily, the fiend's blood in his veins allowed him to see through darkness, but not this time. A magical shroud, then. The moist air slicked his skin.

He was seated, and bindings as cold as ice held him at his wrists, ankles, and waist. He could hardly move. He remembered little. His mind felt sluggish. He tried to summon a small amount of mental energy and transform it into light, but the attempt fizzled. Something was suppressing his abilities as a mind mage.

"He is awake," said a voice. "The suppression cloud is working."

"Then we go," said another.

Before Magadon could ponder what the words meant, he felt the sudden rush of motion and the dizziness that often accompanied magical travel. It reminded him of the times Erevis had moved them between worlds by drawing shadows about them.

When all stopped, he was still in darkness. A smell reached through the ink: salt—sea salt. He heard the telltale creak of a ship at sea, felt the slow roll of the waves.

A twinge of nervousness ran through him. The smell of the sea reminded him of things he would have rather forgotten.

"Show yourself," he demanded, and tried not to betray his nervousness. His dry throat made his voice croak.

The second voice answered, calm and cold. "Soon, mind mage. The magical shroud is a necessary precaution to prevent the use of your mental powers. Be assured, however, that we can see you."

Magadon struggled against the bindings at his wrists and ankles, to no avail.

"We? Who are you?" Magadon asked. "Where are we?"

"My name is Rivalen Tanthul," the voice said from Magadon's right.

The name meant nothing to Magadon. Rivalen went on, and this time his voice was behind Magadon. He must have been circling him.

"Your name is Magadon Kest and you hail from Starmantle. You are fiendspawn and a mind mage. A year ago, you had contact with something that belongs to my people."

Magadon did not understand. "Your people? I do not know what you mean—"

Then he understood. A knot formed in his throat. Rivalen drew the knot tighter.

"We are Netherese, Magadon Fiendspawn," he said.

Fear took root in Magadon's stomach. The Source was Netherese.

"Where are we?" Magadon said, but he had already begun to suspect.

"We are on a ship on the Inner Sea," Rivalen said. "Above Sakkors. Above the Source."

Magadon was sweating. "Why have you brought me here? I will not do anything for you."

"You will," Rivalen answered calmly. "Because I will make you.

I am sorry, but I must." He paused, then said, "The Source . . . it hurt you?"

Magadon shook his head. The Source had not hurt him. It had given him everything he could have wanted, or at least made him think that he had everything he wanted. And that was the problem. Once that feeling was gone, he had nearly killed himself trying to find a substitute for it.

Another voice asked, "How did you come to speak our language, mind mage?"

The question surprised Magadon. He did not realize that he had been speaking Loross. He had learned it from—

"Did the Source teach you our tongue?" the voice asked. "How intriguing. What else did you learn from it?"

Magadon reminded himself of Ssessimyth, the kraken, and how it had been snared in the Source, made content to spend its life in useless indolence, reliving a history that was not its own. Magadon wanted no part of it. He struggled against the bonds, grunting, but they did not budge.

"The bonds are composed of shadowstuff, Magadon," Rivalen said. "You cannot break them. You will only exhaust yourself."

Magadon ignored Rivalen and struggled nevertheless. He had worked so long to regain himself. He would not lose himself again. He would not.

As Rivalen had promised, he soon exhausted himself. The magic in the bonds sapped his energy. Gasping, he slouched in his chair. He prayed that the kraken would surface from Sakkors and destroy the ship, kill them all.

"I cannot help you," he said. "I will not."

Rivalen said, "The Source is torporous, Magadon. How did that happen?"

"Did you do something to it?" asked the second voice.

Magadon almost laughed, as if he could do something to the Source.

The second voice said, "It was attacked. You were here when it happened. I have determined that much. Answer my question. If you lie to me, I will know."

Magadon closed his eyes, tried to convince himself he was dreaming, lost in a drug haze in some smoky basement den in Starmantle.

"Speak," commanded Rivalen.

He was not dreaming.

"Not attacked," he said. "Tapped. An artifact tapped it, drew on its power to serve the wizard who created the Rain of Fire."

"A wizard *created* the Rain of Fire?" the second voice said, astonishment in his tone.

Magadon nodded. "Yes. He was from . . . somewhere else. He used the power in the Source to empower his spell."

"Remarkable," the second voice said.

Magadon realized that he had said too much. He did not want his captors to know of the tower on the Wayrock. Riven might still be there.

"The wizard is dead," he added. "I saw his body, broken and burned to ash by the sun. The artifact he used to tap the Source is also destroyed."

"He is speaking truth," the second voice said, presumably to Rivalen.

Silence followed for a time, as if his two captors were silently conferring. Finally, Rivalen said, "We need you to awaken the Source, Magadon. Only a mind mage can do it. Only you can do it."

Magadon closed his eyes and shook his head.

"I am sorry, then," Rivalen said, and incanted the words to a spell.

Magadon gripped the arms of the chair, braced himself to resist whatever spell Rivalen would cast.

"Help us, Magadon," Rivalen said.

There was magic in Rivalen's voice, power. Magadon could feel it pulling at his will. He fought it.

"No."

"You must. Awaken it for us, Magadon."

Magadon gritted his teeth while Rivalen's bidding wormed its way into his mind. He strained against his bonds, felt them give slightly. His heart pounded hard in his chest.

"It . . . will . . . kill . . . me!" he shouted.

"Careful, brother," cautioned the second voice.

"You must do it, nevertheless," commanded Rivalen. "Awaken it for us, Magadon."

Magadon flailed like a mad thing against his bonds. Rivalen's spell reverberated through his mind, the words like hammer blows. Rivalen's voice soaked his will.

Magadon was weakening.

The words rang in his ears, sank under his skin. He felt himself losing, thinking of how much easier it would be if he simply submitted.

"No! No!"

"Almost," said the second voice.

"You wish to do it," said Rivalen. "I can see it in your eyes. Surrender to it, Magadon. End the pain."

Rivalen's words sounded so much like those spoken by Magadon's archdevil father in his dreams that they shook Magadon to his core. He gritted his teeth so hard he bit his tongue. The sharp flash of pain and the taste of blood brought him an instant of clarity, of freedom. A sliver of mental energy slipped through the power-dampening shroud and made itself available to him. Magadon grabbed onto it like a lifeline and did the only thing he could think of to save himself.

Vermilion light haloed his head, penetrating even the ink of the shroud. His captors shouted. He felt hands upon him.

Magadon grinned even as the pain came. He felt as if he were breaking apart. He screamed as he splintered.

CHAPTER FOUR

10 Marpenoth, the Year of Lightning Storms

Cale dreamed of Magadon, though his friend's voice sounded like Aril's, the halfling boy whom Cale had saved almost two tendays earlier. Cale watched, frozen, as Magadon slipped into a dark void, screaming for help. Cale forced himself from his paralysis, shadowstepped to the edge of the void, dived for Magadon's outstretched hand, and barely caught it. He seized a firm grip, then saw that Magadon's fingernails had turned to black claws, and that his eyes, ordinarily colorless but for the black pupils, were golden.

Startled, he lost his grip. Magadon disappeared into the shadows, screaming. Cale shouted after him, "Mask! Mask!"

But there was no answer. Magadon was gone.

The roll of distant thunder woke him. He lay on his back in bed, heart racing, and stared up at the log crossbeams of the cottage, barely visible in the dark. The dream had set his heart to racing. He had called Magadon by the name of his god. The realization unsettled him.

Mags? he projected, tentatively. As a mind mage, Magadon had easily contacted Cale through dreams before.

No response. Just a dream, then. He exhaled slowly and calmed himself. The deep of night surrounded him. He found comfort in the darkness. A distant lightning flash lit the room and pasted shadows on the walls. Cale sensed every one of them, *knew* every one of them for the instant of their existence.

Midnight was near, he knew. The Chosen of Mask always knew when the Shadowlord's holy hour approached.

He had been asleep only an hour, perhaps two. He had not even bothered to change his clothing before getting into bed. The stink of another night's travels, another night's killings, clung to his clothes.

Varra lay beside him, warm, soft, *human*. Her even breathing steadied his jumbled mind. He often lay awake through the night and listened to her breathe, watched the rise and fall of her breast. Since his transformation into a shade, he needed less and less sleep. But he always needed warmth; he always needed someone near him to remind him that he was still human, at least in part.

He drew the night about him and moved his body instantly across the room into the darkness near the shuttered window. Varra stirred slightly at his sudden absence but did not awaken.

Thunder rumbled again in the distance, the deep-chested growl of a beast. A storm was coming—a big one. It had been a long while since they had seen rain.

In silence, Cale lifted the latch on the window shutters and gently pushed them open. Moonlight spilled into the cottage. Its touch nettled Cale's flesh. Tendrils of darkness swirled protectively across his skin.

A cloud bank loomed in the distance, bearing toward the cottage, devouring the stars as it came. Lightning split the sky, and its afterglow limned the clouds with a purple cast. Cale thought it ominous. Thunder quickly followed and Cale fancied the thunder had a voice.

Everything dies, it rumbled.

He searched the sky for Selûne and found her hanging low in a half-circle over the top of the forest, trailing the glowing cascade of her Tears. Cale could not look at the Tears without thinking of Jak.

Just about a year ago, he had seen the most powerful wizard he'd ever known pull one of the Tears from the Outer Darkness and use it to eclipse the sun. In the end, the wizard's reasons for doing so had been small ones, human ones, though the wizard had been far from human. Cale almost admired him for his reasons. But the admiration had not kept Cale from killing him, because the wizard's small reasons had led to the death of Cale's best friend.

Thunder rolled, soft, threatening, and mocking. *Everything dies.*

The memory of those days darkened Cale's already somber mood. The night answered his emotions and the air around him swirled with black tendrils. Behind him, Varra turned in her sleep.

"I still blame you," he whispered to Mask.

When he looked back on the events involving the wizard, Cale saw the Shadowlord's manipulation in all of it. Through his scheming, Mask had managed to steal an entire temple of Cyric. The whole plot had been little more than divine burglary, petty theft. And it had cost Cale his humanity and Jak his life. Cale could not forgive Mask for exacting so high a price.

Before Jak had died, Cale promised his friend that he would try to be a hero. He had saved Aril and the halfling village, had done similar deeds throughout upcountry Sembia for months. But it did not feel like enough; he did not feel like himself. He missed his friends, missed . . . something he could not articulate.

He looked out on the dark forest meadow. An elm of middling size dominated the oval expanse of low, browning grass. Patches of wildflowers, mostly purplesnaps, daisies, and lady's slipper, dotted the meadow. Varra had tried transplanting the wildflowers into a more orderly arrangement, but the flowers she moved invariably died.

Despite the strange weather and lack of rain, Varra had managed to grow a thriving vegetable garden of cabbages, turnips, carrots, and beans. At Cale's request, she also grew pipeweed. Large stones from the nearby stream walled the vegetable garden to keep the rabbits at bay. The garden did not produce enough to live on, but Varra supplemented their needs with monthly trips to a nearby village, though she had been returning with less and less of late.

A table and two chairs sat under the elm. Cale had made them from forest deadwood. Not bad work. Varra loved to sit in the shade of the tree and watch the flowers in the sun. She had come out of the darkness of Skullport and made the forest cottage and sun-drenched meadow in upcountry Sembia her home. Cale thought her amazing for that.

Cale had bought the cottage and its land from the heirs of a dead woodsman. The place belonged to him, but more and more he knew it wasn't his home. He remembered words Jak had spoken once—*For men like us, friends are home.* Cale missed his friends. The time he'd spent in the cottage had been a welcome respite, but a temporary one. Something was coming for him, coming for him as certain as the storm. He was not sure how he would tell Varra. He looked back on her sleeping form and wondered if she already knew.

Their relationship was unusual. They had lived together a year but Cale knew little about her past, and made a point not to ask. She, in turn, respected his privacy in the same way. They shared a home, a bed, their bodies from time to time, but little else. Cale cared for her deeply, and she cared for him, but he knew he could not stay with her much longer.

He ticked the moments away as midnight drew closer. When Mask's holy hour was imminent, he let the shadows in the meadow steal into his mind, and willed himself into the darkness under the elm, near the two chairs. Always keen of ear, and even sharper of ear in darkness, Cale heard the fauna stalking the woods, the chirp of crickets, the soft coo of the nightjar that nested on the ground under the scrub, the rush of the wind through the forest.

He moved the chair so he could watch the storm approach over the woods. He reached into his pocket and took out the smooth, oval stone that Aril had given him.

"Shadowman," he said, and smiled. He treasured the stone.

The clouds ate more of the sky. Thunder rumbled its promise.

Cale ran his thumb over the smooth stone, thoughtful. He heard the hiss of approaching rain. The wind set the trees to swaying. Lightning cut the sky. Thunder boomed. He wondered if it would wake Varra. After so much time living underground, she still had not grown accustomed to thunderstorms.

He reached into another pocket and retrieved Jak's ivory-bowled pipe, the pipe Cale had taken from his dead friend as a token of remembrance. He took out a small leather pouch of pipeweed, grown in Varra's garden, and filled the pipe's bowl. He tamped, struck a tindertwig, and lit.

Midnight arrived. Cale felt it as a charge in his bones. Rain came with it.

A year ago, Cale would have spent the next hour in prayer, asking Mask to imprint his mind with the power to cast spells. But not any more. Cale had not prayed to Mask or cast a spell since Jak's death. He had created his own ritual for the midnight hour.

He took a draw on the pipe and exhaled a cloud of smoke. He watched the cloud dance between the raindrops and stream off into the night sky.

The elm shielded him from the worst of the rain, but he welcomed the downpour. It washed the stink of his travels from him. It lasted only a short time—the rain never lingered.

Cale spent the next hours in his chair, listening to the wind, and communing not with his god, but with his past.

"I do not belong to you any more," he said to Mask. "And neither does the night."

It belonged to the shadowman.

I awaken in a perfectly square room. A soft red glow suffuses the air, providing light. I see no sign of Rivalen Tanthul and I no longer smell the sea. My bonds are gone.

Have I escaped? I remember shouting, a flash of green, but little else. My mind feels as thick as mud. I know I tried to do something to escape but I cannot remember.

How long have I been here?

The room looks vaguely familiar to me but I cannot place it. I have been here before, though, I am sure of that. The room reminds me of a prison cell. There are no windows and only a single iron-bound door.

Looking at the door, I feel certain that I am supposed to do something. But I cannot remember. The lapse troubles me.

I sit on the floor and the smooth cobblestones feel cool through my clothes. My body aches, as if I have been in combat, or beaten.

Have I been tortured?

I have none of my gear or weapons. I wear only a loose wool tunic, breeches, and boots. Even my hat is gone, and I never take off my hat. I reach up to feel my exposed horns . . .

. . . they are gone.

Startled, I run my hands over my brow. I feel nothing but smooth skin. Has Rivalen removed my horns and healed the wounds? I hold out my arms to examine the rest of my body . . .

The birthmark on my bicep, the sword ensheathed in flames, the brand of my father, is also gone. How is that possible? I tried for years to efface that brand, scarring my skin in the process. Even the scars are gone. So, too, is the patch of scales on the small of my back. I feel only smooth skin, human skin. My heart races.

Someone has stripped my fiendish blood from me.

"This is not possible," I say.

"You have come at last," says a voice behind me.

I scramble to my feet and whirl around. I see no one else in the room. The voice sounds familiar, though, almost . . .

"Up here. On the wall."

I look up and my head swims with dizziness. For a moment, I cannot not focus my eyes. I wobble on my feet, hold out my arms for balance. The feeling passes and I notice a thin, horizontal slit in the stone, more than three-quarters of the way up the wall. If it were not so high, it would be a feeding slit.

I move slowly to the wall, wary for a trick.

"Who are you?" I ask. I keep my voice low for no reason I can articulate.

"Come up so you can see me. I will show you."

The request turns my skin cold. "Tell me who you are," I demand.

"In a moment. Come up, first. I . . . need help."

Help? The word sends a thrill through me. I cannot deny someone who needs help. I study the slit. I might be able to jump up and get my fingers in it, then pull myself up.

"I don't know if I can make it."

"You can," says the voice with certainty. "Do it now."

Without thinking, I jump up and catch the edge of the slit with both hands. I scrabble my boots against the wall for leverage and heave myself up with a grunt. When I can peer through the opening, I find myself staring at another pair of eyes exactly like mine—black pupils, no color. I gasp, startled, and lose my grip. I fall back to the floor in a heap. The impact knocks the breath from me.

"I am sorry," says the voice. "I should have prepared you. Are you all right?"

I climb to my feet, eyeing the slit, stammering, "Your eyes are like mine! How can that be?"

"No," says the voice. "Your eyes are different. I saw them. They are green."

I reel. Green? I am still groggy from the escape, or from the torture, or whatever has happened to me. This does not make sense. How can my eyes be green?

"Are you still there?" asks the voice.

I nod, though the speaker cannot see me.

"Are you a prisoner here?" I ask. "Where are we? Who are you? And why do you look like . . . like I should look?" The speaker sighs, as if at a precocious child. "Listen carefully. What I am about to say will alarm you. Are you prepared?"

I'm sweating, and I don't know why. My skin turns goose flesh.

"Yes," I lie.

The voice says, "There is no 'here' and you are not a prisoner."

CHAPTER FIVE

10 Marpenoth, the Year of Lightning Storms

Word of the emergency session of Sembia's High Council spread through Ordulin like a plague. Rumors ran rampant, most of them hurriedly planted by this or that member of the council. Hushed voices in taverns spoke of the Overmaster's demise and the coming power struggle among the council members.

At Mirabeta's behest, Elyril had hired several trusted rumormongers to suggest that Overmaster Selkirk had been murdered and that nobles in service to Endren Corrinthal of Saerb had been complicit. The countess was portrayed as an indefatigable pursuer of the murderers.

The Highspeaker of the Council delayed the emergency session for more than a tenday, to allow time for the twenty-one members of the High Council to prepare and receive instructions. Mirabeta and Elyril, though impatient to grab power, used the time to good effect. They exhausted Ordulin's messengers by sending queries to fellow members of the High Council, trying to determine where each stood on who should be elected the next overmaster. Mirabeta met face to face with seven of her colleagues. Some were coy, but for the most part, the office seemed destined for either Mirabeta or Endren Corrinthal. Elyril marvelled at the loyalty Endren commanded. Saerb was a trade town of little significance, but Endren Corrinthal was the second most powerful member of the High Council. She did not understand how he'd managed it.

Meanwhile, the overmaster's body was sent in magical stasis to the Tower of the Scales, the small shrine dedicated to his patron god, Tyr. The state funeral was scheduled for a tenday later, a sufficient time to allow outlying nobles to travel to Ordulin to give honor to the dead. The Tyrrans forbade anyone from seeing the body until the questioning before the High Council, and not even Mirabeta dared gainsay them.

Sembia's High Council was at last summoned to session. The elaborate gong tower of the High House of the Wonderful Wheel, Gond's temple, sounded the ceremonial summons. The privilege to sound the summons rotated among the faiths of the city every decade and was determined by lot.

Assisted by their coach driver, Elyril and Mirabeta stepped from their lacquered carriage into the shadow of the Great Council Hall of Sembia. Both wore elaborate, high-waisted satin gowns, the current custom of noblewomen in the capital, though both had selected subdued colors in order to appear respectful of the overmaster's death. They also wore small, enchanted knives on thigh sheaths.

Mirabeta, who ordinarily glittered like a dragon's hoard, had limited her jewelry to a black pearl necklace and matching earrings. Elyril knew both the necklace and the earrings to hold powerful protective and communicative magics. For her part, Elyril wore jewelry that featured amethysts set into antique silver. The purple of the gems and the black of the tarnished metal were Shar's holy colors, Elyril's secret homage to her goddess. Elyril also wore her invisible holy symbol on a neck chain under her gown.

The stately Council Hall, a pentagonal affair, sat amid a tree-dotted municipal district in the center of the capital. Autumn had turned the maple leaves blood red. The gated grounds of the Tower of the City Guard and the impenetrable walls of the Sembian mint, called the Guarded Gate, flanked the great hall to either side. A pair of limestone golems, chiseled to look like oversized Sembian guardsmen in archaic armor, stood to either side of the mint's eponymous metal gate.

The polished limestone facade of the great hall and its five towers gleamed almost white in the setting sun. The glass dome of the central rotunda, known by all to be enchanted with the durability of steel, glittered in the sunlight. Flags flying the Sembian Raven and Silver flapped from the tower tops. Black pennons hung below the flags to mark Kendrick Selkirk's passing. Pairs of uniformed city guardsmen, standing at attention and holding halberds at arms, flanked the various entrances to the hall. All wore black armbands on the left biceps, also in honor of Kendrick. They appeared as miniature versions of the golems guarding the mint.

Each tower of the hall opened into a wide corridor, which featured several side chambers and halls, and each of the five corridors intersected at the rotunda of the High Council. She had always thought the whole thing looked something like a giant fivestar, with the rotunda as the hub, the five towers as points, and the corridors as legs.

The carriages of the council members ringed the hall, and several hundred armed and armored guards milled among them. All wore the heraldry of one or another member of the High Council. Ordinary citizens were being routed away from the municipal district, but Sembian custom allowed each council member an armed escort of up to twenty guards, though this right had been rarely exercised in the past.

Elyril noted the various tabards and recognized that the guards had drifted into two large groups, reflecting the anticipated schism in the High Council. The soldiers serving the members loyal to Endren Corrinthal of Saerb massed to the eastern side of the building, along the Wide Way, while those in service to the nobles loyal to Mirabeta massed on the west, on Norgrim's Ride. Mirabeta had sent her force to the hall in the mid afternoon, and they moved among those on Norgrim's Ride.

The two groups eyed each other. Steel and hostility filled the streets.

"Things could turn bloody quickly," Elyril said to her aunt.

Mirabeta nodded and the coachman pretended not to hear.

A force of perhaps seventy city guards was spread throughout the street around the Council Hall and kept the nobles' escorts at a distance. Unlike the sentries posted at the Hall's doors, dressed in customary ceremonial garb, those in the street bore steel shields, wore chain hauberks under blue tabards, and carried heavy maces. Elyril did not see Raithspur, the tall, grizzled captain of the guard. The captain, it seemed, was wise enough not to wade too deeply into political waters.

The men loyal to Mirabeta cheered upon her appearance—at the urging of Mirabeta's own twenty men—and Elyril's aunt smiled in response. Anything more would have been undignified. The men loyal to Endren scowled and a few even booed. Mirabeta only held her smile.

The pair of guardsmen at the nearest doorway of the Hall left their posts and marched down the flagstone walkway to Elyril and Mirabeta.

"Countess," the middle-aged, bearded guardsman said, snapping to attention. "You are the final member to arrive. By order of the highspeaker, we shall escort you to the doors. The great hall has been cleared. None have been allowed within save the members and their *wolmoners*."

Elyril blinked in surprise. She had not heard the archaic term, *wolmoner*, in many years. Most used the term "vigilman" or "wallman" instead. The custom dated back centuries, when leaders were allowed only one trusted aide, their wallman, in sensitive meetings. Wallmen were originally warriors who served as bodyguards, but as political maneuvering became more important than force of arms, the position shifted to be filled by political advisors like Elyril. The High Council invoked the wallman rule only when a session was politically charged or involved confidential matters.

"My niece is my wallman," Mirabeta answered. "Lead on."

The guardsmen nodded, flanked Elyril and Mirabeta, and escorted them up the walkway through the ring of guards. The two guardsmen resumed their stations at the doors and Mirabeta and Elyril left them behind as they entered the Council Hall.

Mirabeta quickened her stride. Elyril hurried to keep pace. Despite the countess's advancing age—she had seen well over fifty winters, a few less than twice Elyril's twenty-seven—she remained a trim woman, and her walking speed, when she had a purpose in mind, approached a jog.

Their footsteps echoed off the walls of the tower's entry hall. Elyril had never before seen it empty. Usually petitioners, merchants, and minor nobles thronged the building, trying to catch the ear of this or that member of the High Council.

They continued into the long, soaring hall of monuments. Towering statues carved from marble, quarried in distant Yhaunn, lined the hall. The sculptures depicted every Overmaster of Sembia since the founding of the realm. Plaques on the bases displayed their names. Magically colored lighting accented the statues to good effect. The exaggerated, heroic proportions of the sculptures made Elyril think of Volumvax. She licked her lips and looked for him in the statues' shadows.

Mirabeta did not look at any of the statues save the last, that of her dead cousin. There, she stopped. The statue had been completed only two months earlier. Kendrick Selkirk had served as overmaster for just over three years, long enough to get his image carved in stone before dying, but too brief to accomplish anything of note.

"There are no over*mistresses* in this hall," Elyril observed, watering the seed of Mirabeta's ambition.

"There will be," Mirabeta said.

From the far side of the hall, in the direction of the rotunda, came a man's voice. "Gloating ill becomes you, Countess."

Elyril and Mirabeta turned to see Endren Corrinthal walking toward them. The tall nobleman wore a long, ermine-trimmed blue jacket over a collared silk shirt and black breeches. Thick gray hair topped a craggy, careworn face. His overlarge nose had been broken at least once, and his beard and moustache only partially hid a ragged scar that marked his left cheek. A rapier hung from his belt and by all accounts, he knew how to use it.

Mirabeta affected a smile, though the hardness never left her eyes.

"And snide comments ill become you, Endren, who are already so . . . ill-becomed."

Endren chuckled as he crossed the hall. He bowed before Mirabeta.

"It is unfortunate, Countess, that you have never turned that sharp intellect to the public good."

"Quite the contrary, Endren. I have done exactly that for my entire life. And I plan to continue doing so. As overmistress."

Endren's eyes narrowed at Mirabeta's naked statement of ambition but he managed a polite nod. "We shall see," he said, and turned to Elyril and bowed. "Mistress Elyril. You are as lovely as ever. It is a pity you remain unmarried."

Elyril curtsied, wondering as she did how Endren's screams might sound as she offered him to Shar.

"It's a pity your own wife is dead," Elyril said, all innocence.

Endren started an angry retort but a man stepped out of the rotunda and called down the hall.

"Father! The highspeaker is calling for order."

The younger Corrinthal stood a head taller than his father. He displayed a stronger jaw, thicker frame, shorter beard, and no gray hair, but his eyes and nose looked so much like Endren that he could not be missed as the nobleman's son. He wore a heavy blade at his belt—its pommel was a stylized rose—and a holy symbol on a necklace around his throat—another rose, symbol of Lathander the Morninglord.

Elyril hated him instantly. This newcomer's soul shone like the sun. She refused to look at his shadow as he approached them.

"My son," Endren said. "Abelar Corrinthal."

Mirabeta smiled and held out her hand, which Abelar took.

"He could be none other," Mirabeta said. "A pleasure, young sir. I understand you were an adventurer in your youth."

Elyril smiled at the contempt her aunt managed to load onto the word "adventurer."

"A folly of my younger days, Countess. I serve Saerb and my father now."

"And Lathander," Elyril said, and could not quite keep the venom from her tone.

Abelar regarded her curiously. "Indeed. I call the Morninglord patron."

Mirabeta gestured at Elyril. "My niece and wallman, Elyril Hraven."

Abelar's brown-eyed gaze made Elyril uncomfortable. She feared that he saw through her, that he knew her secrets.

"Mistress Elyril," Abelar said, inclining his head. "I have . . . heard your name before."

Elyril could not bring herself to curtsy or speak, though she did force a half-smile. She touched her invisible holy symbol and resolved to kill Abelar at the first opportunity. Abelar regarded her so intently that she wanted to scream, "Stop looking at me!"

Endren saved her by speaking. "Duty summons us, Countess." He gestured for Mirabeta and Elyril to precede him and his son into the rotunda.

They did, though Elyril disliked having the Lathanderian dog her steps. She looked back at him frequently and changed direction as she walked to keep her shadow from falling on him. He answered with the expressionless, knowing gaze that Elyril already despised and feared. Her awkward gait eventually elicited a rebuke from her aunt. With nothing else to do, she bit her lip and endured the Lathanderian's presence.

The gilded doors of the circular chamber stood open. The low murmur of conversation floated from within. Ordinarily, city guards would have been posted at the doors.

"We shall see you inside," Endren said. Father and son stopped short of entering.

Mirabeta and Elyril walked through the doors and entered the chamber. Five pairs of doors opened into the room, and statues of notable council members from the past flanked each doorway.

A grouping of polished wooden tables ringed the raised speaker's dais, which occupied the center of the chamber. The dais was furnished only by an ornate wooden lectern. Glowballs lit the chamber brightly. Blue and silver pennons hung from the walls. Members of the High Council sat at tables and milled about. The Highspeaker, Dernim Lossit, stood on the speaker's dais, his ceremonial baton in hand.

The members' respective wallmen lined the outer edge of the room, away from the tables but near their patrons and patronesses.

All eyes turned at Elyril and Mirabeta's entrance. Half of the assembled members—those loyal to Mirabeta—stood and applauded at her appearance. Mirabeta smiled politely. She gestured for Elyril to take her place along the wall while she greeted her colleagues and found her seat at one of the tables.

A moment later, Endren and Abelar Corrinthal entered from a doorway opposite the one Mirabeta had used. The symbolism was lost on no one.

Again, half the assembled council stood and applauded. Endren accepted their plaudits with a raised hand and took his place at a table, smiling insincerely at Mirabeta. Abelar took his station along the wall, directly across the chamber from Elyril. Elyril felt the young Corrinthal's eyes on her, but she refused to give him the satisfaction of eye contact.

The highspeaker raised his ivory baton for silence and a hush fell. "A quorum being present, this emergency session of the High Council is called to order."

Tension hung thick in the air. Elyril saw it on the faces of the assembled council members. She noticed that almost all of the members and wallmen bore blades—unusual for a session of the High Council.

"Word has come that Kendrick Selkirk has died in office," Lossit said, obeying the formalities. "The realm is without a leader. It is therefore this council's obligation to select a successor from among its members. The dais is open for nominations."

Several members of the High Council stood to be recognized, though not Endren or Mirabeta. Custom demanded that candidates for overmaster not speak on their own behalf.

The highspeaker pointed his baton at Zarin Terb of Selgaunt and recognized him. Elyril knew Terb to be a supporter of Endren.

Terb straightened his long black coat and smoothed his full moustache before stepping from behind his table. He maneuvered his corpulent frame through the circle of tables and stepped atop the dais. The highspeaker surrendered his place and his baton.

"I will not waste time with pontification," Terb said, bouncing the highspeaker's baton on his palm. "The state is without a head, and without a head, the body will die. Now more than ever in our past, Sembia needs wise leadership, *honorable* leadership." He looked pointedly at Mirabeta as he said the last, and several members stirred in their seats. "We all know who among us can best provide that. It is therefore my honor to formally nominate Endren Corrinthal for the office of Overmaster of Sembia."

The hall remained silent and Endren remained still. Terb stepped down from the dais and returned the baton to the highspeaker. As Terb took his seat, Lossit stepped atop the dais and said, "Endren Corrinthal is nominated to the office of overmaster. A voice vote to second the nomination."

Half the assembly shouted loudly enough to make Elyril wince. "Aye!"

"The nomination is formally entered," said Lossit, and he banged his baton on the lectern. "Are there any other nominees to be put forth?"

Three council members stood, all of them loyal to Mirabeta, and the highspeaker recognized the stately, elderly Graffen Disteaf of Urmlaspyr, who stepped to the dais.

Graffen's slow pace and clear diction lent his words gravity. "Sembia has endured many hardships recently and there are many more to come. The Rain of Fire and continuing drought have brought poor harvests in the upcountry and wildfires in the west. The dragon rage brought ruin in the north. The people crowd into the cities, now havens for disease. The winter will prove difficult for the realm."

He took a deep breath and it turned to a cough. When it had passed, he continued. "And yet there is more for us to endure. We know that the elves have returned to Cormanthyr and propose to retake what they think to be theirs. With our aid they have defeated the daemonfey, but who knows now where their ambitions will end? Cormyr, meanwhile, is ruled by an unseasoned girl queen whose nobles rebel in all but name. Now more than ever," he looked at fat Zarin Terb pointedly, "*stability* is needed, steadiness, political wisdom. Kendrick Selkirk provided such, and so too will the cousin who shares his name and blood. I feel it is my duty, therefore, to nominate the Countess Mirabeta Selkirk to the office of Overmistress of Sembia."

The highspeaker called for a voice vote to second the nomination and half the assembled members shouted, "Aye!"

"The nomination is formally entered," the highspeaker said, and banged his baton on the lectern. "Will there be any other nominees?"

The chamber was silent. The battle would fall between Mirabeta and Endren.

"In accordance with custom," the highspeaker said, "we will proceed with the Speaking. Who will advocate for these nominees?"

Almost everyone in the chamber except Mirabeta and Endren stood to be recognized. Lossit selected one member, then another. Elyril heard at least two bells sound from the great hall's belfry while a procession of members rose and extolled the virtues of Mirabeta or Endren. Not all members spoke, but enough did to reinforce what they already knew—the vote would be close.

Throughout the Speaking, Elyril kept her eyes on the doorways, waiting for the priests of Tyr to arrive with Kendrick's body. She knew her aunt had arranged for the body to be brought forth, and Elyril knew that Kendrick would name his murderer. She grew increasingly frustrated when the priests did not arrive. Mirabeta showed no sign of expectation or uneasiness.

During a brief recess, the wallmen left their stations and hurried to their lords or ladies to give counsel and receive instructions.

"The vote will be close," Mirabeta said to Elyril. "Inmin speaks not, nor Weerdon."

"I have marked that," Elyril said. She cleared her throat. "Aunt, when will the priests arrive with Kendrick's body?"

Mirabeta smiled and whispered, "They are now just outside. I arranged for street traffic to delay them."

Elyril could not hide her surprise. "Why?"

Mirabeta tapped her magical earring. "I wanted the arrival appropriately timed for dramatic effect. Watch, niece."

The highspeaker stepped to the dais and called the chamber back to order. Elyril and the rest of the wallmen retreated to their places.

"We will continue with the Speaking," Lossit said.

Before anyone else could stand, Mirabeta broke with custom and rose to be recognized. A surprised murmur ran through the assembly. The highspeaker appeared momentarily discomfitted by Mirabeta's unexpected action, but recovered himself.

"Countess Selkirk. You . . . wish to speak?"

Mirabeta stepped out from behind her table and strode to the Speaker's dais. She put her hands on the lectern and affected a look of dignified grief.

"These proceedings are premature. The overmaster was more to me than the head of state. He was my beloved cousin."

The chamber erupted in shouts. Terb shouted above the tumult. His face reddened and his paunch shook as he spoke. "This is most irregular, Highspeaker! She must not advocate for herself! It is unheard of!"

The highspeaker shouted for order and the chamber gradually quieted. Before he could speak, Mirabeta stared ice at Terb. "I do not wish to advocate for myself, Zarin Terb. In fact, I am withdrawing my nomination."

She paused to let the surprised glances and gasps circle the room. Elyril noticed Weerdon and Inmin paying close attention. Mirabeta continued. "Even if this council deems me fit to hold the office of overmistress, I could not accept it until the questions surrounding the death of my cousin are answered."

No one dared take issue with Mirabeta's words. Elyril smiled, understanding at last, as her aunt continued.

"I—" she shook her head. "No, not just I, but none of us can look to the future until we have answered fully the questions of the past. Rumors swirl through the capital. Can a new overmaster take office with such a cloud hanging over Ordulin, over Sembia? This matter must be put to rest fully and finally, and that should happen before the entire High Council. Let us put all rumors to rest. Only then should we proceed with an election."

As if summoned by her words, the awaited procession of priests arrived. All heads turned. Quiet fell.

The Tyrran High Lord Abbot, Feldinor Jemb, entered first. A white sash cinched his deep blue robe, which featured a scale embroidered in gold on his chest. He wore a white linen glove on his left hand and a glove of black leather on his right. Elyril knew the latter symbolized Tyr's missing right hand.

"Enter, High Lord Abbot Jemb," Mirabeta said.

Jemb nodded and announced, "The Justicar's eyes are upon this assembly. Let none speak falsely."

Several members of the High Council raised their right hands and spoke the ritual answer: "For truth is the tool of the just."

Mirabeta's voice was loudest, her hand held highest. Elyril appreciated the irony.

A group of six junior Tyrrans followed the high priest into the chamber. They, too, wore the blue robes and black and white gloves of their faith, and a warhammer hung from each of their belts. They bore Kendrick's body atop a railed wooden platform. A blue shroud covered the corpse.

"Your timing is impeccable," Endren said to Mirabeta. "And suspicious."

Mirabeta managed to look hurt rather than angry. "I arranged for my cousin's body to be brought before this council, but that is a surprise to none. The highspeaker approved it. The truth must be known to all of us. Would you object to the questioning, Endren Corrinthal?

Endren frowned and sat down. "Of course not."

"I presume none object?" Mirabeta asked, and accepted the silence as acquiescence. "Ascend the dais please, High Lord Abbot."

The Tyrrans walked solemnly through the chamber. The members watched them pass. Mirabeta stepped off the Speaker's dais and returned the baton to the highspeaker. The junior Tyrran priests lowered the platform to the dais and stepped away.

High Lord Abbot Jemb ascended the dais and stood over the body. He offered a prayer and addressed the High Council. "Speaking with the dead is rife with uncertainty. It is not the ghost of the dead who speaks, but a ghost of the ghost, the bit of memory that remains with the body while the soul goes to its reward or punishment. At times the answers given are unclear. Sometimes no answers are given. But where they are given, they are truth."

He eyed each member of the ruling body in turn, then said, "With that caution, I proceed."

The members rose from their tables and crowded around the dais. Even the wallmen stepped forward, though custom forbade them from leaving their posts. Elyril saw Abelar watching the proceedings with care, his brow furrowed. He sensed her looking at him and met her eyes. She looked away.

The high lord abbot peeled back the shroud on Kendrick's body. The overmaster wore only a loincloth. The appearance of his pale body elicited an audible gasp from the council. Elyril grinned, but wiped the smile away when she noticed Abelar's eyes still upon her.

The high lord abbot kneeled and put his hand on Kendrick's brow. Holding his holy symbol, a shield-shaped gold medallion embossed with Tyr's scales, he began to cast the spell. His voice boomed through the otherwise silent chamber.

Power gathered with each word uttered by the priest. The overmaster's flesh began to glow violet.

The members of the High Council, all of them worldly and accustomed to magic, nevertheless stared wide-eyed at the spectacle.

The rhythm of the abbot's cadence sharpened as the spell progressed. His voice grew louder. The violet glow around the body intensified, flared. The High Lord Abbot commanded the body to answer his questions.

Everyone leaned forward, straining to see.

The overmaster's eyelids opened to reveal orbs as black as squid ink.

I hear the voice, but its words make no sense.

"What do you mean, 'there is no here'? That's nonsense."

The voice says through the slit, "There is no time for this. He does not have much time. He has already awakened it and is losing himself even now. You feel as if you need to do something, yes?"

The hairs on my neck rise. My heart beats so hard I can scarcely breathe. "Who . . . who do you mean by 'he'?"

"You feel as if you must do something, do you not? Answer the question."

I back away from the wall but cannot take my eyes from the slit. "How can you know that? Who are you? What are you?"

"I am another piece of the same core," the voice answers. "That does not make sense to you, I know."

I nod but feel silly for doing so. The speaker cannot see me. Or can he?

The voice goes on. "We are personality shards. You and I are all he could spare."

I shake my head in denial. I feel dizzy again. I cannot breathe. "Who is 'he'?" I manage, and desperation seeps into my tone. "Who is 'he'?"

"He is Magadon, the core, the whole. I am his courage, blended with some of his intellect. You are mostly his sense of duty."

My legs give out under me and I sag to the floor, shaking my head over and over again. This cannot be. "That's not possible. That is *not* possible."

The voice goes on, unrelenting. "It is not only possible, it is. And it is the only thing that makes sense. You know that. Here's your charge. Go to the wall. Find the rest of us."

Inexplicably, the words send a thrill through me. I know with certainty that going to the wall is exactly what I am supposed to do.

"You are trying to understand," the voice says. "It is difficult, I know. Stop and evaluate your response to my request. I charged you to go to the wall and you felt complete the moment I tasked you, did you not?"

"No. Yes."

"Yes. Because you are his sense of duty. Fulfilling tasks is why you exist. Go to the wall and find the rest of us. That is your duty."

My response bursts out before I can think. "Where is the wall?"

"Out there, beyond the door," the voice says. "You must break through the wall. Part of us is behind it, untouched by the Source, untouched by the magic of our captors. Make it contact Erevis or Riven."

The names Erevis and Riven trigger a memory. I cannot remember details but I know I have done my duty by them. I know just as certainly that they have done their duty by me. They are my friends, my comrades.

And I know something else: the voice is telling me the truth.

I stand, nervous, but resolved to fulfill my duty.

"How do I break through the wall?"

The voice is quiet for a moment, then says, "I do not know. You must find a way. And . . . what lies behind the wall is dangerous. But there is no choice. You must do it to save all of us."

I say, "Come with me. If it's dangerous, two will accomplish what one cannot."

"I cannot."

"Why?"

"I told you. I am courage. I must stay with him. He needs me more."

"But why me?"

Courage says, "Because you are the strongest of us. You always have been."

The words fortify me. I *am* strong. "You said there is no 'here.' What did you mean? Where is this place?"

"It is not a where but a what. A thought bubble. A microcosm of his mindscape. Go to the wall. Get through it. Find that part of us that is on the other side and force it to call our friends."

I nod, but look uncertainly at my empty hands. "I have no weapon."

"Yes, you do. You are a weapon. And you must hurry. We will all be lost in the Source if you do not hurry."

"What is the Source?"

Saying the word makes me uneasy. It echoes in my mind.

The voice does not answer.

"Are you there?"

No response.

I listen to the silence for a moment before I listen to myself. I know what I must do.

I walk across the room and put my hand to the door handle of the cell. It turns, silently—and I push it open.

CHAPTER SIX

10 Marpenoth, the Year of Lightning Storms

The members of the High Council crowded in close, craning their necks to see. The dead, black eyes of the overmaster stared up at the rotunda dome.

The high lord abbot began his questions.

"Are you Kendrick Selkirk, once Overmaster of Sembia?"

The body's mouth opened and said in a broken tone: "Yes."

Elyril smiled, knowing that Nightseer Rivalen had made a flesh puppet of the overmaster's body. She did not know what shadow creature was speaking through his lips, but she knew it was not the spirit of Kendrick Selkirk.

"Were you murdered?" Jemb asked.

Silence for a moment, then, "Yes."

The chamber erupted in conversation. The wallmen started forward but stopped when the high lord abbot raised his hands. Silence fell anew. The tension in the room made Elyril giddy.

"Do you know who did this deed?"

"Yes."

Another rustle ran through the chamber. Nervous eyes glanced about. Hands went to blade hilts. Elyril licked her lips with anticipation. Mirabeta eyed the corpse the way she might a trove of gold.

The high lord abbot looked out on the assembly.

"Perhaps this question would be better asked in the presence of Raithspur and the city guard?"

"Ask him," Mirabeta said hotly, waving him on. "Do it now, High Lord Abbot. The council holds power in this city and this nation, not Raithspur."

The priest knew better than to challenge Mirabeta. She had too many political weapons with which she could destroy his church, from increased taxation to revocation of the Tyrrans' land charter. He swallowed and nodded.

"Who murdered you, Overmaster Kendrick?"

The corpse stiffly turned its head and fixed the council with its dark-eyed glare. The flaccid lips labored but the words were clear enough.

"Agents of Endren High Corrinthal tainted my final meal with an untraceable magical poison. Endren Corrinthal murdered me."

Elyril almost danced while the chamber exploded into shouted accusations and counter accusations. Mirabeta could not stop smiling.

The members of the Council jostled, pushed, shouted into one another's faces. Endren Corrinthal screamed denials, his face as red as an apple.

"A lie! That is a lie!"

Mirabeta swallowed her smile and took full advantage of her gift. "You are a murderer, Endren Corrinthal!" she shouted, standing behind the high lord abbot and pointing her finger at Endren. "Name those whom you employed to perform this dark deed."

Elyril glanced at Abelar, who looked on with shock.

"A lie!" Endren answered. "Arranged by you."

A melee broke out among several members and knocked Zarin Terb to the floor. Without warning, Weerdon Kost drew his blade and charged Inmin. Other members responded by drawing their own steel and the chamber erupted into a chaos of screams, shouts, and swinging swords. The underpriests swarmed the dais to protect the body and their high priest. The wallmen drew weapons and rushed into the melee. Abelar ran headlong for his father into the confused combat of swinging fists and blades.

Rising to his knees, an enraged Zarin Terb pulled a thin wand from his jacket and discharged a bolt of lightning that cut a swath through the chamber, knocking several members to the floor. A long sword severed Terb's wrist and the wand skittered across the stones. Zarin screamed for aid, clutching the bleeding stump. Someone kicked him in the temple and he toppled to the floor.

Elyril sprinted to the nearest door and shouted down the hall. "Guards! Guards to the Council Chamber! The High Council is attacked!"

She did not wait to determine whether she had been heard. Instead she whispered a hurried imprecation to Shar, charged her hands with dark, poisonous magic, and turned back to the combat to seek a likely target. Abelar Corrinthal stood before his father with his blade at the ready and the rosy glow of protective magics surrounding him. The pair was backing out of the chamber. Elyril guessed that Abelar was either a priest or templar of the Morninglord.

Mirabeta lurked in safety beside High Lord Abbot Jemb, within a circle of the six junior Tyrrans who ringed the dais, warhammers swinging. Both her aunt and Jemb were shouting into the melee but their words were drowned out by the combat. The highspeaker futilely shouted for a return to order.

Elyril spotted Zarin Terb on the floor. He lay senseless in a pool of his blood and his wallman was not nearby.

Elyril pushed through the chamber, avoiding the blades, and knelt at Terb's side. She made the motions of trying to stanch the blood from his severed wrist, but she actually discharged the magical poison of her spell into his veins. He died instantly, and his support for Endren Corrinthal died with him. Elyril watched his spirit exit the body and streak through the roof. She stood and backed away from Terb.

She caught sight of Abelar pulling his protesting father toward an exit. She put her hand to her holy symbol, whispered an imprecation to Shar, and surreptitiously pointed a finger at the Corrinthals. Instantly a swirling, life-draining cloud of black mist took shape around them. Endren Corrinthal shouted and flailed against the darkness as it engulfed him and his son, drank their lifeforces.

The rest of the High Council had little time to pay heed to the fate of the Corrinthals. Steel was flying in the rotunda.

Elyril smiled as she thought of the husks her spell would leave behind, but the mirth vanished when a rose-colored light flared and annihilated her cloud of darkness. The light emanated from a holy symbol in the hand of Abelar Corrinthal. He held his weakened father with one arm and his holy symbol high with the other hand. His gaze fell on Elyril and his eyes narrowed.

Elyril saw in his face that he knew she had cast the spell. She smiled and paid him his overdue curtsy. He said something to his father, lowered him to the floor, and started across the rotunda for her, smashing with his sword hilt any who got in his way. A rosy glow surrounded him.

Elyril put her hand to her invisible holy symbol and snarled. She welcomed the chance to—

The sound of a horn interrupted Abelar's advance and a score of city guards burst in from two of the entrances. They shouted for order and bashed indiscriminately with their shields. Abelar shot Elyril a final glare and retreated to his father's side.

In moments the guards had quieted the melee.

The members and their wallmen stared at one another, gasping for breath. Weapons hung loosely in numb hands. Zarin Terb lay dead. Graffen Disteaf sat on the floor, clutching his chest but still alive. Inmin Dossir's dead body lay blackened and smoking from Zarin's lightning bolt. Four wallmen lay dead.

"What have we done?" asked Vens Derstill of Daerlun. Blood stained his sword.

"Inmin drew first!" exclaimed Weerdon Kost.

"That is not true," said Abelar Corrinthal from near the door, his voice preternaturally calm. "You drew steel first, Weerdon Kost."

While Kost sputtered, Highspeaker Lossit stepped atop the dais. Stopping beside Mirabeta, he dabbed at his bleeding nose.

"That is enough," he shouted, his voice muffled by a handkerchief bunched around his nose. "This will be sorted in due time." He eyed the rotunda, the fallen council members. "Gods, look at this! What will the people say?"

"The people should never hear of it," Mirabeta said, pointing her finger at Endren. "You are responsible for this, Endren Corrinthal."

Endren shook his head, apparently too drained from Elyril's spell to speak for himself. A cut above his right eye would not stop bleeding. Abelar spoke a word and touched his fingertips to his father's face. Endren's wound closed immediately and the color returned to his face. Abelar looked across the chamber at Mirabeta.

"You are responsible for this, Countess. You and your foul niece."

Elyril feigned a gasp.

Abelar continued. "Your niece summoned that dark cloud to try to kill my father. And you inflamed the High Council's passions with theatrics. The two of you arranged for this lie to be spoken."

Mirabeta scowled. "You mind is addled, Abelar Corrinthal. My niece is incapable of casting spells. And it was not I, but the overmaster's corpse that named your father a murderer. You defame two members of my family in a single stroke while you cradle the head of a murderer."

"My father is not a murderer," Abelar insisted, anger in his eyes. "It is a lie. Your lie."

Some of those allied with Endren murmured agreement. Hands tightened around hilts.

"The high lord abbot cast the spell himself," Mirabeta said. "Will you gainsay the priests of the Justicar?"

Abelar stood and pointed his sword at Mirabeta. "I would gainsay *you*, Countess. Who has more to gain from my father's fall than you?" He looked to the other members of the High Council. "There is dark magic afoot here."

"Yes," Mirabeta said. "There is dark magic afoot. And with it, your father murdered my cousin."

"Do not believe her," Abelar said to the members. "You know my father. He is an honorable man. He murdered no one."

Mirabeta's face flushed when several of the members nodded. She turned to the priest. "High Lord Abbot, can you use your spells to detect a lie?"

Jemb nodded.

"Please do so," Mirabeta ordered. "And ask whether I had anything to do with the overmaster's death, and whether I had anything to do with his naming of Endren as his murderer."

Jemb looked at Endren and Abelar, at Mirabeta, at the council members. The highspeaker nodded. Jemb grasped his holy symbol and intoned a prayer to Tyr. When he finished, a nimbus of pale light extended outward from him. Mirabeta stood within its glow.

"None may lie within this light," Jemb said. He looked Mirabeta in the face.

"Mirabeta Selkirk, did you murder Overmaster Kendrick Selkirk, either directly or through an agent?"

Mirabeta let the question hang for a moment before answering. "No. I had nothing to do with it. Nor with perpetrating a fraud in this chamber, as Abelar Corrinthal contends."

Jemb nodded. "She speaks truth."

A susurrous rustle moved through the council and the assembled guards.

"What of her niece?" Abelar said. "Put the question to her."

Eyes turned to look at Elyril.

"My niece is not involved in this," Mirabeta said.

Elyril stood up straight and stepped forward. "It is all right, aunt. I have nothing to hide."

She picked her way through the crowd and stepped within the Tyrran's light of truth.

Jemb said, "Elyril Hraven, did you murder Overmaster Kendrick Selkirk, either directly or through an agent?"

Elyril shook her head. "No. I was not involved."

Jemb nodded again. "She, too, speaks truth."

A rush of conversation filled the chamber. Elyril smiled at Abelar.

"Spells can be fooled," Abelar stated.

"And so can sons," Mirabeta said

Abelar stared cold rage at Mirabeta. "I know what you are, Countess. You and your niece. You will not succeed with this."

Mirabeta smiled politely. "What we are, Abelar Corrinthal, are servants of Sembia, both of us. But you, you are the son of a murderer and traitor." She gestured at the city guards. "Take Lord Corrinthal into custody."

The assembly erupted into protests and calls of support. The guardsmen looked at one another nervously.

Still weakened from Elyril's spell, Endren pulled himself up with aid from his son and spoke on his own behalf. "You do not speak for the High Council, or the city, Mirabeta Selkirk."

Mirabeta's smile never wavered, though her eyes hardened. Without taking her gaze from Endren, she said to Lossit, "Highspeaker, I demand a voice vote on the election of an Overmaster of Sembia."

The chamber erupted. Blades came up anew. Guards rushed forward and disarmed the council members and their wallmen—all but Abelar, who refused to give up his blade, and none dared insist.

"Countess, I am not certain that—" Lossit began.

"I second the demand," Graffen Disteaf said.

Mirabeta raised her hands to calm the brewing tumult and said, "The vote will be to appoint an overmaster for a limited term, until representatives for the vacant seats," she glanced at the bodies of Zarin and Inmin, "can be filled. The appointment shall be valid for nine tendays. Then a new election will be held."

The majority of the members murmured acceptance. Even Lossit said, "A reasonable course, Countess."

The highspeaker called for a new nominee while the priests of Tyr healed the wounded. No one was nominated—Endren refused to allow anyone to stand as his proxy, contending the vote was illegitimate. Mirabeta was left as the only candidate. Lossit called for a voice vote and Mirabeta was elected temporary overmistress by a slim majority. Endren and his two closest allies abstained.

"So noted," said the Highspeaker. "By action of the High Council, Mirabeta Selkirk is hereby temporarily appointed to the office of Overmistress of Sembia for the next nine tendays. The proclamation will go out this evening."

Mirabeta eyed Endren. The elder Corrinthal must have known what was coming. He struck a dignified pose as Mirabeta spoke. "Endren Corrinthal, you are hereby placed under arrest as a suspect in the murder of Kendrick Selkirk."

"No," Abelar said, brandishing his blade. Rosy light emanated from its edge.

"If Abelar Corrinthal interferes, arrest him, too," Mirabeta said.

Five guardsmen hefted their maces and moved toward the Corrinthals. Endren put his hand on his son's shoulder and guided his weapon downward.

"No, Abelar. Not this way."

"You are not a murderer," Abelar said, his eyes fixed on the advancing guardsmen.

Endren eyed Mirabeta. "No. And I will be exonerated."

Mirabeta only smirked.

Abelar looked into his father's face. Endren nodded, smiled, and Abelar sheathed his blade.

Elyril clucked her tongue with disappointment. She had hoped to see Abelar bleed.

Another supporter of Endren, Herlin Sambruar of Urmlaspyr, said, "There are over two hundred citizens on the street outside who will not countenance this, Mirabeta. This is a transparent grab for power."

Before Mirabeta could answer, Endren shook his head. "No, Herlin. We will not turn Ordulin into a battlefield. Unlike the countess, I value our nation too highly as to so casually risk its good order. Highspeaker, I demand that the High Council call a moot for the purpose of electing the next overmaster at the end of Mirabeta's term."

Elyril scowled. So did Mirabeta. A moot would turn the council of twenty into an assembly of seventy or more. Such a gathering would frustrate all of Mirabeta's plans.

"You are in a position to demand nothing, Endren Corrinthal," Mirabeta said. "The High Council has not called a moot of the nobility in over three hundred years. The point of the representative body is to avoid the need for moots."

Endren stared at Mirabeta. "And it has failed. Ordulin has become an insular hive of political backbiting, of grasping politicians who look to their own interests before those of the state. New blood and new perspectives are what the nation needs. I will accede to this arrest—to *house arrest*, at my tallhouse in Ordulin—if and only if my son is left free and the High Council issues a summons for a moot. The next permanent overmaster must be elected by the nobility-at-large, not by this council."

"Seconded!" shouted Herlin. "A voice vote on the question of a moot, Highspeaker."

Lossit, a compromising man by nature, called for the voice vote over Mirabeta's protest. Apparently ready to push the responsibility of electing the next overmaster upon all of Sembia's nobility, every member of the High Council voted for the moot. When Mirabeta saw this, she withdrew her protest and voted in favor of it.

But Mirabeta still had the final word.

"By order of the overmistress," Mirabeta said to the guard and pointed at Endren, "take the murderer into custody."

Endren whispered urgent instructions to Abelar, who nodded while staring daggers at Mirabeta and Elyril.

Cale dreamed of spirits writhing in pits of liquid fire. Horned devils covered in dark scales prowled the pits, flaying the damned at random with sharp knives, grinning as they did their bloody work. Fire rained out of a glowing red sky. Laughter, deep and ominous, boomed over the screaming. Cale found the laughter familiar but he could not place it.

Help me, a voice said.

Cale could not tell if the request was a plea for rescue or an invitation to assist with punishing the damned.

Help me, Erevis, said the voice.

Cale recognized it then.

Magadon?

Before Magadon could answer, something dark and large and terrible entered the dreamscape. The glowing sky dimmed. Damned and devil alike cowered as a shadow fell over the land.

Father, Magadon's mental voice said, and Cale felt the presence of an entity as ancient as the multiverse. The power of it stripped him to his core. He wanted to run, to hide, but there was nowhere for him to go. He knew the entity's name. It was none other than Mephistopheles, Magadon's father.

He is mine, the arch devil said, and his voice made Cale's ears bleed.

Cale awoke to Varra shaking him. He opened his eyes to find shadows pouring from his flesh, swarming the bed. Varra was shrouded in darkness, screaming his name.

"Erevis! Erevis!"

Cale's heart pulsed in his ears. Sweat soaked him. His head was pounding, far behind his eyes. He seized Varra by her wrists and willed the shadows to subside.

"I'm all right, Varra. It was a dream. A bad dream."

But he was not sure that was all it was.

Varra stared down at him, tears in her eyes, concern on her face. "Gods," she said.

"I am all right," he assured her.

She blew out a breath, stared at him a moment, and lowered her head onto his chest. He put his arms around her, hoping she would not hear the hammering of his heart, and he inhaled the smell of her hair. It calmed him.

The cottage was dark. It was still night, perhaps a few hours after midnight.

"You were calling in your sleep, tossing about," she said. "The room went black with shadows. I was frightened. I shook you and shook you, but you wouldn't awaken."

Cale stroked her hair absently, his mind still on the dream. His sleep had been troubled for over a tenday. Again and again he dreamed of suffering souls, but none of the previous dreams had approached the intensity of the last.

"Varra, I think one of my friends may be in trouble."

Varra did not hear him, or did not acknowledge hearing him. She said, "You kept saying the same things over and over again, shouting them."

Cale tried not to ask, but could not help himself. "What did I say?"

"You shouted about a storm coming, about the Hells, and you kept repeating 'two and two are four, two and two are four.' Does that mean something to you?"

Cale felt chill. Shadows played over his flesh. "Yes. No. I mean, I am not certain."

"Your skin is gooseflesh." She ran her hand across his chest. Shadows wove around her fingers.

He stroked her hair. "It is nothing, Varra. Just a dream."

She nodded and asked no more questions.

Cale stared up at the ceiling beams and pondered the dream, the words he spoke in his sleep. The phrase, 'two and two are four' came from Sephris Dwendon, the mad seer of Oghma. Sephris meant by it that there was no escaping fate.

Cale decided that he had to find Magadon. His friend was in trouble. The dreams were some kind of vision, some kind of plea. Magadon needed his help.

His mind made up, Cale waited for Varra to fall back to sleep. When she did, he stole out of bed and silently gathered his clothing, his boots, and his blades, and shadowstepped outside to the meadow. As he dressed, he pictured Starmantle in his mind, the city Magadon called home. He imagined the row of temples that stared down on the dirty, vice-infested trading hub. He pictured the rickety wooden docks teeming with goods and workers, the streets thronged with wagons and carts.

When he had a clear mental image, he surrounded himself in shadows and used them to leap across Faerûn. He traveled leagues in the blink of an eye, leaving Varra and the cottage far behind.

He appeared in a dark alley in Starmantle, his arrival unnoticed by any save a mangy dog. The scruffy pup growled at his sudden appearance and slinked off, tail between his legs.

Cale wasted no time. He prowled the taverns, festhalls, inns, and docks. Sometimes he moved invisibly among the crowds and tables, listening. Sometimes he used coin to pry tongues loose. Other times he used threats to get what he wanted.

All manner of beings filled the establishments in Starmantle. The city aspired to become a great trading center, and so held its gates open to all. Cale questioned not only men, elves, and dwarves, but also towering gnolls, hairy bugbear mercenaries, tusked half orcs, and squeaky-voiced goblin laborers. For the first time in months, he felt like himself, felt like he was doing what he was supposed to do. He met with no success the first night, but his dreams continued, so he returned to do the same, night after night.

He traveled the unnamed drinking holes that festered in the dark places along the docks, ventured into secret drug dens hidden in dank cellars near the city walls, visited the brothels where women and men went for coppers and all manner of tastes were indulged.

And there, as he scraped the bottom of Starmantle's underworld, he picked up Magadon's trail. He heard tell of Magadon as a drunk, a misthead, a babbling madman, or all three.

Cale's worry for his friend grew. The Magadon that Cale had known had demonstrated no weakness for such vices. But that had been before Magadon had melded with the Source. Cale knew that Magadon's contact with the Source had changed the mind mage. But he'd had no inkling of how much.

He followed Magadon's trail to Teziir, and there learned to his relief that his friend—apparently clear headed—had taken work as a guide for the wagons of the Three Diamond Trading Coster. Cale followed that trail from Teziir back to Starmantle. There, he tracked down an overweight merchant named Grathan, the master of the caravan with which Magadon had taken employment. Cale arranged a meeting.

They met across a cracked wooden table in the Buxom Mermaid, one of the few quality inns located in Starmantle's Dock Ward. Cale took the merchant's measure as he sat down. Grathan wore tailored breeches, a dyed shirt, a green jacket, and a threadbare overcloak that had seen much travel. The few pieces of jewelry he wore were of modest quality. Cale concluded that he was well off, but not rich. He wore a gentleman's rapier at his hip, but Cale doubted it saw much use. The man had no hardness in his eyes.

"Thank you for coming, Master Grathan," Cale said. With conscious effort, he kept shadowstuff from leaking from his flesh.

"What is this about, now?" Grathan said. "Are you interested in my goods?"

Cale casually surveyed the inn. He spotted the merchant's guards with little difficulty—two burly sellswords in chain mail vests on opposite sides of the common room, both trying too hard to avoid looking at Cale's table.

"No," Cale said. "But I will compensate you for your time. You headed a Three Diamond Coster out of Teziir?"

"Yes," Grathan said, nodding.

"I am looking for the guide you used. Unusual eyes?"

The moment Cale described Magadon, Grathan wilted and sank into himself. Cale saw the fear behind his puffy eyes.

"You know who I mean," Cale said softly. "I can see it in your face. Where is he?"

Despite his efforts, shadows spiraled from Cale's flesh.

Grathan saw the shadows and his eyes went wide. He scooted back his chair and started to stand.

"I have nothing more to say to you—"

Cale jumped up, grabbed him by the shirt, and pulled him bodily across the table. More shadows spun from him.

"Unhand me, sir!"

Cale nodded at Grathan's guards, who were starting toward the table, hands on daggers. Other patrons stared at Cale in alarm, though none rose to intervene.

"Call them off or I will kill you right now," Cale said, and left no doubt from his tone that he meant what he said. Darkness swirled around them both. "No one can stop me and I will be gone from here before you finish bleeding."

Grathan awkwardly signaled his guards to hold their ground. They did, eyeing Cale coldly.

"I will ask only one more time. Where is my friend?"

The fear in Grathan's wide eyes turned to puzzlement. He looked into Cale's eyes as if looking for a lie. Apparently seeing none, his body went slack.

"Friend? You say you are his friend?"

Cale nodded but did not let the merchant go, though he did loosen his grip a bit.

"Release me," Grathan said. "Let me sit like a gentleman. I will tell you what I saw."

Cale let him slip back into his chair and Grathan waved off his bodyguards. The rest of the patrons went back to their own business.

"My apologies for the rough treatment," Cale said insincerely. He subdued his shadows once more.

Grathan adjusted his jacket, examined it for tears. "Accepted. A man looking after his friend. I can understand that."

"Where is he?" Cale asked.

"I do not know. Something happened on the road."

Cale waited for the merchant to continue.

"We made camp one night as we always did. I'd gone to my wagon for sleep. I left your friend at the fire. I was awakened later by a noise."

"Describe it."

"Like a wind or somesuch, but there was no wind. I sensed something amiss and sneaked from my bed. That's when I saw it."

Cale's fists clenched. "Saw what?"

"Something had happened to the rest of the men. Not one of them stirred. They slept right through the noise. A spell or somesuch, I presume. But this," he touched a silver clasp on his cloak, "protects me from things of that sort, else I probably would have slept through it, too."

Cale gestured impatiently for him to continue.

"Magadon was not affected, either. He rose and shouted challenges into the night. I do not know to whom he was speaking. He could see something that I could not. He fired his bow into the darkness. The arrows glowed red, like they were dripping magic or somesuch. Finally . . ." Grathan shook his head. "It was like . . . the night itself opened up to take him. There was a cloud of darkness above the camp. Magadon looked up at it and dropped his weapons. It descended on him and when it lifted, he was gone. I told the men the next day that he had deserted us in the night. They remembered nothing and I did not want to alarm them."

Cale studied Grathan's face, saw no lie there.

"That is everything? Why did you lie to your men? Why didn't you report it to the watch?"

Grathan looked away in shame. "I want you to know that I asked after Magadon, but quietly. I liked him, for the short time I knew him. But I did not want news of the attack to be widely known. Bad for morale. Bad for trade."

"Trade is no excuse for cowardice," Cale said harshly.

Grathan's face contorted with angry denial but Cale's cold expression froze whatever words the fat merchant might have wanted to utter. Grathan looked away.

Cale stood. He did not bother to control the darkness leaking from his skin or the contempt leaking from his tone. "My gratitude for your time, merchant." He tossed two platinum suns on the table.

Grathan ignored the coins, looked up at him, and said, "I was afraid. So was Magadon. Any man would have been. But I hope you find him, and that he is all right."

Cale heard sincerity in Grathan's voice. He nodded, turned, breezed past one of Grathan's bodyguards, and left the inn. When he found an isolated alley, he drew the shadows about him and rode them back to Varra and their cottage in Sembia, more worried than ever for his friend.

I stand in the doorway and a gentle wind carries the smell of pine to my nostrils. A stream babbles somewhere nearby. I step out of the cell and look about.

I am standing on a hillside, overlooking an unsullied landscape. Conifers blanket the terrain. Ideas, dripping with promise, hang from the branches. A clear stream cascades down the hill into the wooded dale below. Thoughts swim in its current, silver and quick.

I notice the sky and gasp.

A translucent red dome roofs the world and defines its borders. Sharp edges and smooth, flat planes recall the surface of something crystalline. I stand inside a hemisphere—a thought bubble. I recall the words someone said to me once around a campfire: *All men keep a coffer of secrets in their soul.* I realize that I am standing in my coffer.

Flashes of light intermittently flare within the crystal sky, bathing the whole landscape in red light. Whorls of orange and crimson slowly churn within the sky's depths. Dark, pulsing lines trace jagged paths across the glassy surface; they remind me of veins.

I look away, my head swimming. In the distance, I notice the wall.

On the far side of the hemisphere is a wall of black stone. It rises from the earth to the sky, and curves from one side of the hemisphere to the other. The stream flows toward it.

It is immense, and I am supposed to break through it. How can I? I turn, intending to go back into the cell and tell Courage that I cannot do it.

The cell is gone. So is Courage.

I am alone.

Except for some thoughts. Except for some ideas.

A breeze stirs the pines and carries malevolent laughter from somewhere in the distance. I reach for my blade and remember that I have no weapons. I scan the forest, see nothing.

"Who are you?" I call. "Show yourself."

No response but the laughter.

I have a long road to take to reach the wall. I know I need a weapon, something more useful than a club torn from a tree.

I turn inward, searching my mind for any scrap of psychic power that I can use. I find none. I am only a piece of the whole and the core has given me only what I need to exist separately.

The laughter mocks me. I try to ignore it.

Then I remember the words of Courage: *You are a weapon.* I consider the words and think I understand.

Reaching deep into my consciousness, I draw on my sense of purpose, the strongest part of me, ordinarily not a reserve of psychic power. But it is now—in this moment, in this place. Power sparks in my mind, sharp and bright. Not much, but enough. I pull it forth, hold out my hand, and focus my concentration. A globe of pale yellow light forms on my palm. I force my mind into the light, bend it to my will, form it to my purpose.

I am a weapon. I am a weapon.

A single ray of light shoots upward from the ball. I give it an edge with my mind, hone it on my will, and shape it into a blade. At the same time, I close my fist over the globe and squeeze until it is a hilt perfectly fitted to my grasp.

Pleased, I smile and feel no fangs on my lips. I test the mind blade with a few practice cuts. It hums when I swing it and it has little weight. The lack of heft will require compensation. I am accustomed to the weight of steel in my hand. I step to a nearby pine tree and swing the blade downward at a wrist-thick branch, severing it cleanly.

I am ready.

The laughter dies and I take that as a good sign. I start down the hillside, following the stream.

Before I have gone twenty paces, a crack sounds from above, so loud I instinctively duck and brandish my blade. I look up for the source of the sound. There is no missing it.

A jagged crack mars the crystal sky. As I watch, it expands halfway across the world's ceiling. A mass of wriggling black shapes throngs the other side of the crack, trying in vain to ooze through. I do not know what they are and I do not want to find out.

I hurry down the hillside at a run, certain with every step that one of the black things would drop from the sky and fall upon me.

I have a long way to go to reach the wall.

As if sensing my burgeoning despair, the laughter returns and a voice speaks.

"Hurry, now. We are waiting for you."

I stop because I recognize the voice.

It is my own.

CHAPTER SEVEN

28 Marpenoth, the Year of Lightning Storms

Kendrick Selkirk was in the family tomb, Mirabeta was giddy with power, and Elyril stood alone on the third-story balcony that overlooked one of the stone gardens dotting the grounds of Ravenholme, her aunt's estate. Magical lighting of various hues illuminated unnatural arrangements of rocks and boulders, some of them imported from as far west as Baldur's Gate, as far east as Thay. A manmade rill cascaded through the rocks and collected in a small pool at the garden's far end.

Selûne was new, banished from the night sky, a holy time for Shar's servants. Elyril often spent moonless evenings on the balcony staring up at the night, contemplating the majesty of the Lady of Loss, imagining the day when night would shroud Faerûn forever. She reached into an inner pocket and retrieved the invisible disc that served as her holy symbol.

Holding the symbol to her breast, she replayed the Lord Sciagraph's words in her head: *Follow the Nightseer until the sign is given and the book is made whole.* As she had done so often since receiving the vision, she wondered, what sign, what book?

She chided herself for such questions. Shar and the Lord Sciagraph would reveal to her what she needed to know and keep the rest to themselves. Elyril took comfort in the belief that she would know the sign when she saw it, see the book when the time had come.

Still, she wondered when the Lord Sciagraph would contact her again and reveal more of Shar's plan. She resisted the temptation to commit the offense of hope, but recalled fondly Volumvax's touch, the smooth feel of his divine fingers. She felt herself flush.

"I will be the one to free you," she whispered into the sky. She also would be the one to sit at his hand. Together, they would rule in Shar's name.

Elyril did not know how the Lord Sciagraph had been bound to his realm, the Adumbral Calyx, at the heart of the Plane of Shadow. Elyril did not pry into his secrets. She knew only that he could not leave it, not unless Elyril freed him. Until then, she would serve the Nightseer, as Volumvax had instructed her.

She activated her sending ring. When she felt contact with Rivalen, she relayed her news. *Nightseer, Mirabeta is installed as temporary Overmistress. Endren Corrinthal is arrested and under guard.*

Well done, dark sister, Rivalen answered. *Encourage your aunt to aspire to more.*

Elyril considered. Any grab at power by Mirabeta would trigger an uproar in Sembia's nobility. She said as much to Rivalen.

Precisely, Rivalen answered.

Elyril suddenly understood the Nightseer's purpose. *Civil war, Nightseer?*

If the Lady wills it, Rivalen answered. *Find comfort in the night, dark sister.*

The night shroud you, Prince Rivalen.

The sending ended. Elyril's heart raced. Civil war? Could *that* be the sign? If so, what of the book?

She resolved to see it done. Her aunt's ambition could be steered, but Mirabeta was no fool. Elyril would need to be subtle.

Elyril spent the hour before dinner in her chamber inhaling minddust and praying to Shar and Volumvax. Kefil warmed himself before the fire and watched her.

"The Nightseer wishes civil war in Sembia," she said to the dog.

To what end? Kefil asked. His tail thumped the floor.

Elyril shook her head. "The Nightseer keeps his own counsel. But he serves Shar, as do I."

You serve the Divine One.

Elyril cocked her head. "The will of Shar and Volumvax is as one."

Kefil yawned and rolled over on his side. *Perhaps the Nightseer would not agree.*

Elyril glared at the old mastiff. "The Nightseer will not have a chance to disagree because he will never know."

Kefil closed his eyes. *Of course, Mistress.*

"Are you threatening to reveal my secret to him, Kefil?"

Kefil did not look at her. He dared not. *I serve only you, Mistress.*

Elyril nodded. "And I serve the Nightseer only until I receive the sign and the book is made whole. Shar has called me through the Divine One to a higher purpose. When Volumvax is freed, even the Nightseer will bend his knee to him."

And to you, Kefil said. He licked his hindquarters. *Unless you are mad, that is, and none of this is real.*

Elyril considered the dog's words for a moment, dismissed them as nonsense, and returned to her prayers. Later, when it was time to dine, she held her invisible holy symbol in her hand and whispered a spell that would make her words more persuasive. When the spell was complete, she went to the dining hall.

There, she and her aunt enjoyed a meal of stuffed quail and roasted vegetables. Much of Sembia might suffer deprivation, but Mirabeta's fortune allowed for her and Elyril to dine well.

"The huntmaster took the quail yesterday," Mirabeta said. "And the wine is Selgite, from the Uskevren vineyards."

Elyril nodded. Both bird and wine were quite good. This was fortunate, as the lingering effects of the minddust made her taste buds more sensitive than usual. When she thought of Selgaunt, she thought of Zarin Terb, his fat body smoking on the floor of the council chamber. She giggled. Her aunt looked on, bemused.

Two mute serving girls, both the product of Mirabeta's breeding program, lingered at the walls to refill wine chalices and clear away dishes. They had polished the lacquered finish of the dining table to the gloss of a mirror. Elyril smiled at the eyeless, deformed faces that lived in the table. They looked at her from under its surface. She alone could see them—another boon from Shar.

"The nobility should be receiving notice of the moot," Elyril said.

Mirabeta nodded.

Magical missives and official couriers traveling under seal would have dispatched the news to all of the major cities of the realm by the next morning. News of Endren's arrest had no doubt also circulated quickly. Tension lay thick in the capital and would be spreading to the rest of the realm. Despite Endren's claim that he would not turn Ordulin into a battleground, scattered street fights between forces loyal to Endren and forces loyal to Mirabeta had left over three dozen dead.

"The capital borders on chaos," Mirabeta observed. "Too many soldiers and not enough food. The populace is restless."

Elyril sipped her wine, nodded. For years Mirabeta had sounded out her political ideas with Elyril over a meal. The faces that lived in the table told Elyril how to answer her aunt. She looked to them for guidance and they did not disappoint.

"If the safety of the capital is at stake, it is the overmistress's duty to end the threat. Raithspur and the guard answer to you now, aunt."

Mirabeta bit the meat off a quail bone. "Arresting those loyal to Endren could cause a riot."

The faces mouthed a response for Elyril. Her spell made her

words compelling to her aunt. "Perhaps just a few of them, then? The key men, the leaders—Abelar Corrinthal, for certain."

"Abelar has fled the city using magical means," Mirabeta said, making a dismissive gesture. "He has probably already returned to Saerb."

Elyril vented her frustration only with a frown. She would have enjoyed arranging for Abelar to die while in custody. She hated the Lathanderian.

"Not Abelar, then, but the others. The guards could take them from their quarters late at night. You could also arrest a few unimportant men who are loyal to you. That way, you would appear to the commoners to be evenhanded."

Mirabeta devoured her quail, nodded thoughtfully. "The streets would be safe tomorrow if the order went out tonight."

"The citizens would thank you for returning the city to normalcy," Elyril said, while silently thanking Shar and the faces in the table. "You could accompany the announcement of the arrests with the announcement of a new food distribution program. Extra grains could be purchased from abroad and ground in the city's mills. You could order the temples to require that their underpriests use spells to create food."

"The temples would never stand for such a step. They will make food for their loyal worshipers, but not for all."

Elyril finished her wine. "You are the overmistress, aunt," she said simply. "If they refuse to comply, threaten to revoke their land charter, or tax them until they accede."

Mirabeta cocked her head. "An interesting idea."

One of the mute serving girls appeared at Elyril's side and refilled her wine chalice. The ceiling chandelier cast her silhouette on the table and the faces sprouted fangs and tore it to pieces. The mute's shadow, silent no more, screamed as it died.

"Have you determined how best to control the moot?" Elyril asked.

Mirabeta's face tightened. "There is no controlling it. I should not have agreed to it. There is no predicting the outcome of such a thing."

Elyril shook her head somberly and played the fool niece. "I do not understand why we have need of it. An overmistress has been selected. The moot creates uncertainty at a time when Sembia is most in need of stable leadership."

Mirabeta set down her wine glass and nodded. "Indeed."

The faces fed Elyril her next words. "I suppose there is little that could prevent the moot, now?"

Mirabeta tore a wing from a second quail. "Little."

Elyril made a point of pondering. "Aunt, may I be candid?"

Mirabeta regarded her over the rim of a wine chalice. She took a sip and placed the vessel on the table. "Have you not been candid in the past?"

"What I am about to say is of a different cast," Elyril said.

Mirabeta studied her face and turned to the serving girls.

"Leave us," she commanded, and the mute girls scurried from the chamber, leaving behind the Uskevren wine.

When they were alone, Elyril said, "Aunt, you hold power. Deservedly so. You cannot let it slip from your grasp because your election was held hostage to the threats of a murderer. The state will need you for more than nine tendays."

Mirabeta nodded. "Agreed. We are at a critical point in Sembia's history. My cousin and the rest of the High Council stood by in idleness while the elves returned to Cormanthyr, while Cormyr drifted into chaos, while the harvest failed, and while the dragons raged. They were and remain fools. Endren did Sembia a service by killing Kendrick."

Elyril smiled at that. She enjoyed knowing the truth of the murder while her aunt did not. She said, "And now you must do the state a service by holding power."

Mirabeta nodded slowly and bit her lower lip. "I confess to having similar thoughts. There are some among the nobility who would support me in such a move. There are others I could buy. I do control the treasury. But they are too few to ensure my election."

Elyril shook her head in sympathy. She looked up as if struck with an idea. "Then why an election at all? Why not dissolve the High Council?"

Mirabeta scoffed. "Because it will ensure a rebellion, foolish girl."

Elyril recognized the turned soil of the row and planted her seed. "Has not a rebellion already started, Aunt? A member of the High Council has murdered the overmaster and his men do battle on Ordulin's streets. No doubt Abelar has returned to Saerb to raise an army to challenge you and free his father. It appears to me that sitting idly while such things progress is to play more the fool than Endren or the council ever did."

Mirabeta frowned, but Elyril could tell from her tone that she was intrigued.

"You are venturing into deep waters, Elyril."

"But I learned to swim from you, Aunt. Endren's treachery provides the opportunity for a great woman to take power and make her nation great. The time for a council of so-called peers has passed."

Mirabeta took another drink of wine. "The High Council has ever been an ill instrument of state. Speak your mind fully, Elyril. You are holding back."

Elyril rose, took the bottle of wine, and filled her aunt's goblet. She stood beside her and affected a hesitant tone. "Aunt Mirabeta, imagine if some of those invited to the moot did not arrive safely because they were attacked by forces that appeared to be in service to Endren's rebellion, now led by his son. They will be traveling the main roads of the realm. Only a modest guard will accompany them."

Mirabeta stared straight ahead and Elyril could not read her expression. The faces swarmed around her aunt's distorted reflection in the table.

Elyril tried to make the course more palatable.

"I know that such a thing is hard to contemplate. But so, too, is Sembia with yet another weak leader. An attack by traitorous revolutionaries on the nobles traveling to the moot would precipitate an acute crisis. A strong leader could step to the fore and Sembia would thank her."

Mirabeta tapped her fingers on the table. The faces gnashed at her fingertips. Elyril took her seat and studied her aunt. She knew that what she proposed was feasible. Despite its size and wealth, Sembia maintained little in the way of a standing army. Small forces of Sembian soldiers, known as Helms, quartered in the realm's major cities. Their duties consisted largely of patrolling the roads around the cities and supplementing city guards as necessary. The garrisons were decentralized; their commanders answered to the local nobility.

"To what end would forces loyal to Endren attack?" Mirabeta asked.

Elyril waved her hand as if the answer mattered little. "Perhaps they fear the outcome of the moot. Perhaps they are mad for power and are attacking those who would not join in their treason against Kendrick, and now you. The minds of traitors can be fickle."

Mirabeta shook her head. "No one would believe Endren or Abelar to be behind it."

"People will believe what you want them to believe," Elyril answered. "The story need not be true, it need only be plausible. And it is that. Properly characterizing events is critical, but you can control that. Proclamations could go out mere hours after the attacks, blaming them on Abelar Corrinthal and whichever other nobles suit your needs. Most of the rest of the nobility would rally to your cause. Given Sembia's current state, the idea of a war would terrify them. They would want it ended quickly and decisively. The High Council would beg for you to take power as war regent."

Mirabeta shook her head, took another drink of wine. Elyril could see her aunt warming to the subject. Mirabeta said, "The High Council could be made irrelevant. We could hold a rump moot instead. They would elect me."

Elyril finished her aunt's thought. "The very existence of the nation would be at stake. Who in the rump moot other than traitors would risk opposing your election as war regent?"

Mirabeta looked thoughtful. "None." She looked up at Elyril, her eyes gleaming. "It could work."

"It will work," Elyril said. "Sembia will prosper again when the reins of the realm are once more in firm hands. History will name you Sembia's first monarch. Your people will thank you."

Mirabeta leaned back in her chair and stared thoughtfully at the ceiling.

Elyril let the matter rest. Her aunt was taken with the idea and Elyril had done as Rivalen had demanded. Sembia had been a tinderbox for over a year. Mirabeta would be the spark to set it aflame.

The Nightseer would have his civil war.

Another night arrived and so did another dream of fire. Cale awoke, soaked in sweat and shadows, and slipped from the bed. He must not have been thrashing in his sleep because Varra still slept.

He stepped through the shadows and into his sanctuary, the meadow outside the cottage in the dead of night. Stars shone out of a clear, moonless sky.

"Where are you, Mags?" he said, worried.

Cale did not know what to do next. Or rather, he *did* know what to do next, but did not want to do it. He had scoured Starmantle and Teziir but had learned nothing more than what Grathan had told him. With each night that passed, he felt more and more as if he were betraying Magadon by not turning to Mask for aid. Yet he felt that turning to Mask would betray Jak's memory, or worse, betray himself.

Midnight approached and with it came temptation. He could pray to Mask for a spell of divination, use it to locate Magadon. A simple prayer, used one time and never again. He looked at his hands, at the ribbons of shadow that dangled from his fingertips.

He fought the impulse. Magadon would not want him to do it.

He whispered an expletive at Mask and sat in his familiar chair under the elm, surrounded by the night, one with the dark. Crickets chirped. The nightjar cooed. A soft wind stirred the trees.

He withdrew Jak's pipe, the pipe he had smoked at midnight for the last year or more, the pipe with which he defied Mask. Holding it by the handle, he eyed it.

For the first time, he put it aside unused.

Midnight arrived and Cale cursed Mask again but could not

bring himself to smoke. He felt the pull of his god. He resisted, but not for long.

He could not let Magadon suffer due to his own stubbornness. He snatched darkness from the air and carefully formed it with shaking fingers into a mask of shadow, which he placed over his face. The shadows clung to his skin.

He reached out to his god and prayed. He asked for only a single spell, something that would help him locate Magadon.

Mask answered immediately, and Cale could not deny the rush he felt when he connected with his god. He felt a charge in his mind as the power to cast the spell embedded there. Mask tried to give him more power, to draw Cale back fully, but Cale cut off the connection despite the comfort it brought him. He wanted no more than necessary from the Shadowlord.

Heart racing, breath coming fast, Cale wiped his palm through the air and smeared the darkness into a black rectangle that hovered before him. Ready, he murmured the words to the divination Mask had provided. As the spell took effect, Cale picture Magadon in his mind and spoke his name aloud. The magic went out in search of his friend.

Swirls of pitch formed on the lens's surface. Cale powered the spell with his will and again pronounced Magadon's name.

The lens remained dark. Cale tried again and still the spell revealed nothing. He poured all of his desire into the magic, but still it showed nothing.

Cale let the magic dissipate, disappointed and worried. Wherever Magadon was, Cale's scrying magic could not reach him. For the moment, there was nothing else to be done. He removed the mask of shadow from his face and dispersed it.

"Nothing has changed between us," he said to Mask, but he heard the lie in his words. Something had changed. Cale had opened a door he had closed over a year ago, and he liked what he found on the other side. Shutting it again would be difficult.

For the next few hours he sat under the tree and watched the sky, trying to decide his next course. He watched stars rise and set. Hours passed and still he came to no decision.

Dawn was only a few hours away when a tickle started in his ears, then increased to a buzzing. Hope rose in him and Cale rode it out of his chair and onto his feet.

Magadon? Mags?

The buzzing in his ears intensified and Cale did not feel the telltale sensation of mental contact. Instead, he realized the tingle was the touch of an ordinary spell. His hope turned to alarm and the names of several enemies he had left alive throughout the years ran through his brain. Darkness leaked defensively from his pores. He reached to his belt for Weaveshear but realized he had left the weapon in its scabbard back in the cottage. He cursed.

The buzzing grew louder, but it slowed. He recognized it as a voice speaking rapidly, a sending. The buzz continually slowed until it matched the speed of a normal voice. When Cale heard it, he had trouble breathing. He had not heard it in a long while.

Mundane means of contacting you failed, said Tamlin Uskevren, the son of his former lord. *I need help. If you still love my mother, sister, the memory of my father, return to Stormweather immediately.*

Cale's surprise at hearing from Tamlin caused his thoughts to bounce around like crazed bees. A thousand questions coursed through his mind, a thousand memories: of Tazi, of Shamur, of Thamalon, and of Stormweather Towers. A surge of emotion ripped through him, a feeling like he'd known while searching the Dragon Coast for Magadon. He recognized it for what it was: the feeling that things were *right*.

He started to reply to the spell, to ask for some time to consider, but realized that it was nothing more than a one-way sending that did not allow for a reply. For all he knew, Tamlin could have cast it a tenday earlier. The magic could have been seeking Cale for days. Whatever crisis had caused Tamlin to seek him out may already have become more acute, or passed entirely.

He had met his god and his past in the same night. Sephris Dwendon's words bounced around his brain. *Two and two are four.*

He looked to the cottage where Varra was sleeping, and guilt squeezed his stomach. He chided himself for bringing her there. While he had never misled her with words, he knew his actions had given her a false impression. She assumed he would stay with her in the cottage. But he knew that he could not. A cottage in the forest was not where he belonged. Helping his friends, helping his family, that was where he belonged.

Cale considered the implication of the sending. Tamlin had to be desperate to reach out to him. Cale and Tamlin had disagreed often, mostly over the young man's dissolute lifestyle. And while Cale had seen Tamlin change for the better in the months before Cale had left Stormweather Towers, their relationship had never been warm.

Cale looked up at the sky and imagined how it would feel to see the Uskevren again. He realized then that he had already made up his mind. At the moment, he could do nothing more to find Magadon, and Magadon would have told him to go help his family. He would leave at once. And after he had put matters with the Uskevren to right, he would return to the search for Magadon.

He looked back at the cottage and saw Varra at the open window. The sight of her made his heart race. She ducked out of sight and soon a light flared in the cottage. She emerged carrying a small clay lamp. She wore only her night dress and the wind stirred her dark hair. The image reminded Cale eerily of the spirits that he, Jak, Magadon, and Riven had seen on the Plane of Shadow, moving through the ruins of Elgrin Fau—the Seekers of the Sun.

Varra hurried over to the elm. He stood as she approached.

"Did I awaken you?" he asked.

"No," she said. "Not you. Are you all right?"

He nodded, positioned the other wooden chair beside his. She sat and so did he. He saw little good to come from equivocating.

"I received a message."

She looked at him, puzzled. "A message? Tonight? How?"

He cleared his throat. "A spell, from the son of a very old friend."

Varra looked only mildly surprised that Cale had received a magical sending in the dark of night.

"The friend you have been seeking?"

"No. Another."

She stared into the woods. So did he. The distance between them was much greater than that between the chairs.

"What did it say, this message?" she asked.

"It asked for my help," Cale answered.

She nodded. Silence sat heavy between them. Cale wrestled with how to tell her he had to leave. Before he could say it, she asked, "Why don't you share with me, Erevis?"

The question took him off guard. "What do you mean?"

"I mean . . ." she trailed off, searching for words. "Each night when you leave the meadow and do . . . whatever you do, I lay awake, terrified that you won't come back. Did you know that? You have never told me where you go, what you do."

Cale looked at his hands. "I didn't . . . I thought you were sleeping. And you do not want to know."

She looked at him. "Yes, I do. I see the bloodstains on your clothes. You try to wash them off in the brook but I see them. I've asked no questions about it, about anything, but . . ."

She looked away.

Cale said nothing, merely stared at his hands as if they had an answer. Shadows slowly rose from his fingertips. He watched them drift off into the night like smoke and made up his mind to tell her the truth. He turned in his chair to face her.

"Here it is, then. Sometimes when I leave here, I go to help some of the villages around us."

She cocked her head. "Those villages are days away, Erevis."

Cale nodded. "You know what I am, Varra. I can travel very fast through the darkness."

She stared at him, eyes wide, and nodded at him to continue.

"While I'm away, I . . ." he gazed into the night, ". . . kill things. Creatures, mostly. Marauding monsters, trolls and the like. It's gotten worse of late. But sometimes people. It depends. That is the blood you have seen on my clothing."

He saw the shock in her eyes but pushed onward. "They are evil things, Varra. Evil men."

She scooted back in her seat, as far from him as the chair allowed. He doubted she even realized it. He knew then that leaving was the right thing to do for her, too.

"Why do you do it?"

Cale swallowed. "Because I promised a friend once that I would try to be a hero. It sounds absurd, I know. But I meant it. And when I do . . . those things, I'm keeping the promise to save people."

Varra stared into the woods. "The world is too big to save everything, Erevis."

He shook his head. She did not understand. "I do not want to save everything. I just want to save *something*. I need to." The moment the words left his mouth, he regretted them.

Varra's look was sharp enough to cut flesh. She studied his face. "Is that why you brought me from Skullport? Because you needed to save me?"

Cale could not look her in the eyes. His silence answered her well enough.

"You don't love me?" she asked softly, and her voice quavered.

He did look into her eyes, then. He leaned forward and took her hands in his. She was so warm. "Varra, I care for you. Very much. I feel something between us, something . . . wonderful. But there are things I must do, and those things stand between us like a wall. That's why I do not share myself with you. I cannot keep my promise here. It's not enough, what I'm doing. I need to do more." He swallowed, then said, "I felt like myself when I was looking for my friend, Varra. I was talking with people and standing in places that belonged on a street in Skullport, and I felt like myself."

He felt embarrassed saying it, but there it was.

She spoke in a small but resolute voice. "You cannot be yourself here? With me?"

Cale spoke quietly. "I am not a man made to be a husband, to live in a house, tend a garden. Varra, listen to me—I have fought demons, killed creatures from other planes with my hands, these hands." He held up his shadow enshrouded hand, scarred and callused. "I watched a wizard dim the sun, then broke his body as mine broke. I am different from other men. More than in my skin. I've seen forty winters and I will see hundreds more, thousands maybe. But who I am, what I am, was determined in a few key hours scattered over the course of my life up to now. I cannot change that. I do not want to change it."

Varra shook her head. "No, Erevis. Everything you do is who you are, not a few moments. You choose to focus on certain events and let those define you, but they needn't. You are more than that."

Cale looked away. He could not expect her to understand. She did not know what he had seen, what he had done.

She glanced up at the stars. "We are finally talking to one another, but only to say good-bye."

"Good-bye" sounded hard to Cale, but he nodded and said nothing. He could think of nothing else to say.

She took a deep breath and laid her palm on his cheek. "Do you remember what I said to you, back in Skullport, when we first met?"

Cale spoke nine languages but Varra's words then, still stuck in his brain, had confounded him. *"Relain il nes baergis."*

"It means, 'I know your soul.' And I do, Erevis. I do not want you to leave. And I do not think you are as different from other men as you think. You would be a good husband, a good father. Your deeds are different, but not your heart." She smiled and Cale thought her beautiful. "You would stay if I asked you. I know you would. But you would resent me for it. I cannot live with that."

Cale started to protest but knew she spoke truth. They had never lied to each other. He would not start now.

"We are connected, Erevis. I don't know how or why. I just know that we are. Do what you must. Go, help your friends. I'll remain here."

Cale looked into her eyes. "What will you do?"

She smiled and waved a hand at the cottage. "I will keep up the house and tend my garden. I will draw water from the well and put food on the table. This is home for me now. It will not be the same without you, but it will still be home."

"I am sorry, Varra," Cale said, and meant it.

She smiled. Her tears glistened in the starlight. "I know those are not idle words. That is why I love you."

She touched his lips. He kissed her fingers. She closed her eyes and smiled. Without another word, she rose, pushed him back in the chair and climbed atop him.

"Varra . . ."

She hushed him with a finger on his lips. He looked into her eyes and understood—they both knew this was farewell. He surrendered to the moment, wrapping his arms around her, kissing her neck. Her body radiated warmth; his radiated shadows.

Her hands answered his, caressing his shoulders, his hair, the back of his neck. She kissed his ear, his lips. He slipped her nightdress over her head and ran his hands down the length of her nude body. She tugged at his nightshirt.

He put everything out of his mind except her—her smell, her touch, her taste. He wanted to remember them always. She responded with the same urgency. Soon they were lost in each other, and his hands, the blood-stained hands that had killed demons, slaads, and dozens of men, were gentle for a time.

Afterward, they walked naked to the cottage in silence, holding hands. When he entered, he took his gear from his old wooden chest and donned his enchanted leather armor, strapped on Weaveshear and his daggers, pulled on his boots. His gaze fell upon the book he had received from the guardian of the Fane of Shadows. He had not opened it in over a year. The last time he had opened it, he discovered that Mask had placed a black mask within it—a new holy symbol. He held the book in his hands, studying its face. He flipped open the cover.

No mask. He smiled with relief and put the book in his satchel.

Varra watched him throughout. "Must you leave tonight?"

"I think it is better this way, Varra."

She nodded and said softly, "I have something for you."

She went to her night table and took something from the drawer— a piece of cloth, a black piece of cloth.

A mask. Cale's holy symbol.

Shadows swirled around him.

"I found it in the garden two days ago. The wind must have blown it there. I knew what it was but I said nothing. I'm . . . sorry. But I kept it for you. I've known since then that you would leave."

She held it out for Cale.

He hesitated, took it, and stuffed it in his pocket. It lay there like a lead weight.

She looked up into his face. "When I wake up, you will be gone?"

He nodded. "I will wait until you fall asleep before I leave."

"I hope you will return."

He said nothing, kissed her once more, embraced her one last time, and she climbed into bed, into their bed. He sat with his hand on her hip while sobs shook her. He could not stop his own tears. Exhaustion eventually overcame her and her breathing grew steady.

He stood and took a long look around the cottage. He had called it home for over a year. It had been a good year. He looked down on Varra, committed her sleeping face to memory, pulled the shadows about him, and transported himself to Selgaunt, back to the only family he'd ever had.

CHAPTER EIGHT

29 Marpenoth, the Year of Lightning Storms

Cale appeared where he had intended, in a narrow alley off Rauncel's Ride in Selgaunt's Warehouse District. Crumbling mudbrick walls boxed him in. Barrels and crates lay haphazardly strewn through the alley. The smell of old vomit and stale piss hung in the air. Cale almost smiled at the familiarity of the odor. He glanced up and down the alley and saw no one.

"Ao, but you took time enough coming back," said a voice.

Cale whirled around, jerking Weaveshear from its scabbard. Shadows swirled from steel and flesh. He spotted the speaker—a slim, dark-haired man with several days' growth of beard on his face—huddled prone against the alley wall. How had Cale missed him the first time?

The man lifted himself on his elbow and peered up at Cale out of a mass of threadbare, filthy clothes and a misshapen, stained cap. Cale figured him a drunk. He saw no weapons.

Cale lowered Weaveshear, took a few fivestars from one of his belt pouches, and tossed them on the ground near the drunk.

"Mind your own affairs, friend."

The drunk did not even glance at the coins. He had eyes only for Cale.

"Haven't I been doing that all this time?" he asked.

The man's knowing tone made Cale wary. Weaveshear still in hand, Cale approached until he stood two paces from the stranger. Shadows oozed lazily from Cale's blade.

"How do you mean?" Cale asked.

The drunk chuckled and sat up with a grunt. Cale realized that the stench of vomit and piss came from the man's clothing, not the alley. Close proximity made the smell worse. Cale wrinkled his nose.

"Foul, eh?" the man said and looked down at his clothing. "Keeps the stray dogs from bothering me."

The man seemed to notice the coins for the first time.

"Ah," he said, and all three vanished under a single deft pass of his hand.

Cale could tell the man was not what he appeared—he was too clear-eyed, to precise in his movements—though Cale did not yet know whether he was dangerous. He had encountered shapeshifters before and decided to take no chances. He pointed Weaveshear's tip at the man's face.

"Who are you?"

The man seemed unbothered by the shadow-bleeding blade pointed at his face. He reached up and put a fingertip on the edge. Shadows from the steel corkscrewed his finger.

"Nice weapon," the man said. He took his finger from the blade, produced one of Cale's fivestars, and tossed it into the air. He caught it on his fingertip, balanced upright on one of its five corners.

Cale kept the wonder from his face. He knocked the coin from its perch with Weaveshear and it chinked on the stones of the alley.

"I will ask you only once more. Who are you?"

The man frowned at the fallen coin. He looked up and asked, "Who do you think I am?"

Cale said nothing, though something about the man felt familiar.

The man leaned over, picked up the fivestar, pocketed it, and stood.

"Why are you backing away?" the man asked.

Cale had not realized he was.

The man smiled, nodded at the pocket in Cale's vest.

"Is that where you keep it?"

Cale's flesh goosepimpled. "Keep what?"

The man said, "The mask."

Shadows swirled around Cale. How could the man have known of the mask?

"You have been scrying me," Cale said, and tightened his grip on Weaveshear.

The man smiled and shook his head. "No. I left it for you in the meadow and you often keep it in that pocket. I do not need to scry you, Erevis. I know you better than anyone."

An identity for the speaker registered and Cale's heart thumped against his ribs. His breath came fast. Who could have known of the mask? Who could have left it for him in the meadow?

"You are backing away again," the man observed.

Cale held his ground, his mind racing. The idea was absurd. He shook his head. He refused to believe it.

The man examined his fingernails and said casually, "We have not spoken much of late. Remind me again of the reason for that."

Cale grasped at an explanation. "Tamlin sent you to meet me. And you were scrying me, despite your denial."

The man smiled. "No. But you already know that."

Cale was shaking his head. It was impossible. Impossible.

"Why do you not just ask me?" the man said.

Cale just stared, sweating. He dared not ask. He dared not.

"Go on," pressed the man, and took a step toward him.

Cale stood his ground, but only with difficulty.

"Ask," the man said. "I know how you like to ask questions to which you already know the answer. Ask."

Cale licked his lips but his tongue was dry. His thoughts raced through his head so quickly they did not make sense. He felt dizzy.

"It cannot be," he mumbled.

The man chuckled. "But it is. I am slumming," he said, as if that explained everything.

Words crept up behind Cale's teeth and he could not hold them in. He had to hear the man say it. The man smiled, waiting.

"Who are you?" Cale asked.

The man winked and shadows engulfed him. When they parted, the filthy rags had disappeared, replaced by oiled black leathers, high boots, a gray cloak, and several slim blades at his wide belt.

Cale took another step back, eyes wide. His legs gave way under him. He used Weaveshear to prop himself up.

The stink vanished with the old clothing. The man's face went from plain and unshaven to sharp, clean, and handsome. He appeared years younger than Cale. Only his smile remained the same. Cale recognized the face. He had seen it before on a statue in the Fane of Shadows, on the statue of Mask the Shadowlord.

"It cannot be," Cale said. The walls of the alley were falling in on him.

"I have already explained that it *is* possible," said the man—*the god*—as he dusted off his breeches. "Filthy alley." He looked up and stared an accusation at Cale. "I give you power to walk the shadows anywhere you like and always you appear in alleys. Why not a bath-house? Or better still, a high-end brothel?"

Cale could only stare, his mind racing, his heart pounding. To his surprise, the awe subsided, replaced by the seed of something else. He was looking at the god who had caused him to sacrifice his humanity, whose schemes had led to Jak's death.

Anger rooted in Cale's soul, chased away the fear, killed the reverence.

"What is it?" the man asked him, a puzzled look in his eye.

"Speak your name," Cale said, his tone hard. He wanted to hear the name aloud before he did what he had to do. Shadows haloed his body.

Mask looked across the alley at Cale with a frown. "You look upset. You are not still angry about Jak, are you? You know, you have never had a sense of humor. Even as a boy, you——"

Cale snapped like a bowstring, and once loose, his pent-up anger could not be reined. He roared, bounded forward with his shadow speed, and slashed with Weaveshear at Mask's throat. Rage fueled his strength; the blow could have decapitated an ogre.

The god barely moved. He produced a slim black dagger from his belt and parried the larger blade with a casual air and an infuriating smirk.

"Now *that* is amusing. Trying to kill your own god."

Cale gritted his teeth and used his greater size to push Mask against the alley wall.

"Really?" Mask asked. "We are going to go through all this? I wasn't sure, but——"

Cale reached down to his belt, pulled a punch dagger, and drove it into the god's abdomen. The blade sank to the hilt.

Cale stared Mask in the face. Rage made his voice a growl. "Never say his name! Never!"

Mask did not even wince. He glanced down with a surprised look at the dagger protruding from his gut.

Cale twisted it. He had never in his life felt such satisfaction.

Mask looked into Cale's face and anger flashed in the god's eyes.

"That is overdoing it a bit, don't you think?"

The god covered Cale's dagger hand with his own. Cale felt the strength in Mask's grip. The god muscled the blade backward, out of his flesh, and twisted Cale's hand with a jerk. Cale's wrist audibly snapped.

Agony flared; Cale screamed. The dagger fell from his limp hand. His shadow-steeped flesh immediately set to repairing the break.

"Now . . ." Mask began.

Cale ate the pain, threw himself forward, and smashed his head into the bridge of the god's nose. He heard a satisfying crunch.

"Damn it," Mask snarled. He shoved Cale backward to arm's length and kicked him across the alley. The blow hit Cale in the center of his chest and cracked his sternum. The impact with the opposite wall broke several ribs and drove the breath from his lungs.

Cale grimaced from the pain and slid to the ground among a pile of crates. Shadows roiled protectively around him. He breathed with difficulty through the shattered ribs.

Head cocked, Mask stared at him across the alley. Surprise had replaced anger in the god's eyes. His nose was not bleeding and showed no sign that Cale's blow had broken it.

Cale knew then that he could not harm Mask, not permanently, but he did not care. He lifted himself to his feet and brandished Weaveshear.

"Let's finish this," he said. "Now. Here."

Mask studied him for a moment. He put two fingers to the bridge of his nose and tested the flesh.

"That was a good blow," he said, and chuckled.

Cale's flesh had mended his broken wrist and partially repaired his ribs. He took a step forward, blade ready. "I have another one for you."

Mask shook his head and sighed. He sheathed his dagger and held up his hands in mock surrender. "Very well. I will never say his name again. Well enough?"

Cale said nothing but stopped his advance, breathing heavily.

Mask chuckled. "Ao, but you are stubborn. You should have been Torm's Chosen."

A rush of emotion pulled words from Cale. "I should not have been anyone's Chosen!"

Mask scoffed, then sneered. The latter expression looked so like Riven's that Cale would have thought them brothers.

"Come now," the god said. "You are what you are, Erevis. You chose me as much as I you. That is the way of the multiverse. How could it be otherwise?"

Cale recognized the truth in the words and hated it. He *had* chosen Mask. Again and again he'd had the opportunity to walk away. He never did. He never would. He'd left the Uskevren to serve Mask; he'd left Varra to serve Mask.

The anger went out of him. He had no one to blame but himself.

Mask continued. "Chin up now, priest. You have done very well for yourself and for me. And what were you before we met? An assassin dressed up as a butler, preoccupied with the petty goings-on of Sembian nobility. Now the fates of thousands turn on your actions, tens of thousands. Admit it. You would not have it otherwise."

Cale did not bother to respond. Mask knew the truth of the words, the same as Cale. He could not imagine going back to his old life. He did not want to go back to it.

"Why are you here?" he asked.

"You mean why am I sullying my divine form on this drab plane in this revolting alley? In short, I was waiting for you to make up your mind. You can badger a decision as well as Tyr himself."

Cale leaned on Weaveshear to steady himself. "As usual," Cale said, "that is no answer to my question."

Mask smiled. "True. Here is the answer, then. I came here because I wanted to give you something and to ask you for something."

"You can keep whatever you'd give. I've had enough of what you offer."

Mask said, "Ah, but you have already accepted my offer. I gave you a place to put your anger." He looked down and poked a finger through the hole Cale had put in his leathers. "I think that should do it. You feel better, no?"

Actually, Cale did, though he did not say so.

"Good. Now take the mask from your pocket and put it on. Cast a spell. Do what you were called to do. There is no time for your doubts."

Cale thought of Jak, stood up straight, and sheathed Weaveshear. "No."

Mask looked surprised, then puzzled, then angry. "No?"

"In my own time," Cale said. "If ever. You aren't the one to whom I answer."

"That halfling again," Mask said, and shook his head. "Time is running out, priest, your own and that of everyone else. You will learn that soon enough."

Cale held his ground. "In my own time, I said."

Mask glared at him. "Who do you think you are? You are nothing more than my tool, my weapon."

Cale answered the glare with one of his own and dared speak his thoughts aloud. "A bluff. You chose me and I chose you. You said so yourself. I may be your tool, but you are also mine. I am your Chosen, the First of Five. I may need you, but you need me, too."

Mask stared at him, clucked his tongue. Then he shrugged and tried to look casual. "I will get another. The Second will do."

Mask's Second was Drasek Riven, a one-time rival of Cale's, but now a friend.

"A lie," Cale said. "Riven is as loyal to me as he is to you. And we are too far along for a change. As you said, time is running out."

He let that sit.

After a time, Mask nodded and his face softened to a smile. "All right. True. I need you. But as you admitted, you need me, too. So, we need each other. Well enough?"

Cale shrugged. Mask seemed to take it as agreement.

"Things will start happening soon," Mask said. "When they do, you will be glad to be my Chosen."

"Enough riddles," Cale said. "What will start happening?"

Mask said, "The Cycle of Shadows. And that is not as good as it sounds, I am sorry to say. Since this city is where you and I had our beginning, it seemed fitting that it also be where we begin the end."

A pit formed in Cale's stomach. "The end? The end of what?"

Mask made a gesture that indicated all of Selgaunt, or maybe all of Sembia. "This. That. Many things."

Cale shook his head. "You are saying nothing. You make no more sense than Sephris."

Mask raised his eyebrows. "Sephris Dwendon made consummate sense. You know that. That is why you ponder his words so often. You know, I was much like you, once. Rebellious, thinking I had the right of everything." He rubbed his chin. "I was more handsome, of course. And laughed more. And killed less, at least then. But otherwise, we would have been kith."

The words surprised Cale. "You . . . were a man?"

Mask made an uncertain gesture with his hands. "Maybe. More like a god who mistook himself for a man. Took me a while to see the truth." He looked at Cale and winked. "That happens sometimes."

Cale's breath caught. He did not know how to respond.

"Frightening, eh?" Mask asked.

Mask's meanings were impossible to follow. He could be saying one thing, he could be saying another. Cale'd had enough.

"Ask me for what you want," Cale said. "I have seen enough of you. I returned to see my family."

"You *are* seeing your family."

Cale could not form words for a moment. At last, he said, "I mean the Uskevren."

Mask nodded. "I know what you mean. Very well. Listen to me, priest. When the time comes, I want you to recover something for me. I want your word that you will do it."

Cale said, "Do it yourself."

Mask shook his head. "The rules do not allow for that, I fear. I am already breaking them—bending them, at least—by talking to you in person. But things are changing, and who better to bend the rules than the God of Thieves? No, you must do it for me. Your word."

"What is the item?" Cale asked.

"I did not say it was an item. It is something someone stole from me long ago. You will know it when you see it, and when the time is right to take it."

Cale could not help but chuckle. "Someone stole something from the God of Thieves?"

"See! You do have a sense of humor. I knew it."

"Who took it?" Cale asked, and thought immediately of the answer. "Kesson Rel?"

Mask's smile disappeared and he nodded. "Kesson Rel. A most disappointing creature. Most disappointing."

"Why should I do it?" Cale asked.

"Do I have to say it? You will do it because you can do nothing else. Two and two are four and all that."

Cale considered. "Then you must do something for me."

"I have already granted you the satisfaction of wounding me."

"I want something more," Cale said.

"You have been too long among Sembians," Mask said. "You haggle even with your god."

Cale waited. Mask waved him on. Cale said, "Tell me where Magadon is."

Mask smiled and Cale saw the maliciousness in it. "If I tell you, you will not be able to save him, and others— many others— will suffer and die. Shall I tell you anyway? If I do not, I think you will learn it . . ." he smiled, ". . . in your own time. But Magadon will suffer in the meanwhile."

Cale stared into Mask's face. "You are a bastard."

"Yes," Mask said, and bowed. "Much more than you know. But not how you think. Shall I tell you where Magadon is?"

Cale considered, tempted, but shook his head. Magadon would not want others to suffer in his stead.

"No," he said.

"You still must give me your word," Mask said.

"You have it," Cale said absently.

Mask nodded. "Then I will give you this without additional charge: Magadon's fate is tied to Sembia's. Go back to Stormweather and help the Uskevren, as you planned. It will all lead back to Magadon, eventually, though you may not like where it ends up."

Cale said nothing.

"Done, then," Mask said, his tone satisfied.

Cale was struck by the fact that he had just bargained with a god as if he were a street vendor. Mask was not at all what he had expected. He seemed more man than god. He almost said as much, but thought better of it.

Mask grinned and tapped his temple. "I know what you are thinking, Erevis. But this is just flesh, just one of the . . . masks I wear when I move among mortals. Here, have a look behind."

Mask held his arms out wide, stripped away the flesh, and unveiled his divinity.

Cale stared into eternity. He saw, but did not comprehend a consciousness that extended back to the beginning of all. He lost himself in it. He could not breathe. His legs weakened. He was falling, falling . . .

Mask redonned his flesh. "Now you know."

Cale struggled to draw breath. He forced himself to keep his feet, though the alley was spinning. The awe had returned but Cale refused—*refused*—to abase himself before his god.

Mask smiled. "So stubborn, and so prideful. That is why I chose you, you know. That and . . . a few other reasons."

Mask's voice sounded far away. Cale feared he was losing consciousness.

Mask said, "In a few hours, this will start to fade. You will tell yourself it was just a dream, or a trick, or a vision. And maybe it was. But your promise stands. And when events start to speed ahead, remember that I did not create any of this. Others are responsible for it. I am just fiddling around the edges, responding to the inevitable. You do not understand now, but you will, a long time from now."

Cale vomited onto the alleyway and heaved until he had emptied his stomach. When he looked up, Mask was gone.

He spit to clear his mouth and reached back for the wall to steady himself.

He took some time to let his head and stomach settle. Something glinted on the ground: the fivestars he had tossed to Mask. Hadn't Mask taken them?

He needed time to think. His head felt muddled. He had just spoken with a god, looked into the unveiled face of the divine.

Hadn't he?

He stared at the coins, unsure. He left them where they lay and walked out of the alley onto the street.

Shadows cloaked him and Cale found comfort in their embrace. He walked the street in silence. The Shadowlord's words remained in his memory, as light as the fragments of a dream, as heavy as an anchor. Cale sensed the same fatalism in Mask's words that he had heard in Sephris's prophecies but refused to surrender to it. He might not be able to change what was coming, but he would fight his damnedest anyway. That was who he was.

The resolution centered him.

Charcoal street lamps dotted the wide, paved avenue, their fuel burning low. The flames danced in the salt-tanged, late autumn breeze that blew off the bay. Brick warehouses and wood-framed storerooms lined the street, one on top of the other, doors closed, windows dark. Livestock lowed or snorted softly in the stockyards. A few abandoned pullcarts and wagons dotted the pavement.

The dung sweepers were running late. Usually they had already cleaned the city's streets, but Cale smelled the day's waste lingering in the open gutters. He spotted transients sleeping in some of the alleys—more than he had remembered.

He knew that his return to Stormweather Towers would have to wait until dawn. He could not knock on the doors of a noble household three hours before daybreak. He decided to spend the time reacquainting himself with the city he once had called home.

Stepping through the shadows, covering blocks at a stride, he headed south and east, toward the center of the city. He crossed the old crumbling stone wall that symbolically separated transients from residents, and entered the Foreign District.

Inns, eateries, taverns, and equipment shops predominated, so many they made a rickety mob. Despite the late hour, a few merchants, teamsters, and caravaneers sat at tables inside the taverns. Smoke and hushed conversation leaked from the unshuttered windows. Here and there Cale noted the usual thugs, whores, and thieves, but the late hour made even those ragged folk look tired. He kept to the dark places and they did not notice him.

As had been true in the Warehouse District, a surprisingly large number of people slept in doorways or under the trees that dotted Selgaunt's roads. Some were the usual drunks but many were not. Cale had never seen the city so crowded. Everywhere he went he saw huddled forms in the streets, heard throaty coughs, smelled the stink of filthy streets.

He found the bazaar quiet but for the snores of peddlers sleeping in their carts and vendors sleeping in their stalls. His keen ears picked up a few murmured conversations that carried through the night but he ignored them.

He left the Foreign District and moved south, to the area near

Temple Avenue that housed Selgaunt's artists, scholars, and wealthy merchants. The roads narrowed and the inns grew fewer, replaced by well-tended two-story residences and shops. Fewer people slept on the streets, but some were evident. A pair of city guardsmen, Selgaunt's Scepters, dressed in dark green weathercloaks and wrapped in mail, walked the streets with a lantern. They shone its light into alleys as they passed, shooed along any loiterers they found. Cale sank into the shadows as the Scepters drew near. Even in the light of the lantern, the two men passed him by without noticing, though he could have reached out and touched them.

". . . in Ordulin," the shorter one said.

The other shrugged. "Endren Corrinthal? Well, who can say? Damned nobles . . ."

Their conversation drifted away as they continued their patrol. Cale walked through a plaza and got a clear view to the southeast, where the gray stone walls of the old Hulorn's Hunting Garden dominated the skyline. Glowballs and magical violet fires limned the walls. Peculiar statuary dotted the crenellations. The old hulorn's artistic tastes—he favored depictions of strange hybrid creatures such as manticores, chimerae, and others—had long been a subject of conversation in the city. Mad Andeth Ilchammar, he'd been called, and Cale thought the title fitting.

Cale realized that he did not know who currently occupied the office of hulorn. The last he knew, the members of the Old Chauncel had been squabbling over the prize.

The Hulorn's garden looked down on the spires of Temple Avenue. Cale saw the top of the bell tower of the House of Song and the narrow, pennon-festooned spire of the Palace of Holy Festivals. Cale had no desire to see Temple Avenue. He'd had enough of gods for the night. Besides, Temple Avenue reminded him of Sephris. He imagined the mad prophet lying awake in his bed in the House of Higher Achievement, counting the number of cracks in the ceiling, the number of breaths he took in an hour, applying one of his obscure calculations, and deriving the fate of Faerûn.

A few blocks over, the top of a tower rose above the rooftops. Cale recognized it. Decades before it had been the tower home of a minor wizard, Delikor Saan. Subsequently, an eccentric artist—Cale had forgotten his name—had bought it and converted it into an art gallery and curio shop that catered to the city's wealthy. Cale gauged its height at a full six stories, a suitable perch for a view of most of Selgaunt.

Eyeing the top of the tower, he pulled the shadows about him and stepped through them. He appeared on the tower's top. The wind hit him immediately. His cloak billowed out behind him. He crouched low and steadied himself on the tiles of the pitched roof. He looked out on the city.

Streetlamps lit the main thoroughfares: Rauncel's Ride, Sarn Street, Larawkan Lane, the Wide Way. The broad avenues wound their way through the city like glowing snakes. The Elzimmer River ran along part of its northern wall before emptying into Selgaunt Bay.

Cale could see over the wall to the lamplit flotilla of fishing boats, cargo barges, and ferryboats that dotted the far side of the river. The waterway flowed in clean from the northwest, collected much of the city's filth as it passed by the northern wall, and dumped the dredge in the bay. Cale knew many men who had done exactly the same thing—entered Selgaunt clean, gotten dirty while inside, and ended up in the bay.

He looked to the west, to the Noble District and the grand mansions of Selgaunt's ruling noble families, the Old Chauncel. Even from a distance, he could make out the squat turrets of Stormweather Towers, its gated gardens, the meticulously maintained grounds. He had spent many good days within its walls, with Thamalon, with Tazi, with Shamur. He had fought a shadow demon in Stormweather's great hall, then turned to Mask soon afterward.

He felt a pang of nervousness about seeing them again. They had not seen him since he had been transformed. With effort, he could disguise his appearance as a shade, but even under the best circumstances, he knew he looked different. He worried over how they would respond.

Feeling uncertain, he reached into his pocket and took out the mask. He unfolded it, held it before his face, and looked through the eyeholes. Shadows emerged from his fingers, entwined themselves around and through the mask. The wind pulled at his cloak, at his hair, at his soul. He realized for the first time that unless he died in violence, the shadowstuff that made up his body would allow him to outlive everyone and everything he cared about. He would outlive elves. He could find common ground only with gods.

He put his fingers through the eyeholes, tempted, before shoving it back into his pocket. "In my own time," he said.

He turned around and looked out on Selgaunt Bay, glittering in the starlight. Countless piers, like the fingers of giants, jutted into the bay. A forest of masts rose into the night sky. Cale had last been at sea with Magadon and Jak aboard *Demon Binder*. They had discovered the Source and its guardian, the kraken. The beast was still out there, Cale knew. And so, too, was the Wayrock, the island home of the temple Mask had stolen from Cyric. Drasek Riven, Mask's Second, was out there. Cale wondered if Mask had appeared to Riven, too.

The majestic gongs of the House of Song sounded the fifth bell. Dawn was only another bell or so away. Cale decided to watch the sun rise over Selgaunt Bay.

Rather than shadowstep back to the street, Cale dangled himself over the edge of the tower's roof, sought a hold for his toe, and started down. He used the shadows to make himself invisible—he did not want a passerby or Scepter mistaking him for a burglar—but he did all the climbing himself, the old way.

The exertion did him good, reminded him of days when he had still been human. By the time he reached the street, he was soaked in sweat—human sweat. He unwrapped himself from the night and set out for the bay. He kept to the shadows as he moved, out of professional habit, but he did not shadowstep or use the darkness to conceal him magically. He moved like an ordinary man, a human man, a skilled thief and assassin. By the time he reached the docks, he was smiling.

Glowballs and burning braziers lit the wharfs. Caravels and carracks dominated the piers, but Cale spotted several freight barges, a longship, and even a bireme, probably from one of the southern realms. Sailors, dock men, and teamsters were already at work loading and unloading crates, barrels, and sacks. The docks never slept in Selgaunt, though the activity was less than Cale expected.

The workers shouted, grunted, cursed, laughed, and sang as they labored. From time to time, groups of two, three, or four wobbly-kneed crewmen wandered back to their ships from a night in the dockside taverns.

A virtual armada of small fishing boats floated along the length of the bay. Like the sailors on the larger ships, Selgaunt's fishermen were already at work preparing their ships to set out. They would spend the morning at sea and return at midday to sell their catch in the Dock Market. Cale had shopped that market many afternoons, with fat Brilla, the Uskevren kitchen mistress, at his side.

Cale moved away from the larger ships and walked down a small pier. A single-masted fishing boat was tied to its end. A wiry fisherman as thin as a whipblade sat in the boat, tending a net. A young man that Cale took to be his son examined the tiller, the mast, the sail. The youth saw Cale approaching. His eyes went to Weaveshear and he nudged his father. The fisherman turned around and took in Cale's appearance. A knife lay on the bench near him.

Cale tried to look harmless, not an easy task. "Do you mind if I sit? I want to watch the sunrise."

The son could not take his eyes from Cale's blade. The elder fisherman shrugged.

"As you wish," he said, and went back to work on his net. When the boy continued to gawk at Cale, the fisherman said to him, "Mind that tiller, boy."

Cale's presence might have made trained killers nervous, but not a Sembian boatman. Selgaunt's fishermen had a well-deserved reputation for being unflappable. Cale smiled, sat, and let his legs dangle over the pier.

The fishermen cast off before the sun rose. The elder nodded a farewell at Cale, the younger waved, and they released the lines. The son oared them away from the pier.

Cale watched them grow smaller and smaller as the eastern sky turned from black to gray. The sky brightened with every passing moment until the sun peeked over the horizon. Backlit by the dawn, the boat and the two fishermen looked like nothing more than shadows. Cale knew the feeling.

The slate sea turned blue under the rising sun. The light crept across the water and stung Cale's flesh. The rays caused Cale's shadowhand, the hand with which he had driven a punch dagger into the gut of the God of Thieves, to dissipate into nothingness. He had lost the original hand to a slaad's jaws while doing Mask's will. His transformation into a shade had regenerated it, but only in darkness or shadow. It seemed to him fitting that it was the instrument through which he had wounded Mask.

The fight in the alley already seemed like a dream, the recollection hazy and distant. He wondered if the whole exchange had happened only in his head. He had no wounds to show for it, but of course he would not—his flesh effaced wounds as effectively as the sun effaced his hand.

He decided it had been real. It had felt too good to be otherwise. He had stabbed his own god, and the bastard had deserved to be stabbed. How many priests would have liked to have done the same?

He smiled, then grinned, then chuckled. The chuckle gave way to laughter, which transformed into a full-on belly laugh. A passing sailor walking by eyed him as if he were mad, but Cale did not care. He could not remember the last time he had laughed so hard. By the time he finished, he felt better than he had in months.

He waited for the sun to rise fully over the sea, then rose and followed the light west, toward Stormweather, toward his past, toward his future.

He was still smiling.

CHAPTER NINE

29 Marpenoth, the Year of Lightning Storms

Mirabeta and Elyril sat across the table from Malkur Forrin. The rising sun cast blood-red light through the leaded glass windows of the small meeting chamber in Mirabeta's manse, Ravenholme. The mercenary's right eye drooped from an old wound and pale scars crisscrossed his muscular arms. He looked uncomfortable in his attire: the high-collared shirt and vest of a Sembian gentleman. Elyril imagined he would have preferred his mail and helm. He wore his graying hair in a helmcut. A broadsword, rather than a gentleman's rapier, hung from a battered scabbard at his belt.

"You sent for me, Overmistress?" Malkur said.

Mirabeta had employed Malkur's mercenary company, the Blades, often over the years, sometimes as escorts for the caravans of the Six Coffers Market Priakos, a trade consortium in which Mirabeta held controlling interest. Sometimes, she hired him for darker deeds. Malkur had proven his proficiency at bloodletting on several occasions. Elyril thought that he and Mirabeta possessed similar temperaments—ambition unrestrained by moral foibles.

Elyril also knew that her aunt and Malkur had occasional sexual relations. She thought it strange, since they did not appear to like each other much. She suspected the coupling was performed without sentiment. The mental image amused her and she had to swallow a smile.

"How many of the Blades are available at this moment?" Mirabeta asked.

Malkur rubbed his cheek with the back of his hand and pondered. "Three score are away on jobs. I have about a hundred men to hand. And all are eager. Most have been idle for nearly a month."

Elyril and Mirabeta shared a satisfied look. One hundred men would be enough. Elyril knew the Blades to be a diverse force. Most of them were former Sembian and Cormyrean soldiers with a taste for violence, but Malkur also commanded a few wizards, a cadre of warrior-priests in service to Talos the Thunderer, and a handful of highly skilled men who could act as scouts or assassins for the larger force.

Mirabeta said, "Malkur, I have some . . . delicate work that needs to be done. You have the stomach for it. Know that it is for the good of Sembia."

Malkur snorted derisively. "Sembia can sink into the Inner Sea for all I care. And I mean no offense, Countess. I am interested only in the payment."

Mirabeta smiled tightly. "I understand. Then have eighty of your men ride south along the Rauthauvyr's Road. Weerdon Kost has communicated with Lady Merelith already. The Saerloonian delegation to the moot is on its way north. They will skirt Selgaunt. I want your men to attack them."

Malkur did not flinch from the politically sensitive nature of the targets. Elyril thought he would have made a fine Sharran.

"All of them should die?"

Mirabeta shook her head. "No. Attack them from the south, in the guise of Saerbians and Selgauntans, as they move toward Ordulin.

Through my house wizards, I will provide you with magical sendings telling you the exact day. Kill some and let the rest escape northward to me. I want them to bring me news of the attack."

Malkur stroked his whiskers, thoughtful. "You have the uniforms of Saerb and Selgaunt?"

Elyril shook her head. "Uniforms are too obvious."

Mirabeta nodded. "Your men should act in some way to convince the Saerloonians that their attackers are in service to Saerb and Selgaunt. I am sure you will think of something. After the attack, the men should return in small groups to Ordulin. It goes unsaid that none of your men should know of the nature of the attack until it happens."

"It also goes unsaid that none of them should be taken prisoner or left dead on the field," Elyril added.

Malkur looked at Elyril. "My men have never lost a battle, Mistress. Some nobles out of Saerloon and their ceremonial guard are not going to change that." He looked at Mirabeta and leaned forward in his chair. "The proffered payment, Overmistress?"

Mirabeta leaned back in her chair. "I will pay your men twice their normal fee. And you, Malkur, have my promise that when the time comes, you will be reinstated into Sembia's army and named my commander general."

Malkur tried to disguise it, but Elyril caught a flash of interest in his eyes. He had once been a general in Sembia's Helms, but Kendrick Selkirk had dismissed him from his post for excessive brutality in policing the roadways.

Malkur, pretending to ponder the offer, shrugged. "Promises are hard to spend, Overmistress."

"Triple the fee," Mirabeta said, and Malkur smiled. One of his front teeth was missing.

"Done, Overmistress," he said. "I will muster the men and await word from you."

Mirabeta said, "You cannot lead them, Malkur. I have a special task for you and a handpicked group of your men to perform."

Malkur's eyebrows rose in a question. The man fairly sweated greed. "Oh?"

"My informants have located Kendrick Selkirk's sons. They are in Scardale, preparing to journey to Ordulin."

Her words hung in the air, fat with implication.

Malkur's eyes narrowed and he said, "I would enjoy nothing more than seeing the sons of Kendrick Selkirk at the end of my blade."

"Here is your opportunity," Elyril said.

Malkur nodded and looked to Mirabeta. "Some of my Blades are skilled at what you require. And I have a diviner who may be able to locate them on the road. But Miklos Selkirk will be accompanied by his Silver Ravens. You will have a large battle to explain."

Elyril knew that Miklos commanded his own mercenary company called the Silver Ravens. They were less swords-for-hire than adventurers-for-hire. One of the Silver Ravens had been operating as a spy for Mirabeta for the better part of a year. He had informed them of Miklos and Kavin's whereabouts.

"No," Mirabeta said. "He is traveling in disguise, with only his brother. Few know he is coming. He hopes to arrive in Ordulin in secret and perform his own investigation of his father's death before revealing himself to the moot."

Malkur leaned forward in his chair and put his elbows on the table. "Miklos is well known, Overmistress. If word got out . . ."

"Word should not get out," Mirabeta said. "That would put us both in grave danger. That is why we can trust one another, Malkur."

Malkur nodded. "The Selkirk job will cost more. For the men, and for me."

Mirabeta smiled. "I would expect nothing less, dear Malkur. Quadruple the fees, then. A deal?"

Malkur looked pleased. He pushed back his chair and stood. "A deal, Overmistress. I can muster the men immediately."

Mirabeta stood and extended her hand to Malkur. He took it, kissed it, lingered over it.

"It is always a pleasure to be in your company," he said suggestively.

Mirabeta smiled, clucked her tongue, and waved Elyril from the chamber.

"Leave us, Elyril. We have . . . more business to discuss."

Elyril had no doubt. As she left her aunt and the mercenary leader to their lovemaking, she touched her invisible holy symbol and thanked Shar. The plan to employ the Blades to attack the Saerloonian delegation had been largely hers. With one stroke, they would invent a rebellion, make Saerloon a staunch ally, and eliminate Miklos Selkirk, a man who would have stood firmly against Mirabeta's appointment as war regent.

Sembia soon would explode as surely as a Gondsman's firebomb. Elyril chuckled when she considered how easily Sembia would descend into civil war. The tools had been in place for years. They had wanted only someone to wield them.

Daylight showed Selgaunt for the rouge-covered whore she had become. Cale was appalled by how much the city had changed over the last year.

Groups of destitute refugees crept out of the alleys and dark places of the city and sat listlessly on the walkways or streets until shopkeepers or the Scepters moved them along. Many begged alms and almost all of them looked hungry. Surreptitiously, to avoid being mobbed, Cale slipped a few silver ravens into the palms of the women and children he passed.

Selgaunt had been a wealthy city for so long that seeing so many poor on its streets shocked him. Cale guessed they must have come south from the upcountry, fleeing the drought, the Rage, the Rain of Fire, and the daemonfey.

He thought of Varra's words: *The world is too big to save everything.* Looking into the dull eyes of the hungry, he thought she had been as much a prophet as Sephris.

The streets lacked the usual vendors hawking day old bread and browned fruit. The typical smells of breakfasts cooking did not fill the morning air. Instead, stick figures wandered the streets and the air smelled of dumped nightsoil and despair.

Shopkeepers tried to hold up the pretense that Selgaunt was still Selgaunt—sweeping their stoops, setting out their wares—but even they looked underfed. Selgaunt reminded him more of Skullport than anything else.

He made his way as best he could through the deprivation. He knew that he could pray to Mask for the power to cast spells that created food. He knew the priests of other faiths could do the same, and wondered why they had not. At least two score priests lived in the city who were capable of casting the spell.

Perhaps they were seeing only to the needs of the wealthy? Or perhaps they *were* casting the spells for the needy and the magic was not enough. It occurred to Cale that the famine was not simply a problem of feeding the refugee villagers. The villagers had been the ones to feed the city with their crops and livestock. The recent disasters had forced the farmers into the city, and not only did they need food, they were no longer producing food for Selgaunt. The problem would only get worse with time. It would take a small army of priests to feed a city the size of Selgaunt.

A disturbance in the street ahead drew his eye. A wave of people jumped to their feet and pushed toward the middle of the avenue, all racing away from Cale. Many shouted, raised their fists. Cale fought his way through the press to see.

A caravan of mule-drawn wagons from the outlying farms rumbled down the center of the city. Turnips, leeks, and sacks of grain lay piled in the wagon beds. Armed Scepters surrounded the caravan and held the press of people at bay with their shields. Two Scepters rode in the wagon, straddling the food as if it were gold.

"This food is going to the market!" one of the Scepters shouted. "Make your purchase there!"

"Purchase!" a man near Cale shouted. "We cannot afford to pay! A bag of turnips costs a fivestar! We are hungry here, guardsman!"

Many in the crowd shouted agreement and pressed closer.

The Scepters looked alarmed, as did the teamsters driving the wagons. Even the mules looked skittish. The Scepters pushed the press of bodies backward with their shields and brandished their blades. The people fell back and the carts moved onward toward the market, leaving crying children and despondent parents in their wake.

The crowd started to disperse, grumbling in their despair. Cale put a hand on the shoulder of the thin man who had shouted about the price of turnips.

"Did you say a fivestar for turnips?"

The man turned and regarded Cale with hollow eyes. "Aye. The price of food has left all but the rich scraping for dog scraps, unless you are willing to wait all day in a priest's food line and swear to the worship of his god. Where have you been living?"

Cale held his tongue and let the man go.

A year ago, a sack of turnips would have cost a copper, maybe two. But a fivestar! Half of Selgaunt would be unable to eat at those prices. There would be riots.

Cale immediately decided that the new Hulorn was incompetent. He picked up his pace. Perhaps Tamlin could get the Old Chauncel to act.

Halfway to the Noble District, on the sharply angled, shop-lined Adzer's Way, Cale caught sight of a mounted trio of Helms patrolling the streets. They sat atop warhorses and each wore the customary round steel cap and blue tabard emblazoned with Sembia's coat of arms, the raven and silver. Cale stared at them for a moment in disbelief. He had never before seen soldiers of the Sembian army patrolling city streets. Sembia's merchants had always shown a strong distaste for soldiers. The nation's army was small and decentralized and kept deliberately so. Sembia was positioned to conquer through the force of its trade, not through force of arms. The Helms' duties had always consisted of patrolling the trade roads and villages outside of Sembia's major cities.

Cale decided that the new Hulorn was not merely incompetent, he was an idiot. He had put soldiers on the street—not city guardsmen accustomed to peacefully resolving disputes among the citizens, but soldiers, accustomed to answering problems with steel.

Shaking his head, Cale steered wide of the Helms and hurried on. He had been isolated in his cottage for too long. He had not known things had deteriorated so far, so fast. He needed to see Tamlin; he needed to understand what had happened.

The sounds on the streets were strangely subdued, tired, pensive.

Cale moved through the street traffic, dodging thin horses, men pulling empty carts, pedestrians trying to pretend that life was normal. He followed a line of people that snaked almost an entire block until he reached a warehouse with its wagon doors thrown open. Inside, priests of Lathander and Tymora spooned porridge out of huge pots into whatever container the hungry carried. He imagined Temple Avenue must look much the same.

When he reached the Noble District he found the streets dotted with armed men. Patrols of Helms and Scepters walked the streets. The gatehouses of the Old Chauncel manses were manned, not by two or three armed house guards, but by five or six.

Cale endured the suspicious gazes of the soldiers and headed south, past the towering walls of the Old Chauncel manses, toward Stormweather Towers. A group of mail-armored Helms stood in the street before his old home, blocking the walkway that led to the gatehouse. Shields hung from their backs; crossbows dangled from shoulder slings. All bore broadswords at their belts. Cale gauged their number at about a score. The pedestrian traffic—there was little—steered clear of the soldiers. But not Cale. He walked toward them, keeping his hand clear of Weaveshear as he approached. With conscious effort, he kept shadows from sneaking free of his flesh. The Helms saw him coming and three of them detached from the rest and stepped forward to halt his advance.

"The Hulorn holds audiences only on the tenth of each month," said the oldest of the three, a thick-set warrior with a square jaw and hard eyes. "Leave your name with the clerk in the palace and you will be seen in due time."

At first Cale could not make sense of the words. "The hulorn? Why is the hulorn in Stormweather?"

The man's eyes never left Cale's face. The eyes of his two comrades never left Cale's blade hand. "Lord Uskevren resides—"

Cale took a step back, incredulous. "Tamlin Uskevren is the *hulorn?*"

The Helms looked agitated at his tone. "Calm down, goodsir. Of course Tamlin Uskevren is the hulorn—has been these four months past. You are new to the city?"

Cale could not believe that Tamlin had been stupid enough to fill the streets with soldiers. He shook his head.

"No, but I have been away for a time."

Too long, it appeared. He said, "I have business with the Hulorn. He is expecting me."

The Helm took in Cale's appearance and weapons and looked doubtful. "He has not sent word that we should expect a visitor. If you leave your name with the clerk at the palace—"

"I am leaving my name with you," Cale said, a bit more sternly than he'd intended. "Please inform the Hulorn that Erevis Cale is . . ."

Cale trailed off. Behind the Helms, he saw a familiar face emerge from Stormweather's gatehouse.

"That tone will get you a day in the gaol," the Helm said.

Cale ignored the Helm and shouted past him. "Ren! Ren! It's Mister Cale!" Cale raised a hand in greeting. "Here!"

Cale had saved Ren's life a year ago, when slaads had used the young man as a hostage and taken three of his fingers.

Ren, in the attire of an Uskevren house guard, heard Cale's shout and looked around. He saw Cale waving and furrowed his brow.

"Ren! It's me, Erevis Cale."

"Move along," said the Helm, and he put his hand on Cale's chest.

"Mister Cale?" Ren called.

Shadows emerged from Cale's flesh and wrapped the Helm's hand. The man exclaimed, recoiled in alarm, and drew his blade. The other Helms did the same. Cale's hand went instinctively to Weaveshear but he stopped himself before drawing.

"What in the Nine Hells are you?" the Helm said, pointing his blade at Cale.

Cale ignored him and spoke to Ren. "Yes, Ren! It's me!"

Ren wore the blue and gold Uskevren livery over his armor and shield. He hurried down the pathway and scowled at the Helms.

"Scabbard that steel," he said to the Helms. "Now."

To Cale's surprise, the Helms obeyed—reluctantly, and eyeing Cale all the while.

The leader of the Helms said, "This man—"

"Was serving the hulorn when you were still chasing brigands down Tildaryn's Road, Vol," Ren finished.

Vol's lips pursed, but he nodded tightly and held back whatever he might have wanted to say.

Ren regarded Cale, clasped his forearm. "Gods, it is you, Mister Cale. I did not recognize you with the hair." He cocked his head. "And there is something else different, too."

"Dark sorcery," muttered Vol, eyeing his hand where Cale's shadows had touched him.

Cale ignored the Helm. Ren did not.

The house guard held up his hand to show his missing fingers. "You are insulting the man who ensured that I lost only these rather than my life."

Vol looked away. The other two Helms eyed the road.

Cale thumped Ren on the shoulder. He had left Ren an uncertain young man. Now he seemed a senior leader in the house guard. He had grown a neatly-trimmed beard, and he'd put on some weight.

"It is good to see you," Cale said.

"And you," Ren said with a smile.

"My apologies, goodsir," Vol said to Cale.

"Accepted," Cale answered immediately.

Side by side, Cale and Ren walked up the paved walkway that led to the gatehouse. Four other members of the house guard stood at the gate, watching them approach. They were armed and armored like Ren.

Ren said, "The hulorn informed the house guard that if you appeared, you were to be allowed entry at any hour. He neglected to inform the Helms."

Cale did not recognize any of the house guards stationed at the gatehouse. Ren ordered one of them to inform Irwyl, Cale's replacement as Uskevren steward, that Mister Cale had arrived, and the young guard sped off. The other house guards eyed Cale with open admiration.

Ren made introductions and led Cale through the gate and onto the grounds. The estate appeared as Cale remembered it. Topiary, fountains, statuary, and well-tended gardens dotted the swath. The stables, servants' quarters, and other outbuildings crouched along the surrounding walls.

"I told the other guards what happened at the Twisted Elm," Ren explained. "Everyone here knows of it."

Cale nodded, mildly embarrassed.

Ren looked at him sidelong. "I wondered what happened to you after we parted. Were you in Selgaunt all that time?"

"No," Cale said, and left it at that.

Cale could see Ren wanted to speak his thoughts.

"Speak plainly, Ren."

Ren hesitated, but finally asked, "Mister Cale, what happened to the sons of whores that maimed me? I want them dead. Or hurt. Or . . . something."

Cale understood the feeling. He pulled Ren to a stop and looked the young man in the face. "All but one is dead. And I made that one suffer before he escaped. Well enough?"

Ren smiled grimly and nodded. "Well enough."

Cale said to him, "My advice? Leave it in the past."

Ren looked Cale in the face and nodded. "Good advice."

They started walking. Ren asked, "What happened to your hand, Mister Cale? Surely not the same bastards?"

"The same," Cale said, holding up the stump of his wrist. "But the one that took my hand was not the one that escaped."

Ren spat on the ground. "Good news, that. Who were they, Mister Cale?"

"Ask me again another time, Ren. That is a long tale."

Ren nodded and changed the subject. "Things look a bit different, don't they?"

"Stormweather? It looks nearly the same."

"No. The city, I mean."

"Ah," Cale answered, nodding. "Very different."

Ren gestured northward as they walked. "Upcountry was struck hard by the Rage and the Rain of Fire. I heard that wildfires and dragon attacks destroyed entire villages. Some villages were abandoned out of fear. In others, the soil just went bad. The harvest suffered. The villagers headed for the cities in droves but the cities had nothing to offer them. So here we all sit." He shook his head. "I hear Selgaunt is worse than most. I do not know what will happen."

Neither did Cale. He knew only that Sephris had prophesied a storm and he felt as if he were watching it unfold before his eyes. He moved the conversation to smaller matters.

"What are you, second or third in command of the guard? Who heads it? Still Orrin?"

"Second," Ren answered with a swell of pride. "The youngest in the history of Stormweather. And aye. Still Orrin."

Cale knew Orrin to be a good man and a good leader. He had done well to promote Ren. The young man had grown much in the last year. Cale hoped the same was true of Tamlin.

They walked for a time in silence and Cale noticed eyes on himself. Grooms, stable boys, grounds men, all paused in their work to watch him pass. He recognized many of them. They had been on his staff long ago. He nodded. They waved. Gossip trailed in his wake.

"The staff still gossips," Cale said with a smile.

"So do my guards, and neither will ever change," Ren answered, also smiling. "It's good to have you back, Mister Cale."

"Thank you, Ren."

Ahead, Cale saw the raised porch and double-doored main entry-way to Stormweather Tower. Ivy climbed up the manse's curved walls. The Uskevren crest—the horse at anchor—hung over the doorway. Part of Cale's past lurked behind those doors.

Before they reached the porch, a squeal from Cale's left stopped him. He turned to see a bouncing mountain of flesh lumbering toward him—Brilla, the kitchen mistress. She wore a dress as large as a tent, a stained apron like a ship's sail, and a smile as wide as the Elzimmer River.

"Well met, Brilla," Cale said.

Brilla did not bother with words. She wrapped him in the folds of her ample body and gave him a squeeze so hard he was pleased his body had regenerated his broken ribs. Streamers of shadow coiled around her but she seemed not to notice.

"I told them all you would be back, I did. Said this place was in your veins. Said this family was your family. And here you are."

She pushed him away to arm's length. "Let us have a look. Look at this hair! You look so different, Mister Cale. I hardly recognize you."

"I have changed a bit," Cale acknowledged. "But not you, Brilla. You look as lovely as ever."

She turned away and blushed under her gray hair, pulled into a tight bun. "Now, Mister Cale . . ."

Cale smiled and said, "It is a true pleasure to see you, Brilla."

Brilla had always been a rock of sense among the staff. Chatty and stubborn, but always sensible. She beamed. "And you, Mister Cale."

"No need for the 'Mister,' Brilla."

"You will always be Mister Cale to me, Mister Cale."

Cale decided not to argue the point.

"Ah!" she exclaimed. "Your hand!"

Cale pulled his sleeve down over the stump. "It is nothing, Brilla."

"Nothing! How can you say such things?" She took his forearm in her hand, pushed up his sleeve, and examined the stump. There was no point in resisting her.

"It has healed well. How did it happen?"

"Another time, Brilla. Well enough?"

She let his arm go, frowning. "Well enough. Perhaps tonight? I have a torte that you will love, Mister Cale. Ingredients have been hard to come by of late, but I have improvised a little something with grapes from the Storl Oak vineyard and maple syrup. Will you be dining with Tamlin?"

Probably Brilla alone called the Hulorn by his given name.

"I am not certain," Cale said. He did not know exactly what Tamlin desired of him. "But if not, I will make a point to come to the kitchen."

Brilla accepted that with a smile. Most of her front teeth were rotten or missing. "It feels right to see you here again, Mister Cale."

"Thank you, Brilla."

She watched him, smiling all the while, as he and Ren entered Stormweather's double doors.

Irwyl awaited them in the arched foyer, arms crossed, brow furrowed. His short hair hung over a face as pointed as an arrowhead. He wore a prim look, a tailored vest, and linen pantaloons. He looked more a steward than Cale ever had. His eyes widened somewhat at Cale's appearance, but he masked his surprise well.

"You look well, Irwyl," Cale said.

"As do you, Mister Cale. Different, but well. That will be all, Ren."

Ren nodded, turned to Cale, and extended a hand. "For everything, my thanks."

Cale shook his hand. "Of course. I will be around for a while."

"Good to hear," Ren said. He nodded at the butler and took his leave.

"Do you require anything?" Irwyl asked Cale. "A refreshment? A . . . change of clothing?"

Cale smiled. "No, Irwyl."

"Very well. Follow me, then, Mister Cale," Irwyl said, and started for the parlor.

Before they reached it, Irwyl turned around and faced Cale.

"May I be candid, Mister Cale?"

Puzzled, Cale said, "Of course. What is it?"

"Do you intend to take your previous station? I would like to know if I need to seek a new situation. Times are difficult but I suspect the hulorn would be generous with severance."

Cale would have laughed aloud had he not seen how serious Irwyl was. He wiped the burgeoning smile from his face and said, "Of course not, Irwyl. My life has . . . gone in a different direction." He gave Irwyl a friendly pat on the shoulder. "Besides, I would be a poor substitute for you."

A relieved smile broke through Irwyl's stony exterior. "Very good, Mister Cale," he said, in a much softer tone. "Follow me, please."

Stormweather Towers had changed little. Cale felt as if he were walking back in time. Tapestry and art-bedecked halls and walls, carved wooden doors, arched ceilings. All of it seemed so far removed from Cale's life.

Irwyl led him into the parlor, the parlor where Cale often had played chess with Thamalon the Elder, or spent a long night discussing the plot of this or that rival of the Old Chauncel. The book-lined walls and reading chairs remained, as did the ivory and jade chessboard and pieces. Cale felt Thamalon's absence the same way he felt the absence of his severed hand.

"I have informed the hulorn of your arrival," Irwyl said. "He will see you shortly."

While he waited, Cale paced the parlor, examined the spines of the books, the suits of ceremonial armor that stood in the corners of the chamber, the sculptures small and large that dotted the room.

The parlor was still Thamalon's, even more than a year after his death. That pleased Cale. He stood over the chessboard, pondered, and advanced the queen's pawn.

"Your move, my lord," he murmured.

A cleared throat from over his shoulder turned him around.

Tamlin wore a long green jacket, a pale, stiff collared shirt, and the tailored breeches that seemed fashionable in Sembia that season. He wore a number of pouches on his belt—components for his spells, Cale figured. Some gray at his temples accented his otherwise dark hair. Shadows darkened the skin under his eyes, which widened at Cale's appearance.

A man of about the same age stood beside Tamlin. He wore a snugly fitted purple vest with a collared black shirt, and high boots rather than shoes. A rapier and dagger hung from his belt. A short beard masked a tight mouth and small eyes set closely together. He, too, looked surprised at Cale's appearance.

"Mister Cale?" asked Tamlin tentatively.

Cale bowed formally. "Lord Uskevren."

Tamlin approached him, mouth open, but arm outstretched. They clasped forearms.

"Gods, man!" Tamlin said, shaking his head and smiling. "You look so . . . different."

Cale nodded. "Many things have changed since our paths crossed last, my lord."

Tamlin studied his face. "So I heard, and so I see. Same man underneath, though. Yes?"

Cale hoped so. "Yes. You look a bit different, my lord."

Tamlin ran his fingers through the gray in his hair. "Ah, yes, this. Well, heavy is the head that wears the crown and all that, right?" He laughed, a forced sound, and gestured at the man who had accompanied him into the room.

"Do you remember Vees Talendar?"

"Talendar?" Cale paused to think. A rogue wizard of the Talendar family had once orchestrated an attack on the Uskevren. It culminated in a lengthy battle with summoned monsters atop the High Bridge.

Vees flushed. "No doubt you recall my Uncle Marance's unfortunate bout of madness and the consequences of the same."

"Our families have long since come to terms with those events," Tamlin said with a dismissive wave, and Cale was not certain if he was speaking to Cale or Vees. "The Talendar and Uskevren are fast friends now."

"That is something good that came of my uncle," Vees said.

"The past is the past," Cale said to Vees, nodding respectfully. "Lord Talendar."

Vees smiled, a polite gesture but nothing more. "Mister Cale," he said.

Tamlin gestured at Vees. "Vees's advice has been invaluable to me, Mister Cale. Due to him, I was elected Hulorn."

"Indeed?" Cale asked.

"Your own talent got you elected," Vees said, and Cale knew he was silver-tongued. Vees eyed Cale's leather armor, his weapons. "You do not look much like a steward."

"Mister Cale was always more than that," Tamlin said.

"A bodyguard, more like," Vees said. "At least from what I have heard."

Cale recalled that the Talendar family had sent Vees to Waterdeep for an education and he had returned a priest of Siamorphe. Cale thought it strange that he did not wear a holy symbol openly. He knew also that the Talendars had financed the building of a temple to Siamorphe on Temple Avenue.

"How is construction proceeding?" Cale asked, to change the subject.

Vees looked surprised that Cale knew of the temple.

"You mean the temple? Quite well, Mister Cale. The Lady's new home will be completed soon."

"Perhaps then you can give us a tour, at last," Tamlin said with a laugh. He looked to Cale and said, "The priests keep the place locked as tight as a Calishite Pasha's harem room."

Vees smiled and explained to Cale, "There are only two priests other than myself, and the sanctification rites require that the interior be open only to servants of Siamorphe until the process is complete. It is taking quite some time. You understand, I am sure."

Cale did not, but nodded anyway. His god had no temples other than alleys. His god had knife fights with his Chosen.

"Vees could tell us that the rites required nude virgins dancing in the moonlight and I would know no better. Who has ever heard of Siamorphe? You will be pressed for worshipers, my friend."

Vees only smiled. "Perhaps. But we go where we are called."

Irwyl entered with a bottle of Uskevren wine and three goblets.

"Ever timely," Tamlin said. Irwyl distributed the goblets and poured. Cale allowed a fill out of politeness, though he did not intend to drink. Irwyl left the bottle on a side table. He noticed that the pawn had been moved on the chessboard, frowned, and returned it to its original position.

Irwyl asked, "Will Mister Cale be staying in the manse?"

"Of course," Tamlin answered, without consulting Cale. "Mister Cale will serve as an advisor to the hulorn, if he so pleases."

Tamlin looked the question at Cale and Cale nodded. Tamlin said to Irwyl, "See to it that a room is prepared."

"Will your old quarters suffice, Mister Cale?" Irwyl asked.

"They are tiny!" Tamlin said. "I will not hear of it."

"I would prefer it, my lord," Cale said. "That would be fine, Irwyl."

"I will see to it," Irwyl said, and turned to Tamlin. "Will that be all, my lord?"

"Yes, Irwyl," Tamlin said, drinking his wine.

After Irwyl left, Cale decided to move directly to business. "Lord Uskevren, your message asked for my hurried return to the city."

Tamlin set down his goblet and his face grew serious, as serious as Cale had ever seen it. "Kendrick Selkirk is dead. Mirabeta Selkirk has been elected temporary overmistress. Endren Corrinthal of Saerb is accused of murdering Kendrick, but our contacts in Ordulin are not certain of the truth of it. There was some kind of fight in the High Council and Endren was arrested. Zerin Terb was killed."

Vees shook his head. "A shocking, shocking state of affairs."

Cale knew Terb's name. He had been Selgaunt's representative in the High Council for over a decade. Tamlin continued. "In any event, the council has called a moot to elect a new overmaster. I am traveling to Ordulin—"

"My lord?" Cale asked, surprised. The hulorn had always appointed an agent to represent Selgaunt in the High Council or a moot, but never attended personally.

"I cannot tell what is happening there from here," Tamlin said. "Some of our informants there say that Endren's son is raising an army to depose Mirabeta. Others believe that Mirabeta arranged all of this. I need to see it personally before I ask the entire Old Chauncel to journey to the capital for the moot. Something is afoot and I need someone I can trust at my side. You. I want you as my wallman, Mister Cale. What do you say?"

Cale answered immediately. "Of course, but . . ."

"But?" Tamlin asked.

"My lord, Selgaunt is . . . in difficulties. How will it appear if you leave it? Who will govern?"

"We will not be away for long. Two tendays, perhaps three. Vees will speak for me, if needed, but the bureaucracy runs itself. The Old Chauncel will operate by consensus in my absence. In truth, that is another reason that I want to go alone, despite the call for the moot. If the entire Old Chauncel left the city at once, it would be . . . ill perceived. Once I have a handle on events in Ordulin, I will send for the key members of the Chauncel."

"A wise course, Hulorn," Vees said.

Cale was not so sure. Selgaunt felt ready to erupt. Tamlin had called him an advisor, so Cale decided to start advising. He took care to frame his speech appropriately. He had been removed from the niceties of station for some time. The words did not come as easily to him as they once did.

"My lord, may I make a recommendation or two? Actions that you might take before leaving the city?"

Vees snorted into his goblet. "The man is returned for a day and already has suggestions."

Cale stared at Vees. Vees took another sip of his wine and averted his gaze.

"You are my advisor," Tamlin said with a tip of his goblet.

Cale nodded. "The city is overcrowded. The people are hungry."

"There is food in the market," Vees said.

"Little, and it is priced so high that none but the rich can afford to eat," Cale said, trying and failing to keep the coolness out of his voice.

Vees made an uncaring gesture. "Unfortunate, but true. But this is Sembia, Mister Cale. The market is what the market is."

Cale barely resisted the impulse to punch the noble twit in the face. Despite his best efforts, shadows leaked from his skin. The room dimmed.

Tamlin noticed and looked alarmed. So did Vees but he looked more puzzled than afraid.

"I will explain later, my lord," Cale said softly, and with an effort of will, caused the light to return and the shadows to subside.

Tamlin nodded slowly, eyes wide. Vees took another sip of his wine and studied Cale over the rim.

Cale said, "My lord, if your answer is the same as that of Lord Talendar, you will soon have riots. Hunger makes people desperate." Cale thought of Skullport and said, "I have seen it before."

Vees harrumphed. "That is why the Helms are on the streets."

Cale ignored Talendar and addressed Tamlin. He decided to be candid. "If I am going to be of service to you, this all must end right now."

Tamlin looked confused. "I do not understand, Mister Cale."

Cale gestured at the parlor, at Vees, at Tamlin. "This. All of this. The polite speech. The discussions over wine. The clothes. The city is in a crisis, my lord. From what you have told me, all of Sembia is in crisis. We are not discussing a contract for trade. May I be fully candid or not?"

"There is no need for panic," Vees said.

"No, but there is need for hard thinking and bold action," Cale said. "And I never panic, Talendar."

A few streamers of shadows rose from Cale's flesh and dissipated in the air. If Vees thought to rebuke Cale for neglecting the nobleman's honorific, he thought better of it.

"I take your point," Tamlin said thoughtfully. "Let's hear him out, Vees. Mister Cale brings an outsider's perspective on things. Go on, Mister Cale."

Cale plowed forward, eyeing Vees as he spoke. "Get the Helms off the street. They make you look frightened."

Vees said, "The Helms are helping keep order. And are you accusing the Hulorn of being afraid?"

Cale surmised that putting the Helms on the streets had been Vees's idea. "There are not enough of them to stop a riot, if it happened. In the meanwhile, they contribute to the perception that matters are not in hand, that the nobility is frightened." He looked to Tamlin. "My lord, get them off the street. They are tense, and ill-suited to the work you have asked them to do. They drew steel on me outside Stormweather."

"Perhaps justifiably," Vees mumbled.

Cale whirled on him. "I promise you that if another comment like that comes out of your mouth, your teeth will follow it."

Vees flushed, stuck out his jaw, and uttered not a word. Cale turned back to Tamlin. "Put the Helms back on the roads and waterways, where they belong, where people are used to seeing them. Order them to escort refugees into the city."

Tamlin looked startled. "*Into* the city?"

"Out, I should think," Vees said cautiously. "We are already overcrowded."

Cale kept his voice calm. "They are coming anyway, unless you plan to lock down the city. You do not, do you?"

Tamlin raised his eyebrows. "We considered it."

Cale blew out a breath. "Lord Thamalon, you must stop taking steps that suggest desperation. The first thing the people need from you is the sense that you are in control, that things will soon return to normal. You can earn some goodwill by getting the steel off the streets and using it to ensure that your citizens are safe."

"Unwise," Vees said, and hurriedly added, "and I mean no offense, Mister Cale. But the Noble District will be overrun by refugees the day the Helms exit the city."

"Nonsense," Cale said, and Vees stiffened. "Subsidize the cost of food during the crisis. Distribute it through the Scepters. Require the temples to direct their priests to use magic to make food and distribute it."

"They will not do it," Vees said dismissively.

"Some are already doing it," Cale answered. "This is just a matter of forcing the rest. You could lead by example, Talendar. You're a priest, no?"

Vees nodded tightly. "Construction occupies my time, Mister Cale."

Cale scoffed and continued. "Do not make an announcement and force a public fight with the faiths, my lord. Instead, let the high priests know through back channels that if they do not obey, the temples' taxes will increase markedly and you may revoke their charters. You have the tools, Lord Hulorn."

"The gods grant spells, Mister Cale," said Vees. "If the priests say the gods will not grant the spells to make food, then what? Would you have the hulorn hold a blade to the gods?"

Cale did not mention that he had done exactly that in an alley just hours before. Instead, he said, "The gods will not refuse. They need their priests as much as their priests need them."

Vees looked startled by Cale's statement, but Tamlin looked intrigued. "Interesting, Mister Cale. What do you think, Vees?" Tamlin asked.

The sound of hurried footsteps coming down the hall toward

the parlor interrupted whatever Vees might have said. All three men turned to the doorway, and Tazi appeared, breathing heavily.

"Thazienne," Vees said, but she did not even glance at the nobleman. She had eyes, wide eyes, only for Cale.

"Erevis?"

Sweat pasted Tazi's dark hair to her face and she held a riding crop in her hand. She wore tight breeches and boots rather than the more decorous riding dress customary for Sembian noblewomen. The year since he'd seen her last had not changed her at all. She was as beautiful as ever. Her green eyes sparkled under the waves of her hair.

Cale had feared how seeing her might make him feel. To his surprise, he felt only fondness, not desire. He had left his love for her behind when he'd left Stormweather and it had died in the intervening year. He smiled at her.

"Well met, Mistress Uskevren."

She ran a hand through her sweaty hair. "I was just on a morning ride when I heard you had returned. I ran right over." His words registered, and she asked, "Did you call me 'Mistress Uskevren'?"

"Thazienne," Cale corrected with a smile. "Tazi."

"That's more like it," she said with her own smile. She crossed the chamber to embrace him.

Tamlin said, "Tazi, I do not know—"

"What I am cannot harm her, my lord," Cale said, interrupting him and embracing her. She felt tiny in his arms and smelled, as always, of lavender. He kept the shadows from leaking out of his flesh.

Thazienne pulled back and looked from Cale to her brother. "What you are? What does that mean?"

"It means nothing," Cale said softly. "It is wonderful to see you."

"And you," she answered. She eyed his hair, his skin, cupped his cheek in her palm. "You feel cold. And you look so different. What happened to you? Where have you been? Ren told us what you did for him. It seems you have made a habit of saving the members of this household."

Cale felt his skin warm with embarrassment. He had once saved Thazienne from a demon attack within Stormweather's walls.

"Many things have happened," he said. "We can talk about it another time. You look the same as ever. But happier. That pleases me."

She smiled and he saw in her expression the ghost of the shy girl he had watched grow into a bold woman.

"Ahem," Tamlin said. "Tazi, perhaps you and Mister Cale could continue your reunion at a later time. We are discussing matters of state at the moment. Time is short."

She kept her dark eyes on Cale and smiled. "He has grown serious, don't you think? Not as serious as you, but serious enough. Father would be proud, I think."

Cale nodded, though he was not as sure.

"Talbot will want to see you," she said. "But he is away at Storl Oak. I will send word."

"We will speak later, Tazi. Well enough?"

She smiled wistfully. "Over a brandy in the butler's pantry?"

They often had stayed awake late into the night, talking over spirits in the pantry.

"Perhaps in the dining hall?" Cale said. "For a late breakfast? The pantry is no longer my domain. Irwyl is king there now."

"I will see you there," she said. "Brilla has a wonderful torte you should try."

"So I have heard," Cale said.

Tazi grinned, nodded, neglected to curtsy to either Tamlin or Vees, and took her leave.

Cale watched her go, pleased that his heart was steady, that his feelings for her had matured. His mind turned to Varra and he wondered how she was faring.

"As I was saying," Vees continued. "I do not agree with all of Mister Cale's suggestions. I believe he thinks too highly of the refugees and too little of the priesthoods. Do as you think best, Deuce," he said, using Tamlin's nickname.

Cale held his tongue while Tamlin sipped his wine and pondered. Silence hung heavy in the room.

Tamlin stared down at the chessboard for a time, then put down his goblet and said, "My father relied on your counsel for years, Erevis. I will not disregard it lightly. But I will not pull the Helms off the streets," he said, with a nod to Vees. "I will, however, order them to assist with food distribution. And I will send word to the high priests as you suggested. A more serious commitment on the part of the temples should keep people from starving."

Cale figured a partial victory was better than none at all.

"Well decided," Vees said, and Cale disliked the nobleman even more.

Cale asked Tamlin, "When will we leave for Ordulin, my lord?"

"I began preparations upon receiving word from the High Council. Things are taking longer than I had hoped, but we will be ready to leave in the next day or two."

Vees said, "Many other nobles have already left for Ordulin. We know that the Saerloonian delegation is en route already. They passed Selgaunt two days ago, though they skirted the city."

"Skirted the city?"

"Tension appears to be very high in the capital, Mister Cale," Tamlin said. "And it has spilled out into the countryside. The nobles are lining up behind Mirabeta Selkirk or Endren Corrinthal. The Saerloonians do not trust us, so they avoided Selgaunt altogether. Things are sharp at the moment."

Cale took in the words, feeling unsuited to the task of helping Tamlin. He had been solving problems with his spells and blades for so long that politics felt foreign to him.

Tamlin picked up his goblet and drained it. "But all that in due time. I apologize that we will depart so soon. The schedule does not leave you much time for settling in. And my day will be full since I need to sign the orders we've just discussed. We will dine this evening, however. My apologies."

"I will manage, Hulorn," Cale said. "I remember my way around."

"Of course," Tamlin said, and smiled. "I am interested in hearing your explanation about . . . the other events."

"Yes, my lord." Cale said. "My lord, where is Lady Uskevren? I would like to speak with her before we leave."

"She has been away upcountry with Talbot," Tamlin answered. "This city, and the manse, make her unhappy these days. We rebuilt the old upcountry manor house at Storl Oak. She seems to enjoy it there. But she is to return later this morning to see me off. Your presence will be a pleasant surprise."

Cale knew Shamur to be a former adventuress, and she knew him to be more than a steward. They had come to respect and admire each other over Cale's years at Stormweather.

Tamlin continued, "Meanwhile, is there anything you need before we leave tomorrow?"

"No, my lord." Cale had his armor, his blades, his armor . . . and his holy symbol.

"Very good, then. I will leave you to your own devices. Vees, accompany me to the palace. I have orders to issue and we have much to discuss."

Vees offered an insincere farewell to Cale and they parted. Before Cale left the parlor, he again advanced the pawn on Thamalon's old chessboard.

He wandered Stormweather Towers for a time. Servants and members of the house guard nodded and smiled at him when they passed him in the halls. Every room through which he walked held a memory.

Throughout all the events of his life, his love for the Uskevren had been a constant. And he had always known, deep down, that he could return to Stormweather if he had need. It was his sanctuary. The manse was where he had been born, or at least reborn, and it pleased him to be able to return to his birthplace. After wandering for a time, he headed for his quarters to await Shamur's return.

Even when Cale had been Stormweather's steward, he had never done much to personalize his quarters. The room was as bare as he had left it. He opened the shutters, sat in his old reading chair, took out Jak's pipe, tamped and lit. He spent some time remembering with fondness the adventures he and Jak had enjoyed in Selgaunt. He removed the book he had taken from the Fane of Shadows from his backpack—the book that contained lore about Mask, Shar, the Weave, and the Shadow Weave—and opened it.

To his shock, the pages were blank.

He flipped one, another, another. The whole tome was blank except for the final pages. On them were words written in purple ink in a tongue Cale could not read. Staring at the writing made him nauseated, so he slammed the cover shut. He looked at the cover of black scaled leather and assured himself it was the same tome. It was. He blew out a cloud of smoke and replaced the book in his pack. He did not know what to make of the book, but it made him uneasy. Had its magic served its purpose, and was now destroying itself?

Thoughtful, he smoked two bowls of pipeweed before a knock on his door disturbed his reverie. He laid the pipe on the side table and opened the door. Shamur stood in the doorway, still dressed in her green daygown. Jeweled pins held up her auburn hair. Cale thought the lines in her face, around her eyes, and at the corners of her mouth only made her more attractive.

She did not look surprised at his appearance. Perhaps she had been forewarned. "You look well, Erevis."

Cale bowed, embarrassed by the cloud of smoke that billowed out of his room. "And you, Lady, look as young and beautiful as ever."

She smiled, stepped forward, and embraced him warmly. "Mister Cale, you still lie as well as ever."

They separated and he gestured her in.

"Smoking, Erevis? That is new."

"A long tale, Milady," he explained. "A friend got me started. I will put it out."

He moved to the table to snuff the pipe.

"No need," she said. "The smell is not unpleasant. Thamalon enjoyed a pipe, you will recall."

Cale did recall. The Old Owl had not smoked often, but when he had, the entire east wing of the manse would smell of pipeweed for days. In the spring, Cale had the staff open the windows to air out the house. In the winter, nothing could be done but to wait for the stink to pass.

Shamur looked around the room, then turned to face him. "Your quarters look much as you left them, but you have changed a great deal. And not merely your appearance. What has happened to you?"

Cale smiled gently. "Nothing that can be undone or made easier to bear by sharing, Milady. Suffice to say that I have changed, but serve your family still."

She smiled. "Of that I had no doubt. It is good to have you back under our roof, Erevis."

"It is good to be back," Cale said, and meant it. "Please, sit."

Shamur sat in his reading chair. Her hair glittered in the fading sunlight.

Cale did not have another chair in the room so he sat on the bed nearby. Before he could speak, she said, "This house has been dying for a year. It started with Thamalon's passing. Then you left. And Talbot is gone almost always. Tamlin spends most of his day and much of his nights away at the palace. I hate it here."

Cale looked away. He did not know what to say so he broke with decorum and reached out to take her hand in his. Her skin felt warm. Shadows sneaked from his skin and danced over hers. She gasped but did not withdraw her hand.

"What happened to you, Erevis? Tell me."

Cale did not look her in the face. "Milady, I . . . must carry this alone."

She caressed his hand and he felt such a sudden, powerful attraction for her that he pulled away and stood up before it caused him to do something he should not.

"What is it?" she asked.

He shook his head. "Nothing. Nothing at all." He moved the conversation to the purpose for which he had wanted to see her, or at least the purpose for which he thought he had wanted to see her.

"Lady Uskevren, I have reason to believe that things are . . . unsafe in the city."

She leaned forward in her chair. "What do you mean? Have you informed Tamlin?"

Cale shook his head. "No, Milady. It is nothing that we can act on, nothing that I can easily articulate. But I would advise you and

Tazi to leave the city for a time." He struggled to find a better explanation, failed.

"You want me to abandon Stormweather? I have only just returned."

"Not abandon, Lady. I am suggesting only that you retire to the upcountry estate until things settle down here." He grasped for an excuse, found one. "Tamlin would be better served with fewer things to think about. I will watch over him and vouchsafe his person."

"You two are traveling to Ordulin. You will not even be in the city."

"When we return, I mean," Cale said. "Please, Milady."

"What is it that you are afraid of, Erevis?" she asked, leaning forward in the chair.

Cale looked away. Anything he said would sound absurd. He could not tell her that the mad Chosen of Oghma had prophesied a storm, that Mask had met him in an alley and told him something similar. Instead, he offered a half-truth. "Milady, the city is on a blade's edge. The family of the Hulorn is a natural target for those unhappy with the state of affairs. I think you would be safest away from Selgaunt."

She stared at him, considering. He held her gaze but only with difficulty. Finally, she said, "I am always willing to leave Stormweather for the upcountry. And Thazienne *has* found the city stifling of late. Perhaps a vacation is advisable. My carriage is not yet unpacked. It would be easy to return to Storl Oak."

Cale exhaled with relief. "Just for a month or two, Milady. You should leave as soon as possible. Tomorrow. I will inform Irwyl to prepare Tazi's things."

Shamur stood. She studied his face.

"You are not *always* a good liar, Erevis. But I am thankful for your concern." She touched his cheek and exited the room.

Cale remained in his room, thoughtful, until Irwyl came to retrieve him to dine with Tamlin. Irwyl bore a change of clothes in his arms.

"Will you be changing for dinner, Mister Cale?"

The question was clearly a recommendation.

Cale eyed the soft material, the embroidery, the buttons gilded with precious metal. He shook his head.

"No," he answered.

He had worn a facade most of the years he had spent in Stormweather. Those days were behind him. He would wear his own clothing and his weapons. He was a man who wore leather and steel, not linen and gold.

Irwyl only raised his eyebrows and frowned slightly. "Very well."

Cale informed Irwyl that Tazi and Shamur would be returning to Storl Oak on the morrow. Irwyl nodded and led him not to the dining hall but to a private meeting room. Tamlin sat alone at a small table set for two.

"That will be all, Irwyl," said Tamlin. Irwyl bowed and exited.

"Join me, Erevis."

Cale took a seat across from Tamlin. A bottle of Thamalon's Best sat on the table, and a silver platter of roast beef and carrots.

"Help yourself," Tamlin said, and stocked his own plate. "Brilla prepares excellent fare."

Cale cut himself a modest slice of roast. "We are fortunate to eat so well in these lean times."

Tamlin studied his face as if trying to determine if Cale's words had been a veiled insult. Cale kept his face expressionless and let Tamlin conclude what he would.

"Indeed, we are fortunate," Tamlin said. "But it is not all merely good fortune. Some are suited to rule and succeed. Others are not. When times are difficult, the latter often suffer. It is the way of things."

Cale filled his mouth with beef to hold in the sharp retort that wanted to come forth. Tamlin had spent too much time around the likes of Vees Talendar.

Tamlin awaited a reply; Cale offered none. Finally, Tamlin said, "I asked Irwyl to provide you with suitable attire. He is often forgetful. I will—"

"He brought it, my lord," Cale said, his tone overly sharp. "I declined. I deemed my current attire suitable to my situation."

Tamlin's brow furrowed at Cale's tone. "You owe me an explanation, Mister Cale."

Cale did not miss Tamlin's own cool tone.

"About what, my lord?"

Tamlin gestured at Cale's flesh. "About your appearance. About the shadows that flow from your skin. About the hand that appears and disappears from your wrist, about how the light in a room dims when you grow angry. Explain."

Cale set down his fork. Tamlin's tone irked him, so Cale did not mince words. "I am a shade."

Tamlin stared, his fork frozen over his plate. The silence stretched. "A shade?" Tamlin said at last. "Like the Shadovar?"

Cale shrugged. He knew little of the Shadovar. "I cannot say. I am stronger in the darkness." He held up his hand. "My hand regenerates entirely at night or in darkness. I can travel from one shadow to another in an eyeblink, covering a bowshot or thirty leagues. My flesh resists magic. As far as I can determine, I no longer age."

Tamlin gawked. "I do not know what to say. That is . . . wonderful, Mister Cale."

"No, it is not."

Cale's tone tempered Tamlin's exuberance. "How did it happen? Tell me everything."

Cale shook his head. "I am not inclined to share that, my lord. The how and the why do not matter."

"Do not matter?"

"Correct, my lord. And I would be appreciative if you would keep this knowledge between us. I wanted to be candid with you at the outset but I see no reason for others to know."

Tamlin stared, finally managed to say, "As you wish, Mister Cale." They ate for a time in silence.

Tamlin set down his fork and looked across the table. "You do not like me very much, do you, Mister Cale? And you certainly do not respect me."

Cale sipped from his goblet of wine while he considered his words. "You are the son of my former Lord. I will serve you loyally and to the best of my ability."

Tamlin gestured dismissively with his hand. "I know that. But you do not respect me, do you?"

Cale sighed and looked across the table into Tamlin's eyes. "My respect is hard-earned these days, my lord."

Tamlin stared across the table, waiting.

"No, I do not," Cale admitted, and once he opened the gate, the army poured forth. "I do not think you understand the scope of the problems before you, before the city. I could see that after walking the streets for only one day. You still think like a nobleman, not a statesman. And you take counsel from fools like Vees Talendar. And still you—"

He cut himself off. He had said enough. He could see the hurt in Tamlin's eyes, and below that, the angry defiance. Cale knew the expression well. Tamlin often had shown it when his father had demanded something of him. Tamlin had always disliked anyone demanding anything of him.

Tamlin took another bite of beef and said tightly, "You come back for a single day after being gone a year and think to take the measure of me, Vees, and the city all at a glance?"

"My absence did not render me blind," Cale answered. "Or stupid."

Tamlin stared at him across the table. "Thank you for your candor, Mister Cale." He dropped his utensils. "You will excuse me. My appetite has passed."

"My lord—"

"We leave for Ordulin as soon as I can get some final matters resolved," Tamlin said as he rose. "The fool to whom I sometimes listen will not be accompanying us. He must attend ceremonies at the new temple."

Cale nodded. He thought of apologizing but could not bring himself to do it.

"Good eve, my lord."

"Good eve, Mister Cale."

Cale finished the meal alone and in silence.

Afterward, he walked the halls until he reached the kitchen and was warmly welcomed by Brilla. She wiped down a butcher's block, set him down on a stool, and smiled as she watched him eat her raisin and syrup torte.

Vees shed his false face—that of a spoiled dilettante nobleman—and entered the temple through the concealed doorway in the alley. He had murdered the four stonemasons who had knowledge of the secret entrance, using the curved sacrificial knife at his belt to cut their throats.

He closed the pivoting secret door behind him and walked down the steep stairs that led into the secret worship hall below the false temple to Siamorphe. When he reached the vestry off the hall, he donned a ceremonial robe that awaited him there—a voluminous black velvet affair with purple piping. Whispering a prayer to his goddess, he walked the corridor to the main worship hall.

His steps carried him through one of the magically created areas of silence that surrounded the hall. His footsteps on the stone went quiet. A ring of such areas surrounded the worship hall, as did a series of magical screens to prevent scryings. Anything that happened within the hall could be heard and seen only by those in attendance. The secrecy of the design pleased the Lady.

The worship hall of the Lady's temple lay directly below the worship hall of Siamorphe. Like Vees, the temple had a false face. Like Vees, the temple purported to serve one purpose while serving another.

He reached the edge of the area of silence and immediately sensed the change—the whimpers of the sacrifice victim and the murmur of the worshipers suddenly sounded in his ears. He pulled up his hood—none of the worshipers knew his true identity—and pushed open the apse door. A rustle of movement greeted him as the worshipers turned to watch him enter. Even the sacrifice went silent. The large, semicircular worship hall smelled of tallow candles and fear-tinged sweat.

Vees held up his arms and spoke aloud the supplication.

"In the darkness of night we hear the whisper of the void."

"Heed its words," responded the eight worshipers of Shar. "Welcome, Dark Watcher."

"Welcome, dark sisters and brothers," Vees answered, and moved to the altar.

The worshipers lowered themselves onto kneelers, heads down as he passed. No accoutrements of the faith adorned the altar or the worship hall. No windows allowed outside light. The Lady and the Nightseer wished it so.

The room was dark but for the candles that burned in candelabra at the head and feet of the bound and naked sacrifice. Shadows played over the bare walls, the arched ceiling.

Vees assumed the sacrifice—a thin, malnourished man—to be one of the refugees from upcountry. He stepped behind the altar and smiled within his hood. The difficult times in Selgaunt had made sacrifices so easy to obtain.

Sweat glistened on the man's body; he stank of fear. His chest rose and fell rapidly. He stared up at Vees with wide, terrified eyes.

"Do not," he said, his voice a croak. He must have been crying, or screaming, before Vees arrived. "Please."

Vees ignored him and looked out on the worshipers. He moved to one candelabrum and blew out all but one of the candles, then did the same with the other. A deeper darkness settled on the chamber.

"Darkness has fallen and the Lady of Loss is with us," Vees said. "Give her now your bitterness. Lay your losses before her."

He waited while the worshipers confessed aloud the matters that had made them bitter, the things they had lost, the grudges they had developed since the last time the group had met the month before. The hubbub of voices made it impossible for Vees to distinguish sentences or speakers, but Vees knew the Lady heard them all and rejoiced.

When the worshipers completed the ritual and fell silent, Vees said, "The Lady is pleased by your offerings made in this, her new temple. The construction is nearly complete. We turn now to the sanctification of her altar, which requires blood."

The sacrifice writhed, pleaded. "No! No!"

Vees reached under his robes and withdrew the sacrificial dagger. He held it above the man.

The sacrifice fought against his bonds. His breath came so quickly he would soon lose consciousness. Vees could see every tendon in his body, every muscle.

"Your despair is sweet to the Lady," Vees said, and raised the blade for a killing strike.

The sacrifice stared wide-eyed at the blade's point and screamed.

CHAPTER TEN

1 Uktar, the Year of Lightning Storms

Cale awoke in his chamber before dawn. He had not dreamed of Magadon since arriving in Selgaunt and did not know what to make of it. Mask's words haunted him: *Magadon will suffer in the meanwhile.*

Cale dressed and met Tamlin a bit after dawn in the main hall. They exchanged pleasantries and walked side by side across the grounds to the stables. Tamlin wore his father's ermine-trimmed traveling cloak with a rapier, but no armor or shield. Cale recalled that armor interfered with Tamlin's ability to cast spells. A satchel with two thick, leather-bound tomes hung over his shoulder.

Books on spellcraft, Cale assumed with some surprise, since he had never known Tamlin to favor reading. Tamlin had become a moderately accomplished sorcerer over the years. If only his leadership and talent for statesmanship had matured as much as his magical ability.

"Your mount will regret your choice of reading material, my lord," said Cale.

Tamlin smiled tightly. "Just something of interest to me."

For his part, Cale wore his enchanted leather armor, his daggers, and Weaveshear. Pouches at his belt held his lockpicking kit and his coin purse. His pack held his bedroll, rope, and the magical tome he had taken from the Fane of Shadows. He carried the Shadowlord's mask in his pocket.

"I received word late last night that Mother and Tazi arrived safely at Storl Oak," Tamlin said. "I understand that was your suggestion?"

Cale nodded. "Were they escorted, my lord?"

"Of course," Tamlin snapped, an edge in his voice. "I am not a fool, Mister Cale, despite your suggestion to the contrary. Eight members of the house guard rode with them, including Captain Orrin. Five more men plus Talbot await them at Storl Oak."

Cale nodded and said nothing more. They walked the rest of the way to the stables in silence.

The grooms had saddled twelve geldings, all of them stout steeds thirteen hands or more in height. Three pack horses loaded with gear stood with their heads lowered. Ren and nine other members of the Uskevren house guard were loading equipment onto their geldings. All wore chain shirts, helmets, and serious looks. Each bore a blade, a crossbow, and a shield enameled with the Uskevren crest. Their livery, too, featured the Uskevren horse at anchor. They spoke congenially to their mounts as they checked tack, harness, stirrup, and saddle.

"My lord," all of them nodded to Tamlin in greeting. "Mister Cale."

"Men," Tamlin answered.

Ren nodded a greeting at Cale as he stuffed a bedroll into his saddlebag.

The head groom, a tall, thin man with tanned arms and dark hair, moved from man to man, fretting. "I assure you that all is in order with the tack." His annoyed tone made clear that he took extreme pride in his meticulous work, and that the house guards' efforts came as a personal affront.

The men smiled, nodded, and ignored him, adjusting straps and buckles as they saw fit.

A boy held Cale's and Tamlin's mounts by their bits. Cale eyed the horses with apprehension. He had never been a skilled horseman, and riding with only one hand would make it worse. Tamlin noticed his nervousness and smiled smugly.

"Vos is an easy ride, Mister Cale," said the groomsman.

"Very easy, goodsir," said the scrawny boy in an overlarge shirt who held the horse.

"Vos," Cale said, and chuckled. *Vos* was a word from the Dwarvish tongue. It meant "wild" or "unruly," and was usually used to describe a dwarven beer fest. Probably the groom had no idea of its etymology.

"You will be keeping to the roads the whole time," the groom said. "An easy ride."

Cale found small comfort in the fact, but mounted up without embarrassing himself.

Tamlin loaded his gear into his mount's saddlebags and fairly leaped atop his horse. Unlike Cale, Tamlin was an experienced rider. "Ordulin is seven days' ride," he called to the group. "Let's get started. Is all ready, Ren?"

Ren looked to his men, who nodded. "All's ready, my lord."

The house guards mounted up and took station around Cale and Tamlin. Cale smiled at his awkwardness in the saddle. He had climbed eight-story buildings barehanded, but felt uncomfortable perched atop the horse. He did his best to settle in as the group started out.

When they reached Rauncel's Ride, Cale immediately noticed fewer Helms on the street. Before he could ask, Tamlin said, "I reconsidered my course, Mister Cale. At least on the matter of the Helms. A few squads remain in the Noble District, but I stationed the rest at the city gates. They will no longer patrol the streets, but they will be available to Vees and the Old Chauncel should they be needed."

Cale looked Tamlin in the face. "Wisely done, my lord."

Tamlin nodded grudgingly. "The temples responded to my suggestion as you suspected they would. I understand that they are already distributing food—all of them. Temple Avenue is thronged more than during a Shieldmeet festival. The city will still have a hunger problem, but it will not be a crisis, at least not in the short term."

Cale heard both appreciation and resentment in Tamlin's tone and resolved to hold his tongue. He hoped the measures stabilized the city until Tamlin's return. He did not trust Vees and the Old Chauncel to keep good order. In fact, he did not trust Vees Talendar at all.

Groups of Selgauntans gathered to watch them pass. The house guard kept them at a distance from Cale and Tamlin. None showed any anger toward Tamlin—Cale deemed that a good sign—and a few even shouted encouragement. Tamlin must have sent a herald to announce his departure.

"Two tendays ago, they cursed my name and spat on the ground as I passed," Tamlin said to Cale. He shook his head. "The people are fickle."

Cale made no comment and they rode in silence toward the Klaroun Gate. Scepters saluted as they passed. The Helms stationed at the gate did the same. As they climbed the far side of High Bridge, looking down at the glittering, boat-dotted waters of the Elzimmer and Selgaunt Bay, Cale finally asked the question that was eating at him. "How did Vees Talendar come to gain your confidence, my lord?"

Tamlin's mouth tightened and Cale knew he should not have asked. "Vees Talendar has been an asset to me and the city for over a year, Mister Cale. As for anything more, I am not inclined to share it." He looked Cale in the face and said, "The how and the why do not matter."

Cale did not like having his words thrown back at him but he bit back his anger. He did not regret his words to Tamlin over dinner, but he thought perhaps he could have delivered them with more tact. Despite Tamlin's station, he remained in many ways the disappointing son of an accomplished father.

Cale sighed and made himself as comfortable as possible in the saddle. It would be a long ride to Ordulin.

Miklos Selkirk guided his dappled mare around a deep rut in the earth. Kavin skirted it on the other side on his roan mare.

"She is involved," Miklos said across the gap. "There can be no doubt."

Miklos had been saying much the same thing for the previous two days. Kavin knew it was his brother's way of facing the death of their father. Miklos grieved by talking, planning, shouting, acting. He was never one to sit in a corner and wail.

Kavin had always been the more thoughtful of the two Selkirk brothers, and he did his best to check his brother's unwise impulses. He said, "Our contacts in the High Council indicated that the Tyrrans questioned her before the High Council. Mirabeta denied involvement in Father's death, and the high lord abbot pronounced it truth."

Miklos's lips twisted in contempt under his moustache. "Then he is wrong, bought, or both."

"Father's spirit named Endren his murderer."

They guided their horses back together and Miklos shook his head. "You know Endren Corrinthal, Kavin. He is no murderer. Besides, it was Abelar Corrinthal who sent word to us in Scardale and who described the events in the High Council. The man is as right as a carpenter's square. No, this is the work of Mirabeta and that scheming niece she keeps at her side. I am certain of it."

Kavin did know Endren, mostly by reputation. The elder Corrinthal was regarded as an astute politician and an honorable man. His son, Abelar, a servant of Lathander, was above reproach. Abelar had left Ordulin but sent word to Miklos in Scardale, telling him of events, warning him away from Ordulin, and offering him sanctuary in Saerb. Miklos had sent a written reply, thanking Abelar but declining the offer of sanctuary. His place was in Ordulin, he had written.

"We never should have left the capital," Miklos said, pulling at one end of his moustache. "Not with everything that has happened recently. If we had been there, this never would have occurred."

Kavin nodded, though he was not entirely sure he knew which "this" Miklos meant. He said nothing. His brother was given to recriminations and nothing Kavin could say would stop him. Kavin doubted that their presence would have changed much.

"Look at this," Miklos said hotly, and gestured at the field through which they rode. Kavin could not tell from the bare, dried dirt what might have grown there once. He assumed barley, possibly wheat. Miklos snorted. "Fallow. The upcountry fields are fallow all across the realm. Villages are abandoned. Damned drought. Double-damned dragons. And thrice-damned Rain of Fire!" He frowned and said softly, "A realm can bear only so much. Sembia is tottering. I feel it. I fear what will become of it, Kavin."

"Nothing good, with Mirabeta as overmistress," Kavin answered.

"*Temporary* overmistress," Miklos corrected with a wag of his finger. "And we will remedy even that as soon as possible."

"Agreed," Kavin said.

After receiving word from Abelar three days earlier, they had left Scardale in secret and in disguise, cutting southwest across the backcountry to avoid the roads and spies. The travel was slower than by road, but more circumspect. The Silver Ravens—the men of Miklos's mercenary company—had wanted to provide an armed escort but Miklos and Kavin had refused. They hoped to enter Ordulin unnoted and unannounced, assess the political situation and how best to play it, and find out the truth behind their father's death.

"I have arranged a safehouse in Ordulin," Kavin said. "We should have a tenday or more before the moot."

"Time enough," Miklos said.

Kavin agreed, though they would have to move fast to solidify opposition to Mirabeta.

After a time, they dismounted and broke for a quick meal of dried meat and stale bread. Kavin was relieved to be out of the saddle. Hard riding over rough terrain had left him sore.

After eating, they mounted up and continued their cross-country trek, hoping to reach Ordulin by the next night. After about two hours of riding and continued plotting and grumbling,

Miklos pulled back on his reins. His mare snorted and danced a half-circle. He wore a puzzled look.

"What is it?" Kavin asked. He halted his own mount and she whinnied.

"I thought I heard something," Miklos said, staring ahead. "A horse."

"I heard nothing, and we are nowhere near a road. A bird, perhaps?"

The tree-dotted plain ahead looked much like the terrain they had crossed for the past half-league. Uneven ground lay covered in tall whipgrass and scrub, speckled with stands of larch.

"This smells wrong," Miklos said softly, eyeing the way ahead. He put a hand to the hilt of one of his enchanted rapiers. His horse turned a circle.

"We can circle back," Kavin said.

Miklos appeared not to hear him. "The two stands of trees there, to the left and right. Do you mark them?"

Kavin nodded. Two copses of mature larches were separated by perhaps twenty paces. He saw nothing suspicious about them but had learned over the years to trust his brother's instincts.

He uncapped a tube at his belt and pulled out an iron wand that fired blasts of magical energy. He was not a wizard, and could not always get the damned thing to operate, but when it did, it never missed. There was little else he could do from horseback.

As they watched, a dozen or so sparrows alit from the trees on the left, as if disturbed by something.

"Dark!" Miklos swore.

Kavin heard the twang of crossbows and two groups of chain-mailed men and their horses suddenly appeared at the edge of the larches. Kavin caught a glimpse of at least one robed figure among the group—no doubt he had cast an illusion to hide their presence. None of them wore uniforms or symbols revealing their origin.

A shower of bolts hissed around the brothers. Two struck Miklos in the chest and nearly knocked him from his saddle. Neither penetrated his magical mail. A bolt skinned Kavin's roan and she neighed in pain and bucked, but he held his seat. Another passed through Kavin's sleeve but missed his flesh.

Cursing, Kavin leveled his wand and discharged five glowing shafts of violet energy at the robed figure, whom he figured to be a priest or wizard. All five blasts slammed into the figure's chest and he staggered backward then fell to the ground.

The rest of the ambushers slung their crossbows and jumped into their saddles with skill and speed. Kavin marked the men as experienced soldiers.

"Too many to make a stand!" he said to Miklos.

"Ride!" Miklos shouted. He spun his horse and drove his heels into her flanks. She raced off.

Kavin did the same. His mare snorted, turned, and ran like the Hells themselves were at her heels. He spared a glance behind him.

The ambushers spurred their horses after them. He glimpsed a familiar face leading the group.

"Malkur Forrin!" Kavin shouted to Miklos.

His elder brother cursed.

Forrin hated the Selkirk family. Their father had dismissed him from his post in the Helms. Forrin led the Blades, a notorious mercenary company composed of former Sembian soldiers—*skilled* Sembian soldiers.

Kavin steered with his legs and aimed his wand back at their pursuers. He put his finger in the triggering depression and the wand fizzled. A drop of arcane energy drizzled from the tip. He cursed and almost flung it in frustration.

Meanwhile, Miklos reached back and forced open the drawstring on one of his saddlebags. "Stay clear of them!" Miklos shouted. He pulled one of the sacks from his saddlebag and dropped it on the ground, then another, then another, in rapid succession. Upon impact, the bags broke open and the gummy substance within reacted with the air and began to expand. Viscous, sticky fluid pooled in the grass.

Kavin spurred his roan and she leaped the expanding, tangling mess. She hit the ground and he righted himself, then tried again to operate his wand. He succeeded and fired three bolts that hit Forrin in the chest and leg. Kavin grinned. The big mercenary grimaced with pain but continued the pursuit.

"Hyah!" Miklos shouted, and pushed his mare harder.

Kavin did the same and lowered his head along the mare's neck. They were gaining some distance. The mercenaries' horses, bearing armored men, fought against a much heavier load. Kavin and Miklos would outdistance them.

Kavin watched as the mercenaries rode near the spilled bags and two of the horses got caught in the substance. Both went down with their riders in a tumble of legs, shouts, and neighs.

Kavin and Miklos shared a hard grin.

Kavin faced forward in the saddle just in time to see two men rise up in the grass before them. Both wore hooded cloaks that shifted with their movement to match the background terrain. Both wore light armor and held arm-length wooden tubes to their mouths.

Miklos and Kavin's mounts, startled by the unexpected appearance of the men, whinnied and reared up on their hind legs. Both men held their seats, but barely.

"Beware!" Miklos shouted, drawing his rapier.

Kavin pulled one of his throwing daggers and flung it awkwardly at the man nearest him. As he let it fly, he heard a peculiar *whump* and felt a sting in his cheek. The dagger caught the man in the leg and he went down.

Kavin righted his horse, glanced behind—the mercenaries were closing rapidly—and spurred her forward.

"Move, Miklos! Move!"

He brushed at the sting in his cheek and came away with a small, feathered dart. A dark substance and a bit of blood coated its tip and his finger.

He tried to shout for his brother but his mouth was suddenly dry. Events slowed down, blurred. His skin felt thick, numb. He struggled to keep his head up and his hands on the reins. His horse sensed his weakness and slowed, then stopped. One of the men who had been hidden in the grass appeared near her, waving his wooden tube, and she bucked. Kavin could not keep his seat. He fell to the ground. He knew he landed hard but he hardly felt it.

The hooves of the onrushing mercenaries caused the ground to vibrate under him. He felt weight on his chest. He looked up, but saw nothing atop him.

The poison was killing him, he realized.

He caught sight of Miklos. His brother was racing back toward him, his face twisted in anger and concern. The two mercenaries in the magical cloaks turned to face him, drew short blades. One of them limped from the wound Kavin had caused.

Miklos held the reins with one hand and his rapier in the other. He slashed quickly and opened the throat of the man Kavin had wounded. The other dived aside and his cloak caused him to disappear into the whipgrass.

Miklos swung off the horse and knelt beside Kavin. Kavin focused on his tanned face, his moustache, his black hair streaked with gray. The features were like a mask, floating on nothingness. Everything else was a blur. Kavin tried to speak.

"Say nothing," Miklos ordered.

Miklos picked him up and tried to sling him over his horse. Kavin heard the sound of crossbow fire. Miklos exclaimed, stiffened. He dropped Kavin on his back.

Kavin tried to rise but could barely move. He turned his head and saw his brother on his knees with five crossbow bolts sticking from his back. More firing, and three more sank into his chest. Miklos swayed and fell face down beside Kavin. Kavin heard the crossbow bolts snap against the ground as his brother fell.

Tears welled in Kavin's eyes. He struggled to breathe, to pull out his wand. His body would not answer. He felt his heart beating irregularly, failing.

He reached out for his brother. He worked his fingers around Miklos's forearm and inched them down to his hand. He took it in his own and held on with all the strength he had left.

Figures appeared around him. He could hear them, see them as silhouettes, but could not make out details or sounds. He assumed Forrin was among them, and tried to curse him.

He heard his heart in his ears, slowing, slowing. He was floating away.

He squeezed his brother's cooling hand and his heart stopped. For a single moment, he could see clearly.

His last sight was a blue Sembian sky.

Malkur dismounted and looked down on the dead Selkirk brothers. The younger Selkirk's face was blackened and swollen on his cheek from the poisoned dart. He looked at the scorch marks on his breeches caused by Kavin Selkirk's wand.

"That stung," he said, and kicked the dead noble in the head. The men near him chuckled.

Thell, one of his sergeants, stepped beside him to deliver a report. "Dertil is dead to the Selkirk's blade. Whelin broke his neck when the horse went over. Ferd's shoulder came out of joint but that's easily fixed. Xinnen took bolts from the wand but lives. Two horses are down but we've got the Selkirk horses to replace them. That is all."

Malkur frowned. He hated to lose men, especially a skilled man like Dertil. But he had others. "Collect Dertil's gear, especially the cloak." The magical camouflaging cloaks were an asset of the company, not one man.

Thell nodded agreement.

Behind them, Ferd shouted a string of expletives as Millen, a priest of Talos, forced his shoulder back into its joint.

"Where the Hells is Xinnen?" Malkur asked Thell. "The man gets hit with a wand and cannot keep up?"

Xinnen, one of the company's wizards, had located the Selkirks through divinations. His illusions had masked the ambush, which the Selkirks had almost sniffed out.

"Here he is now," said Thell.

Xinnen rode up at a trot, scowling. The men heckled him mercilessly for being out-wizarded by a nonwizard. Xinnen cursed them and called them sons of whores.

"Get down here, Xinnen," Malkur ordered.

The mage dismounted and stood beside Thell and Malkur over the dead brothers.

"Serves them appropriately," Xinnen said.

"Find the magical gewgaws," Malkur said. "We might as well have those."

"The wand is magical, certainly," Xinnen said. He spoke the words to a simple spell and studied the bodies. He turned both corpses over with his foot. He looked up at Malkur and said, "Their blades, their armor, Miklos's boots, and the ring on his left hand. Nothing else."

"Gather it, Thell," Malkur said. "Then search them for coin."

Thell set to his task. Malkur would distribute the booty among his men. A fee on top of their fee.

Malkur gathered his men. "Well done, Blades. Now saddle up. We ride for Ordulin immediately. Dertil and Whelin are coming back with us for a Sembian burial. But these," he nodded at the Selkirks, "these were bury out here. And we bury them deep."

He knew that what could not be found could not be resurrected. As of that moment, Miklos and Kavin Selkirk had vanished from Faerûn's history.

As the men saw to the Selkirks, he said, "And the first man who speaks of this outside the company has his tongue cut out before I gut him personally."

The Blades nodded. They knew he spoke truly.

He allowed himself a smile of satisfaction. He hoped that Lorgan's attack on the Saerloonian delegation went as smoothly.

Lorgan and his commanders sat atop their mounts in a stand of four towering elms, a few bowshots west of Rauthauvyr's Road. The sea of whipgrass that covered the plains snapped in the gusting wind. Slate-colored clouds obscured the afternoon sun. If not for the drought, Lorgan would have expected rain by nightfall. As it was, he expected only clouds.

The rest of the Blades lounged in the grass under the trees, eating, sharpening blades, sparring, jesting.

Two riders approached from the west. Lorgan could not make

out enough detail to determine their identity but he could guess well enough.

"That is Phlen and Othel," said Reht. His sergeant shielded his eyes and squinted into the distance. Reht had an archer's eyes.

"They ride fast," Lorgan said of his scouts. He turned to Enken, another of his sergeants. "Get the men up."

Enken, a scarred, dark-hearted veteran with a talent for throwing knives, turned and gave a piercing whistle.

"Mount up, men!"

As one, the mercenaries left whatever pastime had occupied them, adjusted their armor and weapons, readied their mounts, and climbed into their saddles.

The two riders neared and Lorgan could make out Phlen's long hair streaming behind him and Othel's black leather armor.

The two scouts were racing, Lorgan saw. Both were bent low over their mounts' necks. Each was shouting encouragement at his horse.

"My coin is on Phlen," Reht said, and smoothed his moustache.

"Ten fivestars on Othel," said Gavist, the youngest of the sergeants. He could not yet grow a respectable beard but he had won his rank and the respect of his men in several battles fought in Archendale.

"Twenty," said Reht. "If you've the balls."

"You are looser with your coin than a whore with her favors," answered Gavist with a grin. "Twenty it is."

As the riders drew nearer, the men and horses gathered around Lorgan and his commanders and shifted in anticipation. They knew, as did Lorgan, that the return of the scouts meant that an attack would soon follow. Horses whickered. Mail chinked. Men murmured.

Othel and Phlen tore over the plains. Their shouts carried on the wind. Othel wore his characteristic grin. He spurred his mount and pulled in front of Phlen.

Gavist laughed aloud.

Reht shouted, "Ride, Phlen, you orcwhelp!"

Othel widened the distance and Phlen surrendered the race.

Othel raised a fist in victory. He slowed as he approached the company and pulled his sweating mount to a stop.

"Sir," he said to Lorgan, saluting in the Sembian military fashion. A former Sembian Helm, his military habits died hard.

Phlen arrived in the next moment, chagrined.

"That's ten fivestars to me for outpacing you," Othel said to him.

Phlen ignored him and saluted Lorgan. "Sir."

"Report," Lorgan said.

Othel said, "The Saerloonian delegation is north of us. We watched them pass. They did not see us. They are moving slowly along Rauthauvyr's Road."

"They number about thirty," Phlen added. "All mounted, plus three carriages. I would wager on a wizard or priest in their midst."

"Phlen's wagers are poor bets though, sir," Othel said with a grin.

"Piss off," Phlen said. Lorgan and the commanders chuckled.

"Wizards and priests are both likely," Lorgan said. His own force numbered seventy-six men, including Vors and Paalin—two war priests of Talos—and the Blades' most powerful wizard, Mennick.

"We could let them camp," Reht said. "And come upon them at night."

The Blades often used such a plan. The men were experienced night fighters. With Mennick's spells and several enchanted items possessed by the company's leaders, most of the men could be empowered to see in moonless darkness, and the tactic had worked in many battles.

"No," he said. "If we assault them while camped at night, we will have a slaughter. We want to wound them and send them running northward for their lives. We will attack them on the road." To Phlen and Othel he said, "Fall in with your squads."

Lorgan turned to Vors and Paalin, his war priests. Both wore their brown hair long and tangled; both had deep-set, wild eyes. Lorgan attributed their crazed expressions to their worship of the god of destruction. Each bore a shield that featured the jagged lightning bolt of their deity.

"Hide your holy symbols and leave your shields behind," Lorgan ordered them.

Vors snarled behind his beard. Paalin scowled and said, "I would sooner stick my hand up a dragon's arse."

"Leave them," Lorgan ordered, "or I will stick my hand up yours and pull out your heart. We are to appear as if in service to Saerb and Selgaunt, priest. Are many of your brothers in the faith in service to those cities?"

The priests looked away, grumbling.

"Leave the shields or I will leave you behind altogether."

Lorgan knew the threat of missing the battle would cause the berserker priests to see sense.

"Very well," Vors barked, and tossed his shield to the ground. Paalin did the same. Both of them glared at Lorgan.

Lorgan smiled and looked to his sergeants. "Attack from the rear. Make sure they see you coming for a fair distance. Force them northward to Ordulin. It does not matter how many of them die, so long as some do. Minimize our own losses. Remember, we are not trying to wipe them out, just blood them. The carriages are not to be harmed or attacked and none of our men are left behind, dead or alive. Understood?"

All nodded.

"Let's move out, then," Lorgan said.

The sergeants pulled their horses around and issued readiness orders to the men.

With the rapidity and precision that had won the Blades more than twenty battles, the force moved out. They formed five squads, each led by one of Lorgan's sergeants.

Vors and Paalin pulled colored glass spheres from their saddle-bags and shattered them on an elm's trunk, asking for Talos to find pleasure in the destruction and bless the men in the coming battle. Lorgan thumped both of the priests on the shoulder, mending any hard feelings.

"Reht and the archers to the rear," Lorgan ordered.

Reht and his ten bowmen fell into formation at the rear. Lorgan, the priests, and Mennick fell in behind them.

When the group reached Rauthauvyr's Road—a wide, packed earth road that stretched across Sembia's eastern coastal region like a ribbon—they moved five abreast and accelerated into a gallop. The thunder of hooves shook the earth in all directions.

After a half-hour of hard riding, they spotted the Saerloonian delegation ahead. Enken used hand signals to order the men into a crescent formation. Enken and Gavist's men took the left; Borl and Scorral's took the right. Reht and his archers took their bows in hand and formed a loose line within the crescent. Lorgan, the priests, and Mennick trailed them.

"I want to shed some blood in this, Lorgan," Vors said, thumping a gauntleted fist on his breastplate. Paalin growled agreement.

Lorgan shook his head. "You both are to stay near me. You will see to any wounded and make sure no one is left behind, alive or dead." Lorgan knew that a prisoner or corpse could be questioned and reveal the identity of the attackers. Forrin had been clear about not allowing that to happen.

The priests barked their usual complaints but agreed to do as Lorgan ordered.

Ahead, the trailing riders of the Saerloonian delegation turned and saw Lorgan's forces bearing down on them. Two sped forward and shouted to the rest of the train. A score of heads turned around, alarmed. Men pointed, shouted. Shields were readied, weapons drawn. Heads poked out of the carriages and looked back. Lorgan grinned, imagining the Saerloonian nobles' shock over an attack on their own road.

Gavist sounded a horn blast. The clear notes rang out over the thunder of hooves.

One of the Saerloonian riders sounded a trumpet in answer. Lorgan could see one or two of the riders issuing orders on the fly. The Saerloonian delegation spurred their horses into a hard gallop but the whole train could move only as quickly as the horses could pull the bouncing carriages. The Blades rapidly closed the gap. One rider in the Saerloonian delegation turned in his saddle and pointed something back at the Blades. Lorgan guessed he had spotted a wizard.

"Wand!" shouted several of the Blades.

A jagged bolt of lightning shot from the wand and tore through Borl's men. Three horses and their riders fell, screaming, smoking.

"See to those fallen men!" shouted Lorgan to Paalin, who sped off to assist the wounded. Mennick started to cast a spell to counter the wizard, but Lorgan waved him off.

"Wait," he said to the wizard, and shouted to Reht and his archers. "Archers on the wizard! Archers on the wizard!"

Shooting at a moving target by mounted archers was difficult, but Lorgan knew Reht's men to be very good. Reht's squad pulled their bows and drew the strings to their ears.

"Fire!" Reht said, and eleven arrows buzzed into the sky. Most fell harmlessly to the road but two hit the wizard's mount and it fell onto the road. The Saerloonians did not stop for their downed man.

"Run him down," Lorgan shouted.

Two of Enken's men steered their mounts over the fallen Saerloonian wizard, smashing his skull before he could rise. The Blades drew closer to the Saerloonians. The Saerloonians tried to form up as best they could on the run.

Heads appeared out of the carriages once more. Lorgan could make out their wide-eyed expressions. One shouted something to a nearby rider and ducked back inside. The left door of the rearmost carriage opened and a man stood on the foot rail, facing backward. His blue robes swirled around a breastplate enameled with a symbol of a spoked wheel—a Gondsman. His hand gestures told Lorgan he was casting a spell.

"Beware the priest!" shouted Enken, and the call was repeated across the formation.

"Hit him," Lorgan said to Mennick.

The wizard hurried through an incantation and completed his spell before the priest could. Four glowing missiles of energy streaked from his fingertips and blasted the priest in the chest. The Gondsman grimaced with pain but held his footing and completed his spell. He pointed his open hand at the road behind the carriage and Lorgan saw the telltale ripple of a magical distortion move across the earth.

The road behind the carriage turned to mud in an instant. Most of Gavist and Borl's men could not stop and rode right into it. Their mounts hit the mud and sank to their gaskins in the sludge. The abrupt stop threw the riders head over heels. Panicked and wounded horses neighed and screamed. Some of the men cursed; others shouted in pain.

Lorgan, Vors, Mennick, and the archers yanked their steeds to a halt and steered around the mire, but the spell separated them from the rest of the force.

Meanwhile, Enken and Scorral's squads, unaffected by the mud trap, rode hard after the Saerloonians. The gap between the two groups of Lorgan's forces yawned.

The Saerloonians suddenly went on the offensive. Twenty of the Saerloonian riders wheeled as one to the left, turned, and galloped toward Enken's men. Scorral shouted and his squad moved to intercept them on the diagonal. Meanwhile, the remaining dozen Saerloonians and the carriage sped northward down the road.

The Saerloonian riders wore breastplates and open-faced helms, and carried round cavalry shields. They raised blades high as they closed on Enken's men. Enken's men responded with readied blades of their own.

"For Saerb and Endren!" shouted Enken, and some of his men echoed the lie. Lorgan smiled, pleased that his sergeant had remembered to put forth the ruse.

Flesh and steel collided with thunderous impact. Horses went down; men screamed. Blades fell and came up bloody. A handful of dead were left on each side as they parted.

The Saerloonians wheeled to their right, circled, and headed back up the road. Scorral's squad crashed into their flank. Horses neighed and bucked. Shields collided. Men shouted and died. For a moment, Lorgan could not tell who was who.

"For Selgaunt and Sembian freedom!" Scorral and some of his men shouted.

The Saerloonians put up only a token fight and tried to speed away. Scorral's men let them go and Scorral held up his hand to halt his squad from pursuing. Enken did the same.

"Probably enough," Lorgan muttered to himself. They had drawn some blood and set the Saerloonians to flight. There was no need to risk his men further.

A horn sounded from up the road and a hundred or more riders thundered into view, moving down the road at a full gallop. The sun glinted off their blades and plumed helms. They bore a standard but Lorgan could not make it out.

The fleeing Saerloonians cheered. The cavalry fleeing from Scorral's forces wheeled around as though for a counterattack.

"Who in the Hells are they?" Vors asked.

Reht shouted, "They fly Ordulin's wheel, sir!"

Lorgan cursed. He had too small and too scattered a force to withstand a charge of a hundred cavalry. Besides, his charge had been only to hit the Saerloonians. What in the Nine Hells were Ordulin's forces doing in the field?

"Give the Ordulins some fire, Reht!" he shouted, then hit Mennick on the thigh with the flat of his blade. "And you—earn your keep, godsdammit! You cannot even counter a Gondsman." To the rest of his forces, he shouted, "Get the men, even the fallen, and fall back. Now. Move! Move!"

Ordulin's forces blew another horn blast and formed a charging line.

The Saerloonian cavalry completed their turn and formed up for another pass.

Lorgan's men retreated and scrambled to gather their fallen and those still mired in the mud.

The Ordulin cavalry shouted as it charged. The Saerloonian cavalry did the same. The carriages pulled to a stop and Saerloonian nobility emerged to watch the battle.

Reht's archers fired a volley at the Ordulins and wheeled around to retreat. A few arrows struck home and a few of the charging cavalry went down. Mennick incanted the words to a spell and a curtain of sizzling flame appeared in front of the onrushing Ordulin cavalry. Most of the Ordulins pulled their mounts to a stop in time, but a few did not and three horses and men plunged through the flaming wall. All came out afire and flailing. The horses screamed and fell to the ground, rolling over the burning men.

Mennick intoned another spell and pointed at the onrushing Saerloonian cavalry. A thicket of barrel-wide black tentacles sprouted from the earth in their midst. The magical appendages plucked men and horses indiscriminately and squeezed. The Saerloonian counterattack died in its tracks as horses panicked and men tried to free their fallen comrades from the tentacles' deadly embrace.

Lorgan thumped Mennick on the shoulder. "Well done, wizard! An ale on my coin."

Lorgan shouted encouragement at his men. "Get them up! At it! At it, men!"

In moments, all his fallen men were loaded onto horses. Behind them, the Ordulin forces wheeled wide around the wall of fire.

"Ride!" he commanded. "Ride!"

The Blades kicked their heels into their steeds and tore south down Rauthauvyr's Road. Lorgan scanned his forces and estimated the damage. He had lost fewer than ten men, but left in his wake no fewer than a dozen Saerloonians and a handful of the soldiers out of Ordulin. He would get a firm count from his sergeants once they got clear.

He turned in his saddle and looked behind him. The Saerloonians still struggled with the tentacles and the Ordulin soldiery did not appear keen on pursuing.

He let himself relax. He disliked losing men but they had accomplished what they had hoped and gotten clear. The Saerloonians believed they had been attacked and bloodied by forces out of Saerb and Selgaunt. He would circle back, disperse his force into small teams, and rendezvous with Malkur outside of Ordulin.

CHAPTER ELEVEN

4 Uktar, the Year of Lightning Storms

Nobles from nearby Yhaunn, Tulbeg, Surd, and Ornstar had been streaming into Ordulin for days to attend the moot. The city was thronged. A steady stream of caravans rattled down Tildaryn's Road from Yhaunn's docks, bringing grains from the distant markets of Raven's Bluff and Procampur. Perishable foodstuffs were teleported from distant locales directly to city warehouses. The city's mills turned night and day. The markets were well stocked and prices were only slightly above average. The people cheered their new overmistress for her decisiveness. The influx of nobles and food put the citizens of the capital in an almost festive mood.

Meanwhile, Mirabeta had dispatched Elyril to supervise the arrest of any remaining nobles in the city known to be loyal to Endren. Most had heard of the warrant ahead of time and fled before the Helms could take them into custody, but that bothered neither Mirabeta nor Elyril. Without Endren, the nobles resistant to Mirabeta's ascension were headless. They would hole up in their manses or upcountry estates and accept whatever outcome the moot decided.

The city was firmly in Mirabeta's hands, in Elyril's hands, and indirectly, in Shar's hands. The people supported their new overmistress. The ugliness that had occurred in the High Council and on the streets faded from memory.

Ringed by a dozen armed and armored Helms, Mirabeta and Elyril stood outside their carriage on the cobblestone road near Ordulin's southern gate to await the arrival of the Saerloonians. A crowd had gathered around them, eager to see the Overmistress of Sembia, eager to see the pomp that went along with the Saerloonian delegation's arrival. Mirabeta waved to her citizens and they cheered.

Knowing precisely when the Blades would attack, Mirabeta had dispatched a force of Helms a few days earlier to meet the Saerloonian delegation on the road. Ostensibly the Helms were an honor escort, but Mirabeta's true purpose was to win the Saerloonians' goodwill by providing aid either during or soon after the Blades' attack.

"Sending out the Helms was a masterstroke, aunt," Elyril said, rubbing her temples. She had not been able to snuff any minddust before leaving the estate and her head ached from the lack.

Mirabeta held her smile as she waved to the crowd. "Mind your tongue and feign surprise, niece."

The Saerloonian delegation and the Ordulin Helms appeared in the distance. A rider ahead of the main body sped forward. A cloud of dust from the dry road heralded his progress. The crowd murmured in anticipation. As the rider drew nearer, Elyril recognized his green uniform as that of one of Ordulin's Helms.

"One of Raithspur's men," she said.

Many in the crowd made the same observation. The murmur of the crowd grew louder when the blood on the rider's tabard became visible. Mirabeta and Elyril, accompanied by four Helms, stepped forward to meet the man.

The rider pulled his horse to a stop before the overmistress and dismounted. Road dust covered him. He'd seen perhaps twenty winters and had only a thin beard. He bowed to Mirabeta.

"What has occurred?" Mirabeta asked, loudly enough to be overheard.

"The Saerloonian delegation was attacked, Overmistress," the young Helm said. "We arrived in time to aid them. Several of our men were killed as well as several among the Saerloonians."

Mirabeta put her hand to her mouth in shock. Elyril gasped in feigned surprise, though the matter could not have unfolded better. The crowd grumbled with anger.

"Who attacked?" shouted several voices in the crowd. "Who?"

Mirabeta waved them to silence and asked the young man, "Who were the attackers, soldier?"

The soldier hesitated, then said, "They appeared to be men in service to Endren and the Hulorn of Selgaunt."

The crowd gasped. Mirabeta appeared shocked. Elyril had to control a sudden desire to giggle. Several members of the crowd shouted expletives, cursing Selgaunt and Saerb and Endren. Others looked less sure.

"How many among you are wounded?" Mirabeta asked.

"Nearly a dozen, Overmistress."

Mirabeta turned to the Helm nearest her and ordered him, "Summon Jemb to the gates. I want priests here on the doublequick."

The Helm saluted her and sped off through the crowd and into the city.

The crowd watched in a hush as the rest of the Saerloonian delegation approached. Dust covered the carriages and two of them rode on bent axles. The Ordulin Helms rode in a protective circle around the Saerloonian delegation. Raithspur rode foremost. The broad, bearded captain of Ordulin's guard spotted Elyril and Mirabeta. He spurred his horse forward and dismounted.

"We came upon the Saerloonians while they were under attack from dogs out of Selgaunt and Saerb. They fled when they saw us."

"Did you take any of them alive?" Mirabeta asked.

Elyril tensed, touched her holy symbol.

"None," Raithspur said. "And they collected their dead while their wizard's spells delayed us."

Elyril breathed out. Mirabeta said, "A pity, but well done, Captain Raithspur. I have summoned priests to the gates. Gather any that are wounded and we will see to them."

Raithspur turned and issued orders as the delegation dismounted. The soldiers assisted their wounded fellows. The Saerloonians all eyed Mirabeta with unfeigned gratitude.

The drivers of the Saerloonian carriages stepped down from their seats, placed wooden steps on the ground, and opened the carriage doors. The Saerloonian nobles and their advisors stepped forth, glittering in their finery despite the combat. Elyril thought they looked none the worse for wear. She noted a priest of Gond among their number.

The crowd greeted their appearance with a cheer. The nobles seemed taken aback by their reception but managed smiles and waves.

Elyril recognized only one of the faces, that of Genik Ressial, a wealthy Saerloonian merchant whose family had made its fortune in spices and exotic fruits from the south. Road dust coated his jacket, breeches, and boots. His dark hair hung lank over his pale face.

He must have been the delegation's leader because he approached Elyril and Mirabeta as soon as he recognized them. When he reached them, he bowed. "Overmistress Selkirk. Mistress Elyril. Forgive our appearance. The road has been a hard one."

"Do not be silly, Master Ressial," answered Mirabeta.

"Your troops saved our lives, Overmistress."

"Saerloon is our friend and ally, Master Ressial," Mirabeta answered.

"It was fortuitous that you sent out the escort, Overmistress," Elyril observed.

"Indeed," Genik said with a solemn nod. "We had heard the matter with Endren had reached a head, but we had not expected such treachery. This is civil war!"

"Who *could* have expected this?" Mirabeta answered. "The minds of traitors are impossible to fathom."

Again Genik nodded and Mirabeta smiled.

"But now you are among friends," she said, and touched his arm.

She looked to the rest of the Saerloonian nobles and proclaimed, "You are all among friends now. The traitors failed of their purpose as all traitors must. Your delegation is received with warmth. Welcome to the capital."

The crowd cheered and the nobles bowed and curtsied. Elyril, too, smiled. No doubt the Saerloonians would support whatever Mirabeta wanted to do to put down the "rebellion." As one of Sembia's leading cities, the voices of its nobles would carry much weight in the moot.

Elyril thanked Shar and resolved to reward herself with minddust.

The news of the attack on the Saerloonians burned through Ordulin like wildfire. Mirabeta hired rumormongers to stoke the flames. The news incensed the nobles who had arrived already for the moot. Mirabeta spent the day collecting oaths of loyalty and promises of troops from the nobles. Urlamspyr pledged loyalty, as did the nobles of Mulhessen. Only Daerlun remained neutral, and that mattered little. The Daerlunians were more Cormyrean than Sembian.

Elyril used enspelled rumormongers to start the call among the people that Mirabeta be elected permanent overmistress with war regent authority. She would let the sentiment stew in the heat of the city for a time before encouraging her aunt to broach the subject with the assembled nobility.

She spent the evening with her aunt, creating the edict that would be read throughout the city the next day. It would take Sembia into civil war. Despite the fact that she had been integral in arranging events, Elyril's hand still shook as she read the paper aloud.

"Yesterday, soldiers from Selgaunt and Saerb engaged in a most cowardly and ignoble surprise attack on members of the Saerloonian delegation as they made their way to Ordulin for a moot of their peers. This attack appears to be retaliation for the arrest of the murderer Endren Corrinthal and in furtherance of his and his co-conspirators' attempt to seize power in Sembia through force of arms."

Elyril paused and smiled at the irony. She continued. "This treason will not stand. As of yesterday evening, I have dispatched troops to ensure peace in the nation, see to the safety of the rest of the delegates, and bring the traitors to justice. The assembled nobles have pledged full cooperation and resources. I have called a muster in Ordulin and Saerloon. The leaders of this insurrection will be held accountable for their treasonous deeds.

"Meanwhile, the nobles already assembled here will convocate in a moot—a rump moot—that will determine the next course for the state."

Mirabeta had already asked each of the nobles to dispatch to Ordulin or Saerloon as many men—both Sembian army and city guardsmen—as they could spare. Assembling the army would take time, but the process was under way.

Meanwhile, Mirabeta had dispatched five hundred Helms westward to act as escorts for some of the outlying nobility. She also sent forth the full force of Malkur Forrin's Blades to eliminate the Selgauntans. Mirabeta's spies in Selgaunt indicated that a small delegation had left the city three days earlier. They had no idea of the danger into which they were riding and would be dead before they ever heard Mirabeta's edict. Mirabeta would simply claim that they had been killed in a foiled attack on forces loyal to Ordulin.

Events were unfolding as well as Elyril could have hoped. She knew Shar was driving events. She continued to watch for the sign, for the book. The Shadowstorm was coming, she knew, and she rejoiced.

Mirabeta nodded at the edict. "Get it to the criers."

Elyril preferred to seal it and send it along later. She carefully folded the edict.

"This has been all too easy," Mirabeta said to Elyril. "I suspect other forces at work."

Elyril offered another explanation. "The realm has been on the edge of a sword since the Rage. The drought and Rain of Fire compounded the tension. Sembia has been ripe for change for a generation. You are its agent, Aunt. The only other forces at work are historical ones."

Mirabeta nodded, thoughtful.

Elyril changed the subject lest her aunt start to delve too deeply into causes.

"Aunt, what of Endren Corrinthal?"

Mirabeta looked up and made a dismissive gesture. "What of him? He is under constant guard in his tallhouse. None see him and he sees no one."

Elyril nodded. "But he remains a latent danger. Someone will try to free him. There are many among the nobility who will frown at your ascension but do nothing to stop it, unless they have a leader. Endren is that leader. You must ensure that he cannot ever serve as the lynchpin around which your opposition forms."

Mirabeta nodded thoughtfully. "I could order his execution. His guilt is now beyond doubt. No one will protest."

As much as Elyril wished to see Endren dead—mostly because it would hurt Abelar Corrinthal—and his soul trapped in her holy symbol, she thought an official execution too extreme. Mirabeta had won much goodwill with the people of Ordulin by appearing above politics. Endren's execution would be perceived as political retaliation.

"Perhaps you could make an example of him instead. Imprison him."

"He is already imprisoned."

Elyril shook her head. "He is arrested. I am suggesting that he be imprisoned, not in Ordulin, but in Yhaunn. In the Hole."

Mirabeta looked shocked, then intrigued, then pleased. She smiled. "Endren Corrinthal in the Hole of Yhaunn. The thought pleases me."

"I thought it might," Elyril said. "And if he were to die while serving his sentence . . ." she shrugged. "That would not be surprising to anyone."

The Hole of Yhaunn was the most notorious official prison in Sembia. Few who were sentenced to serve there ever emerged. At one time a mine, the Time of Troubles had left it a zone of dead magic. Elduth Yarmmaster, the overmaster before Kendrick Selkirk, had converted it to a prison and sent his political and mercantile rivals there to labor and die in the dark.

"Well conceived, Elyril. I will order it tomorrow." Mirabeta cocked her head and said, "I think you enjoy the trappings of power, not so?"

Elyril smiled uncertainly and nodded.

"Never forget who holds the true power," Mirabeta said sternly. "You are an advisor to the overmistress. Nothing less. But nothing more."

"I know well who holds the power," Elyril said, and brushed her fingers over the invisible holy symbol of Shar at her throat.

Elyril returned to her room and snuffed nearly a palmful of minddust. The headache that had plagued her all day vanished in an instant. She stripped off everything save her invisible holy symbol and danced with the shadows that painted the walls, while Kefil sang her a dirge and she thought of the Lord Sciagraph's touch.

Later, naked and sweating, she empowered her sending ring. When she felt the connection to the Nightseer open, she sighed with excitement. *War is begun in Sembia, Nightseer. The people believe that Selgaunt and Saerb have taken up arms against the overmistress.*

Rivalen answered, *Well done, dark sister. The night shroud you.*

And you, Nightseer.

Rivalen despised her weakness for minddust but deemed her too useful to discard—yet. He sat in his study and admired his coin collection. He pondered the fivestar he had taken from the dead Overmaster's bedchamber. The date on the obverse was not only the year in which Kendrick Selkirk had died, it was the year in which Shar had lit Sembia afire. Soon, Rivalen would quench the fire with shadow. The most high would have the basis for a new empire, and Shar would have the foundation for the Shadowstorm.

He activated his sending ring and concentrated on the dark brother in Selgaunt. The connection opened.

Nightseer, said Vees Talendar.

Civil war is begun in Sembia, Rivalen said. *The overmistress will make war on Selgaunt and Saerb.*

Rivalen sensed Vees's surprise. As always, Rivalen had provided his underlings with only the information they needed at any given time. Vees processed Rivalen's words and said, *Selgaunt and Saerb cannot stand against the massed power of the rest of Sembia.*

No, Rivalen answered. *But they need not stand alone.*

Silence lay between them. Rivalen knew that Vees was absorbing the implications, looking back and seeing the connections, wondering how he had not recognized the secret for what it was.

I am humbled, Vees finally said. *You are the Nightseer, Prince Rivalen.*

Rivalen said, *When the time is right, I will require an introduction. Lay the foundation with the hulorn.*

Of course, but . . . the hulorn is on his way to Ordulin for the moot even now. He is three days gone. If Mirabeta Selkirk is moving openly against Selgaunt . . .

Who would succeed him? Rivalen asked.

No one as easy to manage as he. The Uskevren pup is a fool, ideally suited to our purposes.

Do what you will, dark brother, just ready the ruler of Selgaunt, whoever that may be, for my arrival.

Yes, Nightseer. A pause, then, *Prince Rivalen?*

Speak, dark brother.

Rivalen sensed Vees's hesitation. Finally the nobleman said, *The night shroud you.*

And you, dark brother.

As the connection closed, Rivalen knew that Vees had left something unsaid. Such was the nature of their faith, secrets upon secrets upon secrets. Rivalen eyed his coins and wondered how much of Shar's plot he did not understand. She too provided her underlings—even her Nightseer—with only the information they needed at any given time.

He pushed such thoughts from his mind. He would need to wear a convincing face when he met Selgaunt's hulorn. It amused Rivalen to think that he would be perceived as coming to the rescue, even as he laid the foundation for conquest.

❖ ❖ ❖ ❖ ❖

Vees had nearly informed the Nightseer of his suspicions regarding the Hulorn's new counselor, Erevis Cale, but decided to keep it to himself. Rivalen would find out in his own time and it pleased Vees to keep a secret from the Nightseer. After all, the Nightseer had kept a secret from Vees. Had Vees known that a Sembian civil war was the Lady's will, he never would have allowed Tamlin to leave the city for Ordulin. The hulorn was too valuable a pawn.

Vees spoke aloud to his shadow, a habit he'd had for decades.

"Erevis Cale is a shade," he said. "I saw the light dim around him when he grew angry, saw the shadows emerge from his flesh when it seemed he might strike me."

Vees did not understand how it was possible, but he knew it to be true. Like the Nightseer himself, Erevis Cale was composed of shadowstuff.

"How can that be, Lady?" he asked Shar, but the goddess kept her own counsel.

Vees drummed his fingers on the walnut desktop thoughtfully. He sat alone, behind closed doors, in the darkened great room of his family's tallhouse on Galorgar's Ride.

"There is something else about Cale that I dislike. Something . . . secret," he said, and smiled. He was not certain he could manage Tamlin with Cale acting as the Uskevren advisor. And Vees would need to manage Tamlin with care in the near future. The Nightseer had told him as much—Vees would need to arrange an introduction between Tamlin and Rivalen.

"I think Cale should die," Vees said. He imagined Cale asprawl on his secret altar, screaming, bleeding shadows and blood as Vees gutted him like a fish and offered him to the Lady.

"Yes. He should die. Unfortunately, I cannot allow that to happen just now."

Vees had no choice but to get word to the hulorn that he was riding into danger. Mirabeta could have dispatched troops already. They had made no secret of Tamlin's departure. He held no fondness for Tamlin, but were he to die or be made a hostage in the first blows of a Sembian civil war, the Old Chauncel would take another six months to elect a replacement. Vees could not allow the city to go leaderless for so long, not when Prince Rivalen wanted an introduction. And he knew that the Old Chauncel would not elect him to the office. He had spent far too long cultivating the perception that he was a dilettante.

He rose, walked to the sideboard, and opened a bottle of Berdusk Red, a full-bodied wine that reminded him of blood. A gobletful always relaxed him. He poured some and returned to the desk. He took a mouthful, swished it, and swallowed.

"Much better," he said. He drank the glass down and resigned himself to saving lives rather than taking them—at least for a while—and rang the brass bell for his manservant.

Zend knocked once on the chamber door and entered. The short, gray-haired steward looked overworked despite his finely-tailored vest and pantaloons. Bags hung under his droopy eyes and wrinkles creased his face. He had been with the Talendars for over two decades.

"My lord?" Zend asked.

Vees pushed back his chair and stood. "Send messengers to the head of each of the Old Chauncel families. All are to meet in the great hall in the Hulorn's Palace within the hour. I have grave news. No advisors, Zend. The heads of the families only."

Zend's eyes widened, but he nodded and turned to his task.

"Wait, Zend," Vees said. "Before you do that, send word to Captain Onthul of the Scepters to attend me immediately. You will find him in the city barracks. Alert him and the city grooms that he is to ready fifty of his swiftest riders for immediate departure. They will be gone several days. I will explain when he arrives here."

Zend waited a moment to see if Vees had any further orders.

"Away, man!" Vees said with a wave, and Zend ran off. "Zend!"

Zend returned, a longsuffering frown on his face.

"Have the carriage readied."

Zend nodded, waited.

"That is all, Zend."

Zend waited a moment longer, turned, and hurried off. Vees

could hear the steward issuing orders to the rest of the staff in the tallhouse.

While Vees waited for Captain Onthul, he changed from his evening coat and loose tunic to a jacket and stiff-collared shirt suitable for a meeting of the Old Chauncel.

As always, Zend proved efficient. The carriage was ready shortly after Vees finished changing his clothes. Captain Onthul arrived soon after.

The towering, bearded captain of Selgaunt's Scepters wore enough mail to cover two men. He had to remove his helm before entering the great room lest he lose it to the door jambs. A broadsword hung at his belt. Scars laced his hands and forearms. He smelled like a stable, but Vees knew him to be a man who took his duty to the city seriously.

"Lord Talendar? You sent for me on a matter of importance?"

Vees nodded. "Captain, the hulorn is in danger."

Onthul stiffened. "Lord Uskevren is three days gone from the city—"

Vees waved away Onthul's words. "I know, Captain. I know." Vees paused for drama. "But our spies in Ordulin have informed me that dark events have occurred there."

"Dark events? Please speak plainly, my lord."

Vees said, "I do not have details, but it appears that the overmistress has seized control of the city and that the army is rallying behind her. For reasons that remain unclear, Mirabeta believes that Selgaunt has allied with Saerb in an attempt to unseat her."

Onthul's brow furrowed. "Impossible. Raithspur would not stand for it."

Vees nodded. "Captain, the hulorn must be informed and recalled. We can sort out events after he is safely returned."

"We have mages in the city who could—"

"No. The hulorn bears magic items that screen him from scrying. Unfortunately, those same items prevent simple magical contact. We must reach him without magical aid."

Onthul seemed dumbfounded by events. His gaze moved here and there, unfocused. He shook his head and spoke dully. "This is . . . unexpected. We all heard of Endren's treachery, but this, this is—"

"*Captain Onthul*," Vees said. "Dispatch riders immediately. They must get to the Hulorn before ill befalls him. Do you hear me, man?"

Onthul focused on him, frowned at Vees's tone, and nodded. "I will dispatch my riders immediately, Lord Talendar."

Vees nodded briskly. "Good man. I will inform the Old Chauncel. The Scepters and Helms should be put on alert. Round up anyone in the city who is on official business of Ordulin or otherwise associated with Mirabeta Selkirk. Off, man. Now."

Onthul nodded and hurried from the chamber, muttering to himself. He hit his helm on the door jamb as he exited, cursed, and continued on without turning around.

Vees poured himself another glass of wine, drank it in a single gulp, whispered a prayer to Shar, and exited his tallhouse.

His carriage rattled through Selgaunt's evening streets—still littered with filth and refugees—to the hulorn's ornate, many-spired palace. Pennons atop the spires whipped in the cold breeze that blew off the bay. The wind carried the promise of winter.

Vees ignored the absurdly grotesque statuary with which the former hulorn, Andeth Ilchammar, had populated the palace. He would have to remind Tamlin to remove it. Assuming the hulorn lived.

The palace chamberlain, Thriistin, met Vees's carriage as it pulled to a stop, and opened the door for him. The middle-aged chamberlain wore formal attire and Vees wondered briefly if he slept in it. He seemed fully dressed no matter the hour. The lacquered carriages of the rest of the Old Chauncel crowded the paved semicircular carriageway that fronted the palace. The drivers stood together in a crowd, no doubt gossiping about the urgent meeting.

"All of the members of the Old Chauncel have arrived already, Lord Talendar," Thriistin said. He had not shaved and a day's worth of whiskers speckled his face. "They are gathered in the main conference room."

"Very good, Thriistin."

Vees hurried up the limestone stairs and through the flagged hallways, his bootsteps echoing off the walls. Thriistin struggled to keep pace with him. Torchlight flickered on the portraits of past Hulorns.

Ahead, the doors to the conference room stood open. The thrum of conversation carried through the doors at the end of the hall. Vees rehearsed his words as he walked. He reminded himself not to appear too decisive. Vees Talendar, after all, was a fop and dilettante.

The moment he entered the high-ceilinged, wood-paneled chamber, all eyes turned to him and the room fell silent. The patriarchs and matriarchs of Selgaunt's leading families regarded him with questions in their eyes. Few wore the jewelry and finery typical of such a gathering, though all wore gowns or jackets. Vees saw the tension in their faces. Recent events in Selgaunt, in all of Sembia, had left the nobility on a blade's edge. They appeared as if they expected a killing stroke to fall at any moment. They soon would get it, Vees thought.

"What is afoot, Vees?" asked the bearish Rorsin Soargyl. His jacket was too small, his head too large.

Vees moved to the head of the table and pressed his palms on the surface.

"I will not waste your time, for there is much planning to do after tonight. I have received word from Ordulin that Mirabeta Selkirk has seized power with the backing of the army and declared Selgaunt and Saerb her enemies."

The table exploded in shouts.

"In Sembia!"

"What nonsense is this?"

"She is mad! This will not stand!"

Vees did not try to shout over the tumult. He waited for the table to quiet. When it did, he said, "You all know of the recent events involving Endren Corrinthal. The overmistress believes that Selgaunt was involved in the assassination of her cousin and Endren's attempted coup."

"Endren attempted no coup, Talendar," said the elderly Thildar Foxmantle, with surprising heat.

Vees acceded the point with a tilt of his head. "I know only what has been reported, Lord Foxmantle."

"What has been reported is a lie," Thildar said, his gray beard shaking. "I know Endren Corrinthal. He is incapable of what he has been accused of."

Vees waved away the objection. "Be that as it may, I wanted this body to be aware of events."

"The Hulorn is riding to Ordulin," said Kelima Toemalar. Diamond pins held her hair up. Her fleshy arms stuck out of the sleeves of her red gown like sausages. "I was planning to leave soon myself. We must send word for him to return. He is in danger."

Vees nodded. "Captain Onthul is assembling a force of cavalry to catch the hulorn's party and escort him back to Selgaunt. They will leave tonight and ride until they find him. We can only pray that they reach him in time. Magical means will not avail us."

"Well done," several of the Old Chauncel said, nodding around the table.

Vees tried to appear humbled by their praise.

Glowering, red-bearded Ruttel Luhn rapped his fist on the table and stood. "How can Mirabeta Selkirk suspect Selgaunt to be involved in Endren's treachery? We have done nothing." He glared at Vees. "Or have we, Talendar? Now is not the time for secrets."

Vees almost laughed at the choice of words. Before he could answer, Thildar Foxmantle stood and glared at Ruttel. The scene was almost comical. The thin elderly Foxmantle stared daggers across the table at the much larger Ruttel Luhn.

"I will not repeat myself, Luhn. Endren Corrinthal committed no treachery."

"So you say," Luhn answered, his deep voice booming. "But you know no more than the rest of us. I will ask again, Talendar: Has the hulorn put the city at risk through some ill-conceived alliance with the traitors in Ordulin? That is something the Uskevren's father would have done."

The table erupted in shouts and epithets. Vees held up his hands for peace and the room settled. "The Hulorn has done nothing to merit Mirabeta Selkirk's suspicion. Perhaps you have, Luhn? You protest the loudest."

"You are a fool, Talendar."

"And you are dividing this council, this city, when it must stand united."

Nods from around the table. Luhn muttered inaudibly and lowered his head. Vees said, "I am certain we will clear up this matter soon enough. Meanwhile, it is imperative that Selgaunt speak with only one voice—the hulorn's voice—and that matters be kept quiet from the rest of the city for now. Let us keep the rumors at bay as best we can. This council will meet daily to stay abreast of events while we await his return."

Heads nodded agreement.

"Thriistin will see to the details and communicate them to you." Vees looked around the table, from one worried expression to another. "There is nothing more to be done tonight, lords and ladies. Return to your homes."

With that, the gathering broke into small, chattering groups. Vees did not linger. He ensured that Onthul's riders had left the city, then journeyed alone to Shar's temple on Temple Avenue. He spent the night offering praise to the Lady and repeating the supplication.

The next day, an edict from Ordulin reached Selgaunt through magical means. Vees and every member of the Old Chauncel received the missive. Vees chuckled as he read it. He knew that no Selgauntan forces had attacked the Saerloonian delegation.

Mirabeta Selkirk had created a war from lies.

No, he thought, and corrected himself. The Nightseer had created a war from lies, and done so in Shar's name.

"In the darkness of night, we hear the whisper of the void," he said, and crumpled the edict into his fist.

The whisper soon would become a scream.

I pick my way through the forest for what feels like hours, or maybe days. I have no way to mark the passage of time. The red glow in the air never changes and the crystalline sky is as still as stone. I keep my eyes away from the dark things that live on the other side of the sky.

I stay along the bank of the brook. As other brooks join it, it turns to a stream. As other streams join it, it turns to a rapidly flowing river that roars over frequent cascades.

Through breaks in the trees, I sometimes catch a glimpse of the wall ahead. As I draw nearer, its dark bulk fills my vision, demarcating the border of the world. A smell in the air grows stronger as I draw closer, a smell like rotten eggs, like sulfur, like . . .

Brimstone.

The voice at the wall returns, mocking me with laughter.

I steel myself by recalling my duty, my promise to Courage. I tighten my grip on my glowing yellow mind blade and continue on. I see no animal life. I am alone in the thought bubble. Or almost alone. I look up at the sky, to the crack, to the black wriggling things that lurk on the other side. I feel them watching me, hungering for me.

Has the crack lengthened? I am not certain.

I push it from my mind and press on. The stink of brimstone grows ever stronger. A haze of black smoke forms in the air and a dark film covers my skin. I tear a strip of cloth from my shirt, dip it in the cool water of the river, and tie it around my nose and mouth to help chase away the smell. The moment I cinch it, a crack like snapping bone sounds from above me. I whirl, stand, and look up.

The crack in the sky has opened into a gash. Wriggling, faceless black forms squeeze through and rain down through the hazy air. Terror seizes me—blind, irrational fear. My heart thunders; my breath leaves me. The mind blade sags in my hand.

"And the sky shat its fears," says the voice at the wall.

I know the voice speaks the literal truth. The things falling from the sky are fears given form, dark and obscene. They can be nothing else.

My legs feel weak under me as one after another of the dark things falls to earth and crashes through the trees. There are dozens, hundreds.

"He is losing himself in the Source, Magadon. Losing himself forever. Part of him does not want you to succeed. His fears are coming for you."

I see the fears in my imagination, sniffing for me through the forest.

"Hurry," says the voice at the wall. "If they catch you . . ."

I nod as if the speaker can see me.

I know I must move faster to outrun the fears. But the terrain is difficult. I am moving slowly. What else can I do?

"The river, Magadon."

"The current is too strong," I say, then realize what I need to do.

I scramble up the riverbank and comb through the forest until I find a trunk of darkwood about the length of a tall man and about as wide around as a barrel. I know the wood to be reasonably strong yet unusually light.

I try to move the log nearer the river but find it too heavy, darkwood or no. I will have to dig it out into a makeshift boat right where it is. I know how. I have seen fishermen in a village on the shores of the Dragonmere turn logs into boats in a matter of hours.

But I do not know if I have hours.

The log will make a poor boat, but I do not need a seaworthy vessel. I just need something that can stay afloat on the river for a time so I can ride the current away from the fears. The river will be safer and faster than the forest.

A scream that trails off into a howl sounds from somewhere in the distance. I hear madness in the howl, and hunger.

The fears are on the hunt.

I look about the forest, see only pine, darkwood, cypress, and stillness. The voice at the wall chuckles.

I curse, pull the makeshift mask away from my mouth, and set to work. I cut at the log with my mind blade and shave off the bark. I hack hunks from what I hope will become the bow and then flatten the top. The mind blade slices through the darkwood efficiently. The sound of my blade chopping wood echoes through the forest. I know the fears will hear me but I press on, deeming the gamble worth it.

By the time I am done with the rough work, I have shaped the log into something that resembles a one-man boat. I stand over it, gasping, sweating. The smoky air causes me to cough but I fight through the fit.

I set to digging out the interior and find my blade ill-suited to the task. Sweating, shaking, angry and afraid, I straddle the half-completed boat and curse.

"Demon's teeth!"

How long have I been at it? The fears must be coming, must be near. "I need a godsdamned axe," I mutter.

In answer to my will, the sword hilt in my hand reshapes itself into a haft. The blade shrinks and transforms from a sword to a large, glowing wood axe.

I stare at it wide-eyed, then set to work.

Each strike throws up a huge divot of wood and I make rapid progress. Lift and strike; lift and strike. My arms burn but I do not stop, cannot stop. I am not precise and the boat looks hollowed out by a drunk, but I think it will do. I just need it to stay afloat with me so I can ride the rapids and escape the fears.

A howl sounds from somewhere to my left. Another answers from somewhere to my right. Both sound near. I freeze in mid strike, gasping. The sweat that coats me makes me go cold.

I examine my work. Good enough. If it floats like a boat, well and good. If it floats like a log, I will just ride it down the damned river.

I straighten up, wincing at the stiffness in my back, and shake the fatigue from my arms. I concentrate on the axe and mold it back into a blade. I tuck it into my belt.

Not far away, something moves in the forest, something dark and predatory. Adrenaline washes away my fatigue but I know the rush will not last. My muscles border on exhaustion.

I bend, grab the front of the dugout, and heave.

I laugh when I lift the front off the ground and it sounds the same as the mad laughter from the voice at the wall.

A howl from nearby. Another. Close. I hear crackling in the woods.

They are coming for me.

"Move," I say to myself. "Move." My arms burn. My legs feel like lead. But I drag the boat through the undergrowth, slipping, struggling, grunting, cursing.

In my mind I imagine the dark things prowling through the forest, following my scent—the scent of fear. The image keeps me going, pushes me on.

I lose my footing, curse, get up, and yank the boat forward another stretch. The strength in my legs is fading. My breath is a bellows. Fatigue makes me dizzy. When is the last time I had water?

I can hear the river's current ahead through the trees.

"Almost there," I say. "Keep moving."

Movement behind me turns me around. I see two black forms perched in the fat lower limbs of two cypress trees. Each is as large as a mastiff. They look vaguely manlike, with a head and four limbs, but their skin looks as smooth as oiled leather.

They howl and their mouths are voids. The sound steals my breath. They leap from one tree to another, deftly landing on large limbs. Leaves shower the earth. The fears' oval heads lack facial features save for three wet vertical slits where their nostrils should be, and a gash for a mouth. Spiderwebs of spit hang between their open jaws.

I cannot help myself—I catch my breath and scream with terror. Pointed tongues emerge from their mouths and taste the air, taste the fear.

Terror energizes me. I fairly pick up the boat and scramble for the river. I hit the bank, see the flowing water below.

I hear the fears leap to the ground and I spare a glance back. Sweat drips into my eyes. The fears howl, and up close, the sound is nauseatingly wet. They bound forward on all fours, leaping through the undergrowth, heads jutting forward, strides eating the distance.

I turn, give a pull for all I am worth, and get the boat over the top of the riverbank.

Behind me, the fears crash through the undergrowth, breaking saplings. I hear their wet respiration. They are nearly upon me.

I push the boat over the bank, run beside it as it descends the slope, and hop in as it picks up speed. The bow hits the water and its movement stalls. I jump out, heart racing, not daring to look back, and get behind it and shove.

"Move, godsdammit! Move!"

The voice at the wall laughs.

"The gods damn you straight to the Nine Hells!" I swear, and push, and push, and push.

"Mind what you wish," the voice says.

The fears growl from atop the bank. I cringe, expecting an impact at any moment. I do not even think to draw my blade; I only want to run.

The boat moves farther into the river and the current seizes it. I lose my grip on it, curse, run as best I can through thigh-high water, grab it, and pull myself in without tipping it.

I lay in it face up, staring at the cracked sky. I realize too late that I do not have an oar or anything else with which to steer but I do not care. Sweating, terrified, I sit up, draw the mind blade, and stare back at the receding riverbank.

I do not see the fears. They are gone.

For the moment.

CHAPTER TWELVE

5 Uktar, the Year of Lightning Storms

Cale, Tamlin, and the Uskevren house guards rode at a moderate pace. By the end of the first day out, they had passed through the ring of villages that surrounded Selgaunt—most of them empty, or nearly so—and entered the rolling, open countryside. To Cale's relief, Vos proved as easy a ride as Stormweather's groom had promised. By the end of the second day, Cale felt reasonably comfortable in the saddle, enough so that he could enjoy the pastoral air and scenery rather than focus on staying seated.

Stands of larch and small woods of oak, elm, and maple broke the monotony of the whipgrass plains. Rauthauvyr's Road stretched before them to the horizon. An overcast sky hung ominously over the land, but the rain held off and the drought persisted.

At Tamlin's instruction, the company skirted the villages and clusters of farmsteads that they passed.

Ordinarily, a village would be expected to provide shelter and hospitality to someone of Tamlin's station. Tamlin did not want to burden the difficult lives of the villagers by requiring that they abide by custom.

"We will sleep under the sky," Tamlin instructed Ren and the house guards. "And eat only our own stores."

Cale credited him for that.

Tension remained palpable between Cale and Tamlin. They spoke only as necessary and Cale feared his candor back in Stormweather had put a wedge between them that would not be easily removed. Cale tried to loosen it. "My lord, if I am to be your advisor, I must be able to speak openly."

Tamlin, riding beside him, did not make eye contact. "You have shown already that you are willing to do exactly that, Mister Cale. When I require advice, I will ask for it."

Cale held his tongue and that was that.

As they traveled farther from Selgaunt, they passed fewer and fewer villages and farms. Those they saw looked as bad as tales had said. The drought and recent catastrophes had left the fields stricken. Most sat fallow or featured sickly crops of shriveled vegetables scrabbling to survive in the cracked, dry earth. Even the barley looked wan, and it ordinarily tolerated dryness. They stopped often at streams and ponds, all of them lower than normal, to water the horses and fill their waterskins.

"I had no idea things were this bad," Tamlin said to no one in particular.

Around midday on the fourth day out, the gray sky departed without dropping any rain and the noon sun emerged to sting Cale's skin. He wore his hood down despite the discomfort, and he often caught Tamlin staring at his wrist. Finally Cale held up the stump, which would regenerate a shadowhand when the sun set.

"It is no blessing, my lord," he said to Tamlin. He spoke softly, so as not to be overheard by the house guards.

Tamlin regarded him coolly. "So you say. But I have been reading what I can of shades and shadow magic." He nodded at the books he had carried from Stormweather, which he kept in his saddlebags.

"You will age as slowly as a mountain. Disease is nothing to you. Your flesh resists magic. That sounds a blessing to me."

The words were as much as Tamlin had spoken to him at a stretch since setting out, but Cale did not welcome them. He had known other men to use the same words when questing for power. Always such ambitions turned out badly.

"I did not endure this willingly," he said, though the words were a half-truth. "And I have heard others speak of power in the same tone you use. I would advise you to spend your energies on more wholesome studies."

"And I did not ask for your advice," Tamlin said, and spurred his horse forward.

Cale let him go but stared at his back, concerned and irritated. Tamlin looked at Cale's transformation and saw only power, not the price Cale had paid for it.

Cale shook his head, felt eyes on him, turned, and found Ren staring at him from atop his horse. Their eyes met. Ren nodded and his glance went to Cale's stump. Cale pulled his sleeve over his hand and nodded back at Ren.

Cale rode for a time in silence. Late in the afternoon, the group crossed paths with two southbound caravans out of the town of Ornstar, but the caravaneers carried no news. The road was otherwise deserted. Cale thought it strange.

Alone with his thoughts as he rode, Cale's mind turned to Magadon. He'd had no more dreams of Magadon since returning to Selgaunt. He was concerned about what it might mean for his friend. Mask had said Magadon would suffer. But he had also said that events in Sembia would lead Cale to Magadon. Cale reached into his pocket, touched his mask, and chose to believe that Mask had not lied to him. He was not sure he was being wise.

That night, the house guards went about the business of setting up tents, tending the horses, starting a fire, and doling out the food stores. Cale kept his regenerated hand covered by his sleeve as best he could, but it proved difficult. Yet no one seemed to notice it but Ren and Tamlin. Cale at last pulled Ren aside and showed him his shadowhand.

Ren eyed it with wonder. "How, Mister Cale? A cleric of Ilmater?"

"No, not a cleric," Cale said.

Ren held up his own maimed hand. "How then? Can I do the same?"

Cale sighed. "We are comrades, Ren—you and I, not so?"

Ren nodded. "Yes. Without any doubt. You saved my life."

"Then I want you to hear my words. The hand regenerates in darkness, and only in darkness, because of what I have been changed into."

He let shadows leak from his skin and Ren's eyes widened. Cale continued. "This transformation I would wish on no one, and certainly not on a man as young as you. It was an accident, happenstance."

Cale was not sure the last was the truth.

Ren looked again at his maimed hand, thoughtful. He looked into Cale's face, his gaze steady.

"I have trouble holding a shield strap. And I still feel them sometimes, the fingers, as if they were still there. Tell me this, Mister Cale—would you sacrifice the hand, even at night, to have yourself back as you were?"

Cale stared into Ren's eyes, considered lying, but decided against it. "No. But only because I need to be what I have become in order to . . . do the things I must do. That is hard to understand but I cannot explain it better, Ren. I do not understand it myself any better than that. If things were different, I would feel differently."

Ren looked at his fingers, chuckled. "Hells, losing the fingers made me the man I am today. It's strange, that. I hear your words, Mister Cale. Sometimes a price is too high. Even Sembians know that."

Cale thumped him on the shoulder. "You are wiser than your years, Ren. And call me Erevis. No more Mister Cale, eh?"

Ren smiled. "Erevis, then. I'll admit it feels peculiar to me."

Cale felt better for having been honest with Ren. Something in Ren reminded him of Magadon, and a little of himself as a younger man.

They joined the house guards around the fire and ate the fare that had been set out—cheese, bread, salted beef and pork. Several barrels of strong ale and bottles of wine from the Uskevren vineyards provided drink. Cale was pleased to see that none of the house guards drank to excess. Ren's men were professionals, as was Ren.

Cale smoked Jak's pipe and jested with the men. One of the house guards, Maur, pulled out his own metal-bowled pipe and lit. He and Cale traded pipeweed. Cale told and retold the guards of his rescue of Ren at the Twisted Elm, of his battle with the shadow demon in Stormweather's great hall. He kept his other stories to himself, even when talk turned to the causes of the Rain of Fire. Most of the men thought it was connected somehow to the Rage of Dragons. Cale knew better.

As was his wont since beginning the journey, the hulorn remained in his tent, reading his tomes on shadow magic until late in the night. Cale looked over at the tent often, worrying about Tamlin.

Though they expected no trouble on a main road through Sembia, the house guards nevertheless set a watch at night. Cale had taken to supplementing the watch. He had little need for sleep. He felt as awake in the deep of night as he did at dawn. Darkness heightened his senses, sharpened his edge, and he had little else to do after moonset.

After retiring for an hour, he awakened shortly before midnight and rose in silence. He willed the darkness to make him invisible and stepped out of his tent. Cloaked in shadow, he sat alone around the dying embers of the night's fire. They had camped in a slight depression near a wood of birch and oak. The wind set the trees to whispering.

Cale intertwined his fingers behind his head and stared up at the stars. His mind turned to Varra, the cottage, Jak, Magadon. He let his thoughts drift. The wind died and the sounds of the night filled his ears: the chirp of crickets and the clicking of an insect he did not recognize, the coo of a whippoorwill from within the wood, the soft hum of the breeze, the—

A metallic sound carried to his ears, very faint, like the rattle of a buckle. He sat up quickly and looked about.

Maur, the house guard on watch, stood at his post to Cale's right but the sound had come from somewhere to the left, somewhere out of sight. Maur showed no sign of having heard anything.

Still invisible, Cale stood and shadowstepped to the high ground at the top of the depression. There, he scanned the plains. The shadowstuff in him allowed him to see clearly by night, but only as far as a bowshot or so. He saw nothing but waving, knee-high whipgrass and some trees here and there.

He remained still and listened.

There. The metallic sound repeated from somewhere out in the grass. Cale acted quickly. He let the shadows dissolve from him so he would be visible and stepped through the darkness to materialize behind Maur. He put his hand around the house guard's mouth and pulled him backward.

The house guard squirmed and grunted for a moment until Cale whispered, "I heard something out in the plains. It's probably nothing. I will investigate. If I do not return soon, alert the camp."

He released Maur and the house guard turned to face him, eyes wide. "Tempus's blades, Mister Cale. You almost stopped my heart."

"Stay alert," Cale said, and without waiting for a reply, stepped through the shadows back to the plains. He was a dagger's throw away from the camp and could see Maur behind him, tense and watchful, staring out into the grass.

He eyed the area around him, saw nothing. He drew Weaveshear, slowly and silently. Shadows leaked ponderously from the blade and dissipated into the night air. Once more he drew the darkness around him.

Invisible and silent, he prowled the grass. The tension drew sweat and shadows from his flesh. A sound from ahead of him, an overloud intake of breath, betrayed his prey's location.

Cale estimated the distance to his unseen foe, stepped through the darkness, covering ten paces with a stride, and found himself standing over a human man crouched in the grass with a knife between his teeth. Cale must have heard him breathing over the blade.

Cale almost missed seeing the man, so well did he blend with his surroundings. The man's cloak perfectly matched the grass and darkness—a magical effect, no doubt—and Cale might not have seen him at all had he not thrown back his hood, revealing a narrow face and short, dark hair.

Cale froze, hovering over the man, blade bare, shadows swirling.

The man tensed and cocked his head as if he sensed Cale nearby. He turned and poked his head above the grass, looking toward the camp, looking through Cale.

Seeing nothing, the man returned to his crouch and used the knife to tighten a loose buckle on his calf-high boots. No doubt the bouncing buckle had caused the metallic sound Cale had heard.

The man pulled up his hood and stood, and his cloak changed appearance to keep him camouflaged. He looked once more on the camp. He appeared able to see despite the darkness, leaving Cale to assume he was magically empowered with night sight.

Seemingly satisfied, the man turned and headed off at a steady run. Cale decided not to kill him—yet. He sheathed Weaveshear and followed in silence.

The magic of the man's cloak masked him well even on the move, but Cale was able to stay close enough to keep him in sight. The man made almost no sound, even at a trot. Cale marked him as a professional—a spy or scout. The man headed directly for a pair of tall larches about three hundred paces off. He slowed as he approached the trees and pulled back his hood.

Cale stayed with him as another man emerged from the darkness of the trees. He was taller, eight or nine winters older, and wearing a cloak similar to the first man's. They hailed each other in silence and did not speak until they were nearly face to face.

Cale crept forward, low to the ground, and strained his ears to hear.

". . . only a single guard. Could have put him down myself and moved through the camp."

Not likely, Cale thought.

The taller man nodded. "Did you mark the livery, Othel? They're Selgauntans and that's certain."

"There's not even a score of men," Othel said.

"Should be easy work," the taller man said.

With that, they set off, moving in a line to the north of the camp. Cale stayed with them. They ran for perhaps half a league and slowed to a walk as they neared a drought-dried pond ringed by tall elms. Both removed their cloaks as they approached.

Cale shadowstepped ahead of them into the trees and saw gathered there a force of over one hundred men. All wore chain hauberks, bore shields and blades, and wore on their green tabards the golden wagon wheel of Ordulin.

Cale crouched low against the bole of an elm and stayed at the edge of the camp.

The group's horses stood in a makeshift pen of rope strung between some trees. All were saddled and ready to ride. The men burned no fires and none slept despite the hour. They only waited.

A murmur went through the camp as the news of the scouts' arrival reached them. All stood. Mail chinked as they adjusted armor and shields.

A tall man with iron gray hair and a thick moustache stalked toward the scouts. Eight other men followed him. Cale noted two unarmored, robed men among them—mages, he presumed—and two long-haired men with lightning bolts on their shields. Cale recognized them as war priests and the lightning bolts as holy symbols, but he could not recall which god was symbolized by the bolts.

The two scouts approached the tall, gray-haired man and saluted.

"Report," said the gray-haired man.

"The Selgauntan delegation is camped half a league to the south," said Othel. "They expect no danger and have posted only a single guard."

Cale saw disappointment in the expressions of many of the men who overheard. Several chuckled and shook their heads in disbelief. Apparently, they were hoping for a hard fight. Cale did not understand why forces from Ordulin would attack the Selgauntans, but there was no mistaking what he'd heard.

"Get the men enspelled for night fighting," the leader said to the two mages. The wizards nodded, reached to cases at their belts, and pulled out metal wands capped with cat's eye chrysoberyls.

"Form up," the blond-haired mage said to the men, and the force shuffled into orderly rows. The two mages started on opposite sides of the formation and began moving efficiently from man to man, tapping each with the wand. Each time, the recipient's eyes flared red for an instant.

Meanwhile, the gray-haired leader said to his sergeants and war priests, "This is a sweep and clean. We approach under sound cover from Vors and Paalin."

"Survivors, Malkur?" one of the priests asked.

Cale recognized the name Malkur from somewhere but could not place it.

"No prisoners," Malkur answered. "As I said, a full sweep and clean."

The mages finished their work and Malkur turned to one of his sergeants, a scarred, dark-haired man fairly covered in throwing knives.

"Give the order, Enken. Let's mount up."

Enken nodded. "Aye, sir." He turned and issued orders to the men to mount up and take positions by squad.

The men moved briskly to their horses and checked their gear. Cale figured the Selgauntans had half an hour, maybe less, before the force of soldiers swept down on them. He wrestled with the notion of killing a few of the leaders before leaving, but decided against it. He did not want them to know they'd been discovered. The Selgauntans could not fight; they'd have to run, and Cale knew killing a few leaders would make no difference.

His mind made up, he drew the shadows around him, imagined the Selgauntans' campsite in his mind, and rode the night there in an instant.

He found himself standing before the glowing embers of the campfire with his holy symbol in hand. He stared at the mask, puzzled. He had not taken it from his pocket, had he? He had no time to consider. He let the shadows fall from him so he would be visible.

Maur still stood at his post at the top of the depression, looking out over the plains.

"Maur," Cale called, and the house guard eyed him with wonder. "Get down here."

Maur hurried down, his long hair flapping behind him.

"Where did you come from, Mister Cale? I was watching the approaches."

Cale did not bother to explain. "Saddle the horses, Maur. As fast as you can. We will soon be attacked."

Maur's expression turned to alarm. "What? How do you—"

"Do it," Cale said. He left Maur and moved from tent to tent. "Up, men. Now! Up. On your feet."

Groggy heads emerged from tents.

Cale did not shout but spoke loudly enough for his voice to be heard. He clutched his mask in his shadowhand. "This campsite will be overrun by cavalry in less than half an hour unless we are gone from here. Gear up and mount up."

Cale could not keep the shadows from bleeding out of his flesh. No one seemed to notice in the darkness.

The house guards asked no questions. They shook the sleep from their heads, stepped out of their tents, and pulled on hauberks, belted on blades, and donned helms. They moved with alacrity, one man helping another.

Cale saw Ren slipping into his hauberk. Cale went to him and reported what he had learned.

"One hundred horsemen are north of us and are planning to attack. Get some men to help Maur with the horses. We need to move. This instant."

"Dark," Ren oathed, fastening the buckle on his weapon belt. "How do you know this?"

"I spotted one of their scouts at the edge of our camp and followed him back."

Ren nodded, capped his head in a helm, and started barking orders at the men. "Leave everything except arms and armor. Get the horses saddled. My lord," Ren said, turning to face Tamlin, who had emerged from his tent.

"What is happening?" Tamlin asked, looking around the bustling camp. He had already put on his boots and thrown on a cloak.

"We must ride south, my lord," Cale said. "And we must do so quickly. Gather only your essential things."

"Maur!" Ren called above the tumult. "Ready Lord Uskevren's horse! Daasim, help Maur with the horses."

Tamlin watched with bemusement as a house guard hopped by, pulling on his boot as he moved toward the horses.

"Stop," Tamlin said, but no one listened. He grabbed Ren by the shoulder and said, "Explain what is happening."

Before Ren could reply, Cale answered, "My lord, nearly one hundred mounted men wait not far from here. Seasoned men. They have priests and wizards among them. They wear Ordulin's colors and mean to attack us."

Shadows streamed from Cale's flesh as he spoke and Tamlin watched them spiral into the night. Cale's words appeared to register with him.

"Ordulin's colors?" Tamlin asked, and shook his head. "That does not make sense, Mister Cale. If they wear Ordulin's colors, then they must be an escort."

"Lord Uskevren, they are no escort. I know with certainty that they mean to attack. I heard them say as much. I cannot explain why but it is so." He gestured toward the horses. "Please, Lord. I will gather your things."

"You heard them?" Tamlin asked. "How? Were you away from the camp?"

"My lord," Ren said to Tamlin, and tried to steer him toward the horses. "I think we would be well-advised to heed Mister Cale."

Tamlin turned to Ren with ice in his eyes. "You would be better served by heeding *me*, house guard."

Ren let his hand fall from Tamlin's arm and stammered, "Of course, Hulorn. I meant only . . ."

Cale cut him off. "We are wasting time on irrelevancies."

Tamlin glared at Cale. "Did you say 'irrelevancies'?"

Cale could not keep the anger from his tone. "Yes. This is not about what is between you and me. Your own safety and that of your men is at stake. Ten times our number is going to ride down on us. You must run. All of us must run or die."

"Run? I am no coward. And I did not think you were, either."

Cale's anger flared at Tamlin's false bravado. He grabbed him by the shirt and lifted him from his feet, regretting it almost instantly. Shadows swirled around them both.

Ren looked shocked. The camp fell silent. Cale felt the eyes of the house guards on him. Tamlin looked first afraid, then enraged.

"Take your hands from me, Mister Cale," he said tightly. "Now."

Cale calmed himself, released him, and offered a half bow.

"My apologies, my lord. I am . . . concerned. It is not cowardice to flee from a superior force. If you try to make a stand here, all of us will die."

"I am not convinced that these riders you think you saw mean us ill," Tamlin said coolly.

Cale struggled to keep his voice level. "I stood invisibly among them, Hulorn. Their leader is called Malkur. I do not merely *think* I saw anything. I do not merely *think* I heard anything. I did see, and I did hear. Again, if we stand, we die."

Ren looked at Cale intently. "Malkur? Malkur Forrin?"

Cale shrugged. He did not know the man's surname. "Tall, gray haired, with a moustache."

"Yes, that is him," Ren said, and turned to Tamlin. "My lord, Malkur Forrin is a former general in the Sembian army. He now heads a mercenary band. They have a dark reputation."

"But they wear Ordulin's colors," Tamlin said. "How could Malkur Forrin—"

"Ignore the damned colors they wear!" Cale snapped. "If the riders meant you no harm why would they approach by night? Why not await the day? Why not sound a greeting? Surely an escort force would do exactly that. These are mercenaries, whatever colors they wear."

Tamlin opened his mouth to speak, closed it, and frowned. "A good point," he acknowledged at last.

Cale seized on the opening. He could not waste any more time with further discussions.

"Move out as quietly as you can," he said to Ren. "I will delay them."

"Delay them?" Tamlin and Ren said simultaneously.

Cale reached into his pocket and clutched his holy symbol.

"Leave it to me. I will catch up when I can."

"Catch up?" Tamlin asked. "You intend to remain?"

"I work best alone, my lord," Cale answered. "I will catch up. I can move very quickly when I have need. Faster than the horses. You know that."

Ren oathed. Tamlin eyed Cale thoughtfully, nodded, and said, "Yes, of course."

To Ren, Cale said, "Take Vos with you. I will not need him until we rendezvous. Ride due south, cut across the countryside. Do not take the road. Move fast but quietly. I do not want them to know we have abandoned the camp until they are upon it."

Ren nodded and Cale turned to Tamlin. "My lord? Will you go? Now, please?"

Tamlin nodded. Cale said, "Do not use your spells unless you must, otherwise you will betray your position."

Tamlin glared at him. "You are not to issue orders to me, Mister Cale."

Cale did not give voice to his anger lest he say something to further sour their relationship.

Ren tried to diffuse matters by gesturing at the horses. "My lord, your horse is ready. Please, this way."

Cale and Tamlin stared at one another a moment longer before Tamlin turned and walked to his horse.

As the men formed up, Cale called to Ren and Tamlin, "Stay as quiet as you can until you know they have marked you. If we are quiet, they may miss us in the darkness." He paused, then said to Tamlin, "We must return to Selgaunt, my lord."

Tamlin nodded absently.

Ren reached down to take Cale's forearm. "Tymora watch you, Erevis."

Cale knew it was not Tymora's aid that he would need, but Mask's. He said, "And you, Ren. And you, Lord Uskevren."

Tamlin said nothing and the men spurred their mounts and rode due west at a moderate gallop. Cale winced at the noise they made, though they were as quiet as they could be.

He shadowstepped to the top of the declivity and looked north. He did not see the mercenaries, but his nightvision extended only so far. Given their numbers, he knew he would hear them before he saw them.

He looked at the mask in his hand. He remembered the Shadowlord's words to him: *Do what you were called to do.*

Cale donned the mask.

He calmed himself and opened his mind to the Shadowlord. It was after midnight—the time he would ordinarily pray for spells—and he did not have time for his usual meditations, but he hoped Mask would answer his request nevertheless.

He sent forth his consciousness and requested that Mask fuel his mind with the power to cast spells, spells that would harm and mislead. He took a deep breath, let the shadows enfold him, and repeated the request.

Power rushed into his mind, one spell, another, another. He tensed as the familiar rush filled his brain; he grinned at the familiarity of it.

A voice from beside him whispered in his ear, "You are late, as usual. But welcome back. Almost there, now."

Cale whirled and looked to his side, but saw only darkness, only shadows. His skin was goose pimpled.

He looked north across the plains and saw the entire company of mercenaries bearing down on the campsite at a full gallop. They made no sound as they approached; their clerics must have silenced them. The whipgrass hid the horses' legs from view. The whole force looked as if it were floating.

Cale stood, his request for spells only partially answered, and drew Weaveshear. He pulled the shadows about him until they masked him from sight. He shadowstepped to the south side of the slope, putting himself between the Selgauntans and the mercenaries. There, he crouched in the grass, the power of his god sizzling in his mind.

The mercenaries charged in a crescent formation, blades bare and shields at station. About a spear's cast from the campsite, one of the riders made a cutting gesture with his hand and the magical silence ended. The thunder of hooves and the battle cries of the mercenaries filled the air. No doubt they expected the surprised Selgauntans to rush from their tents and be cut down. Had the Selgauntans been in the camp, none of them could have escaped the charge.

The mercenaries barreled into the campsite, shouting challenges. When they found only empty tents, they pulled up and searched about. Curses and questions replaced battle cries. The mercenaries trampled the Selgauntans' tents and gear. Malkur, the priests, and the wizards appeared at the top of the declivity opposite Cale. The company's archers held formation behind them.

"They were here not too long ago," called Othel, atop a horse in the midst of the campsite.

Malkur frowned and looked out over the plains. "They cannot be far."

One of the priests beside Malkur smashed together two glass spheres and incanted a spell. He turned his horse in a semicircle and stopped when he was facing south, the direction the Selgauntans had fled.

"There," he said, and pointed past Cale. "Three long bowshots, no more."

The priest galloped around the declivity in the direction in which he had pointed, toward Cale.

"Form up," Malkur called to his men, and several sergeants echoed the command.

Cale had hoped to get the mercenaries in a more compact formation, but decided he could not wait any longer.

"I see them!" the lead priest called. He was no more than a dagger toss from Cale, and alone. "Due south. Two bowshots."

"Form up for pursuit," Malkur said to the rest of the men. "Archers at the ready."

Before the men could reassemble, Cale intoned a rapid imprecation to Mask. A cylinder of fire and searing divine power engulfed the entire declivity in flames, heat, and light. The moment Cale completed his spell, the shadows enshrouding him peeled away and left him visible.

The flames caught almost a score of men in the thick of the blast, including Malkur, the mages, and one of the priests at its edge. Men and horses screamed and the stink of burning flesh filled the air. The horses not caught in the flames, including those of the archers behind Malkur, reared and bucked.

The flames whooshed out of existence as fast as they had appeared, leaving burning tents and the bodies of over a dozen men and horses scattered across the campsite. Screams of pain rose into the night. The unwounded men cursed, tried to control their horses, and looked about warily.

"What in the Hells?"

"Where did that come from?"

The priest near Cale, unaffected by the fire, noticed him.

"Here!" he shouted, and spurred his horse toward Cale. "He is here!"

The mercenaries responded to the priest's words with professional speed. Before Cale could pull the concealing shadows back around him, half a score arrows hissed toward him. Four missed and sank to their fletching in the grass. The shadows that sheathed him deflected two arrows, but four buried themselves in his chest, shoulder, arm, and thigh. The impact drove him backward and knocked him to the earth. He hissed with the pain even as his flesh started to spit out the arrows and heal the wounds.

The cleric appeared above him on his horse. His axe and lightning bolt-emblazoned shield hung from his saddle. He pointed a hand at Cale, fingers outstretched.

Cale could not interpose Weaveshear in time and an arc of fire shot from the priest's fingers and seared Cale's face and chest. His flesh was not able to repel the priest's spell and the flesh of his eyes and lower jaw—those parts of his face not protected by the mask—blistered and peeled. The damage sealed his eyes shut.

"There's fire for your fire, whoreson," said the priest, and he called back to his fellows with a wild laugh. "He is alone!"

Cale could hear the priest's horse thumping in the grass near him. He pulled the arrows from his body by touch, grunting with each one.

"Run him down," Malkur ordered. "Vors, see to the fallen. The rest of you, after the Selgauntans."

Cale braced himself with his arms and tried to rise but the priest's horse slammed into him, knocked him flat, and rode over him. The war horse's hind legs stomped his chest and snapped several ribs. Cale hissed at the pain. The priest laughed maniacally as he galloped off.

Cale felt the ground vibrating as the rest of the horsemen galloped out of the hollow and toward the Selgauntans. They rode directly at him, he knew. His body was healing itself, and just in time, he could open his eyes and see.

Hooves were all around him, throwing up clods of dirt. He rolled to his side, resisted the instinctive urge to cover up, and did the only thing he could. He moved from the darkness on one side of the declivity to the darkness on the other.

He arrived across the campsite behind Malkur, the wizards, the priest, and the departing archers. He held his silence and took as deep a breath as his damaged body allowed. He watched the mercenaries speed off after Ren, Tamlin, and the house guards.

He lay on his side, sheathed in shadows, and let his flesh heal for a few moments. In the campsite below, he saw one of the priests moving from one burned corpse to another, presumably looking for signs of life. The priest's horse followed him, tossing its head at the stink.

Cale winced as his ribs knitted together. He whispered a prayer to Mask and channeled healing energy into his wounded body. He ran his fingers tentatively over his face and found it nearly healed. He rose into a crouch, Weaveshear in hand.

The priest kneeled over another of the fallen. The back of his neck was exposed between helmet and mail. Cale had killed dozens of men in exactly that position. He was about to add another to the number.

He took Weaveshear in a two-handed grip and in a single stride, moved into the darkness directly behind the priest. The priest's horse snorted at Cale's sudden appearance but before the priest could turn, Cale slashed downward and decapitated him. The priest never uttered a sound. The blood pumping from the stump of his neck soaked the corpse he had been checking.

Cale sheathed his blade and hurried over to the horse. It backed off and whinnied, throwing its head.

"Steady," Cale said. "Steady, now."

The warhorse stood taller than Vos by five hands. Cale took hold of its reins and whispered soothingly as he moved to its side. It backed up, snorting.

"Steady," Cale said again, and patted its neck. It seemed as calm as he could hope for, so he put his foot to the stirrup and swung himself up. The horse danced under him but he held his perch. The stirrups were too short but he did not have time to adjust them.

He pulled two daggers from his belt and took one in each hand, all while holding the reins. He spurred the horse and it raced after the mercenaries so fast it almost dismounted him. Probably it found him a lighter load than usual. The priest had been shorter but fully armored.

Cale leaned forward and bent low, his head along the horse's neck, and encouraged it onward. He could see the mercenaries ahead, moving at a full gallop, and ahead of them, the Selgauntans, also at a gallop. The mercenaries' wizard must have cast a spell on the Selgauntans to mark them, for all were covered in glowing, golden dust. Cale could make out Tamlin and Ren even at his distance.

The mercenaries, arranged in a wide column, were gaining. Stormweather's horses were bred for strength and endurance, not speed. It was only a matter of time before Tamlin and the house guards were caught. They needed to find favorable terrain to make a stand. Meanwhile, Cale was gaining on the mercenaries, slowly but inexorably.

He saw Ren shouting orders to his men and gesturing, and they cleared out from behind Tamlin. Tamlin turned in his saddle and pointed a finger back at the mercenaries. A bolt of lightning tore through their ranks. Two men and horses fell in tumbling, smoking heaps. The rest veered around the fallen, as did Cale, and continued the pursuit.

"Hyah!" Cale called to his horse, and spurred it harder. It snorted and found a reserve of speed. Cale closed more of the distance.

Shouted orders passed through the mercenary ranks and the group of archers, in the rear of the column, drew their bows.

A flight of arrows arced up and rained down on the Selgauntans. A horse went down and its rider tumbled. Another arrow sank into the shoulder of a house guard. He sagged but held his seat with one hand.

Cale gained a few more strides and figured he was close enough to walk the shadows. He eyed one of the last men in the formation, an archer. He leaned forward and moved through the darkness from his saddle to that of the archer. He appeared behind the man, on the horse's backside. Cale did not even try to stay atop the horse. He drove both daggers through the mercenary's mail and into his kidneys. The man gave an aborted shout and the horse's motion threw him and Cale.

Cale hit the ground in a roll. The impact drove the air from his lungs and displaced his shoulder. He ignored the pain, jumped to his feet, and started sprinting after the mercenaries. His regenerative flesh popped his shoulder back into its socket as he ran.

Cale ran a handful of steps, picked another man at the end of the formation, jumped into the air, and stepped through the shadows to the darkness behind the archer. Cale appeared in midair and wrapped his arms around the throat of the rider. The mercenary uttered a muffled scream for aid as he and Cale fell from the horse. Both grunted as they hit the ground and tumbled. Cale felt a bone crack in his ankle and forearm, but his body quelled the pain as it repaired the break. He gained his feet, located the groaning mercenary, and drove a dagger into his chest and another into his throat.

He stood, prepared to repeat the process, and saw that two of the mercenaries must have heard their comrade shout. They peeled off the formation and charged at Cale, blades high.

Cale held up his shadowhand and intoned a prayer to Mask. An arc of dark energy went forth from his palm and struck both men. Wounds opened in their exposed skin—gashes like mouths spitting blood. Their bones twisted and shattered. Both screamed and fell from their horses. One snapped his neck on impact. Cale drew Weaveshear, bounded forward, and drove the blade through the second rider's chest.

He grabbed the reins of one of the neighing horses, calmed it, swung himself up, and started after the mercenaries once more. He was not close enough to shadowstep, so he spurred the horse on.

He gritted his teeth as another volley of arrows from the mercenaries killed another house guard. The mercenaries' horses stomped his fallen body into the ground as they pursued. Cale saw five glowing magical darts shoot from the fingers of the wizard riding near Malkur and slam into Tamlin's back. He arched with pain but held his saddle. Tamlin turned to look back on the mercenaries, moved his hand through a series of intricate gestures, and pointed.

A blinding cloud of sleet and ice formed and swirled around the mercenaries' center, affecting fully a third of the force. The icy ground sent half a dozen horses down and their riders with them. Men shouted, cursed, railed. Horses neighed, whinnied, bucked.

Cale grinned, thinking the Selgauntans had just improved the odds and might yet escape.

The mercenaries' wizard answered Tamlin's spell with one of his own, and a thicket of fat black tentacles squirmed up from the plains in the Selgauntans' midst. Their horses reared and bucked, and many fell. The house guards shouted, hacked at the tentacles with their blades, all to no avail. The squirming limbs grabbed at everything that moved. Some plucked riders from their mounts, others plucked mount and rider together and lifted them off the earth. In the span of three heartbeats, every Selgauntan was wrapped in a black tentacle. The limbs began to squeeze and the Selgauntans began to scream.

The mercenaries slowed and approached at a more leisurely pace. Cale cursed. He would have to kill the wizard.

He sheathed his daggers and intoned a prayer to Mask. When he finished, dangerous energy charged his hands. He closed the distance to the mercenaries until he was less than a bowshot behind them. He checked the darkness behind the mage and rode the night onto the wizard's horse.

The moment he appeared, he clamped both hands onto either side of the wizard's head and discharged the baleful energy. Wounds erupted all over the wizard's face. Blood spurted from his ears, eyes, and mouth. Cale felt the man's skull crack under his fingertips. The wizard managed only a choked, gurgling scream before Cale let him fall, dead, from his horse.

Malkur's horse and others near Cale whinnied and reared in surprise. The men near him cursed, tried to turn their mounts and bring their blades to bear.

Cale met Malkur's eyes for a moment before he pulled the shadows around him and stepped through them to the edge of the tentacles, ahead of the mercenaries.

The thick limbs entwined men and horses and both screamed as the tentacles continued to constrict. The glowing dust that had covered the Selgauntans no longer shone. Cale held up his hand and intoned a prayer to Mask, pitting the power of his magic against that of the wizard, attempting to undo the wizard's constricting magic.

He felt resistance when his magic met the wizard's spell but Cale's abjuration prevailed. The tentacles vanished in a blink and the men and their mounts fell to the ground, groaning. The bray of a battle horn sounded behind Cale and he turned to receive the mercenaries' charge. The Selgauntans were all going to die, but he would take Malkur and as many mercenaries with him as he could.

But instead of facing the charging mercenaries, Cale saw a second force of spear-armed horsemen streaking across the plains from his right, directly at the attackers. Cale guessed their number to be about double that of Malkur's men.

A rosy glow illuminated the riders and they looked almost celestial galloping through the high grass on their leather-barded warhorses. The glow emanated from the upraised blade of an armored figure who rode at their head—a sandy-haired man in a mail hauberk, helm, and enameled breastplate. He alone bore a blade rather than a horse spear. In his left hand he carried a standard and it billowed straight out behind him: a silver horse rampant on a violet field, the heraldry of Saerb. The rider beside him blew a note on his horn and the Saerbians spread into a line.

"For Saerb!" the riders shouted in unison.

Cale saw a nervous ripple make its way through the mercenary ranks as horses turned circles and men sought orders. Malkur and his sergeants issued commands and the mercenaries formed a makeshift line. The archers let fly a disorganized volley of arrows that found no targets in the onrushing Saerbians.

A few of the house guards behind Cale recovered themselves enough to let out a cheer.

"Huzzah!" shouted one.

Cale thought the mercenaries might make a stand. He considered shadowstepping into their ranks to kill Malkur but did not want to get caught in the Saerbian's charge.

The Saerbians let loose another horn blast and lowered their spears. The thunder of charging hooves vibrated the ground under the Selgauntans' feet.

Malkur shouted an order, turned his horse in a circle, and signaled a retreat. As one, the mercenaries whirled their mounts and sped off. The Saerbians let out another blare of their horns and thundered after.

A second wizard in the mercenary company cast a spell as he rode and the air between the two cavalry forces froze solid into a curtain of ice that rose fully twenty paces vertically and stretched several bowshots across the plain. Its edge nearly reached the Selgauntans. Cale could feel the cold it radiated.

The glowing rider at the head of the Saerbian forces shouted and pulled his mount to a stop. The others did the same, and two hundred warhorses reared and pawed. The chill air near the wall of ice made their snorts visible as frozen mist.

The mercenaries, heads down, galloped away as fast as their horses would bear them.

From behind Cale, Tamlin incanted a spell and shot a lightning bolt at the fleeing mercenaries. It hit a horse and rider squarely and sent them careening head over heels and smoking into the turf. His fellows did not slow.

"After the bastards!" shouted one of the house guards.

Ren echoed Cale's thoughts. "Leave it, Maur. It's over."

Cale turned, nodded at Ren, saw that Tamlin and several of the house guards showed wounds from arrows or spells. He hurried to Tamlin's side.

Tamlin eyed him with a question on his face and Cale remembered his mask. He removed it, held it in his hand, and uttered a healing prayer as he touched Tamlin. The pallor left Tamlin's face and he breathed more easily.

"A shade and a priest," Tamlin said. "You provide one surprise after another." He looked at the mask. "Which god do you serve, Mister Cale?"

Cale mumbled something incomprehensible and moved to the wounded house guards, healing each in turn. None of the men asked him any questions, but merely mouthed gratitude. Cale felt Tamlin's eyes on him throughout.

The rumble of approaching hooves heralded the Saerbians' arrival. Cale, Tamlin, and the house guards rode forth to meet them. Although he was no astute judge of horseflesh, even Cale could see that the Saerbian horses were magnificent. Leather barding protected muscular bodies covered in reddish brown fur. The riders bore short spears and mail. All wore serious looks, but none more serious than their leader.

An enameled rose decorated his breastplate and a similar symbol hung from a chain at his throat. Short, sand-colored hair topped an angular face spotted with several days' growth of beard. He sheathed his glowing blade and handed the standard to one of the men beside him. Cale could not shake the impression that the man was still aglow, though he could see plainly that he was not.

"The gods keep Saerb," Ren said with a smile, and many of the Saerbians smiled.

The leader dismounted and said, "I am Abelar Corrinthal. And these are men of Saerb. You are Selgauntans, no?"

Cale, Tamlin, and the house guards answered with nods and ayes.

"You have our thanks," Cale said to Abelar, and extended his hand. "I am Erevis Cale."

Abelar regarded him with a furrowed brow but extended his hand anyway. No shadows emerged from Cale's skin at Abelar's touch.

"Corrinthal?" Tamlin said. "You are kin of Endren?"

Abelar nodded and a challenge lit his eyes. "His son."

Cale gestured at Tamlin and said, "You have saved Selgaunt's leader. Thamalon Uskevren the Second, Hulorn of Selgaunt."

A murmur went through the ranks of the Saerbians.

"The hulorn himself is on the road?" Abelar asked.

Tamlin nodded. "Traveling to Ordulin for the moot. You are far from home, Abelar Corrinthal."

"We have been many days on the road," Abelar answered with a nod. "When we heard that the Saerloonian delegation had been attacked, we—"

"The Saerloonian delegation was attacked?" Tamlin asked. "By whom?"

Abelar answered, "I suspect by the same forces that attacked you, Lord Hulorn."

"But the forces that attacked us wore Ordulin's colors," Tamlin said.

"Mirabeta Selkirk is behind it," Abelar said. His men nodded, grunted agreement.

Tamlin stared at him for a moment. "That is preposterous! Mirabeta Selkirk is the Overmistress of Sembia. Why would she make an enemy of Selgaunt?"

Abelar said, "Because she wishes more power for herself and knows that Selgaunt will not support her. Just as she knows that Saerb will not. Events are moving quickly, my lord. You have been away from your city only a few days and matters have run ahead of you." He reached into a pocket and removed a folded piece of parchment. He handed it to Cale, who handed it to Tamlin. "This is a proclamation issued by Mirabeta Selkirk five days ago. When I heard of it, I expected an attack on your delegation. We have been riding after you since."

Tamlin unfolded the parchment, read it, and his expression went from puzzled to angry.

"That is absurd! Forces out of Selgaunt did not attack the Saerloonians!"

"Nor did any man from Saerb," Abelar said. "I assure you of that."

Tamlin handed the letter to Cale and he read it to himself.

Yesterday, soldiers from Selgaunt and Saerb engaged in a most cowardly and ignoble surprise attack on members of the Saerloonian delegation as they made their way to Ordulin for a moot of their peers. This attack appears to be retaliation for the arrest of the murderer Endren Corrinthal and in furtherance of his and his co-conspirators' attempt to seize power in Sembia through force of arms.

Cale did not bother to read the rest.

"She is lying!" Tamlin sputtered. "Lying!"

Abelar nodded. "It is all a lie. My father did not murder the Overmaster, yet Mirabeta has condemned him to the Hole of Yhaunn." Uncomfortable glances passed between the men from Saerb at that news.

Abelar continued, "Selgaunt and Saerb did not attack the Saerloonians, yet we are named traitors to the nation. The truth no longer matters. The people and the nobility believe the lie because they prefer where it leads. Mirabeta has made you, and Saerb, the enemy that she will use to secure her rule."

"I will not have it," Tamlin said, shaking his head. "Sembia will not have it."

"It is already done, my lord," Abelar said. "Most of the nobility in the realm are behind her. Only Daerlun stands neutral, but that's only because it contemplates secession to Cormyr. Mirabeta has won the rest with promises, fear, and false patriotism. Already she has sounded a muster in Ordulin and Saerloon, and troops from all over Sembia are gathering. Come spring, Selgaunt and Saerb will be assaulted by her two armies. You have two options. You can accept her lies and go meekly to the gallows or you can fight. There is no other way."

"Fight?" Tamlin said. "Fight other Sembians?"

"Civil war, my lord," Abelar said, nodding. "It is already upon us though the armies have not yet met."

Tamlin was flushed, sweating. The combat and the news from the capital left him foundering.

"I need time to think," Tamlin said, rubbing his temples. "This is . . . unbelievable."

Cale stepped to Tamlin's side, prepared to steady him by his presence if not his arm. "Where are you camped, Abelar?"

Abelar regarded Cale coolly. "Not far from here." He turned to his men. "Regg, have the men assist the Selgauntans in gathering their dead. Then we ride for the camp."

The Selgauntans, aided by the Saerbians, set about collecting their fallen. Afterward, the entire force rode south for the Saerbian camp. Tamlin, Cale, and Abelar trailed the main body.

"You spoke of civil war, yet you ride far east of your home to rescue us?" Cale said to Abelar.

Abelar looked at Tamlin as he answered. "I needed to ensure the safety and loyalty of the leader of my only sure ally. I have done the former. I hope I have done the latter?"

Tamlin nodded absently. Abelar glanced at Cale, then back to Tamlin.

"You keep unusual company, Lord Uskevren," he said.

Tamlin took his point. "Mister Cale is a trusted advisor and . . . priest."

"Oh?" Abelar said, eyebrows raised. "Whom do you serve, Erevis Cale?"

"Yes, whom do you serve, Mister Cale?" Tamlin asked.

Cale came within a blade's width of punching Tamlin in the face. Had Tamlin not been Thamalon's son, had Cale not figured Magadon's fate to be tied up in Sembia's, he would have left Tamlin to his own counsel then and there.

He looked Tamlin in the eyes, then Abelar. He took the mask from his pocket and held it up for both of them to see. "I serve Mask the Shadowlord. I have for over two years." Tamlin looked shocked. Abelar frowned. Cale glared first at Tamlin then at Abelar. "I can read your face, Corrinthal. Say what you would."

Tamlin, perhaps thinking better of his verbal ambush, said, "Mister Cale has proven his worth to my father and to me countless times, Abelar. His loyalty is beyond question, irrespective of the god he serves."

Abelar held Cale's gaze throughout Tamlin's defense. Cale credited him for not faltering. If nothing else, he recognized Abelar as a man he could respect.

Abelar said, "I judge men by their deeds, Cale. Not their gods and not their blood." He looked at Cale's skin as if he could see Cale was not a mere man. "But Lathander has empowered me to look in men's souls, and there is darkness in you. It is apparent to anyone who can see."

Cale knew the words to be true but was too angry to acknowledge them aloud. "There is a darkness in every man, Corrinthal," he answered. "And I, too, judge men by their deeds. That holy symbol you wear carries no weight with me."

They stared at each other a moment longer. Finally Abelar nodded. "Well enough," he said.

"Well enough," Cale answered.

When they arrived at the Saerbian camp, Tamlin, Cale, and Abelar took counsel in private around the fire, amidst the Saerbian tents. The house guards and Saerbians assigned men to a watch and the rest prepared for sleep.

Tamlin looked from Cale to Abelar. The firelight highlighted the circles under his eyes.

"If we fight . . ." he eyed Abelar, ". . . and I say 'if,' because even if I agree with your course, I do not have plenary authority to send Selgaunt to war. The Old Chauncel must ratify any such decision."

Abelar said "They will fight. An army will arrive at your walls. They will fight or die."

Tamlin sighed, continued. "Who else can we count on as an ally?"

Abelar leaned back and shook his head. "No one. The nobles have either sided with Ordulin or are trying to stay neutral until the storm blows over."

Cale found Abelar's choice of words ominous. Abelar continued. "Even the nobles in and around Saerb have lost their nerve. My father could rally them, but he is in the Hole of Yhaunn—and I am not him." He looked at Tamlin steadily. "I have two hundred and eleven men in this company. Another two hundred, perhaps three, would rally to me back in Saerb. That, combined with your forces, is all that stands against Mirabeta."

Tamlin shook his head. "You have four hundred men? Five hundred at best? Mirabeta will have thousands. I can muster perhaps two thousand men, not many more, assuming all the Old Chauncel agree that war is the only course."

"It is the only course," Abelar affirmed, and Cale found himself in agreement.

"How do we know that?" Tamlin asked, still grasping. "Perhaps Daerlun has the right of it. We stand by peacefully and let events unfold."

Before Abelar could reply, Cale said, "My lord, you read the proclamation. Mirabeta has declared Selgaunt and Saerb enemies of Sembia. If Abelar speaks truth, most of the nobility appear prepared to back her play."

"I always speak truth," Abelar said to Cale.

"We will see," Cale countered.

Abelar said to Tamlin, "Mirabeta Selkirk does not want war. She *needs* it. It is the pretense for her to seize and hold power. I have looked in her eyes, Hulorn, seen into her soul. Nothing else matters to her. And her plotting is furthered by her niece, Elyril Hraven, and that one serves a dark patron. There is more afoot here than a mere grab for power by Mirabeta Selkirk."

Cale agreed but kept his thoughts to himself. *It all leads back to Magadon,* the Shadowlord had told him. *But you will not like where it leads.*

Abelar continued. "If we stand idle, we will hang as traitors. There will be no peace before there is war. Mirabeta cannot allow it."

Abelar's words weighed on all three men. They sat in silence for a time.

"What of Cormyr, or the elves of Cormanthyr?" Cale asked.

"No doubt both would be pleased to see Sembians fighting Sembians," Abelar said. "Perhaps one or the other would enter the war at some point, but not until the murk clears."

"I will send out envoys nevertheless," said Tamlin. "We need allies from somewhere."

"Aye," Abelar said. "That we do, unless Sembia is to fall under the rule of Mirabeta and whatever dark god she serves." He brightened. "In the meanwhile, we have one another, and Lathander."

And Mask, Cale thought, but did not say.

The next morning, a mounted force out of Selgaunt rode into the Saerbian camp and informed them that they were in danger of attack. Cale almost laughed.

CHAPTER THIRTEEN

6 Uktar, the Year of Lightning Storms

The next day, Abelar, Cale, Tamlin, and the combined force of Selgauntans and Saerbians rode quickly for Selgaunt. The sun stole Cale's shadowhand. Cale did not bother to hide it and Abelar noticed.

Cale looked him in the face and said, "I am a shade, Corrinthal."

He offered no further explanation. Abelar stared at him for a time, then said, "Lathander and Mask, light and shadow. War sometimes makes odd allies."

Cale looked at Abelar. "That it does. Let's find a few more and send Mirabeta to the gallows in our stead."

"Indeed," Abelar said grimly. "And her niece."

The journey to Selgaunt was somber but uneventful. Cale stayed near Tamlin but they spoke little.

"Mister Cale," Tamlin said to him as they neared the High Bridge. "I wish another were Hulorn."

Cale understood the feeling and appreciated that Tamlin had confided it to him. He'd had similar thoughts after becoming a Chosen of Mask.

"Responsibility is heavy, my lord. You will bear it."

"You must," Abelar said. "Or Sembia will fall to darkness."

Tamlin made a dismissive gesture. "You are seeing events through the lens of your religion, Abelar. This is not a battle between good and evil. This is politics. Nothing more and nothing less."

"You are mistaken," Abelar said with a soft smile, but left it at that.

Cale suspected that Abelar was nearer the truth than Tamlin, but did not say so.

Abelar reined in his mount near the monumental arch that spanned the Elzimmer. "This is as far as we go, Hulorn," Abelar said to Tamlin.

"What? No. You must enter the city with me. Your forces will join ours."

Abelar shook his head. "I am doing all I can to rally men to our cause, Hulorn. The nobility may stand with Mirabeta or cower, but individual men will join us. We need all we can get. I will return to Selgaunt or send word within two tendays. Mirabeta will not start her war in winter. We have until spring to recruit men to our cause. After that, there will be blood."

He clasped Tamlin's hand, then Cale's. He held Cale's longer.

"I would have thought you and I more likely to cross blades than raise them together. I am . . . pleased it is otherwise. Let it stay that way, eh?"

"Agreed," Cale answered.

They parted, Abelar to raise as many men as he could to stand against Mirabeta, Cale and Tamlin to muster Selgaunt's forces and prepare a defense.

"We must send for your mother, Thazienne, and Talbot," Cale said.

Tamlin nodded. Both of them knew it was safer to be in the city than outside of it.

✦ ✦ ✦ ✦ ✦

Elyril watched from her position along the wall of the High Council Chamber as her aunt made her way through the crowd to the Speaker's dais. She wore a flattering but unpretentious green daygown. Elyril wore a violet gown, her amethysts, and her holy symbol

The council chamber was filled. The open doors revealed more nobles and their servants and wallmen packing the surrounding halls. Sunshine poured in through the domed ceiling, glittering off the dragon's hoard of finery and jewels. Almost all of Sembia's nobility was represented, either in person or by proxy. Much of the western nobility had sent word of allegiance to Ordulin and support of the overmistress. Only the nobility of Saerb, Selgaunt, and secessionist Daerlun were unrepresented, but they did not matter. Saerb, traitors in kind with Selgaunt, answered to Endren Corrinthal, and Endren Corrinthal was rotting in the Hole of Yhaunn.

Advocates for granting Mirabeta plenary power as Sembia's war regent had already spoken. No one had risen in opposition. All that remained was for Mirabeta to accept.

As Mirabeta ascended the steps of the Speaker's dais, the chamber hushed and Elyril silently thanked Shar. Only a few stray coughs broke the silence.

Mirabeta did not smile. She looked grim, as befitted the circumstances.

"You offer me a great honor, and great responsibility. My inclination is to turn it down. Sembia has not had a war regent in centuries."

Conversation rushed across the chamber, speculation that Mirabeta would refuse to serve. Elyril knew better.

"But I have recently received word that Abelar Corrinthal rides the countryside, rallying traitors to his standard, and terrorizing ordinary Sembians."

Elyril knew most of the words to be lies. Abelar was raising a force of riders in the northwest, but he had terrorized no one.

"I have also received word that Selgaunt is raising an army to withstand the will of this body. It does not please me, but if Selgaunt and Saerb wish war, then war they shall have. We refuse to let Sembia fall into the hands of traitors and thugs."

The chamber erupted into applause. Mirabeta nodded and waited for it to die down.

"Under these dark circumstances, in these dark days, I feel dutybound *not* to follow my inclinations. Accordingly, I hereby accept this august body's directive to act as War Regent of the realm throughout the term of the insurrection."

Several hundred of Sembia's merchant nobility rose to their feet as one and fairly rattled the dome with their cheers.

The next days became a blur to Cale. Tamlin met with the Old Chauncel assembly, with individual members of the Old Chauncel, with high priests and powerful wizards. He sent out word of a muster, dispatched envoys to Cormyr and Cormanthyr. Peaceful overtures to Ordulin went unanswered. It seemed Abelar was correct—Mirabeta would have her war. They expected no aid but sought it nevertheless.

Agents were sent abroad as far as Baldur's Gate, Ravens Bluff, and Arrabar, seeking to hire mercenary companies. Selgaunt's treasury was no match for Ordulin's, but it was a wealthy city nevertheless. Surely some swords would answer the call of coin.

Such events turned Cale's shadowy past as a guild "letters man" into a valuable asset to the Hulorn, who used Cale and Vees Talendar to help him compose the constant stream of orders and proclamations that went forth from the palace.

Everyone in the city soon realized that war was imminent, that the matter could not be peaceably resolved. Some Helms abandoned their posts to join with the forces marshalling in Saerloon, and others arrived in Selgaunt seeking to join against Ordulin. The brewing civil war provided an excuse to bring long-buried regional and familial rivalries to the fore. Many in Sembia had long been jealous of Selgaunt's prominence.

Tamlin declared martial law and posted Helms and Scepters at the gates and along the walls. Trade came to a standstill. Everyone entering and leaving the city was questioned and checked. Repair crews worked on long-ignored defensive bulwarks. Captain Onthul and the Helms drilled and re-drilled the soldiers. All ships of the Sembian navy in Selgaunt Bay were pressed into service.

"It is not enough," Tamlin said to Vees and Cale as they sat in the parlor in Stormweather.

"No," Vees said. "It is not."

Their spies told them that the muster in Saerloon would result in several thousand troops, with hundreds of cavalry among them, and that the muster in Ordulin would result in half that again. Selgaunt would be outnumbered four or five to one, not accounting for hired mercenaries.

"We have not yet heard from Abelar and the Saerbians," Cale said.

"If only he could rally those loyal to his father," Tamlin said. He sipped at a goblet of Storm Ruby, the heaviest wine in the Uskevren cellar.

"He will bring a few hundred men, no more than that," Vees said, and topped off Tamlin's goblet.

"We do not know what forces he will bring, Talendar," answered Cale.

"If he does not hurry, he will bring nothing," said Tamlin tiredly. "The snows will soon arrive. He will not be able to reach us at all if he does not arrive soon."

"Perhaps he does not intend to," said Vees casually.

"What? What do you mean?" Tamlin asked, alarmed.

Cale glared at Vees, then said to Tamlin, "I read Abelar as a man of his word, my lord. He said he would return or send word. He will do so."

Tamlin nodded absently. "He could be dead, Mister Cale. We would not know it."

To that, Cale could say nothing. Abelar *could* be dead.

Vees leaned back in his armchair and looked at the ceiling.

"Deuce, I have something . . . controversial to say."

Tamlin set down his goblet and looked a question at Vees. Cale did the same.

"It is a bit embarrassing to admit," Vees said. "But . . . my family has indirect trading ties with . . . no, never mind."

"Speak, Vees," Tamlin commanded.

Vees looked to Tamlin, to Cale, and said, "Very well. My family trades with the Shadovar of Shade Enclave."

He tried to look embarrassed but Cale saw through it.

"The Shadovar?" Tamlin exclaimed. "How? What kind of trading ties?"

Vees said, "A Shadovar trade emissary contacted me while I was in Waterdeep taking the rites. They wanted dressed stone—marble and the like—so we supplied it. The relationship grew from there. It has been quite lucrative."

"The Shadovar?" Tamlin said, sounding more intrigued than appalled. He glanced at Cale, at Cale's shadowhand, and returned his gaze to Vees. "Why have you never spoken of this before?"

Vees shrugged and smiled sheepishly. "As I said, it is embarrassing for the family. The Shadovar are held in low regard, but as my father always said, 'coin is coin no matter its source.' And the Shadovar are desperate for trade, Deuce. They live in a floating city above a desert. They need almost everything, but they lack trading partners."

"That is because they attack their neighbors," said Tamlin.

Cale knew that forces out of Cormyr, and even some Sembian soldiers, had battled the Shadovar, but he did not know the underlying reasons.

"I think much of that may have been a misunderstanding," Vees said. "These things happen in politics, Deuce. Look at what is happening in Sembia now. Ask ten people outside of Selgaunt who started this whole affair, and eight of them will point at Selgaunt and Saerb."

"They would be wrong," Tamlin said.

Vees nodded. "And that is my point. What is said of the Shadovar does not square with my experience."

Cale said, "What relevance does any of this have to events, Talendar?"

Vees did not look at Cale. He said to Tamlin, "The Shadovar are aware of our plight. They have indicated to me that they would be willing to assist us if we were willing to entertain a formal and open trade and political alliance."

Tamlin stared at Vees for a long while. Cale noticed for the first time how much the gray in his hair had multiplied.

Cale said, "I like this not at all, my lord. From what I have heard of the Shadovar, they are not trustworthy."

"I have heard the same of priests of Mask," Vees said.

Cale rose, shadows bleeding from his skin. Tamlin laid his hand on Cale's forearm.

"Please, Mister Cale. We are all tense."

Cale glared into Vees's smug face, at his dull eyes and weak chin. Vees only smiled.

Tamlin said, "I fear we are in no position to be selective in our choice of allies."

"I have found them trustworthy, Deuce," Vees added, and looked at Cale. "For whatever my word is worth."

"It is worth much," Tamlin said.

"I will get us aid elsewhere," Cale said suddenly.

Vees scoffed. "From where? We stand alone. Only the Shadovar have stepped forward to offer aid. Tamlin, I can arrange a meeting as soon as tomorrow."

Cale did not like the eager undertone to Vees's words.

"The nobility around Saerb and near the High Dale," Cale said. "They will rally to Endren Corrinthal."

"Endren Corrinthal is rotting in the Hole of Yhaunn," Vees answered. "He is a murderer. And honestly, what are we talking about here? The northern nobility are little more than retired old men and their house guards."

Cale knew Talendar was at least partly correct. Merchants, not soldiers, retired upcountry. Still, it was a better course than an alliance with the Shadovar.

"I would wager Endren is no more a murderer than we are

traitors," said Cale. "Mirabeta Selkirk arranged all of this, built one lie on another. I will get Endren out of the Hole. The northern nobility will answer his call."

Tamlin sat up in his chair. "You can do this?"

Shadows leaked from Cale's flesh. "I can do it."

He would need help, but he knew where he could get it.

"Then do it," Vees said, and turned to Tamlin. "But Deuce, do not let the possibility of aid from one quarter dissuade you from aid from another."

"You seem eager to put the Shadovar before the Hulorn," Cale said, and shadows swirled about him. "Too eager."

Vees glared unadulterated hate at Cale. He touched his throat as if something hung from it, though there was nothing. "I am eager to save our city, Erevis Cale."

Before Cale could respond, Tamlin said, "How soon can you arrange the meeting, Vees?"

Vees said, "As early as tomorrow."

"Do so," said Tamlin. "I want to hear what the Shadovar have to say. Mister Cale, it will take you days, perhaps tendays, to arrange a rescue of Endren Corrinthal. I need to—"

Cale shook his head. "No. I will have him back in Selgaunt within two days."

Tamlin stared at him, agog. So did Vees.

"You cannot," Tamlin said.

"I can and I will," Cale vowed.

"Good-bye, then, Mister Cale," said Vees.

Cale had had enough of the twit and his smug tone. He stood, took Talendar roughly by the shirt, lifted him from his chair, and steered him from the parlor over his protests.

"The hulorn is tired from the day's work, Lord Talendar. Begone from here."

Vees resisted but his strength was no match for Cale's. Cale deposited him in the hallway, said, "See yourself out," and shut the parlor door in his face.

"You are unnecessarily harsh with him," Tamlin said. "I do not approve."

"He is a fool and dissembler. I do not approve of that."

Tamlin, perhaps too tired to argue, merely took another gulp of wine. Cale stared at him, trying to frame in his mind what he wanted to say. Tamlin anticipated his words. "Do not bother to try to dissuade me, Mister Cale. My mind is made up."

Cale started to speak but Tamlin interrupted him.

"Do you not see what will happen here? If we do not get assistance, Mirabeta's forces will take the city. We are too few. We will die. Perhaps not you, since you can vanish into the shadows, but I, and the rest of the Old Chauncel. And all for what? So she can hold power? I did not ask to stand in her way."

Tamlin's words surprised Cale. They sounded as timid and self-absorbed as something he might have said years ago.

"We do not always get what we ask," Cale said. "And this is not about you, Tamlin. This is about the city, about Sembia."

About Magadon, he thought, but did not say.

"No!" Tamlin said, and slammed his hand on the table. Wine sloshed over the brim of his goblet and stained the tabletop crimson.

"This *is* about me, because *I* will hang if we are taken. Not you. Me. Do you understand?"

Cale stared at Tamlin. He could see the younger man was in deep water and unable to swim. "I understand too well. You are afraid."

The words caused Tamlin to redden but he nodded. "Yes, very well, I am afraid. I do not want to die." He looked at Cale, anger in his eyes. "But you are not afraid, are you? No, of course not. The fearless Mister Cale, the competent Mister Cale, the Mister Cale my father always respected and loved more than his own son, the Mister Cale who vows to pull a man out of the Hole of Yhaunn."

Cale heard years of resentment bubbling up in Tamlin's tone. He took a deep breath and spoke calmly. "You are fatigued, my lord. You should rest now. Things will appear different in the sun."

Tamlin rubbed his temples. "I am going to meet with the Shadovar, Mister Cale. If they offer military assistance, I will give them whatever trade concessions they wish."

"You should not. They are not to be trusted. Vees Talendar is not to be trusted."

"Why should I not trust the Shadovar?" Tamlin said, with rising anger in his voice. "Because some of them are shades? So are you. Because they use shadow magic? So do you."

Cale drew himself up and said, "The difference, Tamlin, is that I serve you and by extension, the city. They do not."

"Do you?" Tamlin snapped. "Do you, really?"

Cale held his anger in check but the shadows leaking from his skin betrayed him. "I will return with Endren Corrinthal. Do what you will with the Shadovar. If you need me in the meanwhile, reach me via magical sending, as you did before. And understand something, Lord Uskevren. I have been afraid, for myself, for my friends, for my family. But I do not let it overwhelm me or cloud my judgment."

Tamlin seethed and waved Cale out.

Cale turned and left the parlor, left Tamlin, and after gathering his gear, left Stormweather Towers.

My boat cracked on the rocks . . . how long ago? I do not know. It could have been months. It feels like months. I know only that I must keep moving toward the wall. The fears are behind me, hard on my heels. My use of the river has opened some distance but not enough. I can feel them behind me in the woods, stalking me.

Sweating, gasping, covered in dirt, I dash through the forest. Limbs slap my face. Welts cover my exposed skin. I trip repeatedly but rise each time and run onward. The smell of brimstone is so intense that I cannot escape it, but I have become inured to the stink. I notice it, but it no longer bothers my lungs.

Behind me, the fears howl, one, another, another. They are unrelenting.

I scramble up a tree-lined slope . . . and stop in my steps.

An open, grass-covered plain stretches before me for maybe a fifth of a league. It ends at the wall. I did not know I was so close.

The dark edifice rises from the plain and stretches to the sky.

Thin cracks line its face. Black smoke leaks from them. To my surprise, ice rimes the cracks.

Abutting the wall, at its base, is a small stone structure. It looks much as I imagine the cell in which I awakened must have looked. Like the wall, it is composed of dark stone. It features only a single, windowless door.

If the door is not barred, the cell will offer shelter from the fears and a place from which I can work to breach the wall.

And I will breach it. That is my task.

The fears howl again, right behind me. I can hear them crashing through the undergrowth, chuffing, slobbering. I have no choice. I take a deep breath and sprint onto the plain.

Before I have taken twenty strides, the fears howl and burst from the treeline behind me. I spare only a single glance backward and wish immediately that I had not.

Hundreds of black forms bound and roil over the grass behind me. They are closing.

CHAPTER FOURTEEN

10 Uktar, the Year of Lightning Storms

Cale bade the house guards at the gate goodeve, strode down the walkway, and stepped out onto the darkness of Rauncel's Ride. Street torches pasted shadows over the cobbles, the sides of buildings. A few wagons rumbled up the streets and dozens of pedestrians walked the avenue. All of them wore worry on their faces. There was barely enough food to prevent starvation through the winter, and spring would bring war.

Cale adjusted his pack. He checked his weapons and his mask, and thanked Mask again for the spells that filled his mind. He walked the street until he found a deserted alley. It stank, of course, as all alleys did these days. Despite his grim mood, he smiled, thinking of Mask's request to him that he cease appearing and disappearing from alleys.

"Old habits are slow to die," he said, and pulled the

darkness about him. He imagined the Wayrock in his mind—a rocky, gull-covered isle jutting from the blue expanse of the Inner Sea, with the temple that Mask had stolen from Cyric pointing up from its center.

Cale had not returned to the Wayrock since killing the Sojourner, since Jak had died. He knew he would find Riven there, serving Mask, and he would also find Jak's grave. He had not helped bury his friend—the pain had been too sharp, then—and he regretted it. He had never said good-bye, not really.

Remembering the halfling, how he had felt, cold and lifeless in Cale's arms, sent a swell of emotion through Cale like a fist in his throat. He beat back the tears and reached down to touch the pipe in his belt pouch—Jak's pipe. For a moment, the smell of pipeweed was so powerful that Cale could have sworn Jak was standing beside him.

But it was only a phantom, a memory, and it vanished with the breeze. Cale tried to send his grief with it. He had work to get done.

He reached out to make a connection between the night in Selgaunt and the night at the Wayrock, found it, and moved across the Inner Sea in a moment.

He appeared near the center of the island, just outside the tower. The surf murmured in the distance. The smell of fish and sea salt spiced the air.

The spire, a gray stone cylinder unmarred by windows, looked much the same as the last time he had seen it, when it had channeled enough magical power to pull one of Selûne's tears from the Outer Darkness. The drawbridge was lowered and the open archway leered. Torches burned on either side of the entry and the flames danced in the wind. Cale saw no guards. Mask's temple appeared abandoned.

A figure materialized out of the darkness of the archway. Cale recognized Riven from his stature and stance, from the two sabers that hung from his weapon belt. He wore a black cloak rather than his usual crimson.

He did not bother to hail Riven and Riven did not bother to hail him. Cale started up the drawbridge; Riven started down. Cale was Mask's First; Riven was Mask's Second. They met in the middle, cloaked in the night.

"He told me you were coming," Riven said. "I have been waiting."

Like the tower, Riven looked much the same as the last time Cale had seen him—short, muscular, and precise. He wore his long black hair pulled back and tied. The scarred hole of his right eye looked like a pit in the swarthy skin of his face. The signature sneer and stained teeth nested in a black goatee. He wore a black disc on a chain around his throat—a symbol of Mask.

Cale did not waste time with niceties. "I need help, Riven."

Riven cocked an eyebrow over his empty socket. "What kind of help?"

"I need to pull a man out of the Hole of Yhaunn."

Riven scoffed until he saw that Cale was serious. "You came here for that? No one comes out of the Hole, Cale."

"He must, and soon."

Riven raised his eyebrows to ask why.

"Long tale," Cale said. "There is much at stake."

"For who?" Riven asked.

"For Mask. For Magadon."

Both struck bone. Riven's eye narrowed. "Magadon's in the Hole?"

"No. Magadon's missing."

"Missing?"

Cale hesitated, then dived in. "Have you . . . dreamed of him?"

Riven's eye widened and he nodded slowly. "A blizzard of ice, devils. He's falling. They stopped, though. A while back."

"For me, too," Cale said, nodding, though Cale had dreamed of flames, not ice. "But it's all related somehow: the dreams, the Hole, Mask." He stared into Riven's face. "I need your help, Riven."

"You are the First," Riven said, and the words surprised Cale, for he heard no envy in them. Riven stroked his goatee. "The Hole is dead to magic. Spells do not work there. Magical weapons or toys. Nothing."

Cale had not known. The fact complicated matters. "Nothing works?"

"Nothing," Riven answered. "When I was with the Zhents—just starting out—they considered trying to get a man out of there but called it off. They thought it impossible. It's not the guards. There aren't that many. It's that it's in a city, with only one way in and out, and no way to use magic."

"Nothing is impossible."

"True," Riven said. "But it can't help but be ugly."

"That's why I need you," Cale said.

Riven smiled at that. "We'll need to be fast."

"Speed is critical," Cale said, nodding. "We take a guard and force him to tell us where our man is. We get him and get out."

Riven looked him in the face. "Who's the target?"

"A Sembian nobleman. Endren Corrinthal."

Riven's face showed no recognition.

"Ordulin is making an armed play for all of Sembia. It's all lies, but Selgaunt and Saerb are the falls. Endren would rally some of the neutrals to Selgaunt and Saerb."

"Civil war in Sembia," Riven said, shaking his head. "Coin counters at war. They're in for some hard lessons." He looked at Cale. "I'll do this because you're the First and because you believe it ties back to Magadon. I care nothing for a Sembian civil war."

"Well enough," Cale said. He would get no better from Riven.

"When do we move?" Riven asked.

Cale considered. "Tomorrow night. Do you know the layout from your Zhent days? The number of guards?"

Riven shook his head. "I wasn't part of the Zhents' planning. Just muscle, then."

"Then we go in blind and improvise," Cale said.

"So we do," Riven said. He offered his hand. Cale was surprised, but took it. They had said good-bye with the same gesture after Jak's death.

"Welcome back," Riven said, and the words sounded almost exactly like those Mask had whispered in Cale's ear before the battle with Malkur Forrin's mercenaries.

"Almost there, now," Cale said softly, echoing Mask's words.

"What did you say?" Riven asked.

"Nothing. It's good to be back," Cale said, and meant it. He had come to rely on Riven, his Second, and Riven had not let him down.

Riven gazed into the night, licked his lips. "There are some things you need to see. Things have happened since you were last here."

Riven was rarely cryptic and his words raised Cale's curiosity. "Such as?"

"Follow me," Riven said.

They turned and walked up the drawbridge side by side. Before they reached the tower's archway, two short-haired hounds darted out of the tower and dashed toward them. Both had birder in them, judging from their ears and black and brown spots.

"My girls," Riven said by way of explanation. His voice held a surprising softness.

Cale kneeled as the canines rushed toward them. Riven half-heartedly ordered the dogs to heel and neither even slowed.

Cale held out his shadowhand to the dogs. They sniffed it suspiciously, whined, and backed off, but Cale persisted and the larger came back again to tentatively sniff, and the smaller followed suit. Moving slowly, Cale rubbed the larger one on her muzzle, the smaller on her flanks.

That did it. Tails wagged and they licked his fingers. Cale gave them a final pat.

"They're good dogs," he said, standing.

"Loyal," Riven answered quietly.

"A good quality," Cale said, not necessarily meaning the dogs.

"That's truth," Riven said.

Tongues lolling, the dogs bounced from Cale to Riven, and the assassin stroked each of their heads in turn. They licked his hand and both fell over and showed their bellies. Riven scratched each. Cale found the scene entirely incongruous. Until then, he had never seen Riven gentle with anything.

"I never understood your fondness for dogs," Cale said good-naturedly.

"And I never understood your fondness for Jak Fleet," Riven said as he stood.

Anger chased Cale's smile and hot words formed on his lips. He started to speak but Riven shook his head, held up his hand, and cut him off.

"That's a lie. I did understand it. Fleet and I . . . reached an understanding before the end. I'm sorry for those words, Cale. Old habits return when I see you."

"Old habits are slow to die," Cale said, echoing the words he had spoken to Mask moments before.

"Go on," Riven said to the dogs, and gestured at the archway. The dogs turned and darted inside, tails wagging. Riven watched them go, then turned to Cale.

"Let's say we end all this, beginning now."

"End what?"

"The posturing," Riven said, making a frustrated gesture. "All of it. We've been through too much, Cale. You are Mask's First and I am his Second, and that's the end of it."

Cale managed a nod through his surprise. They *had* been through too much. "Well enough," he said. "We are past it. Starting now."

Riven stared at him, nodded, and they walked up the drawbridge.

"I presume we'll hit the Hole after midnight?" Riven asked.

Cale nodded. "Well after."

Guards would be not only fewer, but tired in the small hours. Cale had killed many men during the sleepy hours before dawn. He knew Riven had done the same.

They strode through towering iron doors and into the temple's foyer. The dogs were gone. The bare entryway appeared exactly as it had when Cale had last seen it. A pair of wooden double doors stood opposite them, with a wide stairway beyond it leading up into darkness.

"I had thought to fit the place out," Riven said by way of explanation. "Transform it into a temple for Mask. I thought that was what he wanted."

Cale knew that guessing at what Mask wanted was a fool's game. "But it wasn't?"

Riven shook his head. "I don't think stealing this place was about getting a new temple. Or at least it was only partially about that." He looked at Cale sidelong and said, "I think it was about us."

They walked through the double doors and started to climb the wide stone stairway beyond.

"Us? What makes you think that?" Cale asked.

"They do," Riven said, and nodded at the top of the stairs.

Cale stopped in his steps.

At the top of the stairs stood seven men clad in darkness. Long dark hair hung loose around clean-shaven brown faces. At first Cale thought each wore a mask over the top half of his face but he realized it was a tattoo of a mask. The dark eyes looking out of the tattoos featured the eyefolds typical of those from the far east.

All wore gray cloaks, gray breeches, and soft leather shoes. None wore weapons, but all showed battle scars on their hands and forearms. Torchlight from the hall behind them backlit their silhouettes.

"They said a vision brought them here," Riven said.

"A vision?" Cale walked up the rest of the steps, Riven beside him, until he stood face to face with the foremost of the seven men, whom Cale took to be the leader. The man, smaller and less muscular than Riven, gave a nod and the others bowed slightly. All seven regarded Cale with open curiosity, though they said nothing.

"What kind of vision?" Cale asked the leader.

The man said nothing, merely studied Cale's eyes, the shadows that leaked from his skin, the darkness that flowed around him like fog.

"I asked you a question," Cale said.

"They arrived two months after you left," Riven explained. "They almost never speak, but I know they call themselves shadow-walkers. They may not be shades, but I have seen them move and they are damned close."

"What are they doing here?" Cale asked Riven, though he continued to eye the shadowwalkers.

" 'Waiting,' is all they would say."

"Waiting?" Cale asked. He stared into the leader's dark eyes.

"For what?"

"They won't answer you, Cale. They're just here . . . waiting. And they won't help us with Yhaunn. I have tried to enlist them before. Whatever they are waiting for, it hasn't happened yet."

"And you think it has to do with us?"

"With you."

Cale turned to him. "Me?"

"They aren't priests," Riven said, nodding at the shadowwalkers. He pulled the tie out of his hair and let it fall down his shoulders. "Hells, I don't know what they are. But they serve priests, or they did. They're from Telflamm, Cale. Mask has a large temple there, a large following. When they arrived, they said the Shadowlord had stopped answering the prayers of the priests. When they learned of that, they had the vision that led them here. They say they follow the Twilight Path."

Shadows leaked from Cale's skin as the implications of Riven's story settled on him. Mask had not stopped answering *his* prayers. Mask had chatted with him in an alley, or at least he thought so.

He looked at Riven and said, "Sometimes gods do not answer the prayers of even their priests."

Riven shook his head. "This is not one wayward priest. They said none of their priests received spells. None."

Cale shook his head, his mind spinning. What if he was the only priest to whom Mask spoke?

"What about you?" Riven asked, his voice quiet. "Does he still grant you spells?"

Cale hesitated, turned back to look at the shadowwalkers.

They were gone.

"I told you they were good," Riven explained. "What about it, Cale? Does he still grant you spells?"

Cale answered Riven with a question of his own. "What about you? Can you still heal with your touch? Does he still grant you that?"

Riven nodded. "That . . . and the rest."

Riven's candor surprised Cale. The assassin had been surprising him since Cale had appeared on the island. Cale decided to be honest.

"Yes, I can still cast spells. Though I went a long while without praying."

Riven's face showed first relief, then a question. "Why a long while?"

Cale could hardly believe Riven was asking the question. "Why? Because Jak is dead. Because I'm . . . this." He held out his arm and let the shadows spiral around his flesh. "Because he did it all so he could steal a thrice-damned temple."

Riven's face remained calm.

"I told you this was not about the temple. There's more to it."

Riven's calmness only stoked Cale's anger. "What if there isn't, Riven? Hells, why don't you *question*? What kind of faith doesn't doubt? Look what he took from us!"

Riven shook his head. "What kind of faith *always* doubts, Cale? And look what he *gave* us."

Cale blew out a breath and looked away. Riven said, "No Cyricists have come to take vengeance for the theft of the temple."

Cale said nothing and Riven repeated himself, as if he thought his words significant.

"Did you hear me? No Cyricists have tried to take back the temple, Cale. Not one, not ever. They're either ignorant of what happened or occupied with something bigger. I think it's the latter. Something is coming, Cale. You feel it. I know you do. I feel it, too. So do the shadowwalkers. That's why they're here."

"A storm," Cale said absently, and rubbed the back of his neck. For some reason, his mind turned to the book in his pack. "Sephris called it a storm."

"Sephris? The old prophet?"

Cale nodded.

"Cale, that's why Mask is withdrawing from his servants. All but us. This temple, the Sojourner, all of it was designed to prepare us. Don't you see that?"

Shadows leaked from Cale's fingers. He watched them dissipate into the darkness. "Prepare us for what?"

"For the storm," Riven said. "For whatever is coming."

Cale shook his head. "No. Not even gods plan that well.

Besides, he's preparing himself, not us."

"It's the same thing," Riven said. "Let me show you something else. Come."

Cale took Riven by the shoulder. "I don't need any more surprises."

Riven looked him in the eye, his expression . . . soft? "One more," he said.

Riven led Cale through the darkened temple. Although the structure lacked any formal accoutrements of Mask's faith, Cale figured the Shadowlord found the darkness and shadows of the windowless temple pleasing. Torches lit their way through bare stone corridors and rooms.

Riven led Cale up a flight of stairs to a closed wooden door. Cale recognized the room and his throat caught. They had laid Jak's body there. He looked a question at Riven.

"Open it. You'll see."

Cale studied Riven's face.

"Open it," Riven insisted.

Slowly, reluctantly, Cale pushed open the door. When he saw what was within, his heart rattled in his ribcage and words stuck in his throat.

I sprint through the grass, my legs burning, my breath rattling. The stone cell is just ahead.

I hear a fear just behind me and lash out blindly backward with the mind blade. I feel it bite flesh and the fear wails with pain and anger.

Twenty paces to the door. Ten. Five. I lose my footing, fall to all fours, and scramble frantically the final few paces. I slam into the door, praying it is not locked.

It opens.

I fall in, throw the door shut behind me, and brace my back against it.

It's freezing inside.

The fears throw themselves against the door and drive it ajar. Grunting, I press my body against it, shut it again, and feel around desperately for some kind of lock, anything. My fingers close on a rusty frigid iron bar on the floor near the door. I find the bracket on the door by touch and slide the bar in.

The fears again throw themselves against the door. It shudders under the impact but the bar holds and they howl their frustration. Thumps on the roof and walls tell me they are looking for another way in.

Breathing heavily and sweating, I hold up my mind blade and look around the interior of the cell. Thankfully, I do not see any other means of ingress.

The wall opposite me is *the* wall and a crack runs through it from floor to ceiling. It is lined with smoke-blackened ice. Otherwise, the cell is a mirror of the one in which I had first awakened. Empty, with a bare stone floor.

The fears hit the door with such impact that it rattles on its hinges. Others beat at the roof, at the walls.

"Magadon," says a voice, the voice at the wall, coming from behind the crack. "Come here. To the crack."

I do not move. I stare across the cell at the crack in the wall while the fears try to beat their way inside.

"Terrifying, are they not?" the voice asks, and chuckles. "Come here, Magadon."

Clutching the mind blade, I cross the cell and stand before the wall. The crack cuts a jagged, irregular path down its face. Stink and cold leaks through—brimstone mixed with the fetid, rotting odor of a charnel house. I put my hand on the stone and find it icy to the touch.

"The wall is weakest here," says the voice eagerly. "You can break through it. Use your weapon."

The fears beat against the cell in a frenzy. The walls vibrate; the door rattles; the roof shakes. I am concerned that the whole structure may soon collapse. In my mind's eye, I imagine the black forms of the fears coating the cell like a layer of oil, encapsulating it in terror.

"You must hurry," says the voice. "Time is short."

I will the mind blade into the form of a large pickaxe and start chipping away at the wall, expanding the crack.

Jak lay on the same bed that they had placed him on soon after his death.

"This is not possible," Cale said, and shadows spiraled out of his skin. His legs felt weak. Jak should have been buried, decomposed. It had been over a year.

Despite his better sense, he allowed himself to hope and called, "Jak?"

The little man did not move.

"Go in, Cale," said Riven.

Cale entered the room in a daze and walked cautiously to the bed. His friend looked exactly as he had in life. His small frame barely put a dent in the bed. A mop of red hair framed a face that could have been sleeping. He looked at peace.

Cale fought back tears, and kneeled on his haunches at the head of the bed.

"Jak?"

The scab peeled away from his grief and the hole in his gut yawned. The tears came then. He could not stop them. He reached out a hand, tentatively, and touched Jak's cheek. He recoiled with a gasp.

Riven's voice sounded behind him and gave him another start.

"He is still warm," Riven said. "I could not bury him like that. So I left him there. I check him every day. Nothing has changed."

Cale nodded but did not turn. Shadows bled from his skin, swirled around him. He stared at Jak, hoping, fearing, wondering. What did it mean? He thought Jak's eyes could open at any moment. Did it mean that Jak wanted to come back?

"This is not possible," was all he could manage.

Riven stepped beside him and stared down at Jak. "And yet, there he is."

Cale shook his head. "Why? How?"

Riven eyed him sidelong. "Cale, I think . . . that he is waiting, too. Like the shadowwalkers."

"For what?" Cale started to say, but could not find his voice at first. "For what?"

"For you to let him go." Riven gestured at Jak. "He is as you left him when you stopped your resurrection spell in the middle of casting it. Let him go now."

Cale's eyes welled. He reached into his pocket and put his hand on Jak's wooden pipe. He had said good-bye to his friend but he knew he had never let go, not fully. That's why he had attacked Mask in the alley. That is why he burned a pipe at midnight every night. And it was the reason that he carried the dead weight of regret around in his gut. He had asked Riven to bury Jak. He had never even returned to visit the grave, or what he thought was a grave.

Cale thought of his promise to Jak and the words came out before he could stop them.

"I promised him I'd try to be a hero."

Riven neither sneered nor laughed, surprising Cale again. "You will keep that promise. I will help you because you are the First. That is my promise. Now . . . let him go."

Cale shook his head and the tears flowed. Riven put a hand on his shoulder. "You must. Whatever is coming, there is no more room for doubt, no more room for questions. There is room for you, me, and the Shadowlord. Nothing more and nothing less."

Cale heard the truth of his words, *knew* the truth of his words.

"Who in the Nine Hells are you?" he asked Riven, and tried to smile. "This temple has gone to your head."

Riven looked him in the eyes. "It has, but not in the way you think. Cale, I am the Second of Mask. We are more than comrades, more than friends. I am at your shoulder through whatever comes. Now . . . be the First."

Cale stared into Riven's good eye and remembered Mask's words to him in the alley in Selgaunt. *Do what you were born to do.*

"Be the First," Riven repeated.

Cale swallowed, steadied himself. "This is the way it will be, then?"

"It cannot be any other way."

Cale looked at Jak, back at Riven, and nodded. He put his hand over Jak's.

"Go," he said to Jak, and meant it. "Thank you for the second chance. You are my friend, always. But that's enough. Rest, now."

Jak's flesh began to cool in his hand. Cale did not recoil. He held Jak's tiny hand in his own, took a deep breath, and turned to Riven.

"Spades?"

Riven nodded. "Somewhere."

"I will carry him," Cale said. "Also, bring something small and sharp."

Riven looked a question at him but Cale did not explain. He picked up the body of his friend and carried him out of the room, down the stairs, and out of the temple. When he got outside into the night, he walked like an ordinary man up to the top of a small hill near the temple. It afforded a view of the island but not the sea, which was just as well. Jak had disliked the sea.

Cale sat on the earth and awaited Riven. Jak was growing colder; his body was stiffening.

Riven soon arrived, bearing two metal spades. His dogs followed. Together, the First and Second of Mask dug a grave and gently placed a friend and priest of Brandobaris in it. They had no coffin. The dogs watched it all.

Cale threw the first shovelful of dirt over Jak. Riven said nothing, merely helped him fill the hole. The dogs howled. They worked until Jak was buried. Cale started to put Jak's pipe on the earthen mound as a marker, but Riven said, "He'd want you to keep it."

Cale looked at the pipe, nodded, put it in his pocket.

"Did you bring what I asked?" he asked Riven.

Riven produced a small, flat-bladed knife with a rounded tip.

"Small and sharp," Riven said.

Cale tested the edge and found it satisfactory. He kneeled at the side of the grave and started to cut his hair, first cutting it to a short, choppy length, then to stubs, then shaving it off with the knife. The wind blew it away and the dogs chased it. Cale opened countless gashes in his scalp, but the bleeding and pain lasted only a moment before the shadowstuff in his flesh repaired the damage.

Riven watched it all in silence.

When Cale had finished the job, he stood, returned the knife to Riven, and ran a hand over his bald pate. Shadows leaked from him and he felt like himself.

Riven eyed him, nodded.

Cale took out Jak's pipe, stuffed it with pipeweed, and smoked graveside. Riven pulled a wooden pipe from his belt pouch—a pipe like the one Jak had once given the assassin—and joined Cale. Afterward, they collected the spades and walked back to the temple.

The shadowwalkers awaited them on the drawbridge. Shadows swirled around them, around Cale, around Riven. The wind blew their cloaks.

Cale approached the leader. "Tell me your name."

"Nayan," the man said, his voice as soft as rainfall.

"Nayan," Cale said, testing the word.

Nayan turned to his fellows and indicated each in turn. The men bowed as their names were spoken. "Shadem, Vyrhas, Erynd, Dynd, Skelan, and Dahtem."

"Erevis Cale," Cale said.

"Drasek Riven," said Riven.

Nayan nodded to each, and held up both hands as he said, "You are the right and left hands of the Shadowlord and he still speaks through you."

"That is so," Cale said, and preferred Nayan's words to "First" and "Second."

Nayan said, "We are servants of the Shadowlord and therefore servants of his Chosen."

"You're offering to help us?" Riven asked.

Nayan nodded once.

Cale looked the shadowwalkers in the eyes. "You have been blooded. Anyone can see that. But being blooded is not enough. Where are your weapons?"

Nayan held up his hands again, touched his elbows, his knees, his feet. Cale understood—the shadowwalkers fought without weapons.

Cale knew some men could do it, but it took years of training and discipline. Cale decided to be candid with Nayan.

"We are not . . . kind men, Nayan. Do you take my meaning?"

"I know what you are," Nayan said, and held Cale's gaze.

Cale stared into Nayan's face, studied his impassive expression. He had known many killers through the years and all of them had the same cold, dead look in their eyes. Riven had it. Cale had it.

Nayan had it.

Cale nodded and looked to Riven. "They come. All of them."

Riven said to the shadowwalkers, "Get some sleep and prepare your gear. We hit the Hole of Yhaunn tomorrow night."

After they were gone, Riven said, "Looks like they are done waiting, too."

CHAPTER FIFTEEN

11 Uktar, the Year of Lightning Storms

At Vees's urging, Tamlin decided to meet the Shadovar representative unaccompanied by other members of the Old Chauncel.

"The Shadovar prefer quiet negotiations," Vees told him.

Tamlin stood behind a polished conference table in a meeting room in the palace. Magical protections shrouded him, and the chamber itself was screened against scrying and magical transport. Glowballs in the corners of the chamber provided light.

The Shadovar delegation had arrived at twilight by magical means. A score of dark-armored men with wide swords had walked out of the night and entered Selgaunt through its Mountarr Gate. A ceremonial guard of Scepters escorted the delegation through the city's streets, and the dark strangers were the talk of the taverns. Tamlin provided the Shadovar with lodging in the eastern wing of the palace. After allowing them time to get settled, he requested a formal meeting with the Shadovar ambassador, Rivalen Tanthul, a prince of Shade Enclave.

Tamlin did not know what to expect. He had never met with anyone from Shade Enclave, and the stakes could not have been higher. Selgaunt needed assistance from outside of Sembia, or it would fall to the gathering army of the Overmistress. Tamlin, his family, the Old Chauncel, and the nobility of Saerb would all hang as traitors.

He calmed himself by recalling the words his father had oft spoke before important trade meetings: *No matter their station, all men are men.* Tamlin whispered the words to himself as he listened to the approaching footfalls of Rivalen Tanthul.

Vees stood beside him. Both men wore their finest jackets and stiff-collared shirts. A silver tray of sweetmeats, bread, cheese, and two bottles of red wine had been laid out on the table. A banner bearing Selgaunt's arms hung from the ceiling. Tamlin thought the room was lacking in the ceremonial trappings merited by the meeting, but they had done what they could on short notice.

"Here we go," Vees said to him softly. "Their appearance is unusual. Do not let it alarm you."

The door to the chamber opened and Chamberlain Thriistin, dressed in his finest attire, announced the ambassador.

"My Lord Hulorn, I present Rivalen Tanthul, Prince of Shade Enclave, emissary of the Shadovar."

The darkness swirled like mist around Thriistin as a towering figure strode past him into the chamber. Rivalen Tanthul stood only slightly shorter than Mister Cale. Golden eyes shone out of a dark, angular face that featured a large, sharp nose. Long black hair hung loose to his broad shoulders. His drab cloak did not hide the narrow sword at his hip. Darkness alternately clung or flowed from him.

Tamlin realized immediately that Rivalen was a shade, like Mister Cale. He managed to meet and hold the Shadovar's gaze.

"Prince Rivalen," he said, and bowed.

"Hulorn," the Shadovar said, and his deep voice sounded as if it had emerged from the bottom of a well.

Thriistin scurried around Prince Rivalen, poured wine into three goblets, and took his leave.

"Please sit," Tamlin said, and gestured at the comfortable armchair before the table. "And enjoy the food. The wine is from my personal vineyards."

Rivalen walked up to the table but did not sit. He brought the shadows with him and the light in the room dimmed.

"You are gracious, Hulorn," Rivalen said. He lifted the wine and inhaled its bouquet but did not drink.

"I regret the informality of our reception," Tamlin said. "I hope you understand."

"Formality is a crutch for the foolish," Rivalen said, and held up his goblet. "To Selgaunt."

Vees handed Tamlin a goblet. He raised it and said, "To the Shadovar."

"And to a new friendship between us," Rivalen said.

"Indeed," Vees said with enthusiasm.

The three men sat. Vees started the discussion. "It is a pleasure to see you once more, Prince Rivalen. I trust the Talendar stone has met your expectations?"

Rivalen nodded. "It has." He eyed Tamlin. "My Lord Hulorn, I know it is customary for ambassadors to exchange gifts and pleasantries before discussing weighty matters, but I propose—since we are dispensing with formality—that we ignore such trivia and move directly to the point."

Tamlin nodded. He said, "Very well, then. You are a shade."

Vees choked on his wine. "Hulorn, that is—"

Rivalen held up a dusky hand to silence Vees. He wore several rings, all of them silver or platinum and of archaic design. One of them was an amethyst ring not unlike the one favored by Vees.

"That is so," Rivalen said. "In the interest of serving the good of all our citizens, a fortunate few among my people are selected to become shades."

Tamlin could not hide his surprise or keep in his words. "Fortunate? I have heard others describe the transformation as a curse."

Rivalen smiled and Tamlin noticed his fangs for the first time. He presumed they were an affectation but could not be certain. "Only those who do not understand it would so describe it. Where have you heard such a thing?"

Vees cleared his throat and shifted in his seat.

Tamlin hesitated. "I . . . read of it. I have studied what I could of shadow magic. A trifling amount, I assure you."

Rivalen regarded him with a half-smile. "Your reading habits are unusual, Hulorn. I am impressed."

Tamlin could not help himself. He preened. Rivalen continued. "The transformation into a shade is no curse, nor is it painful. It is a blessing. But it demands of its recipient a lifetime of service to the city."

Tamlin well understood the burden of service. "Intriguing."

Rivalen breathed in the wine. "I could arrange for you to learn more. Perhaps a tour of Shade Enclave at some later date?"

"I would like that," Tamlin said, and found that he liked Rivalen Tanthul, liked him a great deal. He seemed . . . certain of himself.

"We were about to discuss weighty matters," Vees offered.

Tamlin dared one more personal question. "You said the transformation demands a lifetime of service. How long is that lifetime? How old are you, Prince Rivalen?"

Vees looked agog. His mouth hung open.

Rivalen's eyes flared but he did not hesitate. "I am nearly two thousand years old."

Tamlin's mouth fell open then. "Two thousand," he said softly. He leaned back in his chair and sipped his wine. To live so long, to be immune to disease, to regenerate wounds. Tamlin well understood how Rivalen could call the transformation a blessing. Mister Cale was a fool.

"I can see you are interested in learning more, Hulorn, and I am pleased by your interest. Most of those we have encountered since our return are small minded about such things. They see darkness and assume evil. Let us plan further discussion of it later. Not as representatives of our governments, but as friends."

Tamlin smiled, quite pleased with the offer.

"I see I needn't have been here to broker anything," Vees said with a laugh. "You two already are boon companions."

Tamlin leaned forward in his chair and decided to be frank. "Prince Rivalen, you are aware of recent events in Sembia?"

Rivalen nodded. "Of course. A most unfortunate turn." He shook his head and looked thoughtful. "It is difficult to know in these days who works for good and who for ill."

"That it is," Vees said sadly. "That it is."

Tamlin could not keep the indignance from his tone. "I assure you that I am no traitor to my nation, Prince Rivalen, if that is what you mean, nor is any noble of Selgaunt. Or of Saerb, for that matter. Mirabeta Selkirk has lied and murdered her way into a civil war so that she can seize and hold power."

Rivalen looked across the table at Tamlin. Shadows swirled around him. Tamlin wanted to quail before the golden eyes but held steady.

"What you describe is consistent with some reports that we have received. The overmistress wishes to be queen, it would seem. I have lived a long time and seen her like before."

"The things some will do for power," Vees said, and shook his head.

Rivalen continued. "But even had I not heard those reports, still I would have believed you. Even our brief exchange here has shown me your measure. You are no traitor."

The words gave Tamlin great satisfaction. He hid his pleasure behind a drink of his wine. "Yes, well . . . I am but one man, and Selgaunt is but one city. We are in need of aid. Military aid."

"If I may be so bold, you are in need of much more than that," Rivalen said. "Your city is overcrowded, filthy, rife with disease and hunger. Your priests hold disease and starvation at bay but for how long? How will they cope with winter, or when the siege begins and their spells are needed for other things?"

Tamlin neither acknowledged nor denied Rivalen's words, though both of them knew the Shadovar spoke truth. Rivalen continued, "The situation in Selgaunt, indeed, in all of Sembia, is dire. I am authorized by my father, the Most High, to offer assistance."

"What form will the assistance you offer take?" Tamlin asked.

"We are a magical people, my lord," Rivalen said, and shadows swirled around him, as if to make his point. "Many powerful priests and wizards work for the betterment of our city. And while the military forces with which we could aid you are not numerous, they are nevertheless formidable, and highly mobile."

Tamlin had no doubt, but he feared the price to be paid.

"What do you ask in exchange?"

Rivalen leaned back in his chair and gestured casually with his hand, as if he were requesting trifles. "I ask that the ties between our people become much closer. I would need a formal treaty between our cities, an embassy in Selgaunt, and an informal position as advisor to the hulorn. We also would request a trade alliance—the specific terms of which would be negotiated, of course—and use of your port for importing and exporting goods. Should the conflict in Sembia turn in favor of Selgaunt—and with Netheril's assistance, I believe it will—we would expect you to advocate a similar arrangement with a few other key cities of the realm."

"Netheril?" Tamlin asked, puzzled. "You mean Shade Enclave."

Rivalen shrugged noncommittally and Tamlin let the issue die. In truth, nothing Rivalen had requested surprised Tamlin, nor did anything cause him concern. The Shadovar could have asked for much more and he would have given it. Tamlin was not in a position to haggle. He said, "We would expect a reciprocal arrangement with regard to the embassy. And the port access would be subject to an annual usage fee, of course."

"Of course," Rivalen said.

Tamlin shared a glance with Vees before saying to Rivalen, "Your offer is not unreasonable, but I would need a show of good faith to take to the Old Chauncel."

"I understand," said Rivalen. "I can arrange for significant amounts of food to be transported into the city. Shadovar troops can have it here in a matter of a few days. At the same time, their presence will bolster your defenses. Would that serve?"

Tamlin was not certain how much he liked the idea of Shadovar troops entering Selgaunt, but the city did need the food.

"That is a start," he said.

"Here is an end, then," said Rivalen. "Vees informed me that you have organized an attempted rescue of Endren Corrinthal, the nobleman of Saerb. He is imprisoned in Yhaunn, I believe."

Tamlin eyed Vees with disapproval, but said to Rivalen, "Vees's tongue is loose, but that is correct."

"We can be of assistance with that as well."

"Indeed? How?"

"I have men who . . ."

Tamlin shook his head. "Out of the question. My agent would not welcome that kind of assistance."

"He is a bit unstable," said Vees.

Rivalen pressed his lips together, thoughtful, and said, "A distraction, then? At the moment of the attack? Surely that would assist your man? And a free Endren helps our cause greatly."

"It would have to be quite a distraction," Tamlin said, half-jesting.

Rivalen smiled and showed his fangs. "As I said, Lord Uskevren, we are a magical people. Yhaunn is allied with Ordulin against you and therefore against Shade Enclave. Consider it the first blow of our new alliance. I will endeavor to make it a memorable one. You need only alert me when the rescue is about to occur. I will see to the rest."

Tamlin nodded and smiled, feeling satisfied. He had made the decision that gave Selgaunt its best chance of survival. He said, "We have reached agreement in principle."

"Excellent," Rivalen said.

"Very good," Vees said.

Rivalen said to Vees, "I understand the temple your family has financed is nearly complete."

Vees nodded. "Indeed. Nearly so. When it is, I would be honored to give you a tour. There are some architectural flourishes that I am sure you will appreciate."

Rivalen nodded in agreement.

"And speaking of a tour," Tamlin said to Rivalen, "I intend to take you up on your offer of a tour of your city, Prince Rivalen."

Rivalen smiled politely. "I shall look forward to it."

❦ ❦ ❦ ❦ ❦

Cale awakened at midnight inside Mask's temple. Shirtless, he sat cross-legged on the floor and prayed to the Shadowlord for power. He also offered his gratitude for the opportunity to truly say goodbye to Jak, to bury him. On the Sembian plains, Mask had whispered to Cale that he was almost there. Cale was all the way there now.

Spells filled Cale's mind, sparked in his brain. Cale knew he would not be able to use the spells in the attack on the Hole, but he would use them before they got in and after they got out.

He remained awake the rest of the night, smoking Jak's pipe. When morning arrived he dressed, checked and rechecked his gear, sharpened his blades, and sought out Riven.

He found him outside in the sun, watching the dogs roll in the grass. The wind off the sea was cool. The dogs noticed Cale, ran over and sniffed him. They whined at the stump of his wrist, but he patted them with his other hand and they licked him in greeting.

Riven and Cale discussed final points of strategy while the dogs played. They would enter quickly and quietly, take a guard alive, and force him to take them to Endren. The Hole did not keep many prisoners, so Endren would not be hard to locate. After they had him, they would get the hells out.

Easy. Except that it would be hard.

In the distance, Cale could see the hilltop where they had buried Jak. Riven followed his gaze.

"We could have used Fleet on this job," Riven said.

Cale nodded. "The shadowwalkers?" he asked.

Riven shook his head. "I only see them at night. They'll be along."

They spent the rest of the day preparing themselves. Cale knew they would have to kill guards to get Endren out. He told himself that it was justified, that he was trying to rescue an innocent man for the greater good of Sembia. But he knew that was a lie. He was prepared to rescue Endren and kill guards because he thought and hoped that it would somehow lead him to Magadon. Mask had promised him that Sembia's plight would lead back to Magadon, and Cale believed the Shadowlord. And if Cale had to kill strangers to get to his friend, he would do it. He would not like it, but he would do it.

Late in the day he and Riven took a meal together. Cale found it strange to be doing something so ordinary with Riven, something friends did together. He was not sure if Riven was his friend, but he knew they understood one another as no one else did, save perhaps Mask himself. If that was not friendship, it was still something Cale appreciated.

Before they finished their meal, a familiar buzzing sounded in Cale's ears—a sending. He tensed, shadows swirled. Tamlin's voice spoke in his mind.

The Shadovar offer a distraction at Yhaunn. When will you make the attempt? My spell allows you to respond. Use fewer than two score words.

Cale frowned, still displeased that Tamlin had taken Vees's advice and made common cause with the Shadovar. He debated whether to respond at all. Riven must have read his expression.

"What is it?" the assassin asked across the table.

"Tamlin Uskevren and the Shadovar are offering to provide a distraction to coincide with our move against the Hole."

Riven's eye narrowed. "The Shadovar? What kind of distraction?"

Cale shook his head. They stared at one another across the table. Both knew the attempt on the Hole was dangerous. A distraction could help.

"Take it," Riven said.

Cale considered, nodded, and responded to Tamlin:

After moonset tonight, he sent, and the buzzing in his ears stopped.

"That will have to be something special to be worth our while," Riven said.

Rivalen Tanthul's voice echoed through the corridors of Ssessimyth's mind.

Swim for Yhaunn. After moonset, destroy the harbor and dock ward.

Ssessimyth knew where Yhaunn lay. He knew the location of most every city on the coast of the Inner Sea, at least those that had existed before he had been bonded to the Source.

Thinking of the Source pained him distantly. He still longed for it. He sometimes felt as though the Source were still bonded to him, still one with his flesh. But he knew the sensation to be a phantom created out of his memories, out of his hopes. Rivalen and his shadowy brothers had magically removed the crystal from his flesh, torn it out in a shower of blood and veins and brain matter and pain.

But Ssessimyth knew it was for the best. Rivalen meant him well.

He undulated, propelled a vast amount of water into and out of his body, and cut through the cold depths. Had he been hunting, he would have kept to the deepest water and knifed surfaceward only after spotting prey, only for the kill. But he was not hunting and he made no effort to disguise his bulk or his passage. The cluster of his tentacles trailed behind him, waving rhythmically with each undulation. The sea cleared out before him. Nothing in the water could challenge him. He was supreme in his domain.

He headed east and north along the Sembian coast. His pace devoured the leagues. He swam silently under ships, and past outposts of sea elves and warbands of tritons. He grew hungry and dived for the depths. He coasted near the bottom, the motion of his body tossing up a churn of sea floor behind him. Whalesong sounded in the distance, a poem of love and loyalty. Ssessimyth swam for it, spotted a mother humpback and her nearly grown calf far above him.

He angled upward for the whales. Before the mother saw him, he was upon her. He rammed his head into her abdomen, whirled, and wrapped his tentacles about her body and squeezed. He was ten times her weight; she had no chance. She spun in his grasp, sang in terror, but could not escape his strangling hold. She grew exhausted quickly and issued a single command to her offspring.

Flee!

The calf sped off into the deeps, singing despair for its mother. Ssessimyth allowed the calf to escape and held the mother in the net of his arms until she suffocated. He devoured her, tearing off huge chunks of her flesh in his beak. Blood and fragments drifted toward the sea bottom but scavengers did not approach. They would wait until Ssessimyth departed.

After he completed his meal and let the humpback female's bones sink to the bottom, he sped for Yhaunn. As he approached, he twisted his tentacles into an arcane arrangement and recited the words to a spell known to all of his kind. Magical energy went forth from him and sped surfaceward to summon a storm.

An hour later he breached the surface. Clouds blocked the stars and a cold winter rain pounded the sea. The rain cooled the warmer waters near the surface. Cool water better allowed Ssessimyth to control his buoyancy. In the distance, he spotted through the rain the cluster of lights that was Yhaunn.

He sped toward the harbor, gaining speed as he went.

After sunset, Nayan and his shadowwalkers returned. When the darkness grew deep, Cale, Riven, Nayan, and the shadowwalkers rode the night into an alley within the walls of Yhaunn.

Wind-whipped rain thumped against their cloaks, so cold it was nearly sleet. The group pulled up their hoods and stepped out of the alley and onto a main thoroughfare.

Two- and three-story wooden buildings with steeply-pitched tile roofs lined the paved street, crammed so closely together they fairly melded into one long structure that ran the length of the block. Streams of the city's effluvium raced down the city's open sewer channels on either side of the street. The downpour slicked the stone.

The late hour and freezing rain left no passersby on the street. A few wheelbarrows dotted the walks, and an unhappy horse, soaked and shivering, stood tied to a hitching post outside a shuttered inn. Lights burned in a few second-story windows. Lanterns hung from hooked poles that lined the avenue. The rain had put out several. The others shook in the wind.

A boy holding an oversized cloak over his head darted out of an alley and untied the horse from its hitch. Cale and his companions sank into darkness out of habit and the boy never noticed them.

"Here," the boy said to the horse, and pulled the recalcitrant animal down the alley.

They continued down the street until they reached a plaza that featured a bronze statue of a wizard in the midst of casting a spell. Sleet glazed the statue's outstretched arm and hand. From the plaza, Cale got a good look at the whole of the city.

Yhaunn lay in the bottom of a shallow, sloped quarry, not unlike an immense bowl. The city was sectioned into tiers built in stages down the quarry's slope like giant steps leading downward to the sea. Walled earthen ramps bridged the tiers. At the bottom of the city stood the deepwater harbor, the piers, and the ramshackle buildings of the poor. Ships crowded the piers and despite the rain and hour, Cale could see several forms moving along the piers in quivering lantern light. Beyond the piers the Inner Sea stretched into the distance, dark and foreboding.

The tall towers and mansions of the wealthy stood atop the highest tier. From that lofty perch the rich were afforded a pleasant view of the sea and a less pleasant view of their less fortunate citizens. Yhaunn's buildings, even its noble mansions, did not show the architectural variety of Selgaunt. Most were square with a rounded turret or two, and all featured the pale limestone that once was pulled out of the quarry.

Between the two extremes of the mansions and wharves stood the cramped wood-and-brick forest of buildings in which lived Yhaunn's laborers, traders, craftsmen, and artists. A four-domed mansion in the center of the city and the tall, magically-lit spires of a guildhouse just above the wharves created a meager skyline.

The city gave Cale the impression of being overstuffed, of overflowing its bowl. The buildings sprawled over every square of ground within the quarry and crawled up the sides.

Cale turned and looked behind them. Overlooking the noble manses, and built not within the quarry but on top of its cliff wall, stood the Roadkeep—Yhaunn's treasury, barracks, and gaol. A ramp of piled earth and crushed stone led down from the Roadkeep into Yhaunn. No traffic moved upon it. The night was too old, the sleet too heavy.

Cale knew they would find the Hole under the Roadkeep. He led his team through the city, walking the shadows to avoid using the ramps that led from one tier to the next.

They moved quickly and reached the highest tier of the city. The wide earthen ramp that led up to the brooding spires and walls of the Roadkeep lay before them. Torches and lanterns burned on the Roadkeep's walls. Cale saw a few soaked Watchblades—Yhaunn's guardsmen—walking the walls. The cliff face fell away beneath the castle. At its bottom lay what Cale assumed to be the Hole.

The Hole stood on one side of the ramp that led up to the Roadkeep, against the northwestern wall of the quarry. From the outside, the entrance to the political prison appeared as little more than a fortified stone box built against the cliff face. The mine entrance must have lay within, leading down into the quarry. A portcullis was the structure's only means of ingress. A handful of Yhaunn's Watchblades guarded it. All wore weathercloaks and a signal horn. Cale had no doubt that many other guards were stationed down in the mine.

The clouds hid the moon, but Cale assumed moonset to be near.

"Let's get into position," he said over the hiss of the sleet.

Gravel and loose stone covered the area around the small stone building. A few heaps of cast off stone and rubble provided cover.

Cale pointed, his team nodded, and all of them walked the night to an area behind one of the heaps.

"We wait," Cale said.

The shadowwalkers, still holding their silence, sat cross-legged on the ground and closed their eyes. The rain and cold seemed not to bother them. Cale presumed they were meditating. It reminded him of Magadon, which reminded him of his purpose.

Riven peeked at the mine over the heap of loose stone. "This is no dwarven delve," he said. "It can't be that deep. We'll be in and out quickly."

Cale nodded. He joined Riven in eyeing the structure. Five

guards leaned casually on their halberds, their hoods pulled low against the weather.

"Where does magic stop working?" he asked Riven.

Riven shook his head. "I do not know."

Cale decided to learn what he could. He held his mask in his hand and intoned the words to a simple spell that allowed him to see magic. The shadowwalkers opened their eyes and crowded around him as he cast. The mask tattoos on their faces gave them a sinister appearance.

When the spell was complete, Cale perceived a glowing aura around enchanted items. Cloaks, rings, earrings, amulets, boots, and gloves worn by the shadowwalkers glowed in his sight, as did Riven's blades, his armor, a gold ring on his left hand, and two or three small items in a belt pouch.

Cale looked over the stone at the guards. Two of the guards bore swords that glowed. The portcullis, too, showed enchantment. Magic functioned at least up to that gate. Cale informed his team and all nodded. They waited for the distraction the Shadovar had promised.

A rumble shook the city. At first Cale mistook it for thunder. He looked up but realized the sound came not from the sky but from near the docks. Shouts and screams followed, audible even over the sleet. The sound of snapping wood and crashing stone carried through the city.

Cale, Riven, and the shadowwalkers rose to their feet, looking toward the docks. In the heavy rain, they could see little.

More shouting, screams, rending stone, snapping wood. The entire city shook.

"What in the Hells is happening down there?" Riven said.

Cale was curious, too, but resisted the impulse to view the docks. Instead, he waited for an opportunity to attack.

Above them, the guards on the walls of the Roadkeep pointed down at the docks. Pairs of armed men on horses thundered down the ramp, shouting. Cale could not make out their words. More and more shouts sounded, screams, the rumble of crashing stone.

The guards before the Hole's portcullis shared nervous glances. They shouted something to an unseen comrade within the stone structure and one finally sped off in the direction of Cale and his team. Cale, Riven, and the shadowwalkers melted into the shadows and the man passed by without noticing them.

Another impact sounded and the ground vibrated under their feet. Cale waited for the guards at the entrance of the Hole to abandon their posts, but it appeared they would not budge.

"It's not going to get any better," Cale said to Riven, who nodded. Whatever the Shadovar had done, they had to take advantage. The rest of the city appeared occupied, at least.

"I will get inside," Cale said. "Clean up those outside."

Riven nodded. Nayan nodded.

Cale wrapped himself in the night, turned invisible, and charged the Hole. The guards did not see him and he shadowstepped within the structure. The entryway opened onto a hallway that lead to a watch station fitted out with wooden chairs and several tables. A dozen or so guards stood about, sat, or chatted. Cale could see that the noise outside had interrupted some gambling—loose coins and playing cards lay scattered on two of the tables. All eyes—tired eyes—focused on the portcullis. They looked right through Cale.

A swinging iron gate stood at the back of the room. It opened onto a large, archway-shaped hole in the cliff face—the entrance of the mine. Lanterns lit it and Cale could see that it was not a vertical shaft. It was a sloped tunnel that led downward.

Using his magic-finding spell, Cale checked the men for magical gear. Several items glowed in his sight. The gate to the mine did not, however, and Cale wondered if the gate denoted not only the entrance to the mine but the point at which magic ceased working.

"Phraig," a bearded guardsman said to a younger man. "Go see what in Helm's name is happening."

Cale flattened himself against the wall as Phraig hurried past him, then caused the darkness to eat the light in the room. It turned pitch, though Cale could see through it clearly.

"What the—?"

The men leaped to their feet and drew weapons. Fatigue made their movements awkward, imprecise. Cale moved among them, unseen, silent, the perfect killer.

"Back to back," shouted the bearded man.

"I can't see to go back to back," answered another.

Outside at the portcullis, Cale could hear the shadowwalkers and Riven battling the guards.

Phraig drew his blade and shouted a belated alarm.

"We are attacked!"

Cale moved behind his first kill and raised Weaveshear. He stared at the back of the guardsman's throat . . . and hesitated.

Recalling his promise to Jak, he reversed his grip on Weaveshear and slammed the hilt into the head of one guard, then another, then another. They fell hard to the floor, collapsing in a heap of armor and the clatter of dropped weapons. Cale could not be certain that all of them would live—he'd had to hit them hard to ensure unconsciousness—but surely most of them would.

Outside, Cale could hear fists thumping into flesh, men grunting, crying out.

Cale dodged a few wild swings taken blindly in the dark, but his work was easy. The guards were men-at-arms of limited experience. Cale and Riven could have cleared the room almost as easily even if they had walked in and announced themselves. In moments, he had all of them down except Phraig, who stood with his back against the wall, panting with fear, blade held before him.

"Belum? Corz? Who still stands?" Phraig called.

Cale moved silently beside Phraig and put Weaveshear to the young man's throat. "Be still or you will die."

The young man gave a start. His brown eyes were wide in the dark. His lip trembled and he lowered his blade. Sweat pasted his brown hair to his forehead. Cale let the light return and Phraig's eyes went wider still when he saw all his fellows down and only one other man in the room.

"Open the portcullis," Cale said to him.

"No need," Riven called.

The shadowwalkers appeared around Cale and Phraig, stepping out of the darkness.

Phraig gasped at their sudden appearance. Riven, too, winked into existence. Cale questioned Riven with his surprised eyes.

Riven pointed at the gold ring on his left hand. "From the Sojourner. Works a few times per day. How else could I get supplies to the island, Cale? I've a few other items, too."

Phraig eyed the shadowwalkers' tattooed faces, the disc Riven wore at his neck.

"You're priests of Mask," he said.

"Endren Corrinthal," Cale said. "Take us to him."

Fear in his eyes, Phraig said, "I don't know where he is."

Cale saw the lie. So did Riven, it seemed.

Riven stepped before him. "Lie again and I will split you, boy. Clear?"

Phraig looked into Riven's face and must have seen the seriousness in the assassin's eye.

"I know where he is."

Riven nodded, looked around the room. He saw that Cale had left the guards alive. Cale expected a rebuke, but Riven simply said to Nayan, "Bind them."

The assassin had vowed to help Cale keep his promise to Jak. It appeared he would.

The shadowwalkers each produced rope from their packs and rapidly bound the guards.

"This one is dead," said Nayan, holding the body of one of the guards.

"And this one," said Dahtem.

Cale cursed. Phraig softly spoke the names of his fallen comrades.

"Corz and Draeg. He was just married three months ere."

Cale said nothing, nor did Riven. The shadowwalkers left the dead where they lay and arranged the rest along one of the walls. None of the guards stirred throughout the process. Cale had put them out cold.

"Asir has the key to the mine gate," Phraig said, indicating one of the guards near Nayan. The shadowwalker skillfully rifled the guardsman's pouches and pockets, collected the key from a pouch, and tossed it to Cale, who threw it to Riven.

"Let's move," Cale said, putting the dead guardsmen behind him.

The moment Riven placed the key in the mine gate, a sound carried from outside, a shriek so loud it froze them all, a shriek that Cale had heard once before. Shadows boiled from his flesh. The hairs on the nape of his neck rose. He put his hand over Riven's and prevented him from turning the key.

"What?" Riven said.

"Wait here," Cale said. "Right here."

Heart pounding, hopeful and fearful, he shadowstepped past the portcullis, past the dead guards outside, and into the city. He scanned the skyline, selected the first tall building he saw, and walked the darkness to the roof of a three-story inn. From there, he looked down at the docks, at chaos.

The fleshy gray mound of the kraken's enormous body fairly filled the harbor, displacing so much water and mud that the lower tier of the city had flooded. The whole dock ward was little more than a soup of bodies, broken ships, and destroyed buildings. The beast must have swum into the harbor at full speed and run itself partially aground on the docks. Tentacles flailed through the city streets, toppling buildings, crushing people and animals. The gash in its head—the open wound in which the Source had once lay—had scarred to a thick rubbery line. The Source was gone.

Panicked citizens thronged the streets, rushing up Yhaunn's slope for higher ground. At the same time, groups of Watchblades tried to move down the slope and control the chaos. Others fired crossbows into the kraken. It was like throwing pebbles at a dragon.

The earthen ramps that led from one tier to the next filled with terrified people. The low stone walls that lined the edges of the ramps did not prevent the mob from forcing a few people over to fall to their deaths.

At the harbor, a trio of wizards zipped about in the air above the kraken, raining fire, lightning, and glowing bolts of energy onto its body. The spells seemed not to trouble the gargantuan creature. Groups of armed men, wizards, and priests gathered here and there and started down the slopes. The city was organizing its defenses rapidly.

For Cale, all the connections suddenly fell into place, all Mask's words. The Shadovar commanded the kraken and the kraken was no longer bonded to the Source. The Shadovar therefore had the Source. For what purpose, Cale could only guess. And only one man alive had previously contacted the Source and lived—Magadon. Mask had told Cale that Sembia's fate was tied to Magadon. Tamlin had thrown in with the Shadovar.

But there was more.

The kraken shrieked again and the sound sent hundreds of panicked people roiling forward. Cale saw many citizens cowering on rooftops, swimming through the debris.

He turned to go back to the Hole—he still had to get Endren out—but stopped. He watched another building topple, watched a woman get crushed between a floating timber and the side of a building.

He had to help.

He shadowstepped to the entrance of the Hole. Riven had the gate open. Skelan was eyeing the passage.

"Magic doesn't work beyond the gate," Riven said, then noticed Cale's expression. "What is it?"

"The Shadovar have Magadon," Cale said to Riven.

Riven's eye narrowed. "The Shadovar? How do you know?"

"The kraken is destroying the city. The Source is gone."

The words took a moment to register with Riven. "The gods-damned kraken? Dark and empty!" He looked into Cale's face. "Let's go have a chat with these Shadovar."

Cale nodded. "Afterward. We get Endren first. How many men do you need?"

Outside, the kraken's shriek again split the night. The whole city shook under its onslaught. Cale got a disturbing mental image of all of Yhaunn sliding down the quarry's slope and sinking into the sea, just as Sakkors had slid off its floating mountaintop to lie in a heap.

"What do you mean?" Riven asked. "What are you going to do?"

The shadowwalkers watched them closely.

"Help get some people out of the way of that monster," Cale said. "How many do you need to get Endren?"

Riven stared for a moment at Cale, then turned to Phraig and grabbed him by the shirt. "How many guards are down there, you little pissdrip?"

Phraig stuttered, finally managed, "A score and a half."

"How far is Endren?"

"Not far," Phraig said.

"Not far and thirty guards," Riven said, considering. "Leave me half."

Cale nodded. "Nayan—you, Erynd, and Dahtem are with me." To Riven and the shadowwalkers, Cale said, "Kill only if you must."

Riven frowned.

"Only if you must," Cale repeated.

Riven looked into his eyes and nodded.

"If we are not out in half an hour . . ." Riven started.

"We'll come in after you," Cale finished.

"If we're not out in a half-hour, there won't be anything to come after."

Cale nodded, and the First and Second clasped forearms. Then Cale, Erynd, Dahtem, and Nayan moved through the shadows to perch on nearby rooftops. From there, they got a full view of the destruction.

Squads of Watchblades rolled ballistae down the streets, forcing them through the ocean of terrified citizens, trying to get a shot at the kraken. Meanwhile, more than a dozen wizards flew in the air above the harbor, firing destructive energy at the creature. Entire platoons of Watchblades perched on the edge of one of the lower tiers, firing clouds of crossbow bolts.

The huge creature shrieked again and the entire city rumbled. A tower collapsed in a pile of dust and falling stone. Two tentacles rose into the air, flailing for the wizards. The enormous limb struck a wizard and he spun into the harbor, broken and lifeless.

"Pull out any trapped citizens," Cale said, pointing at stranded women, children, and men cowering on rooftops or in alleys. "Get them to higher ground."

Nayan looked at him, a puzzlement in his dark eyes. "That is not our way," he said.

"It is now," Cale replied. "Do it."

The shadowwalkers nodded, and all four men rode the shadows down to the harbor.

Riven put a punch dagger against Phraig's back.

"Do you have a wife, boy?" Riven asked him.

Phraig hesitated, but a prod of the blade elicited a nod.

"Here it is, then. We're going to move fast. You're going to tell anyone we see that everything is fine. That will keep you alive for your wife. You say anything I don't like or slow us down and my steel finds your kidney. You'll bleed to death in less than a thirty-count. Your wife will grieve for a while but she's probably a young woman. She'll find another husband while you rot in the ground."

Phraig looked Riven in the face, defeat in his eyes.

"Understood?" Riven asked.

"Understood," answered Phraig in dull tone.

Riven knew his team's survival depended entirely on speed and surprise. He intended to leave the guards in the mine no time to think, no time to plan.

"Let's go," Riven said to his group.

The moment they stepped through the gate, Riven felt something go out of him. The feeling may have been of his own invention, but he knew that magic no longer functioned.

The tunnel descended at an increasingly steep angle. Wooden timbers reinforced the ceiling. The widely spaced lanterns hanging on the walls left alternating patches of darkness and dim light.

"Two in front of us, two behind us, along the walls," Riven said to the shadowwalkers. "Stay dark."

He had seen the shadowwalkers operate. With or without magic, they were the best he'd ever seen in wearing the night.

Shadem and Vyrhas hugged the wall to his right, Dynd and Skelan to his left. As he expected, they merged with the darkness of the corridor. Their footfalls made no sound.

Riven prodded Phraig with the dagger and they moved double-quick down the corridor. The shadowwalkers led them, invisible as ghosts.

"No surprises," Riven whispered to Phraig.

The young guardsman nodded. "There's a drop shaft ahead, with a lift. It . . . it's guarded."

"How many?" Riven asked.

"Two," Phraig said.

"Shadem, Vyrhas," Riven said. "Take them down. They live, if possible."

Ordinarily, Riven would leave no one alive behind him. But he had made Cale a promise, and as much as he disliked it, he intended to keep it. He clutched his saber in his fist. Its missing magic made the otherwise enchanted blade feel heavier than usual. He made no effort to mask the sound of his approach. Ahead, he could see that the tunnel opened onto a larger chamber.

"Talk, boy," he whispered to Phraig.

"Two coming down," Phraig called.

Riven hustled Phraig down the tunnel. It opened onto an irregular, rough-hewn chamber with a large hole in the center of its floor. A low stone wall circled the hole and a four-legged frame of timbers straddled it. Thick hemp lines hung from pulleys set into the frame, directly above the shaft. Riven guessed the lines to be attached to a lift at the bottom of the shaft.

Two guards with tired eyes stood near the lift mechanism. Chain hauberks draped their fat bodies. Blades hung at their belts. Their helms lay on the stone wall at the edge of the lift. Both looked curiously at Riven as he and Phraig walked into their view.

"Well met," Riven said, as disarmingly as he could manage. He prodded Phraig and the boy said, "Birg, Nilmon, this is—"

Shadem and Vyrhas stepped out from behind the men. Each grabbed a man in an armhold around the throat and leaned back to lift them off the ground. The guards did not so much as gag. Their legs kicked, and their eyes went wide as the shadowwalkers choked them into unconsciousness.

"Well done," Riven said.

"Gods," Phraig said softly.

Riven knew the guards would not remain unconscious for long. He left Phraig for a moment and smacked each man in the temple with the hilt of his dagger. That would keep them down for a time.

"How many at the bottom?" he asked Phraig.

Skelan and Dynd looked down the shaft.

"Uh, another two, at least," Phraig said. "And . . ."

Riven heard the hesitation in the boy's tone and knew Phraig had not told them everything. He stalked over to Phraig and held the punch dagger before his face.

"Speak it, boy."

"I may have . . . misspoken when I said there were only thirty guards."

Riven's eye narrowed. "How many?"

"Twice that," Phraig said, and winced as if he expected a blow.

Riven almost gave it to him. Instead, he looked to Shadem, Vyrhas, Dynd, and Skelan. None of them looked concerned. They were in it all the way. He liked them more and more.

Riven turned back to Phraig. "Sixty men? Even at this hour?"

"At all hours," Phraig answered. "The Nessarch is well paid to ensure that no one escapes. This duty pays the guards double their usual draw. We choose lots to see who'll get it each month. I'm lucky to have the work."

Riven's anger rose and he could not keep it from his face. Phraig blanched.

"You feel good about being part of this, boy?" Riven said. "Enslaving these men? Working them until they die?"

Phraig's eyes looked everywhere but Riven's face. "Slaves? No. I am . . . I mean, I'm just doing my job."

Riven sneered and pricked Phraig's cheek with the dagger. The boy recoiled, bleeding. "Me, too. Is this lift the only way in or out?"

The boy nodded, dabbing at his cheek. "There used to be others, but they were sealed off."

Riven said, "Guards at the bottom, what else?"

Phraig answered so fast Riven knew he was not lying. "The barracks, mess, and supply rooms are in the large, finished tunnel to the right. The cells are to the left. They will not be guarded at this hour. The prisoners are chained within them. The rest of the tunnels are for mining."

"How many prisoners?" Riven asked.

"A dozen, maybe," Phraig said. "They don't last long. Every tenday some new ones walk in and some old ones are carried out."

Riven glared at him. "Just doing your job, right?"

Phraig looked away and made no answer.

Riven considered having his team scale the shaft but felt it unwise to put his whole team at risk for a fall. He said to Dynd and Skelan, "We need the lift."

The two shadowwalkers nodded in understanding. Both stepped atop the low wall, leaped out to take hold of the ropes, and shinnied down. Vyrhas and Shadem stepped up and looked over the edge of the platform. Riven and Phraig joined them.

Dynd and Skelan slid rapidly, silently, little more than black smears in the darkness.

Dim light from the bottom showed that the shaft descended perhaps two bowshots straight down. Riven had no idea how the original miners had sunk such a shaft. The ropes fell like plumb lines to a winch inset into the wooden lift that sat at the shaft's bottom.

About three-quarters of the way down, Dynd and Skelan swung toward the wall, released the rope, and fell. Phraig gasped. Riven cursed. But both used their hands and feet against the wall to control their otherwise precipitous descent. They landed atop the platform with a hollow thump.

Riven heard a curse from below and the two shadowwalkers bounded out of sight.

A shout of alarm was cut short and the light trickling up the shaft flickered as men fought in the torchlight. The dull thud of fists and elbows finding flesh and the chink of armor sounded up the shaft.

Silence.

Vyrhas and Shadem shared a look and started over the edge of the shaft, but Dynd reappeared on the lift. He examined the winch for a moment and started to crank. The mechanism clinked with every turn of the crank arm. Riven winced at the sound.

It seemed to take a lifetime before Dynd got the lift up the shaft. The winch cylinder was geared to allow even a single man to lift a heavily loaded platform.

"Well done," Riven said to Dynd. "Skelan?"

"Below. He lives," answered Dynd.

Riven, Phraig, and the three shadowwalkers climbed onto the lift and Dynd cranked them downward. When they reached the bottom, they found Skelan crouched over three guards. He was bleeding from a wound on his arm and a scratch on his face. The guards' helms and blades lay scattered on the ground. From the angles of their necks, Riven knew the guards were dead. Skelan held a finger to his lips for silence and pointed past them down the tunnel.

Riven turned to see a long, wide corridor, well lit with torches, extending into the distance. He could hear snatches of conversation coming from down the hall. He leaned in close to Phraig and said, "Even a croak I don't like and you die. Take me to Endren."

The guard nodded, fearful, and led them down the damp, cramped corridor. There was no light, so Riven removed a bronze sunrod from his pack and struck it on the ground. Its tip, treated with an alchemical substance, burst into light as bright as a candle.

The damp air got in his lungs and tickled his throat but he held down the cough. "Same as above," he said to the shadowwalkers. "Get on the walls ahead of us. Move, boy."

The shadowwalkers vanished as they hustled through low, timber-reinforced passages that stank of loam, stagnant water, and some pungent indefinable odor. Phraig led them first left, then right. They reached a corridor that looked newer and less meticulous than the rest of the mine.

A score or more wooden doors with small barred windows dotted the corridor. The stink of vomit, piss, waste, and rot hung in the air.

Two hulking half-orcs with axes lunged from a side corridor with a snarl. They wore leather jacks and skullcaps.

Riven shoved Phraig to the ground, sidestepped a downward chop that would have severed his arm at the shoulder, and slashed open the half-orc's throat. Blood sprayed but the creature kept his feet and swung backhand at Riven's head. He ducked under the blow and stabbed the half-orc through the chest with his saber. The creature expired on his blade, snorting blood. Riven drove his punch dagger into the creature's temple, just to be sure.

Meanwhile, Dynd, Vyrhas, and Skelan emerged from the darkness and unleashed a flurry of kicks, elbows, fists, and throws that disarmed the half-orc, broke his jaw, shattered a rib, and finally crushed his windpipe.

Riven grabbed Phraig by the scruff of his neck and jerked him to his feet.

"I don't give second chances, boy," he said, and raised the punch dagger.

"No! I didn't know! The half-orcs are jailors. I assumed they stayed with the guards at night, not near the cells. I didn't know."

Riven gritted his teeth and controlled his desire to kill the boy. None of his team had been hurt. He let Phraig go.

Coughs sounded from behind the cell doors, and a few moans.

"Which is Endren's?" Riven asked.

Phraig pointed at a door about halfway down the corridor.

"Get the keys off those," Riven said to Vyrhas, pointing at the dead half-orcs, each of whom bore a large ring of keys at his belt.

They hurried to Endren's cell, tried a few keys until they found the right one, and opened the door.

Endren Corrinthal looked up at them, bleary-eyed, blinking in the light of Riven's sunrod. Filth covered him. He wore only a frayed tunic and leather breeches. Sores and bruises covered his exposed skin. Circles shadowed his eyes. An unkempt gray beard sprouted from his cheeks. A rusty iron manacle ringed his left wrist and a thick chain attached the manacle to a ring in the wall. A tin plate lay near his feet. A puddle of rancid water was near enough that he could drink from it.

"Who are you?" he croaked, and the question ended in a fit of coughing. Endren couldn't have been in the Hole more than a few days and already looked near death.

"We're taking you out of here," said Riven.

"Out? Out?" Endren leaned forward, the chain rattling. "Did my son send you?"

"No. Shadem, Vyrhas, get him free." To Endren, Riven said, "Be still and quiet."

Shadem and Vyrhas hurried into the small cell and examined Endren's manacle. The half-orcs' keys didn't work. They pulled a pouch of pries, pliers, files, and picks from their pockets and set to the lock.

"Me, too," moaned a voice from across the hall. "Me, too."

"Silence," Riven barked, but it did no good.

Another voice joined the first, and another. Soon voices in every cell were pleading to be rescued, coughing and moaning.

"There is no more time," Riven said to Shadem. "Can you get it?"

Shadem looked back at Riven and shook his head.

A shout sounded from somewhere down the hall, then a cry of alarm. Someone must have found the guards at the bottom of the lift.

Riven cursed.

"Cut it," Endren said.

"What?"

"Cut it," the old man repeated. "I would have done it myself if I'd had a blade. Cut the damned thing off."

Riven did not hesitate. "Tear me off some cloth to use as a tourniquet."

Shadem ripped strips from his cloak. Together, they tied off Endren's forearm as best they could.

"Prepare yourself," Riven said.

Endren laid his wrist over the block and stared into Riven's eye, unflinching.

"Do it."

Riven chopped downward and severed Endren's hand at the wrist. The old man gritted his teeth and grunted. Blood spurted from the stump. Skelan stanched it with a piece of his cloak.

Riven and Skelan lifted Endren to his feet. The old man was already a shade paler. Riven did not know how long he would last.

"We go."

The shouts in the hall were joined by the tramp of booted feet, the chink of armor. The prisoners continued to moan and plead.

Riven, Phraig, Endren, and the shadowwalkers emerged from the cell and hurried down the corridor. From the direction of the lift, they heard the sound of voices, the tramp of boots, the ring of armor. A whistle sounded, ringing off the walls.

"Shadem, check it."

The shadowwalker disappeared into the darkness toward the voices. Riven and the rest of the team waited a twenty count and Shadem reappeared.

"Two score armed men," he said. "They stand between us and the lift. They are moving methodically and quickly, with a lot of light. There is no way to hide from them."

Riven knew they could not fight their way through, not with Endren.

"Where else?" he said to Phraig.

The young guardsman shook his head. "There is nowhere else. The rest of it is work tunnels for the prisoners. None of them lead out."

"Where do they lead?"

"Nowhere. Most of them are dead ends. The Nessarch doesn't care if the prisoners produce any ore. They're just here to work until they die."

"Most of them are dead ends? What are the rest?"

"What?"

"You said most of them lead nowhere. If I die here, boy, you'll go with me. Think!"

Phraig must have heard the truth in Riven's words, for his eyes showed fear. The shouts from the approaching guards were drawing closer.

"Now, boy!"

"There's a shaft at the end of the northwest work tunnel. It's old. No one knows how deep it is."

"We go," Riven said. He would figure something out when they got there.

A shout from behind them said, "Here they are! Here!"

Riven whirled to see a half-elf in the tabard of a Watchblade pointing at them and shouting over his shoulder. He bore a blade but no torch.

Riven flung his punch dagger—awkwardly, since the weapon was not balanced for throwing—and struck the half-elf in the thigh. The guard grunted and turned to run, but Skelan ran him down, knocked him over, and while the man shouted to his comrades, broke his neck with a hard twist.

But the damage was done. Riven could hear the guards approaching. The light from their lanterns fell on the walls.

"Move!" Riven said.

"He is unconscious," Vyrhas said.

Riven cursed and checked the old man's body. He was alive but there was no way they would escape carrying his unconscious form.

"You cannot make it out," Phraig said.

Riven's glare shut the boy up. "We need time," Riven said to the shadowwalkers.

They understood. Skelan said, "I will give you some. Go."

The shadowwalker took a position at the intersection of the tunnels and melded with the darkness. He had not even frowned at the idea of sacrificing himself.

Riven did not like it, but there was little else to do.

"Lead us, boy," he said to Phraig, and drew his other saber. "Fast."

Vyrhas bore Endren. Riven and his team rushed through the corridors. His saber kept Phraig at a run. They darted down corridors, Riven's light leading the way. The remaining shadowwalkers moved in front of them and behind.

After a few moments, they heard shouts and the sound of combat behind them. Riven froze, turned. The chink of steel, the shout of men. He almost ordered his whole team back to rescue Skelan, but thought better of it.

"Keep moving," he said. He did not intend for the sacrifice to be in vain.

They reached a rough-hewn work tunnel. The sounds of combat had faded but the shouts and bootstomps had not. The guards were still after them.

A few mining tools lay scattered about and loose rock dotted the floor. At the end of the corridor, a hole in the floor opened like a mouth. They approached it cautiously, gasping, sweating.

Riven pointed his sunrod down the shaft. No bottom was visible. He dropped the rod and it fell and fell. After a time, its light vanished.

"They say the miners found it when they constructed the mine," Phraig said. "They say it leads to the Underdark."

Riven ignored the boy. "Can you climb with him?" he asked Vyrhas, the largest and strongest of the shadowwalkers.

"Yes," Vyrhas said. "But not fast."

Riven knew the guards would not follow them down the shaft. They would follow it to the bottom and find a way out from there. Perhaps magic would function farther down in the mine, making escape easy.

"Start downward," he said to his team. To Phraig, he said, "This is where it ends for you, boy."

The young guardsman held up his hands. "No. I did what you asked."

"Just doing my job," Riven said, and brandished his saber.

Phraig would have run but Dynd blocked his retreat. "Don't!" the boy gasped.

Riven held his saber before the young man's face. "Those words are scant comfort when you're on the wrong end of them, aren't they?"

Before Phraig could reply, Riven slammed his pommel into Phraig's cheek. The boy fell like a sack of turnips. Riven hoped the boy would rethink his course when he awakened. He did not mind killing or worse, but he despised anyone who purported to do so only because it was their job.

Shouts sounded from down the corridor. Light bobbed from lanterns. He lowered himself over the edge of the shaft and started down after the shadowwalkers.

Cale materialized atop a two-story building. The entire first floor was flooded. The kraken's body filled his vision, filled the harbor, filled the city. It shrieked and the sound nearly knocked him flat. More fire and lightning fell from the wizards flying overhead.

Cale spotted a woman and two adolescent children, a boy and a girl, perched atop the steep roof of a three-story shop. Cale could not save everything, but he could save something, and would. He stepped through the shadows and materialized in their midst.

The woman screamed and the children recoiled.

"There is nothing to fear," Cale said as the kraken shrieked and destroyed a building across the street. Shouts from all around, screams. The kraken shrieked again.

Cale stepped near the family, pulled the shadows about them, and stepped through the darkness to the uppermost tier of the city.

Before the stunned woman and her children could do anything more than marvel, he shadowstepped back to the building on which he had found the family and looked about for others trapped by the kraken's rampage. A block away, one of the kraken's tentacles wrapped around a spire, flexed, and pulled it down.

Cale spotted an elderly man struggling in the churning water. He walked the darkness to him. The man grabbed at him in a panic, taking them both under. Cale pushed him away, surfaced, and used the shadows to move them both to safety.

The man, soaked and shaking, said in a trembling voice, "The gods bless you."

And so it went for a half-hour that felt like a lifetime. While the Watchblades, wizards, and priests of Yhaunn fought the kraken, managed the panic, and tried to save their city, Cale pulled more than two score citizens from the creature's path, and the shadow-walkers did likewise. Throughout, Cale kept an eye on the Hole, waiting for Riven.

"Come on," he said, willing Riven to emerge. "Come on."

Voices sounded at the top of the shaft. Lantern light trickled down. Riven and the shadowwalkers froze in silence, tried to merge with the stone.

The beam from a lantern shone down the shaft, scoured the sides. It fell on Riven, on the shadowwalkers.

"There!" said a voice. "There!"

More shouts and the twang of crossbows. A bolt skipped off the stone near Riven. Another. One sank into Dynd's thigh. He grunted with pain, slipped, but held his perch.

"Faster," Riven said. "Faster!"

But he knew they were too slow. Endren was slowing Vyrhas and the smooth walls made climbing difficult. The crossbows continued to sing. Bolts skittered off the walls. Head-sized chunks of rock joined them, crashing and bouncing down the shaft's sides. One clipped Dynd on the shoulder. He lost his grip and started to fall but Shadem grabbed him by the wrist and planted his hand on the stone. Both men slipped a body length, but both steadied themselves.

More rocks fell, coming like rain. One whizzed by Riven so close he felt the wind of its passage. Another shower of bolts whizzed around their heads.

"You're all dead men!" shouted one of the guards, and the rest laughed.

Riven could not argue the point. They were dead if they kept climbing. And they had no other choice.

Riven steadied his footing, steadied his heart, and took his magical knife from his belt pouch. The magic it held usually caused its edges to glow red, but it lay dark in his hand, inert in the magic-dead Hole.

"Let go," he shouted to the shadowwalkers.

They eyed him across the shaft, their tattooed faces dark in the lantern light from above.

More bolts sizzled down the shaft. One nicked Vyrhas. He grunted with pain. Endren slipped, but Vyrhas held him.

"If it's deep enough, the magic may work before we hit bottom. I'll use my ring. You use the shadows. It's all we have."

The shadowwalkers shared a look, nodded.

Riven pushed himself away from the wall and went into a free-fall. The air roared past his ears and he plummeted downward into darkness. He held his holy symbol in his right hand, the dagger in his left, willing its dark blade to spark back to life.

From somewhere far below, he saw a dim light. His sunrod. The bottom.

He cursed as the bottom rushed up and his dagger blade began to shine.

Cale saw Riven's team materialize out of the shadows outside the Hole's entrance. They bore a body and they were missing one man. Either they had not gotten Endren out, or one of them was still in the mine. Cale cursed and rode the shadows to their side.

He saw that Riven was alive and the relief he felt surprised him. Dirt and blood covered the assassin. Vyrhas carried the limp body of a gray-haired man dressed in filthy, tattered clothes. Cale assumed him to be Endren and could see that the man was bleeding. A bloody rag wrapped the stump of his wrist. Shadem and Dynd both bore wounds but seemed unharmed. Skelan was missing.

The darkness swirled around them and Nayan, Erynd, and Dynd stepped from the shadows.

"What happened?" Cale asked.

"Guards," Riven said. "Skelan bought our escape. He's not coming out."

"Hells," Cale cursed.

Nayan put a hand on Cale's shoulder. "It is our honor to die in service to the Shadowlord."

"The Hells it is," Cale said.

The kraken shrieked from down in the bay, the city rumbled, and spell explosions lit the sky. Cale decided that he had done all he could for Yhaunn. The city would drive off the kraken sooner or later, or it would not.

Cale took Endren by the hair and pulled back his head. The man's eyes fluttered open, rolled back in his head.

"You'd better be worth it," Cale said, and intoned a healing prayer. The energy flowed into Endren and his breathing steadied. To Nayan, Cale said, "Take him to the Wayrock and await us there. If we don't return, get him to his son. Riven, you're with me."

"The Shadovar?" Riven asked.

Cale nodded and pulled the darkness about them. The shadow-walkers did the same.

CHAPTER SIXTEEN

11 Uktar, the Year of Lightning Storms

Cale and Riven stepped through the shadows to Selgaunt, to an alley off Rauncel's Ride. Cale strode onto the street, shadows pouring from him, and stalked up to Stormweather's gate.

"Mister Cale!" said one of the house guards whose name Cale did not know.

"Where is the hulorn?"

The man seemed so surprised by Cale's appearance and tone that he could not speak. His eyes moved from Cale to Riven.

"Where is Lord Uskevren?" Cale repeated. "Now, man."

The house guard said, "At the palace, with Vees Talendar and the Shadovar ambassador."

"At this hour?" Cale asked.

The guard shrugged and said, "Is all well, Mister Cale?"

"No," Cale said.

He had visited the hulorn's palace many times in his life. He pictured it in his mind, drew the shadows around him and Riven, and transported them.

They materialized on the walkway before the palace's main entry. He and Riven drew blades and took the stairs two at a time. They pushed through the palace's double doors and the graying chamberlain, Thriistin, appeared from a side room. He appeared to be awake, though . . .

His eyes widened with surprise. Cale knew Thriistin but they had not seen one another for some time. Four Helms emerged from concealed watchposts around the doors, blades bare.

"May I . . . help you, Mister Cale?" Thriistin asked. "The hour is late and weapons are not—"

"Where is the hulorn?" Cale demanded.

"I am certain that I could—"

Cale took him by the shirt, pulled him close, and looked into his face. Shadows boiled from his hands. The chamberlain paled.

The Helms advanced but Riven held his blades up and said, "I wouldn't."

Cale said to Thriistin, "You know me, and my connection to the Uskevren family, Thriistin. Tamlin is in danger. Where is he?"

"Danger?" asked one of the Helms.

The chamberlain stammered, then managed, "In the great hall, with the Shadovar emissary and his guards."

Cale released the chamberlain and rushed down the hall with Riven, the Helms rattling after them. Cale could see a faint light leaking under the double doors of the great hall. He kicked them open and strode into the room.

Glowballs provided light. Tamlin, Vees Talendar, and the tall Shadovar ambassador stood over a long wooden table. A large vellum map lay stretched out atop it. A plate of fruits, breads, and cheese lay on the table.

All three men looked up. Vees Talendar's face twisted in a snarl. Tamlin's face showed only surprise. The Shadovar's angular face showed nothing, but his glowing, golden eyes narrowed.

Shadows swirled around him like a cloak.

Cale realized immediately that the Shadovar was a shade.

"Mister Cale!" Tamlin said. "You are returned safely. Is Endren—?"

"Endren is safe," Cale said, eyeing the Shadovar and closing the distance. "But you are in danger." He looked at the ambassador. "Step away from him."

Cale moved around the table toward the ambassador and five Shadovar bodyguards—shades, like their master—materialized out of the darkness to cut off Cale's approach. Their hands went for wide blades. Cale had forgotten Thriistin's mention of the guards but it did not matter. He walked the shadow space and in a single stride found himself behind the bodyguards and eye to eye with the golden-eyed Shadovar ambassador.

"Mister Cale!" Tamlin said.

"Gods," Vees Talendar said.

The shadows around the ambassador flared into a protective shroud; the shadows around Cale responded, leaping outward toward the Shadovar. Energy crackled where the shadows touched.

The ambassador's expression showed no fear. His voice was steady and cold. "The hulorn is in no danger from me." He held up a dark hand to halt whatever the bodyguards might have intended.

"No, not anymore," Cale said, and brandished Weaveshear.

The ambassador cocked his head. He said softly, "You are a shade," and his gaze moved for an instant to Vees Talendar. "Strange that I have not heard of this earlier."

"Magadon Kest," Cale said. "You have him. Where is he?"

The ambassador said, "Magadon is a friend of yours, I assume?"

Cale grabbed the Shadovar by his finery and almost jerked him from his feet with one hand. The shadows around the two men spat purple sparks.

The Shadovar bodyguards appeared around them, blades at the ready.

The ambassador's eyes showed brewing anger but he shook his head and the bodyguards did nothing.

"It is fortunate for you that we are where we are," the ambassador said.

"What is going on here?" Tamlin demanded, circling the two so he could see Cale's face. "Mister Cale? Cease immediately."

Riven moved around the table into Cale's field of vision, eyeing the Shadovar. Three of the bodyguards turned to face him, shadows swirling around them. Riven chuckled.

The three Shadovar, as silent as shadows, spread out for combat.

Cale glared into the ambassador's face. "If anyone dies in this room, I promise that you will be among them."

The Shadovar's face hardened. Shadows as black as midnight streamed from his flesh, swirled around Cale.

"You are playing a dangerous game, child."

"Mister Cale!" Tamlin said. "You are assaulting an ally of Selgaunt and an ambassador of a foreign state." To the Helms standing in the doorway, Tamlin said, "Arrest him."

"Stand your ground," Cale said, and did not hear the Helms advance.

"You seem tense," Riven taunted the Shadovar, turning a circle in their midst, feinting to elicit movement. "What color is your blood, I wonder?"

"The same as yours," the ambassador called to Riven. "We are men, as you. And we are allies of your lord."

"He's not my lord," Riven said with contempt.

"Unhand him, Erevis," Tamlin said. "Now. This is Rivalen Tanthul, a prince of Shade Enclave, and his people are Selgaunt's ally."

Rivalen nodded at Cale. "I arranged the attack on Yhaunn so you could succeed in your rescue of Endren. Is that not evidence of where my loyalties lie?"

Cale shook his head. "It is evidence only that you are a skillful liar. I do not know your game, but I know your like."

Rivalen's eyes narrowed. The room darkened.

"Release him, Erevis," Tamlin said. "And apologize. You are in the wrong."

"Very in the wrong," Rivalen said softly.

Riven scoffed.

"Erevis?" Tamlin said.

"Fear not, Lord Hulorn," Rivalen said. "This is a trifling matter."

Despite his reassuring words, his eyes smoldered. "Mister Cale does not understand that Magadon is no prisoner. He is performing a service for us. Voluntarily."

Cale reluctantly let Rivalen go, though he still held Weaveshear at the ready.

Riven spat on the floor of the great hall and said, "A lie."

Cale nodded. "You lie."

"Tell him the nature of the service," Tamlin said to Rivalen.

"You will forgive me, Hulorn, but the matter does not concern Selgaunt or Sembia at this time."

Tamlin seemed at a loss for words.

"Bring him to me," Cale demanded. "Now."

Rivalen's eyes flared. He studied Cale's face. "I will take you to him, if you wish."

Cale smelled the trap but had little choice. He needed to learn where Magadon was being kept.

"No," he said. "You tell me where he is and we will go ourselves. I have my own methods of travel."

Rivalen stared into Cale's eyes. Cale answered with his own stare.

"He is in Sakkors," the Shadovar said.

"I'm unfamiliar with—" Tamlin started to say.

Cale held Weaveshear's point at Rivalen's chest. "Sakkors is three hundred fathoms under the Sea of Fallen Stars."

"Not anymore," Rivalen answered. "See it for yourself, shadeling. The enclave's name should be enough to allow you to use the Fringe to take you there. Scry it first if you wish. There are no wards to stop you."

Cale studied the shade's face, seeking the lie. He could determine nothing; Rivalen's face was a mask. He looked to Riven, who said, "We can kill them all now and figure it out afterward."

Cale smiled at the thought. The Shadovar bodyguards tensed. Leather creaked. Armor clinked.

"Sheathe your weapons," Tamlin commanded. "Do it. Now."

Cale ignored him, as did Riven, as did the Shadovar bodyguards.

Cale stared into Rivalen's face and leaned in close. "Know my mind, shade. If you have harmed him, I will kill you."

"Know mine, shadeling," Rivalen answered. "You live only because of my respect for the Hulorn. Were we not in his presence, things would be otherwise."

"Yap, yap, little dog," Riven said, and Cale saw real anger behind Rivalen's eyes.

Cale stared into Rivalen's face and saw the familiar dead space behind the shade's eyes—like Cale, Riven, and Nayan, Rivalen had a killer's eyes.

Cale knew with certainty what would happen in Sakkors. The Shadovar would not turn Magadon over to him, not willingly.

"We go," Cale said to Riven, and both of them backed away. To Tamlin, Cale said, "You are allied with serpents, my lord."

Tamlin snapped, "No. I have done the only thing that can preserve this city. You are dismissed, Mister Cale. Do not return."

"You are making a mistake," Cale said to Tamlin.

"I am correcting one."

Cale's hand twitched but he resisted the urge to knock Tamlin down.

"You shame your father," he said, and Tamlin blanched.

Cale had knocked him down after all.

The darkness in the room deepened as Cale and the Shadovar drew it about them. Each stared at the other as they started to meld with the shadows, each making the other hard promises.

Cale tightened his grip on Weaveshear and thought of Sakkors. When he felt the correspondence, he moved himself and Riven there.

Chunks of stone fly off with each strike of the pickaxe. I make rapid progress. The stink of brimstone and rot grow worse but I dare not open the door for ventilation. The fears are still outside. I strike the wall again and again, drowning out the sound of the fears, quelling my own. The sweat freezes on my skin, the air is so cold.

"Hit it, Magadon," encourages the voice. "You are almost through! Hit it!"

The fissure in the stone grows deeper and wider. I strike it again, again. The wall crumbles under my onslaught, the debris gathering around my feet, the dust filling the air of the cell.

At last I pierce it and the head of the pickaxe pokes through to the other side.

Orange light rushes into the room, a blast of air so frigid it burns. There follows the sound of screams, and smells like a thousand graveyards. I gag, recoil, vomit.

"Again, Magadon! It is too small for me to get through."

I wipe my mouth, sore, spent, and shivering. I want to look through the wall, to see what lies beyond. I cast aside the pickaxe, step to the wall, and look through the hole.

I catch a glimpse of pits of flame carved in ice and filled with agonized souls, then a form blocks my view.

"Don't look, Magadon," says the voice. "None of that matters."

But I have already looked, have already seen. Horror lies on the other side of the wall. Darkness. Evil.

"You must free me, Magadon," says the voice.

Aghast, I shake my head. I cannot open a door to *that*.

"You must," says the voice.

I steel myself and peer through the hole again. I must be sure.

"Show yourself," I command. "Back up so I can see you fully."

"No."

"Do it or I will walk away. I will give myself to the fears. Show me."

Silence from the other side. Then, "Very well."

The form backs away from the wall until I can make him out in the light of the flames. I cannot contain a gasp.

He is me, but not me. Fine red scales cover most of his skin. His horns are so long they curl back on themselves, and membranous wings sprout from his back. Fangs protrude from his hateful mouth. His eyes, my eyes, radiate malice and madness.

"You are a devil," I say, unable to look away.

"No. I am Magadon," says the devil. "Part of him. The same as you. Nothing more. But I am the only part not lost to the Source. You must free me. That is your duty."

I shake my head. "I won't. You are not the only one free of the Source. *I* am also free."

"But only for the moment. Listen."

The fears have gone silent.

"Open the door of the cell," the voice says. "The fears are gone. Even they are lost. Look outside, Magadon. See what is coming. Hurry. He is almost gone. And so are we."

"You are liar," I say.

"Quite so, but he could not live without the lies."

I do not understand. "You make no sense."

The devil laughs. "He calls himself a 'tiefling' but he knows that is not true. A tiefling is touched by a devil's blood. *Touched*. He has a devil for a *sire*. He is a half-fiend and then some. The lies are all that make it tolerable. Without me, without the lies, he would be lost."

I shake my head again. "With you, he's lost."

The devil does not dispute it. "Go look outside, Magadon. Do it now. See what comes."

Despite the dread that floods my chest, I move to the door and listen. I hear nothing. Are the fears truly gone? I have to know.

Heart thumping, I slide back the lock. When the fears do not renew their assault, I open the door a crack.

Still nothing. I take a breath and throw it wide.

"Look at the far side of the bubble, Magadon."

I do and see the bubble dissolving. It is as if a horizon is moving across the world, annihilating everything behind it.

"Loose me and I will save him. I will call his friends to him."

I say nothing and watch death approach.

"They are near," the devil says. "I called them long ago through the crack but I cannot do it anymore, not unless I am freed. He is too far gone. Let me out. Let me out now, or it will be too late."

I cannot. I will not.

"No," I say. "I know what you are. He locked you away for a reason. You are evil. It's better for us to be lost. All of us."

"No," the voice says, and I hear real fear in the tone. "Think of all that will die. Darkness, yes, but light, too. Goodness. Lost forever. Would you let that all die to spite me? Would you? All men harbor a darkness. It's what makes them men. Save him. Save us. You must."

I stand in the doorway and watch the world dissolve.

"I can't," I say. "I can't."

"There is no more time," the devil says. "We are all going to die. You, me, him, all of us. Do you want that to happen? Can you allow it? Choose. Do your duty or die. Choose!"

CHAPTER SEVENTEEN

11 Uktar, the Year of Lightning Storms

Cale and Riven materialized on the edge of a floating city shrouded in darkness—Sakkors, newly raised. The mountaintop that Cale had last seen at the bottom of the sea had been lifted from the depths and positioned so its flat top faced the night sky. Cale leaned over the edge to see the Inner Sea, still and black, far below them.

Sakkors had been rebuilt somehow. Shadows twined around thin spires, thick walls, along wide boulevards, through the windows of shops, residences, and noble manses. The city was nothing but dead stone; there was no greenery of any kind. Something about it reminded Cale of Elgrin Fau.

In the distance, he could hear the sounds of workers—hammers banging stone, shouts.

"Quite a feat," Riven said, looking around.

Cale nodded. "They will attack the moment they appear."

"Of course they will," Riven said. "I saw his eyes."

Riven reached into a belt pouch and removed two small stones—one a deep purple, one a light purple. He tossed them into the air and both whirred in a tight orbit around his head.

"More from the Sojourner," he explained to Cale.

Cale nodded, grasped his mask, and incanted a spell that made him faster, stronger. He expected an immediate attack from Rivalen and his bodyguards. The delay worried him.

They moved away from the edge of the mountaintop to give themselves room for combat. Before they had taken ten strides, the darkness around them deepened, swirled, surrounded them. Even Cale had difficulty making out shapes within the darkness.

"Here we go," Riven said, assuming a fighting crouch.

"Rivalen lives," Cale said, "but only until he tells us where Mags is."

A pair of golden eyes formed in the black, then a series of dark forms. Rivalen and his five shade bodyguards emerged from the murk. The bodyguards bore blades, and Rivalen held a black disc with a purple border in his hand, a holy symbol. Cale saw power crackling around it.

Cale charged. Riven read his lead and engaged two of the bodyguards nearest him, blades whirling. Before Cale had taken two strides, Rivalen pointed his holy symbol and said, "Die."

A gray beam shot from the shade's symbol. To Cale's surprise, Weaveshear did not absorb it and the dark magic hit Cale's chest, entered his flesh, and twined around his heart. Cale gasped but kept his feet and continued forward. He lunged and offered a weak overhand swing with Weaveshear. Rivalen dodged backward but not before Cale's blade opened a gash in his chest. Rivalen hissed with pain.

"Not enough, shade," Cale said through gasps. Despite the magic seizing his heart, he pressed ahead and stabbed at Rivalen's stomach. The shade sidestepped the blow and Weaveshear only skinned his side.

Rivalen grabbed Cale by the wrist and held it to keep Weaveshear away from him. Cale struggled but found Rivalen's strength to be a match for his own. Purple light shot through the darkness that swirled around them.

"You are a priest," Cale said through gritted teeth.

"And more," Rivalen answered, and intoned a prayer.

Cale recovered enough to chant a prayer of his own. Both completed their spells at almost the same moment. Dark energy flared in both their free hands and each reached for the other. Their hands met and both spells discharged harmful energy.

Wounds erupted from both of them. Cale's spell opened rips in Rivalen's arm, chest, and face. Rivalen's spell twisted Cale's organs and tore gashes in his arm and face. Both men shouted with the pain as their flesh struggled to regenerate. Neither released the other. Cale struggled to free Weaveshear for a killing strike but the Shadovar would not let him loose.

"*You* are a priest," said Rivalen through the pain.

"And more," answered Cale. He butted his head into the bridge of Rivalen's nose, heard a satisfying crunch, and used his greater size to drive the shade backward.

The Shadovar, his nose gushing blood, tried to shake his hand loose to cast a spell but Cale held him tight. The struggle spun them around and around and Cale caught intermittent glimpses of Riven dueling with the shade bodyguards. The shades blinked in and out of the shadows around Riven, but the assassin kept his blades moving so fast that the Shadovar could not gain an advantage.

Cale grunted, tried again to free Weaveshear. Rivalen grunted in answer, tried to free a hand to draw his own blade. They shoved, spun, grunted, and whirled. Shadows enveloped them. Violet sparks shot through the darkness.

Finally Rivalen gave up trying to draw his weapon and intoned another prayer. Cale answered with one of his own. As the dark energy of their spells manifested in their hands, as they spun and whirled, shouted and strained, they fell over the edge of Sakkors.

Both shouted with surprise as they fell. Cale caught a glimpse of the sea far below them. Starlight reflected off its surface. Their grips on one another loosened as they plummeted toward the placid water.

Rivalen jerked his hand free and slammed it against Cale's chest.

Cale's body exploded with pain. He screamed, his body contorting with agony. Blood poured from his ears. He responded instinctively, lashing out with a blind stab from Weaveshear. He felt it sink into flesh and Rivalen's scream joined Cale's as they fell.

The dark water rushed upward to embrace them.

Despite the pain and blood loss, Cale recovered enough to use the shadows around him to transport back to Sakkors. He appeared, bleeding and spent, ten paces from Riven.

The assassin saw him appear and unleashed a flurry of saber blows that drove back the shade bodyguards. He feinted at one in front of him and unleashed a backhand crosscut to the one on his right. The blow nearly decapitated the man and he fell at Riven's feet. Before Riven could choose his next move, the shade to Riven's left stabbed the assassin through the side. Riven grunted, waved his sword defensively, and staggered backward, bleeding and favoring his side.

For a moment, Cale let himself hope that Rivalen had perished in the fall. But the shade priest stepped from the shadows on Cale's right, breathing heavily and bleeding. Their eyes met and each glared hate at the other.

"Where is Magadon?" Cale demanded.

Rivalen only smiled.

Cale stepped through the shadows and appeared beside Riven. A shade bodyguard lunged at him, blade low. Cale parried the man's blade into the ground and punched him in the face with his other hand.

"We go," he said to Riven, and drew the darkness around them.

They shadowstepped across the city to the roof of a distant shop. Both men stood in the darkness, surrounded by a dead city, gasping, bleeding. Cale's flesh worked to close the score of tears in his body.

Riven peeled back his cloak and shirt to check the wound in his side. It was deep and pouring out blood. He closed his eyes, concentrated for a moment, and the dark purple stone circling his head flashed. The wound in his side healed completely.

"Stores a spell or two," he explained to Cale. "Someone has to cast them into the stone but I can trigger them after that."

"Useful," Cale said. He held his holy symbol and cast healing magic not into himself—his flesh would take care of his wounds—but into the whirling stone. The magical gem flashed as it absorbed the spell.

"Healing magic," Cale explained, wincing as more of his wounds sealed shut. "I don't want you dying on me."

Riven grinned. "We're in agreement on that. Now what?"

Cale was working one step at a time. "We find Magadon and get clear."

"How?"

"With spells," Cale answered, but he was not confident. He had tried magic before. He could only hope that proximity to Magadon would allow his divinations to function more effectively.

"Got to stay alive for that," Riven said. "Be quick, Cale. The shades will be after us."

Cale knew. They had almost an entire city to search—assuming Rivalen had told them the truth about Magadon—and Cale did not know where to begin. He tried mental contact before casting a spell. If Magadon had reached him in dreams, perhaps he could sense him now.

Magadon, Cale projected. *Magadon, where are you?*

The darkness deepened around them and ten shade soldiers charged out, blades bare. Cale rolled to his left and stabbed upward with Weaveshear. The blade pierced the Shadovar's armor, his gut, and poked out his back. Before Cale could pull it free, a blade sliced open his shoulder. Another stabbed him through the side. He spat the words to a harmful prayer, held forth his palm, and sent an arc of black energy into the Shadovar standing over him. They grunted and recoiled as the baleful force of Cale's spell cracked ribs and rent flesh. Cale pulled Weaveshear free of the Shadovar, rolled to his side, and gained his feet.

Riven shouted a series of power-laden syllables of the Black Speech and the Shadovar quailed, covering their ears. Riven slashed the throat of one near him and Cale decapitated another.

"Leave the rest," Cale said to Riven, and intoned a prayer to Mask. As he pronounced the last syllable, he shadowstepped with Riven from the roof to the top of a spire across the street. In his wake, his spell summoned a column of flame that drenched the rooftop and the Shadovar soldiers in fire. He knew that their flesh resisted magic, like his, but he hoped the spell incinerated at least a few.

Magadon, I need you to tell me where you are. Magadon!

Riven cursed as Rivalen and two other Shadovar, both with glowing metallic eyes, flew up from street level and hovered in the air less than a long dagger toss from the spire. One of them bore an archaic greatsword as long as Cale's leg. The other held a staff that bled shadows. Darkness swirled lazily around all three.

Riven hurled three daggers in rapid succession but the shadows around Rivalen deflected them.

The staff-bearing Shadovar leveled its tip at Cale and shot a swirling beam of yellow energy. Cale interposed Weaveshear but the blade absorbed nothing. The energy slammed into him, lifted him from his feet, and pushed him backward to the edge of the rooftop. His magic-fighting flesh deflected whatever other injury the spell might have caused.

Cale spared a glance down at the street below and saw a virtual army of dark-skinned, muscular bipeds with pointed ears charging down the streets toward the spire. They caught sight of Cale, pointed upward, snarled, and roiled forward.

"Riven!" Cale said.

"I see them!" Riven said. "Too godsdamned many, Cale!"

Cale agreed. They would have to leave without Magadon. Desperate, he tried once more to reach out to his friend.

Mags, where are you? Tell me now or we'll have to leave you.

The darkness near Riven swirled and a greatsword-wielding Shadovar stepped out of it. He twirled his black-bladed sword with such ease and speed it might as well have been a whipblade. The weapon trailed frost in its wake. His eyes burned orange. He stood as tall as Cale but as broad in the shoulders as a half-orc. The symbol of a stylized sword decorated the dull gray breastplate he wore.

Riven turned to face him, whirled his own sabers in answer, and intoned a short prayer to Mask. When he finished, his blades bled dark power.

"Let's dance," he said to the Shadovar warrior.

Magadon! Cale called in a last, desperate attempt.

The cell crumbles to nothingness around me. I look up into the sky and see the annihilating line rushing across the thought bubble, eating the world. I will be destroyed. The devil will be destroyed. I smile, laugh, and then remember . . .

Magadon will be destroyed, too.

The devil is frantic behind the wall. "We will all die, Duty! All of us! Unless you let me out! Let me out!"

My arms hang slackly, still holding the pickaxe, watching the world end.

"Let me out! Let me out!"

I see my choice clearly: To save the man, I must save the devil; to kill the devil, I must kill the man.

Where does my duty lie?

I do not know.

All men have a darkness in them, or so the devil had said.

I know the devil was a liar.

But I know that the devil had spoken truth. All men *did* have darkness. Some wore it in the form of horns. Some bore it invisibly as rot in their souls.

I can let myself die, but I cannot let the core die. Too much good lives in the core.

I make my decision, heft the pickaxe, stride to the wall. I strike it with all my might. Stink and cold boil out of the fissure. I strike again, again, again.

"Yes! Let me out!"

Riven and the sword-bearing Shadovar moved so rapidly Cale could scarcely follow. The Shadovar swung overhand; Riven side-stepped, slashed with his off-hand saber. The Shadovar spun a circle and unleashed a reverse slash at Riven's throat. Riven ducked under and landed both blades on the Shadovar's chest. The magic powering Riven's blades opened twin gashes in the Shadovar's armor. The shade warrior recoiled, surprise in his eyes.

"Rethinking it now?" Riven asked with a sneer.

"If all of me were here, this would be finished already," the shade said.

Cale didn't know what to make of that and didn't care. He shadow-stepped to the Shadovar's side and stabbed with Weaveshear. The blade sliced through the shade's armor and sank deep into flesh. Grunting, the shade slashed backhand at Cale with such speed that Cale could not avoid it. The steel opened a gash in his throat and the magic of the weapon froze his skin. Blood and ice sprayed and he staggered backward.

Riven leaped forward, slashed the Shadovar's sword arm, nearly severing it at the bicep, and kicked him off the edge of the tower.

"Cale?"

Cale's flesh worked to close the hole in his throat. He signaled with a hand that he was all right.

Behind Riven, the staff-carrying Shadovar completed an incantation and shot a bolt of black energy at Cale and Riven. Cale leaped to his feet and tackled Riven. The bolt missed them and both came up in a crouch as the energy melted a stinking hole into the spire's roof.

"If we stay, we die," Riven said to him.

"I know," Cale managed, his voice awkward from the throat wound.

There was nothing else for it. Cale wrapped himself and Riven in darkness and prepared to flee. A voice rang out in his head, so loud it drove him to his knees.

Let me out!

Riven clutched his ears, as did every other creature on the street. Cale recognized the voice, though its tone was different.

Mags! Show me where you are!

Magadon answered, *Erevis? Erevis Cale? Are you here? Can you be real?*

Now, Mags! Now!

A mental image formed in Cale's mind—a hemispherical chamber deep within Sakkor's floating mountain. Cale reached for the connection between where he stood and where he wanted to go.

At that moment Rivalen completed his spell and gestured at Cale with both hands. A wave of gray energy poured forth from Rivalen's hands and hit Cale's body, penetrated the magical protection of his flesh, and burst him from the inside. His skin ruptured and blood, tissue, veins, and arteries exploded from him in a stringy shower of gore. He tried to scream but choked on his own blood.

He fell to his knees in the wet mess, gagging, coughing, agonized. Woundshock was setting in. He was drifting, falling. Riven cursed and leaped to his side. Cale caught a flash of purple as Riven pulled a healing spell from his stone. Cale's vision cleared. The pain remained and his flesh struggled to regenerate the rest.

"Get us out of here, Cale," Riven said, looking up at the shade warriors. Behind Riven, Cale saw the greatsword-wielding Shadovar. The door to the spire's roof burst open and a column of snarling, muscular humanoids burst through. Their white fangs stood out starkly against their black skin. The lead creatures raised their blades, shrieked, and charged.

His face sticky with blood, his mind cloudy with pain, Cale let himself sink into the darkness. He rode the shadows to the place Magadon had shown him.

He and Riven appeared in a hemispherical chamber bathed in red light. The mammoth, glowing crystalline mythallar hovered unsupported in the center of the room. Whorls of orange and red flowed within the facets. Waves of magical energy poured forth from it with the regularity of a heartbeat.

Cale's ears throbbed with each pulse. The room vibrated with arcane power and ropes of shadow floated from Weaveshear toward the mythallar. The weapon pulsed in Cale's bloody hand in perfect time to the magical vibrations.

Cale's skin continued to close, pulling the exposed threads of his veins and arteries back into his flesh. Darkness swirled protectively around him, comforting him, sheltering him. Riven's hands darkened and he touched them to Cale. More healing energy flowed into him.

With Riven's aid, he stood.

Magadon stood under the mythallar, small and emaciated. He looked as if he had not eaten in days. He held his thin arms up so that his hands touched the crystal's surface. Black veins grew out of the mythallar and twined into Magadon's hands, forearms, and biceps. It looked as if the crystal were eating Magadon, one small bite at a time, beginning with his fingertips.

Magadon wore a vacant expression and his pupilless eyes showed no white; instead, they glowed red, the same red as the mythallar. The horns in his brow had grown a full finger's length since the last time Cale had seen him. The tattoo on his arm—a red hand shrouded in dark flames, the symbol of Magadon's father—stood out markedly against his pale skin.

"Get him free of it," Cale said to Riven. His voice was wet with gore.

Magadon cocked his head and said slowly, "Erevis?"

Cale gritted his teeth as his body painfully knit back together.

"We're here, Mags," Cale said, and nearly fell. "Riven and I are both here. Get him, Riven."

He knew Rivalen would be coming.

Riven moved warily under the huge crystal and put his hands on Magadon's shoulders. Riven was as gentle with Magadon as Cale had seen him with his dogs.

"It's part of him," Riven said, nodding at the Source's veins that grew into Magadon's flesh.

"Leave me," Magadon said, and grinned like a madman. He showed fangs for eyeteeth. "There's power here. And wonders. Leave me. I am content."

Cale remembered the kraken, its mind lost in the false world of the Source. He remembered Magadon had said to him once that contact with the Source exacted a price. He was seeing it firsthand.

Get me out, Magadon said in Cale's mind.

Cale tried to walk, found that his legs could support him, and moved to Riven's side. He threw aside his cloak, soaked as it was with blood.

"We pull him out or cut him out," Cale said.

"I will harm you if you try," Magadon said absently.

I will not allow it, but you must hurry, Magadon projected.

The shadows across the room started to deepen and churn.

"Pull him," Cale said in alarm, and whispered a healing spell to accelerate his recovery. Mask's healing energy warmed him, eased the pain.

Riven tried to pull Magadon free, failed. Cale assisted and the two Chosen of Mask tried to pull their friend free of his addiction.

The veins of the Source started to give way. Magadon screamed as the strings grew taught, ripped his flesh. Blood oozed from his arms. Cale watched glowing eyes form in the darkness across the chamber. Riven saw them, too. They pulled harder. Magadon groaned as a number of black veins, glistening with blood, snaked out of his skin, but Magadon did not come free. He dangled there, a macabre marionette.

"Stop! Leave me and I will give you what you need to defeat the Shadovar, Erevis. The whole power of the Source channeled into one weapon. Here. Now."

Magadon and the Source flared and pulsed rapidly.

Power went into Weaveshear. The blade vibrated in Cale's hand. Shadows poured from it, darker than before, and spiraled around them. With so much power diverted from the mythallar to Cale's blade, Sakkors began to slowly descend.

Cale watched Rivalen and the two other Shadovar emerge fully from the darkness, their glowing eyes wide as their city started to lower back into the sea.

"Your blade," Magadon said, his voice far away. "It will absorb even their shadow magic spells. Cut them down, Erevis. The power of an entire city is in your hand. Just leave me. You are my friend. Leave me."

Cale hesitated, tempted. Magadon grinned, nodded, his eyes pulsing in time with the Source.

Free us! Magadon screamed in Cale's head. *He is almost gone!*

Rivalen pulled a thin black blade from the scabbard at his belt. The pommel, inset with an amethyst, was tinged with purple light.

"Give me the power of the Source, Magadon," Rivalen said.

Magadon laughed. "No. I gave it to him. I am free of you."

Rivalen's eyes widened and all three shades began to incant.

"Pull him loose," Riven said to Cale.

"No. You are my friend," Magadon said again. "Leave me."

"I am your friend," Cale said. "That's why I can't leave you."

Cale slashed the exposed veins hanging between Magadon and the Source.

Magadon screamed and collapsed. The sinewy cords spat sparks of red energy and squirmed back into the crystal.

Rivalen's companion fired a blistering beam of green energy that hit Cale in the chest. Cale's flesh repelled the magic and it dissipated harmlessly.

"I will return for you," Cale said to Rivalen, and pointed the charged Weaveshear at him.

"We will be here," Rivalen said.

Cale imagined the Wayrock in his mind. His mind was cloudy, the image faint. He held onto it as best he could, wrapped Magadon and Riven in his darkness, and stepped through the shadows.

When the darkness parted, they were not on the Wayrock. They were sitting atop a hillock of ash-covered ice, under a steel gray sky, overlooking an icy plain dotted with pits of hellfire. The souls of the damned squirmed in the pits, screaming their agony into the sky. The smell of brimstone polluted the freezing air. A frigid breeze stirred up a cloud of ash and ice and carried with it the stink of a charnel house.

"Welcome to Cania," said a voice.

Mephistopheles's voice.

Shadows bled from Cale's skin. A trickle of blood leaked from his ears.

Magadon began to laugh.

FORGOTTEN REALMS®

R.A. SALVATORE'S WAR
OF THE SPIDER QUEEN

THE NEW YORK TIMES BEST-SELLING SAGA OF THE DARK ELVES

DISSOLUTION BOOK I
RICHARD LEE BYERS
While their whole world is changing around them, four dark elves struggle against different enemies. Yet their paths will lead them all to the most terrifying discovery in the long history of the drow.

INSURRECTION BOOK II
THOMAS M. REID
A hand-picked team of drow adventurers begin a journey through the treacherous Underdark, all the while surrounded by the chaos of war. Their path will take them through the heart of darkness and shake the Underdark to its core.

CONDEMNATION BOOK III
RICHARD BAKER
The search for answers to Lloth's silence uncovers only more complex questions, allowing doubt and frustration to test the boundaries of already tenuous relationships.

EXTINCTION BOOK IV
LISA SMEDMAN
For even a small group of drow, trust is the rarest commodity of all.
When the expedition prepares for a return to the Abyss, what little trust there is crumbles under a rival goddess's hand.

ANNIHILATION BOOK V
PHILIP ATHANS
Old alliances have been broken and new bonds have been formed. While some finally embark for the Abyss itself, others stay behind to serve a new mistress – a goddess with plans of her own.

RESURRECTION BOOK VI
PAUL S. KEMP
The Spider Queen has been asleep for a long time, leaving the Underdark to suffer war and ruin. But if she finally returns, will things get better... or worse?

For more information visit **www.wizards.com**

THE FIRST INTO BATTLE,

THEY HOLD THE LINE, THEY ARE...

THE FIGHTERS

MASTER OF CHAINS
Once he was a hero, but that was before he was nearly killed and
sold into slavery. Now he has nothing but hate and the chains of
his bondage: the only weapons he has with which to escape.

GHOSTWALKER
His first memories were of death. His second, of those who killed him.
Now he walks with specters, consumed by revenge.

SON OF THUNDER
Forgotten in a valley of the High Forest dwell the thunderbeasts,
kept secret by ancient and powerful magic. But when they're discovered
by the Zhentarim, a young barbarian must defend his reptilian
brethren from those who would seize their power.

BLADESINGER
Corruption grips the heart of Rashemen in the one place they thought
it could not take root: the council of wise women who guide the people.
A half-elf bladesinger traveling north with his companions is their only
hope, but first, he must convince them to accept his help.

For more information visit **www.wizards.com**

THE WATERCOURSE TRILOGY

THE NEW YORK TIMES *BEST-SELLING AUTHOR*
PHILIP ATHANS

A MAN CONSUMED BY OBSESSION...
DRIVEN BY AN OVERWHELMING VISION OF
WHAT MIGHT BE.

THE WIZARD
Pledged to the Red Wizards of Thay from boyhood, he will do anything
for anyone who can give him more power.

THE SENATOR
A genasi, he has fought his way up from the gutter and will never go back.

THE MAN
A master builder, he walks the coast of Faerûn, and the waves whisper to
him of a mighty work, a task worthy of his talents.

WHISPER OF WAVES
November 2005

LIES OF LIGHT
September 2006

SCREAM OF STONE
June 2007

For more information visit **www.wizards.com**